4TH AND FIXED

A NOVEL

4TH AND FIXED

A NOVEL

REGGIE RIVERS

SOURCEBOOKS LANDMARK™
AN IMPRINT OF SOURCEBOOKS, INC.®
NAPERVILLE, ILLINOIS

Published by Sourcebooks, Inc.
P.O. Box 4410, Naperville, Illinois 60567-4410
(630) 961-3900
FAX: (630) 961-2168
www.sourcebooks.com

Library of Congress Cataloging-in-Publication Data

Rivers, Reggie.
 4th and fixed : when the mob tackles football, it's no longer just a game / by Reggie Rivers.
    p. cm.
  ISBN 1-4022-0219-9 (alk. paper)
  1. Football—Betting—Fiction. 2. Organized crime—Fiction. 3. Gambling—Fiction. I. Title: 4th and fixed. II. Title.
PS3568.I833 F68 2004
813'.54—dc22

                              2003023432

        Printed and bound in the United States of America
               BV 10 9 8 7 6 5 4

**For my parents
Frankie and Phyllis Rivers**

ACKNOWLEDGMENTS

Several years ago, I decided to write a story about a crime family trying to fix NFL games. In typical fashion, I didn't create an outline, map out chapters, or otherwise plan the book. I just started hammering away at my keyboard.

Everything was going great until I got about two-thirds of the way through the story. Suddenly, I realized I had set up a series of events that I wasn't sure how to resolve. I stopped writing and thought about this problem for months. I literally did not type a single word. Finally, I gave the manuscript to my brother Mike, and he called a week later with the answer.

"Reggie," he said, "X is the key to the story. Everything pivots around this point."

He was absolutely right. Thanks to Mike's insight, I had a fresh perspective and was able to finish my first draft. Once it was done, my friend Kristie Kauerz slogged through the mess and helped me clean it up. Chuck Thomas, a former FBI Agent and NFL Security officer, helped to ensure that the details about the NFL's gambling prevention efforts were correct. Vinnie Magliulo, who ran the sports book at Caesar's Palace for fourteen years, gave me some crucial instruction about the point spread, how it's set, and how it works.

Brett Hoff contributed ideas for a couple of scenes, and creative writing teacher Esteban Martinez put me on course for my best re-write. Tom Rouen, who punted for the Denver Broncos for ten years, gave me invaluable advice for a scene about punters and kickers, and, as always, my publicists Sharon and Steve Cooper delivered a steady diet of support and encouragement.

I owe a tremendous debt of gratitude to my agent, Bob Diforio, who signed me back when *4th and Fixed* was just twenty pages long and didn't look like much. Once the book was completed, he quickly found a home for it. Thank you to Sourcebooks editor Hillel Black, who read the manuscript, saw through its flaws, and helped carve it into a tight, action-packed story. Laura Kuhn, the Magenta Mama, has been a terrific lead editor and a joy to work with.

4TH AND FIXED

A Novel

"He's gonna bolt," Michael Gasca said.

"I heard you the first time," Roscoe Evans said through clenched teeth. He had the largest head Michael Gasca had ever seen on a human. Roscoe also had a chest like an engine block, a neck as thick as a church pillar, and a thunderous heavy stride; when Roscoe walked it looked as if he could hammer nails into the concrete with his feet. At the moment, Roscoe was wedged into the driver's seat of a Lincoln Town Car going as fast as he could, which was a little slower than he normally backed out of his driveway. He looked out the windshield at five lanes of traffic stacked up in front of him going nowhere.

"I'm just saying," Gasca continued, "if he walks in and we're not there, he's gone." Michael Gasca was a normal-sized human being at five-foot-ten, 170 pounds, but he looked like a child sitting next to Roscoe.

"You see all these cars or you got your eyes closed?" Roscoe's deep voice rumbled like distant thunder. There seemed to be one long, tense muscle running from his forehead, back over his skull, down his spine, and out each of his arms and legs. He had an elbow out the window, and he was leaning on the wheel with the kind of force he wished he could apply to the accelerator—or Michael Gasca's neck.

"I see the cars," Gasca said, overly patient, "but I was wondering if you heard me twenty minutes ago when I said 'Don't get on the highway'?"

"Yeah?" Roscoe countered. "And I was wondering if you heard me when I told you not to schedule a cross-town meeting at rush hour?" Roscoe Evans drummed his fingers on the wheel and glared at the traffic. Suddenly, he leaned on the horn and stayed on it for about ten seconds.

"Roscoe." Gasca sounded like a father admonishing an errant son. Roscoe Evans stared back at him and showed his teeth in an unfriendly way. Michael Gasca pointed at the car next to them. "Look what you've done to her."

Roscoe looked over and saw a woman in her early forties carefully not looking at him. She had a panicked manner about her that made him regret his impatience. He thought about what this must look like to her—enormous black guy filling up the front seat like an elephant stuffed into a circus car. He's caught in traffic, blowing his horn as if he's about to charge, and she's wondering what she did wrong to end up stuck next to him.

Roscoe took a deep breath and let it out slowly. "You got a backup plan for when he ain't there?"

"You know," said Gasca, putting it together. "Remember the article I showed you in *Fortune* magazine?"

Roscoe thought about it for a moment. "The one with Kinneson on the cover smiling like he just got laid?"

"That's it," Gasca said. "You remember what the story was about?"

Roscoe thought about the article, which detailed the career of San Antonio Stallions owner Jonathan Kinneson, but he came up empty. He shook his head.

"The headline on the cover was 'Because My Time Is More Important Than Your Time!'" Gasca said from memory. "The whole article was about how Kinneson is always late for meetings. This could get interesting if he gets to the country club before we do."

■ ■ ■

Ken Buckius was built like a floor lamp. He had a long, skinny frame and a wolfish face topped with a bushel of black hair, which he groomed constantly. He'd been the head valet at the Verdant Hills Country Club for five years, and he treated the guests who pulled up in their Mercedes, Ferraris, and Maserattis as if they were his peers. He dismissed the drivers of lesser vehicles as if they were homeless people panhandling for change.

A few minutes after 5 P.M., a Rolls-Royce Bentley Azure Silica convertible with wild berry piping eased up the drive gracefully, the twelve-cylinder engine barely audible behind the shield-shaped grill. A delighted sigh slipped from Ken's mouth. He hustled around the car, allowing one gloved hand to trace along the Bentley's flank. He snapped the door open the moment the car came to a stop.

"Good afternoon, sir," Ken said. "Welcome to Verdant Hills."

Jonathan Kinneson climbed out of the car without ever looking at Ken Buckius—he never looked at servants. Kinneson's face bore deep furrows carved by more than fifty years of scowled demands and screamed orders, but no one—not his doctor, his three ex-wives, nor the Division of Motor Vehicles—knew exactly how many years over fifty. He stood a shade under six feet tall and had lush brown hair—the best money could buy—that looked as natural as the head of a man half his age, however old that was.

The Bentley was on loan from a local dealership. Kinneson had three Rolls-Royces at home, and he'd be damned if he was going to rent a Chrysler when he traveled.

"Will you be staying for dinner, sir?" Ken Buckius wondered pleasantly.

Jonathan Kinneson didn't answer. He pulled on a cashmere sports jacket, shot the cuff at his left wrist, and looked down at a diamond-encrusted Rolex without really noticing the time.

"I'll keep your car up front," Ken said confidentially as he slid into the luxurious driver's seat, closed his eyes and moaned as the supple leather embraced him.

Jonathan Kinneson had already turned away. He marched through the building without making eye contact with anyone. Kinneson was a dot-com billionaire and the much-ballyhooed owner of the San Antonio Stallions, so it was no surprise that several men sitting at the bar tallying their scorecards recognized him. They called out and invited him to join them. Kinneson just waved without really seeing them—a king gesturing to peasants. A steward led him to a carefully decorated meeting room at the back of the building and Jonathan Kinneson was three strides into the room before he realized it was empty. He stood still and raised his wrist in front of him. This time he stared at his watch for far longer than was necessary to read the time.

He took a lap around the room, walking slowly with his head down. It had been decades since he'd had to wait for anyone, and he wasn't sure how to handle this bizarre situation. After the initial bubble of rage, he calmed down and considered the facts. It was Thursday, and the first part of the contract had to be fulfilled on Sunday. If he didn't stay for this meeting, he'd have to reschedule, and that wouldn't be practical. It was inconvenient enough to leave San Antonio and fly all the way to Philadelphia for a meeting that surely could have been conducted by telephone, but Michael Gasca had suggested that this wasn't the sort of conversation he wanted recorded on an FBI wiretap, and Kinneson had been persuaded by that sober logic. Leaving was not an option.

Jonathan Kinneson walked out into the hallway and flagged down the steward. "Has the man I'm meeting already been here and gone?" It was a fair question; Kinneson was nearly an hour late.

"No, sir," the steward assured him. "You're the first to arrive." And that infuriated the Stallions owner all over again. How could Michael Gasca be an hour late for a meeting with one of the richest men in the world?

Kinneson strode back into the room, plopped down in an armchair and looked at his watch a third time. The pretty diamonds twinkled in the light. He tried to console himself with the possibilities this presented. Gasca undoubtedly would try to squeeze him for a million dollars, but Kinneson would use his tardiness as a negotiating point. He'd start at a two hundred thousand and see how things went.

■ ■ ■

Roscoe Evans pulled off the highway at Commerce Street and got on two wheels going around the corner on to Esplanade. This, Roscoe thought, was more like it. They were out in the open, cruising now.

"What I don't understand," Roscoe said, "is why Kinneson needs you to help him with the coach. Why doesn't he just fire the guy?"

"The coach," Michael Gasca said, referring to Stallions head coach Max Starnes, "has the best contract in pro football. Got a guaranteed five-year deal with a lock-in clause if he makes the playoffs in any of those first five seasons."

"Kinneson gave him that contract?" Roscoe asked. That didn't sound like the shrewd negotiator he'd read about in the magazines.

"No, Alan Feld, the previous owner, did. Coaches' contracts have gotten more complicated the past ten years or so. Used to be that if you were the owner, you signed the coach, and if you decided you didn't like him, you fired him. But now coaches get guaranteed contracts, and owners are sneaking around and hiring coaches out from under each other in ruthless bidding wars."

"So what's Starnes's deal?"

"Coach Starnes insisted on a contract that would survive the sale of the team," Gasca said. "It's complicated with a lot of variables, but in simplest terms, he gets five years guaranteed. If he makes the playoffs even one time in those five years, it turns into a ten-year guarantee. If he gets fired in the first five years or after he's made the playoffs, Kinneson has to give him a fifteen-million-dollar severance package."

Roscoe whistled. As far as he knew, pro coaches usually lasted about as long as the shirt on an exotic dancer. "So this is the fifth year?"

"Yep. And there's a sneaky little clause in the contract that Kinneson wants to take advantage of this weekend."

"So he needs the team to lose on Sunday."

"That's right."

"But he still wants to win the Super Bowl this season."

"Right again."

"And he's willing to risk the Super Bowl for the chance to get rid of this coach?"

"He figures this is just one loss early in the season."

"But it's not just one loss," Roscoe said. "They've already lost two games, so this'll be number three."

"True, but Kinneson's willing to gamble, because when we get the Stallions to the Super Bowl, he doesn't want Starnes coming along for the ride and earning the right to stay for five more seasons."

▪ ▪ ▪

The problem with Max Starnes, Jonathan Kinneson thought, was that the coach didn't show him the proper respect. Kinneson had a sterling record of success in the business world, but Coach Starnes refused to allow the owner to participate in any decisions regarding football operations.

"I'm the owner of the team!" Kinneson had once complained.

"And I'm the coach," Starnes replied. "You don't like that, you can fire me." *And pay me fifteen million dollars.* Those words went unspoken, but Kinneson heard them just the same. Coach Starnes wouldn't share the game plan with the owner; he'd locked Jonathan Kinneson out of the draft room in April, and Coach Starnes had actually canceled practice a few weeks ago—*canceled practice!*—when Kinneson refused to leave the field.

Jonathan Kinneson flinched at the memory of that humiliating day and tapped one Italian loafer against the hardwood floor. He snatched up his cell phone and spoke slowly.

"He...is...not...here!" Kinneson listened with pursed lips. "If he's not here in..." His words trailed off as the door creaked open. Kinneson snapped his phone shut and slouched back in the chair. He crossed his legs and propped his chin against his hand, as if he were relaxed. But when the door came fully open, it wasn't Michael Gasca. It was the steward carrying a menu.

Jonathan Kinneson rose, snatched the book away from the young worker, and grunted as he launched it across the room. It was a heavy, three-ring binder full of thick laminated pages, which crashed against the wall with a fat *thwack!* The steward backed away from the older man, then turned and ran from the room. Jonathan Kinneson dusted off his hands and sat back down with a satisfied grin.

■　■　■

"He ain't gonna wait this long," Roscoe Evans said. They were an hour and fifteen minutes late, and he was whipping the Town Car through residential streets.

"He'll be there," Gasca said, his voice infused with confidence.

"You wanna put something on it?"

"Of course," Gasca said. "I'll even give you ten-to-one odds."

Roscoe looked over at Michael Gasca and wondered where this skinny little white boy got his balls. "You're that sure?"

"That sure."

"Then I got a hundred bucks, but you gotta tell me why you think a billionaire would wait so long to meet with you?"

"I'm not so sure he's a billionaire."

"Come on, he's the richest dude in Texas!"

"He was," Gasca conceded. "He was one of those amazing dot-com success stories, but now all he has is the team, and he needs to milk as much money out of the Stallions as he can."

"That doesn't explain why he would wait for you."

"You ever watch the Discovery Channel?"

Roscoe shrugged. He didn't see what this had to do with anything. "Yeah, I check it out sometimes."

"You see *Wild Discovery*, show about all the animals?"

"Yeah," Roscoe smiled. "Saw one the other day about cheetahs. They're bad dudes!"

"Few weeks ago, I watched a pride of lions jump on a buffalo. Four, five lions hit him like linebackers swarming a running back. They clawed his back, chewed on his legs, bit him in the ass. The buffalo kept swinging around trying to gut the lions with his horns, but they stayed behind him, out of reach. After a few minutes, the rest of the herd came running over and chased off the lions. The narrator said that lions normally wouldn't risk fighting with a herd of pissed-off buffaloes. If they can't keep one animal isolated, they'll move on to smaller prey. But the lions had already made an investment. There was blood dripping from their mouths and staining their fur. They could see the buffalo they'd attacked was limping and moving slow. So the lions didn't move an inch. They lay down in the tall grass and waited. A few minutes passed, then half an hour, then an hour, and still they sat and waited. It took more than two hours, but eventually the herd moved on and the injured buffalo couldn't keep up. The lions raced in for the kill."

Roscoe waited for more, but Gasca was finished. "That's it?"

"That's it."

"That's your explanation for why Kinneson is waiting for you?"

"A man's like a lion," Michael Gasca said. "Once he gets the taste of blood in his mouth, he'll wait as long as it takes."

■ ■ ■

Ken Buckius brushed lint off the front of his trousers and looked up when he first heard, then saw, the Town Car screeching around the corner. The engine growled as the car came up over a curb and tore several branches off a manicured hedge. The car raced toward the front door as if the driver was about to drive right into the building, and Ken Buckius cowered behind his valet stand. Suddenly, the brakes locked up, and the Town Car slid forward, nose angled sharply toward the ground, leaving a pair of ten-foot skid marks on the clean concrete driveway.

The car was panting loudly as an impossibly large black man squeezed out of the driver's seat and towered into the sky. Ken peered over the valet stand, hardly believing his eyes. Another man (this one normal-sized) got out on the passenger side, but Ken barely noticed. He couldn't take his eyes off the hulking figure coming around the car. Ken set his chin and came out of hiding. He would handle this right here and right now. These two men, whoever they were, would not be permitted to sully the interior of the Verdant Hills Country Club.

"Gentlemen," Ken said, putting so much disdain on the word he hoped they'd understand he was using it facetiously.

They barely looked at him. The black one, who looked too big to fit through the door, tossed Ken the keys.

"*Gentlemen!*" This time Ken Buckius really didn't mean it. He positioned himself in front of them, and said, "How can I help you?"

Roscoe looked at the valet carefully and spoke with a voice of such deep timbre that Ken's glasses vibrated: "Keep it close. We ain't gonna be long."

Hopefully that would be true, Ken thought. But before he could say another word, they walked around him, through the front door, and down the hall. Ken Buckius watched them go and considered calling the police, but then thought better of it. He looked at the keys in his hands, then at the ticking, wheezing Town Car. He definitely would not keep the car up front. That was a privilege reserved for vehicles that cost more than a quarter million dollars.

"Here we go," Michael Gasca said.

"That's if he's still in there," Roscoe said. He was looking forward to the $1,000 he'd collect if Kinneson were gone.

"He'll be there."

"You hope."

Roscoe Evans walked into the room first, and the hulk of flesh eclipsing the door caught Jonathan Kinneson by surprise. He blanched as if he feared he were going to be robbed…or worse. From behind this monster came Michael Gasca with his hand out, offering no apology.

"Mr. Kinneson, I'm Michael Gasca, and this is Roscoe Evans. Please don't get up."

Jonathan Kinneson's heart returned to a normal pace, and so did his outrage. He'd had no intention of standing up and it irked him that Gasca didn't realize that. But before he could launch into it, Michael Gasca turned to Roscoe and said, "You got that hundred?"

Roscoe grumbled and reached into his wallet. He looked at Kinneson and said, "You should be ashamed of yourself."

Ashamed of what? Kinneson wondered. Before he could ask, Gasca picked up the phone. "Man, I'm dying of thirst," he said, then into the phone, "Hello, yes, we're in the Alameda Room. Could you please bring me a glass of iced tea and…you want anything, Roscoe?"

"A Coke."

"And a Coke and . . ." Gasca looked at Kinneson, who glared back at him. "And a menu…Oh…" Michael Gasca said, surprised. All three men stared at the menu sitting in a jumble in the corner, and Kinneson, to his credit, didn't even blush.

"Didn't like the selection, huh?" Roscoe said, chuckling.

"I see we already have a menu," Gasca said into the phone. "Just the drinks, please."

"How about another hundred on the menu?" Roscoe Evans said.

Gasca smiled, pointing with the one hundred dollar bill he'd just taken from Roscoe. "Not only are you on," he said, "but I'll give you the same ten-to-one odds."

"Without using physical force," Roscoe stipulated.

"Of course not," Gasca agreed.

Jonathan Kinneson watched the two men, but didn't understanding what they were talking about, and he couldn't tolerate being ignored.

"Mr. Gasca, you've kept me waiting more than an hour and that is unforgivable," Kinneson said, standing up.

Michael Gasca and Roscoe Evans looked at each other. *Unforgivable?* Gasca knew Kinneson's first wife had left him over unforgivable. Roscoe had once had a car repossessed over unforgivable. They were nearly two hours late for a meeting with guy who was still waiting for them when they arrived. That didn't sound like unforgivable.

"But you're still here," Roscoe said.

"I could leave!" Kinneson threatened.

Roscoe thought this was getting ridiculous. If the guy was gonna leave, he should have left a long time ago. But now that they'd arrived, Jonathan Kinneson would not be permitted to leave.

Michael Gasca said, "Mr. Kinneson, why don't we start over? I'm sorry we're late. We underestimated the traffic coming across town. Let's sit down, have a drink, maybe get some food and figure out what we're going to do."

Jonathan Kinneson let out a breath through his nose, somewhat mollified.

"You wanna go pick up that menu?" Gasca asked.

Kinneson thought Gasca was talking to his big bodyguard, but when he realized the two criminals were staring at him, he said, "*Me?*"

"You threw it over there."

"What makes you think I threw anything anywhere?" How did they get on this track?

"How else would a menu get in the corner like that?"

"Maybe it was trying to escape," Roscoe offered, erupting with deep gurgling laughter that filled the room and prevented all conversation until he was done.

"The menu," Kinneson said finally, "is immaterial. I've come a long way for this meeting, and you're late! Can we please get down to business?"

"This is business, Mr. Kinneson," Roscoe said. "See, what we're thinking here is that the menu in the corner is a whatchamacallit for our whole arrangement."

"A whatchamacallit?"

"He means a metaphor, Mr. Kinneson," Gasca explained.

"That's right. A metaphor," Roscoe said.

"Mr. Kinneson," Gasca said, "if we go forward, I give the orders and you follow them. If you don't do what I tell you to do, things aren't going to work out the way you want, and it's going to cost you more money."

"Mr. Gasca—"

"It's gonna be expensive to help the Stallions win, so we need to work out the details," Gasca said. "But first, I need you to put that menu in my hand."

Jonathan Kinneson looked around the room for hidden cameras. This had to be a joke. Surely, a man of his elevated stature couldn't end up in a country club arguing with a couple of low-grade hoods about who was going to pick up a stupid menu.

"What's so hard about fixing a few games?" Kinneson said, changing the subject. "After all, the Stallions are going to win some on their own, so you only have to worry about the games that are questionable."

"That's true," Gasca agreed, "but you're talking about the NFL. It's the hardest league to crack, the toughest line to beat and the riskiest bet to collect if you win. The NFL makes more money than all the other pro leagues, so it spends more money on security. The whole system is hyper-sensitive to any sort of manipulation."

"Well, it sounds impossible," Kinneson said impatiently. He hated subordinates who complained that their jobs were difficult. He'd be damned if he was going to sit and listen to them bitch.

Michael Gasca smiled. "It sounds impossible, but we're here, and you're here."

"And so is the menu!" Roscoe interjected.

"Yes, so is the menu," Michael Gasca said. "What's the likelihood that you're gonna get out of that chair, walk across the room, and deliver that menu to me?"

"Zero," Kinneson said through clenched teeth.

"That's 'cause you've got pride," Gasca said. "Every player we deal with this season is gonna have pride, too. They don't wanna get pushed around. These young guys have a lot in common with you, Mr. Kinneson."

Kinneson grunted. He found that highly doubtful.

"You're one of the best businessmen in the world," Gasca continued, "and they're among the best athletes in the world. They've succeeded their whole lives, and they've got money, fame, women, and everything they've ever dreamed of. So I'm gonna walk up and say, 'Hey stud, I know you've got the world by the tail, but I want you to pick up a menu for me like a servant.' It's gonna take some persuasion to get them to do that. So here we are sitting in a beautiful country club, having a nice conversation, with our metaphor sitting patiently in the corner waiting to see how our ten-million-dollar deal will be resolved."

"Ten million!" Kinneson sputtered, turning crimson. "Are you crazy?"

"Not at all," Gasca smiled.

"Your services are worth, at most—*at absolute most!*—one million dollars to me!" *Easy! Slow down!* Kinneson tried to catch his breath. He'd intended to start at two hundred thousand and work his way up. Somehow he'd blurted out one million and that wasn't good at all.

Michael Gasca was still smiling. "So you flew all the way up here from San Antonio in your private jet and waited nearly two hours so we could talk about getting your coach fired and getting you into the Super Bowl. In the process you'd become a media superstar, get the taxpayers to build you a new stadium, and make a whole lot of money, and for all of that, you figured you'd give me a million-dollar gratuity?"

"A million is probably too much," Kinneson said. Maybe he could still repair the damage.

"I'm selling this the wrong way," Michael Gasca said. "If I wanted to, I could make sure Coach Starnes gets a win this week, and that he wins every weekend through the middle of the season. I could get the Stallions into the playoffs, but then make you lose in the first round. You'd get no Super Bowl, but you'd be stuck with Starnes for another five years and you probably wouldn't get your new stadium. So how much would you pay me to not do that?"

Jonathan Kinneson shook his head. "You don't have that much control over the games."

"Mr. Kinneson, you're here in Philadelphia because you know I have exactly that much control. Now the deal is ten million, but the menu has become a major point. You don't pick it up, the price is going to eleven."

Jonathan Kinneson clenched his jaw and looked carefully at Roscoe Evans. Kinneson wondered what would happen if he tried to leave.

"How are you going to make sure Starnes doesn't win this weekend?" he asked.

"You leave that to me," Gasca said.

"I need to know," Kinneson said. "If it's obvious the league will investigate."

"It'll be subtle," Gasca assured him.

"Well, if it's so subtle, how will I know you did anything? You could just sit on your ass and try to collect if the Stallions lose."

Gasca said, "You wanna gamble on the Stallions losing this weekend, go right ahead. With me, you get a guarantee. It'll be subtle, it'll be effective, and it'll get Starnes out of your way."

"Why don't you tell me what you're going to do, that way I'll know it when I see it?"

"I can do that," Gasca agreed. "But if you want that information, you're gonna have to pick up that menu."

They all stared at the notebook in the corner.

The steward entered the room with an iced tea and a Coke on a tray.

"Ah," Gasca said. "Thank you."

Kinneson took advantage of the interruption. To the steward he said, "Pick up that menu." Kinneson locked eyes with Gasca and smiled victoriously. The younger man smiled back and took the notebook from the steward. He looked at it for a long time before ordering two pieces of chocolate cake—one for himself and one for Roscoe.

"Anything for you, sir?" the steward said to Kinneson.

The Stallions owner shook his head without looking at the servant.

Michael Gasca took his time ripping open a packet of Sweet 'N Low and stirred it into his tea. "I've heard a lot about you." He took a sip and watched Kinneson over the rim of the glass. "Hard-charging, take-no-prisoners type of guy. School superintendent, then president of an Internet company, then billionaire, then owner of the San Antonio Stallions. It must be killing you to have a coach you can't fire and team that's guaranteed to lose in the first round of the playoffs. Must be wondering if you've lost your golden touch."

"I haven't lost anything!" Kinneson snapped. "I *will* have a Super Bowl championship, with or without you!"

"And now the economy has leveled off," Gasca said, "and the value of your company stock—which I think we can all agree was grossly over-valued—"

Roscoe raised his hand. "I agree."

"Plummeted from seventy-eight dollars a share to just seventeen," Gasca continued, "and you went from being a multi-billionaire on Forbes's list of the world's richest, to just a pretty wealthy guy who can still get laid on South Beach, but you can't run with the big boys anymore. All of a sudden the football team you bought as an expensive trophy has become your prime source of income, and you're just starting to realize that owning a franchise doesn't generate the kind of take-home cheddar you need to maintain the lifestyle that you've become accustomed to. Am I close?"

Too close, the Stallions' owner thought. He didn't like Michael Gasca.

"So let's talk pay schedule, because you need this a lot more than I do," Gasca said. "It's an eleven-million-dollar package, and you pay as you go. There's—"

"Whoa!" Kinneson had a hand up like a school crossing guard. "First it was ten million and now it's eleven? I got you the menu." He sounded like a whiny little boy.

Gasca smiled. "You delegated to the waiter."

"Yeah," Roscoe said, rubbing his hands together, "and in the process, you made me a grand." Roscoe thought it was typical of Michael Gasca to lose a thousand dollars on the bet with him, but make a million off Kinneson. Somehow, Gasca never lost.

Kinneson looked at Roscoe Evans, confused. *What grand?* "I never agreed to ten million, and I'm certainly not going to pay eleven just to satisfy your ego."

He stood up and moved toward the door, but Roscoe stood with him and blocked the exit.

"Move!" Kinneson said, glaring up at Roscoe.

Roscoe smiled down at him. "No, I think it's your move."

"You can't leave, Mr. Kinneson," Gasca said.

"Like hell I can't." Kinneson tried to push Roscoe out of the way, but he might as well have been trying to push a building out of his way. After a moment, Roscoe bent down and enveloped the owner in his powerful arms. He squeezed, lifted Kinneson into the air, and carried him back to his chair. Roscoe was holding on just tight enough to keep the Stallions' owner from taking a breath. Kinneson's face turned red, and he flailed his arms helplessly. When Roscoe let go, Kinneson coughed and hacked for half a minute.

Michael Gasca set his iced tea on the table and brushed lint off his knee. "Mr. Kinneson, the menu cost you a million. Just accept it, and let's move on."

"I won't pay that!" Kinneson said with all the breath he could muster.

"Not only will you pay, but you'll make a deposit right now," Gasca said. "Give Roscoe a thousand dollars."

Roscoe rubbed his hands together. Kinneson's eyes went wide. "I …don't have a thousand dollars."

"How much you got?" Roscoe asked.

"That's none of your business!"

Roscoe walked over to Jonathan Kinneson, and the Stallions' owner cowered back with his hands up in front of him.

"What are you doing?" he squealed. He desperately did not want to get another hug.

Roscoe grabbed Kinneson by his ankles and dragged him slowly out of the chair. When the Stallions's owner was on his back, Roscoe lifted his ankles into the air, inverting Kinneson, who was frozen stiff with fear and indignation. His jacket fell down around his head, his cell phone clattered on to the floor, change jingled out of his pockets, and his bill-fold hit the floor with a plop.

Roscoe dropped Kinneson and picked up the wallet. He whistled when he saw the thick stack of bills inside. He extracted exactly one thousand dollars.

Michael Gasca said, "What you've gotta understand, Mr. Kinneson, is that you're not in control of this situation." He pulled a small card out of his pocket. "Tomorrow you transfer one million into this account. Once I get the confirmation, I'll make sure Coach Starnes loses this weekend."

The steward returned with two slices of chocolate cake and tried very hard to keep his eyes off Jonathan Kinneson sprawled on the wooden floor.

"Thank you," Gasca said, rubbing his hands together as he looked at the cake. When the steward departed, he continued, "After I get rid of Coach Starnes, you'll make million dollar payments according to the schedule on the card, with the final three million due in a lump sum after you win the Super Bowl."

"Eleven million is too much," Kinneson said weakly. Roscoe almost felt sorry for the guy.

"It's a pittance compared to the money you're going to make over the long haul." Gasca took a bite of his cake. "But if it'll make you feel better, I'll tell you what to watch for on Sunday."

"What?" Kinneson said, desperate for anything.

"Actually it's not a *what*, it's a *who*," Roscoe corrected.

"You're right," Gasca said.

"Who?" Kinneson insisted.

"Caleb Alexander," Gasca said.

"Caleb Alexander?" Kinneson asked, hoping for more details.

"Caleb Alexander!" Roscoe repeated, laughing loudly.

2

Officially, Steven Oquist wasn't parallel parked in the middle of a long row of cars on Gustavson Avenue. Officially, he didn't have his baseball cap pulled down tight over his eyes, with a small pair of binoculars trained on the entrance at Lenny's Grill. Officially, Steven Oquist didn't know about the early morning thunderstorm that had rolled through Philadelphia, filling the streets with greasy puddles that jumped up with every passing car and painted the side of his league-issued Lexus with grime that would harden into brown barnacles by the end of the day. Officially, Steven Oquist was in San Diego attending his wife's aunt's funeral, and he'd return to the office when his wife of twenty-seven years felt strong enough to be alone. Steven Oquist was conducting this stakeout unofficially, because officially, he'd been told on too many occasions to count to back off of Michael Gasca—stop the surveillance, quit responding to tips about the man, and spend his time dealing with real threats to the NFL. But Steven Oquist ignored these instructions and continued to study the man who had become his sole passion in life.

Oquist's eyes locked on a gray Lincoln Town Car turning onto Gustavson Avenue three blocks down. That had to be Michael Gasca. He didn't always arrive in the same vehicle, but it was always a Lincoln Town Car—different colors, different appointments, different years, but always the same brand and always the same driver: Roscoe Evans. The Town Car bounced through waterlogged potholes and eased indifferently into a no-parking zone in front of Lenny's Grill. Oquist settled back to enjoy an event that had become a small pleasure in his life—

watching Roscoe Evans extricate himself from a Lincoln Town Car. Oquist didn't know Roscoe Evans's height or weight, but he knew the big man had to duck to get through doorways, he barely fit in the triangular cavity of a revolving door, and when he drove, the left side of the Town Car slumped toward the ground at a precarious angle.

At the moment, Roscoe was wedged into the driver's seat like a sweater crammed into an overstuffed drawer. Oquist had a camera the size of a lipstick cylinder perched under his rearview mirror; it could zoom in to read a suspect's expression from a hundred and fifty feet. A fiber optic wire delivered images to a laptop computer in the passenger seat, and Oquist watched the screen as Roscoe Evans opened the door and let his feet fall out of the car. His impossibly long, high-top sneakers hit the pavement with a flat *thwaap* that spattered water out to the middle of the street. Roscoe didn't move for a moment and Oquist imagined the big man must be resting and building up his strength for the remainder of the task. Roscoe's arms came next, two long columns of blackened steel extending straight out of the car and bending as he hooked his elbows in the frame and levered himself up.

Oquist thought Roscoe looked like a strange, giant crab who might walk away with the car still attached to his back. But then Roscoe stood up, detached himself from the vehicle, and turned toward the building.

"What's gonna happen if you ever have to get out of the car in a hurry?" Michael Gasca asked.

"Gimme a for instance," Roscoe said.

"Like if the car was on fire or went into the water?"

Roscoe Evans shook his thick head. "That only happens in the movies."

"Sometimes it happens in real life, too."

"You ever known anyone whose car caught on fire or went in the water?"

"Not personally, but that's not the point, Roscoe," Gasca said. "The point is that if you ever had to get out in a hurry, you couldn't do it."

Roscoe nodded. "You ever had to get out of a car in a hurry?"

"No," Gasca said, rolling his eyes. "But if I had to I could."

"How do you know I couldn't if I had to?"

"Because I watch your big ass struggle every time we stop!" Gasca thought Roscoe would be more comfortable in an SUV, but Roscoe had always insisted on a Town Car. He'd tried a Chevrolet Suburban a few years ago because he got a deal on it from a guy who was good at starting cars without keys. The Suburban had plenty of room inside, but Roscoe thought it rode too far off the ground, and he didn't care for the way it dipped and swayed when he pushed it around corners. The Town Car had tight, nimble handling, and it fit Roscoe like a tortoise's shell, which was exactly how he liked it.

A puddle, propelled by a passing garbage truck, attacked Steven Oquist's side window with the sharp staccato of machine gun fire. Oquist uttered a tiny, frightened moan and dove across the center console, sprawling into the passenger seat. After a moment, he sat up and chuckled nervously, pulling the jumbled laptop computer back into place. Oquist ran a hand along his stubbled jaw. He had dark, bushy eyebrows and close-cropped gray hair. He wore his standard uniform: button-up dress shirt, open at the collar, under a navy blue V-neck sweater, with pleated khaki pants and an old bomber's jacket. He would have looked like a college professor if not for blue eyes that had a hard, calculating glint that never went away, even when he smiled, even when he made love to his wife.

The rattling garbage truck continued down the street, launching a storm of puddles, and Michael Gasca seemed to gaze past the truck and look right at Steven Oquist. The former FBI agent knew he was too far away to be seen, but instinctive fear nibbled at the back of his throat. After a moment, Gasca's eyes turned away and he and Roscoe marched into the restaurant.

Water sluiced off the roof of Oquist's Lexus down onto the windshield; he turned the key in the ignition and flipped the wipers once to clear the view. It had been fifteen years since he had first developed an interest in Michael Gasca, about seven years since that interest had turned into an obsession, and a little over two years since that obsession had cost him his job.

Oquist sometimes dreamed that he had his hands wrapped around assistant director Ken Parsley's fat neck as fat veins bulged out of his fat forehead and his fat face bloomed purple while his fat eyes bulged out of their fat sockets. And after Ken Parsley's fat body lay dead on the floor, Oquist would say, "No, Ken, you fat fuck, I do not want to be promoted to regional director. I want to stay out in the field, where I belong. Where I can keep an eye on Michael Gasca."

But his business cards read: Steven Oquist, Regional Director, NFL Security. The organizational chart for NFL Security used to go from director Don Burk to assistant director Ken Parsley to all of the agents out in the field. But at Parsley's suggestion, a new post was created to take Oquist off the street and made him the glorified overseer of the investigations wing. Oquist was the third man down in the NFL Security hierarchy, which sounded important, but he had no real power.

Steven Oquist had spent two decades catching people for the FBI, and when he retired from the bureau seven years ago, he came to work for the NFL. His wife initially hadn't understood his position. When she'd heard the words NFL Security, she'd thought he would attend football games and keep drunks from running on the field—unless, of course, the drunks happened to be players. It didn't sound like the sort of assignment befitting his age, training, or status. Over the years, she'd learned that the words, "My husband is a special agent with the FBI," was a line she could lay down at a luncheon and stop the crowd. She shuddered to think what would happen the first time she confessed that her husband worked security at football games. But Oquist had assured her that his new post was dignified.

"I monitor gambling," he had explained patiently, "just like I always have." NFL Security had a staff of thirty-three officers—one for every NFL city plus Las Vegas; they'd all spent decades with the FBI, where they'd investigated racketeering and organized crime.

Since the promotion to regional director, Oquist seemed to monitor gambling less than ever. He didn't enjoy sitting in an office taking reports from other agents. He needed to be on the street talking to bookies, running surveillance and letting his instincts lead him to the action.

Oquist released an angry breath in the car. If they'd let him stay on the street, he could have kept close tabs on Michael Gasca; he could have stopped this infiltration before it began. But Ken Parsley had pulled him away from his beat. Pulled him away from an area he'd worked most of his life.

"Fat fuck!" Oquist spat, riled, as always, by the mere thought of the assistant director. Oquist had first called Ken Parsley a fat fuck about five years ago, and he had used the appellation more frequently and with more vigor as Parsley continued to shake his fat head to deny investigations focused on Michael Gasca. Steven Oquist had used the moniker so often that word eventually got back to the assistant director, who called him in to explain, with a straight face, that he had a gland problem.

Oquist thought the only overworked glands in Parsley's body were his salivary glands, but he kept that thought to himself, offering instead an apology that sounded sincere and a promise to cease and desist.

"Because if I hear through the grapevine," Parsley said, and Oquist thought it typical that the assistant director's metaphor would reference food, "that you've been calling me a fat fuck, I will fire your ass. You hear me?"

"Of course I hear you." Oquist wondered why Parsley so often asked people if they heard him. Maybe the fat around his ears made it difficult for him to hear himself, so he assumed that his words sounded muffled to others as well.

"What I mean," Parsley persisted, "is do you understand me?"

"Of course I understand you," Oquist said, holding Parsley's gaze without blinking.

They waited each other out. Parsley hoped for another affirmation; Oquist hoped that Parsley's hunger pains would cut short this ridiculous meeting.

In the days that followed, Steven Oquist called Ken Parsley everything but fat fuck, and it was the name Corpulent Copulator that stuck. Soon everyone in NFL Security referred to Parsley as C.C., and though the assistant director had heard the acronym, no one had yet confessed its meaning.

Oquist looked at his card again. Regional Director. The title served mostly as a restraining order to keep him away from Michael Gasca. And since Oquist was the only person who believed Michael Gasca was a serious threat to the NFL, his new title meant that the league no longer had a sharp focus on the man who could destroy professional football.

■ ■ ■

Lenny's Grill was an L-shaped space tucked between a check-cashing facility and a dry cleaner. It had Formica tables with cracked maroon vinyl benches along the windows and a long bar with twenty high-back swivel stools welded to the scuffed linoleum floor. Lenny's offered second-hand smoke, profanity, and cholesterol as menu items, and it had no shortage of customers. Roscoe Evans and Michael Gasca walked through the door and saw Lenny in the back working the grill. He had a net over his long black hair and an unlit cigarette perched on his lips. He raised a spatula in their direction; they waved back.

"Hey fellas," Jennifer Winesett said in her familiar singsong.

"No need to fuss over us, Jennifer," Roscoe said, stopping her before she could come around the bar. "We got it." He grabbed a couple of menus from the hostess stand and led the way to a booth in the corner. Jennifer met them at their table with water and silverware.

"Haven't seen you boys in a while." She had hazel eyes, auburn hair, and a clear, unblemished face.

"Which is our loss, 'cause you're lookin' fine as ever." Roscoe squeezed his massive frame into the booth. Every time Roscoe and Gasca came into Lenny's they remarked that the place would be dingy if not for Jennifer.

"Well, thank you." She made a small curtsy. "What can I get you?"

"I'll take black coffee and pancakes," Gasca said.

"You already had breakfast," Roscoe said, pointing at a clock over the bar, which read nearly 1 P.M.

"Yeah," Gasca agreed, "but that was bacon and eggs. When I come to Lenny's I like to have pancakes."

Roscoe thought for a moment. They'd been to Lenny's many times over the years, and he didn't recall any consistent theme in Gasca's previous orders. "You didn't have pancakes the last time you were here."

"Yes, I did." Gasca had an unfaltering confidence about past events that always piqued Roscoe's competitive instinct.

"No, you didn't."

"What you got to put on it?"

"I got a hundred bucks," Roscoe said.

"Jennifer," Gasca said, "you remember what I had the last time I was here?"

Before she could answer, Roscoe bellowed, "That ain't fair!" His deep voice roared like a sudden clap of thunder, and everyone in the restaurant looked up, startled. "You've poisoned the well! She's gonna say pancakes 'cause you said pancakes."

"All right," Gasca agreed. He was always too agreeable, Roscoe thought. "Let's do it this way. You tell Jennifer what you thought I had. That way she can think about both options and pick the one that sounds right."

"He had a corned beef Reuben," Roscoe said without hesitation. "It was a Friday night, and you were working a double shift like you always do on Fridays and Saturdays. We were sitting right here waiting for Giovanni, and he had a Reuben."

Gasca said, "Jennifer?"

"I think Roscoe's right. I remember you saying you hadn't had a Reuben in a couple of years and it was the best one ever."

"Ha!" Roscoe slapped the table. "That's my girl!"

Gasca smiled. "Yes, I did have a Reuben when we were here on Friday the 17th. But that wasn't the last time we were here. Roscoe, the following Monday, we had to pick up Porter at the airport. You remember? That was the morning he was coming back from Chicago. We sat over there at the bar and had pancakes."

"Oh," Jennifer said, "that was when Lenny came out of the back with a cigarette in his mouth—"

"And I asked him not to light up until I finished my pancakes—"

"—and he said he'd quit smoking and just had the cigarette in his lips for comfort."

"Then I asked him when he'd quit—"

"—and he said, 'this morning.'"

Roscoe said, "What are you guys, some kind of stage routine?" This little back and forth made him think that he'd been suckered.

"He's right, Roscoe," Jennifer said. "I remember that."

Roscoe shook his head and slid a hundred dollar bill across the table. He should have known better than to bet against Michael Gasca's memory. There didn't seem to be any limit to the things Gasca could hold in his head and pull out at a moment's notice. Roscoe liked to drag Michael Gasca and his memory into bars to hustle cocky young businessmen, standing with their jackets on and their ties loosened as they sipped micro-brewed beers. The yuppies were always slapping each other's backs, laughing with wide-open mouths and telling stories about their important jobs. Every now and then, one of them would reach into his pocket, pull out a fat wad of cash, taking his time with it, making sure the ladies could see it, saying, "This round's on me!"

On a recent occasion, Roscoe walked over and squeezed between four guys in slick suits. They were chuckling about something, and Roscoe started laughing with them. They ignored him at first, but his voice, coming from so deep in his enormous frame, was hard to ignore. When Roscoe laughed it sounded like a Harley-Davidson idling at a stoplight; it tended to drown out everything else. Soon, the yuppies lost their patience and stared up at Roscoe with hard eyes.

The apparent leader of the bunch had blond hair with a cowlick in front. "Hey, look!" he said. "It's the Himalayas!"

His buddies chuckled nervously, but when Roscoe smiled at the joke, they laughed with a little more enthusiasm.

"Aren't you getting mounted by sherpas tonight?" Cowlick continued. That brought another peel of snickering.

"I'm not part of the Himalayas," Roscoe said with good humor.

"No, he's the Pyrenees!" said a suit wearing black-rimmed glasses.

The yuppies, feeling emboldened by Roscoe's affable response, smiled in earnest.

"Look," said a guy in a yellow tie, "it's Sasquatch!"

That's it, Roscoe thought. He stepped forward and brought the ball of his foot down on Yellow Tie's square-toed Kenneth Cole loafer and pressed down. Yellow Tie squealed and dropped his beer on to the counter. It tumbled over and rolled across the bar, spilling amber liquid out of the neck before another patron set it back on its bottom.

"What you gotta remember," Roscoe rumbled, "is to stay on the theme. You understand?"

Yellow Tie had tears in his eyes as he tried to push Roscoe off his foot, but Roscoe's granite frame didn't budge.

"No," Yellow Tie said, suddenly realizing that he'd compared Roscoe to a big ape, which wasn't what he'd meant at all. "I didn't mean to offend you sir. I was just joking."

"I know," Roscoe said, leaning in a little harder. The other men watched the confrontation from a careful distance. Roscoe still had another foot and two free hands—a limb for each of them. "What did your friend call me?" He pointed at Cowlick.

"He…he…called you the Himalayas."

"That's right."

"Then this young man here with the glasses. What did he call me?"

"The Pyrenees."

"So you see your mistake? You see how you didn't stay on the theme?"

"Yes sir. I think so."

"Sasquatch ain't a mountain, is it?"

"No, sir." Yellow Tie thought the arch of his foot might snap at any moment.

"You wanna try again?"

"Sir?"

"Think of something else to call me?"

"No, sir. I think I'm done calling you names."

"Come on. Gimme something good, and we'll call it a night."

Yellow Tie's eyes danced around the room wildly, but he could not think of a single mountain range.

"The Rockies," Cowlick offered.

"The Appalachians," Black-rimmed glasses said.

"No help from the gallery," Roscoe said. "He's got to come up his own answer."

"Please, sir. I'm so sorry." Whatever joy Yellow Tie had felt a few minutes ago was gone; he didn't imagine he'd be happy again for a long, long time. He just wanted to get this giant off his foot.

Roscoe said, "I'm waiting."

"Mt. Saint Helens," Yellow Tie said suddenly.

"Mt. Saint Helens?" Roscoe asked.

"It's a volcano," Black-rimmed glasses said.

Roscoe laughed. "Hey, I like that. That's a good one!" He eased back off Yellow Tie's foot. Yellow Tie groaned and grabbed his ankle as blood rushed back into his foot.

"What I was wondering," Roscoe said to the other three men, "was whether you boys might be interested in a little wager?"

"What kind?" Cowlick asked, keeping his distance.

"See that little white boy sitting over there in the corner?" They all looked at Michael Gasca alone in his booth with a cocktail in front of him. He didn't look like much. "That's the smartest man on the planet,"

Roscoe said. "He can remember the final score of every NCAA football game since 1976. I'm willing to put up fifty dollars that says you can't stump him."

As usual, it didn't take much more than that to get the carnival rolling. They walked over to the table—Yellow Tie limped—and dug into their memories.

"In 1984," Black-rimmed glasses said, "my alma mater, Stanford, played Northeast Louisiana—"

Before he finished the sentence, Michael Gasca spit out, "It was October 3rd. The line on the game was Stanford by 21, but Northeast Louisiana scored a late touchdown. Final was 30-14 Stanford, but Northeast Louisiana covered the spread." Just like that, Roscoe Evans picked up fifty dollars. Roscoe didn't like it when Gasca answered so quickly, because he thought they might quit. But they were competitive young men with an audience of young ladies watching the exchange; they wouldn't surrender easily. So the yuppies doubled down—and lost. Then doubled again—and lost. And again. And again.

After a while a pile of money was heaped on the table and someone had run out to his car to get a Palm Pilot. He had wireless Internet access, and the yuppies were ready to find some games that Michael Gasca wouldn't know. They threw out "Angelo State versus Texas Lutheran College in 1981."

Gasca said, "Which month?"

That's when they thought they had him. Roscoe could see the predatory shine on their teeth when they smiled. By then they were down a thousand dollars, but at double-or-nothing, they needed to stump Gasca only once to win back all their money.

Michael Gasca said, "Because they played twice that year. The first game on September 12th got called in the third quarter because of lightning. The score was 17–10 Angelo State. They played a re-match on November 14th and Angelo State won that one 20–14. Which one were you talking about?"

Roscoe laughed again; this time the Harley roared up to 30 mph. He watched the yuppies carefully, and he knew they had the same thought everyone had when they first met Michael Gasca: *Who the hell is this guy?*

Now they had to decide what to do. Cowlick glared at Roscoe and said, "Double or nothing."

"You got another grand on you?" Roscoe wondered pleasantly.

"I have this." Cowlick pulled off his Rolex. Roscoe looked at it for a while, then handed it to Michael Gasca, who studied it and nodded.

Cowlick said, "It's worth three grand. I'll put it up to cover the double here, and I'll take the cash off the table."

Roscoe laughed again, longer this time, and if possible, deeper. The Harley sped up to 60 mph. "We don't give change," he said, chuckling. He handed the watch back. "Maybe we'll just take the cash and call it a night."

"Wait a second!" Cowlick said. He huddled with his buddies. Roscoe could see that the other three wanted to cut their losses and run, but Cowlick wouldn't let them. He sounded like a coach trying to motivate his players. He told them that they had a computer. They'd take their time and search for the right game. They'd find a couple of little division three schools that played fifteen years ago in a game that no one could possibly remember. "We're not gonna let that *cocksucker* take our money!"

They turned back to the table. Cowlick put his watch on top of the cash and said, "The watch entitles us to two chances." He glared at Roscoe—they all did. Despite Roscoe's intimidating size, looking at him was easier than locking eyes with Gasca. When people stared at Michael Gasca, they got headaches.

"Tell you what," Roscoe said generously. "For the watch, you get four chances."

It didn't matter. Michael Gasca never missed.

■ ■ ■

Jennifer brought their food out from the kitchen.

"Here ya go, boys," she said, sliding the plates onto the table.

"We haven't taken any money from any stupid drunks in a while," Roscoe Evans said nostalgically.

"What are you talking about?" Gasca said, "I took some money from *you* ten minutes ago."

Now that hurt.

Before Roscoe could respond, Michael Gasca's cell phone rang. He pulled it from the clip on his belt and spoke softly. Gasca had a new phone every week, and each came equipped with a digital scrambler to keep the FBI from eavesdropping.

"How's Texas?" Gasca said. He'd sent two trusted men down to Texas to do some advance work. Mostly they were building dossiers on the Stallions' players and coaches, but one of their priorities was tracking down adequate living quarters for Gasca and Roscoe.

"So you found it?" Gasca asked, smiling with the phone pressed to his ear. "Oh, don't worry about that, she's in love."

Roscoe couldn't hear the question, but he smiled appreciatively. In their business, love was more deadly than guns.

"No, don't go anywhere near Trevor," Gasca said. "We'll take care of that ourselves."

▪ ▪ ▪

Steven Oquist kept his camera rolling throughout the lunch inside Lenny's Grill. After the men walked out, he watched Roscoe squeeze laboriously back into the Town Car. Oquist waited a full twenty minutes before starting his car.

3

Steven Oquist hadn't spoken to Susan Rich in years; he hoped she wasn't still angry with him. He dialed her number as he angled across town.

"Susan, this is Steven Oquist with NFL Security."

"Hello," she said coolly. Susan was in her late forties with short dark hair and big, compassionate eyes. She worked mostly with families who had recently learned of a child's disability.

"I was hoping you could do me another favor," Oquist said. "I've got a tape that I—"

"Mr. Oquist," Susan interrupted. "I told you several years ago that I don't do that sort of work." She typically met with desperate parents who walked through her door shell-shocked and scared.

"I know that," Oquist said. "I wouldn't ask if it weren't important. But we've got an emergency here. If you could just take a look at the tape, it would really help a lot."

Susan closed her eyes. She'd first met Oquist when he worked for the FBI. He'd needed her help catching a notorious gangster. She'd agreed because the investigation sounded important, but the experience had taken too much from her. She didn't like spying, even on people who deserved to be caught. She often told her students that they should always have respect for other people and never use their ability to intrude on private conversations. She'd worked with Oquist on three occasions, and each time, she'd found the work so distasteful that she vowed never to repeat. But once again, he had dialed her number.

"I can be at your place in fifteen minutes," Oquist said.

"Fine," Susan sighed. "But this is the very last time, Mr. Oquist. I hope you understand that. The absolute last time."

"Believe me, Susan, I won't ever ask again."

He had said that before.

"I don't have much time," Susan said. "I have students coming over this morning."

"The tape's not long at all," Oquist promised.

■ ■ ■

The videotape had been shot with a telescopic high-definition camera. Lynn watched as Roscoe Evans and Michael Gasca climbed out of a Lincoln Town Car, walked into a restaurant, and sat down at a table near the window. Roscoe had his back to the camera; Gasca faced it.

Susan Rich spoke the words as she saw them. She was one of the nation's leading audiologists and speech pathologists. She'd given up a career as a traveling lecturer so that she could teach deaf children to read lips. Susan could instantly match words to the movement of any mouth speaking English. In the same way that each key on a piano had a unique and identifiable tone, so too did each arrangement of the lips, tongue, and teeth. A composer might watch a muted videotape of someone playing the piano and imagine the melody in his head just by watching the pianist's hands; Susan could watch a man talk for fifteen minutes and know not just what he'd said, but whether he'd said it with an accent.

Steven Oquist took notes as she spoke. She repeated only Michael Gasca's half of the conversation, but it gave them an idea of what was happening. Oquist smiled all the way to his toes when he heard Michael Gasca—through Susan Rich—say that he would head down to Texas to work on Trevor. Oquist knew only one Trevor in Texas worth talking about—Trevor Deale, the first-round draft pick and starting quarterback for the San Antonio Stallions.

Oquist thanked Susan profusely and promised to throw away her phone number, which they both knew was a lie. He called Ken Parsley's office.

"Elizabeth, it's Steven Oquist. Is C.C. in?"

The assistant director's secretary was immediately on edge. Oquist hadn't called in a while, so she was out of practice at fending off his requests.

"He's, uh. . ." she stumbled.

"Listen, this is serious. I really need to talk to him."

"He's not available."

"I'm in New York," Oquist interrupted, which was not quite true. He was still in Philadelphia, but he could be at the NFL's Park Avenue office in a few hours. "Tell him I'm coming by today. I have a videotape to show him."

"What's on the tape?" Elizabeth asked.

Oquist took a deep breath and wondered why he had to put up with this continuous inquisition. "It's for C.C.'s eyes only."

"When I tell him you're on the phone, he's going to ask me what you want," Elizabeth said, her tone mimicking the impatient tone C.C. would have when he asked the question. "I need to be able to give him a snapshot."

"I've got a known crime family member mentioning the name of a prominent NFL player." That ought to get the alarms clanging, Oquist thought.

"Is the known crime family member Michael Gasca?" Elizabeth prodded, even more condescending than usual.

"As a matter of fact, *E-liz-a-beth*, it is. Do you want to get C.C. on the phone or do you want to keep pretending that you're the assistant director?"

"I'm just doing my job."

"And I'm just doing mine!" Oquist screamed. "Put the fat fuck on the phone!"

The line clicked, and Oquist feared that he'd been cut off, but then he heard delicate hold music. Finally, Elizabeth returned and told him in curt tones that he could have fifteen minutes with the director at 4 P.M. She hung up before he could respond.

Steven Oquist walked into Ken Parsley's office with his old swagger back. The assistant director extended his pudgy hand over the desk, and Oquist shook it without conviction. Parsley's hand had the consistency of play dough.

"I've got a few things to show you," Oquist said. "But before I do, I want your word that if you're persuaded by what I have here, you'll take it to the director and put me back on the street as part of the investigating team."

"If this has to do with Michael Gasca—" Ken Parsley's neck jiggled as he talked.

"Of course it does, C.C., but before you roll your eyes, I want you to watch the tape." Oquist pulled a videotape out of his bag. He'd used an editing program on his computer to add the transcript as a lower-third graphic.

"Why do you call me that?" Parsley said.

"Call you what?"

"C.C."

Oquist shrugged. He didn't plan to tell the Corpulent Copulator anything. "I can't remember how it got started, but everyone's called you that for so many years, why are you asking about it now?"

"Because no one else will tell me."

"Maybe they don't remember either."

"Maybe they didn't make it up."

"You think I did?"

"I know you did. I just don't know what it means."

Oquist pretended to think about if for a moment. "It probably has to do with the fact that you get CCed on every memo. You're the top dog, no man cometh unto the director but by you. So you're C.C. That's how I remember it."

Ken Parsley eyed Oquist suspiciously. "Because if it's any reference to my weight . . ." He left the threat hanging.

"Of course not," Oquist said. "By the way, you look good. Have you lost a few pounds?"

Parsley perked up. "About ten on the protein diet."

"Lost?" Oquist said, "or lost *sight* of?" Oquist believed everything below the assistant director's prodigious stomach might be written off as missing if Parsley didn't occasionally consult a mirror.

"You should be careful," Parsley warned. His eyeballs jiggled with rage.

"You wanna watch the tape?"

Parsley let out a breath and seemed happy to leave the topic. "Who did the translation?"

"Susan Rich."

Ken nodded, which sent a ripple down the front of his body. If Susan Rich did the lip-reading, he knew he could trust the script implicitly.

As the tape rolled, Ken Parsley recognized Michael Gasca and Roscoe Evans, but their faces didn't surprise him. He figured this was more of Oquist's usual stuff. Only at the end of the tape when the script revealed the words "Texas" and "Trevor" did Parsley become interested.

"Where is Michael Gasca now?"

Steven Oquist watched Parsley with a sly look on his face. "Are you going to let me be part of this?"

"Is he in San Antonio?"

"Are you going to put me back on the street?"

Parsley sighed, which sounded to Oquist like a whale shooting air out of its blowhole. "Steve, I promise, I won't shut you out on this. But right now I need to know what you know."

"I'm guessing they're in San Antonio, but I'm not positive. I know this much—they were out of town for two weeks. They came back three days ago, and they're probably leaving again soon."

"Could have been on vacation."

"True."

"Or working in Vegas or Atlantic City."

"True again, but no one saw them in either of those cities, and—"

"Or in Europe like the last time you sounded an alarm and had us scouring the nation, and it turned out they were sitting on a beach in Barcelona."

"I know," Oquist said quickly. He didn't want Parsley to get rolling on all of his past failures. "But why would they meet to talk about the Stallions if they weren't making a move?"

"Maybe they're fans," Ken said.

"Come on."

"Maybe they knew you were watching."

"No way. I'd been on the stakeout for three days, shifting locations, and I was all the way down the street. They had no idea I was there."

"Who authorized the stakeout?"

Uh-oh, Oquist thought.

"Listen, Ken. I did this on my own time, okay? I got a tip from a friend, so I started watching for myself. The tip produced this lead."

"I thought you were in San Diego at a funeral."

"Ken," Oquist said. He looked out the window, but couldn't find any words.

"How do you know the tipster wasn't working with them?" Ken Parsley said. "Get you down there with your camera, so that you can record them talking about Trevor Deale and Texas. You go running off to San Antonio, dragging NFL Security's focus with you while they target some other team?"

Steven Oquist let out a long, slow breath. "No one knows Michael Gasca the way I know him. I've been watching this kid most of his life, and this feels as real as anything I've ever seen. I'm telling you, they're on their way to Texas right now, and the fact that Roscoe Evans and Michael Gasca are handling this themselves tells me that it's big."

Ken Parsley doodled on a piece of paper. "Have you talked to Jerry Powers?" He was the NFL Security agent in San Antonio.

"Not yet," Oquist said. "I was hoping to talk to him in person."

Parsley watched Oquist carefully. "Powers is a good man."

"Yes, he is, but—"

"And Roscoe Evans isn't the kind of guy who can hide in a crowd. If he was in San Antonio, Powers would know about it."

"Probably—"

"So maybe we should just call Jerry Powers and see what he says."

Oquist rubbed a hand down his face.

Ken Parsley dialed the phone. Oquist could hear only part of the conversation, but it was clear that Jerry Powers had not seen anything. While he talked, Parsley replayed the end of the surveillance tape. The words "Texas" and "Trevor" stuck out in the script.

The assistant director put the phone back on its cradle. "Not yet."

"But what if they—"

"If anything strange happens, we'll take a closer look."

"You'll call me in on it?"

"I'll put you on it," Ken promised.

"Thanks, Ken."

"But Oquist, I don't want to hear any more about you running your own operations. You don't do stakeouts unless I authorize them. I don't want you doing any investigations of this matter without clearing it with me first. Is that understood?"

4

Trevor Deale cruised slowly down streets lined with magnificent oak trees, tall hedges and homes the size of apartment complexes. He had to remind himself that he wasn't just a gawker any more—he was wealthy enough to purchase any home on the block. As the number-one pick in the draft and the new starting quarterback for the San Antonio Stallions, Trevor had signed a six-year, forty-five-million-dollar contract with escalators that would increase the deal to nearly sixty million if he performed as well as everyone hoped he would. The sun winked through thin clouds, and Trevor pulled his Nike shades down over his eyes. His mother chattered away on the cell phone. He hadn't told her about the house he was planning to visit because the price embarrassed him. Trevor had lived in dire poverty for so long that the opulence that now surrounded him felt a little ridiculous.

His contribution to the conversation didn't require much, just a few "uh-huhs" and a chuckle every now and then. Trevor craned his neck to look at a castle sitting back from the road, hidden by trees and perched on a small rise in the land. Some of the homes in the Dominion—with a golf course that was a regular PGA Tour stop—sold for four to five hundred thousand dollars, but the entry price was a bit too low for the multi-million-dollar upper crust seeking true segregation from the great unwashed masses; the Estates at Dominion offered a gated community within a gated community, plus most of the homes had private security gates—the Jehovah's Witness would have to work pretty hard to get to the front door. The minimum bid for a house in the Estates was two million dollars, and Trevor's girlfriend, Vanessa Patterson, had chosen a home worth three times the ante.

"Uh huh. . ." Trevor said into the phone. He looked over at Vanessa. They'd been together a year and a half, and looking at her still made his pulse race. She had a nose that angled down her face with perfect pitch between high cheekbones that were always flushed with natural blush. A few light freckles dotted the bridge of her nose, and dappled green color danced in her eyes. She had plump, supple lips and a long, feminine jaw that framed the bottom of her face and gave warning of the beginning of her succulent neck. Vanessa had the type of body that inspired the makers of low-slung, hip-hugger jeans and tight, midriff-baring shirts. Her high, firm breasts easily filled a C-cup bra. She had a sculpted waist and a tiny bubble butt that looked great in jeans.

Trevor had brownish-blond hair, clear blue eyes, a square jaw and a six-foot-four-inch muscular frame that made it appear that he'd just stepped out of a beer commercial. He and Vanessa had been a royal couple on the University of Oklahoma campus, and now they were both excited to be shopping for the house they might share for the rest of their lives.

"Trevor, the house is beautiful," his mother continued on the phone. Kathy Deale was talking about her own new home—five of which would have fit inside the mansion Trevor and Vanessa were about to tour. Trevor had promised to buy his mother anything she wanted. He had assumed that she'd want to move out of Lamesa, Texas, but she had refused to leave the small town where she'd spent most of her life. Even more surprisingly, Trevor's sister, Mandy, wanted to stay in Lamesa.

Mandy was a dark-haired twenty-one-year-old whose soulful brown eyes still shined with hope despite the years of despair she'd endured. Childhood undernourishment had left her slightly too skinny. But she had a pretty face that showed few traces of her adolescent acne. Mandy wasn't a stunning creature like Vanessa, but what she lacked in raw beauty, she more than made up for with a kind spirit, quick-witted intellect, and generous heart. Trevor wanted nothing more than for Mandy to fall in love, and now it seemed to be happening. She'd recently started dating a man who worked as a consultant at the state prison, and from everything Trevor had heard, he sounded like a keeper.

"The fridge's got more food in it than I've ever seen," Kathy Deale said. "It looks like a grocery store in there." Her new 2,000-square-foot home had been constructed adjacent to the old house. It had taken six months to build, and Kathy and Mandy had moved in a couple of weeks ago.

"There's wall-to-wall carpeting in the whole house and tile in the bathrooms!" Kathy exclaimed. "And a garage that opens all by itself. I got the car parked in there." She said this in a hushed whisper, as if she feared someone might discover the secret hiding place of her Honda Accord. Trevor had offered to purchase any vehicle she wanted. He had thought she'd want a luxury car or a big SUV, but after checking with Consumer Reports, Kathy had determined that a Honda Accord LX had everything she needed.

"It's reliable and it gets good gas mileage," she'd said.

Trevor hadn't expected gas mileage would be so important to her, since she traveled only two miles to work each day. But his mother had been poor most of her life and Trevor's sudden wealth hadn't displaced her natural frugality. However, her new possessions had changed her perspective on property ownership. She was more nervous now. She worried about the car every day. She'd read in the paper and seen stories on TV about cars thieves, "and there are a lot of guys at the prison who got there by stealing cars," she'd once reported. Her husband had stolen her last car when he deserted the family years ago, and she was determined to never again lose her mobility. She hid the Honda in the garage like a woman secreting family heirlooms in safe.

"If there's anything y'all need, you just let me know," Trevor said. He would give every penny to his mother if she wanted it.

Vanessa pointed off to their right, and Trevor pulled through a gate, easing up a long driveway toward a Mediterranean mansion sitting serenely among a grove of oak trees. The house had tan stucco walls, a red tile roof, and the relaxed air of an exotic resort hotel.

Trevor smiled at Vanessa and took her hand. She was wearing a cream-colored silk skirt with an off-the-shoulder black shirt. She'd pulled her terracotta hair up seductively, polished her tan skin to a shine, and framed her green eyes with liner and mascara. She squeezed his hand and smiled back lovingly. They couldn't wait to start this new chapter in their lives.

"I'm so proud of you, Trevor," his mother said. "All those years in the backyard throwing your football at that tire really paid off. You were always so confident that you would be a quarterback in the NFL, and now look at you. You've gone and done it. You made your dream come true."

Trevor blushed. "Mom, I gotta go, but I'll call you later."

"Okay, honey. I love you."

"Love you, too."

"Oh! Did you end up getting that truck you wanted?" She was suddenly interested in vehicles of all types—an expert on transportation.

"Yeah, I picked it up a couple of days ago."

"You made sure it had a good warranty, didn't you? I keep hearing about cars that break and the company won't fix 'em, saying it's your fault the car won't run."

"I got a warranty, Mom."

"Does it get good gas mileage?"

"It does okay."

"I hope it has airbags! That's important 'cause if you get into a crash they could save your life. The little bags just inflate and cushion ya."

"It's got airbags, anti-lock brakes, and four-wheel drive. It's a good car."

"I hope it's not too fancy. Car thieves like those fancy cars, you know?"

"Nothing fancy, Mom, I promise. Just something to get me from point A to point B. I've got to run, Mom, but I'll call you later."

Trevor hung up the phone and climbed out of a black Range Rover 4.6 HSE.

"So what do you think?" Vanessa waved her arm across the view as if she were a *Price is Right* model.

"It's beautiful, honey," Trevor said.

Trina the Realtor flung herself out the front door racing toward them with her arms extended to give hugs all around. "Oh, you found it!" she exclaimed. "I got here early just to make sure everything was perfect for you, and believe me, it is ab-so-lute-ly perfect!"

She ushered them inside for a forty-five-minute tour of the compound, and Trevor grew more quiet with ever step. The house was overwhelming.

"A lot of people go for the traditional Mediterranean style on the outside of the home, but use an entirely different style on the inside," Trina explained as if she were describing something as gauche as lipstick on a dog. "But here, the original owner carried the Mediterranean theme throughout the house. It's just wonderful!"

"It's really quite authentic," Vanessa agreed.

"Something from every country in the region," Trina sang.

They spoke so reverently Trevor was tempted to say, "Amen."

Trina pointed out the Greek architecture in the master suite, while Vanessa gushed over the Italian marble in the guesthouse. Vanessa asked about the Moroccan stones surrounding the swimming pool; Trina drummed her long painted fingernails on the Spanish tiles in the chef's kitchen; Vanessa caressed an elaborate Sicilian banister while Trina raved about an archway modeled after France's Arc de Triomphe.

"I think," Trevor said when the exhausting tour was over, "that this might be a little more than we're looking for."

Vanessa shook her head. "For an estate this size, six million dollars is a steal."

"Just a few months ago," Trina said, "a compound slightly smaller than this one, and not nearly as nice, sold for just over seven million."

"Sounds like property values might be going down," Trevor suggested.

"Sounds like the perfect time to buy," Vanessa said.

■ ■ ■

"We can't buy that house," Trevor said when they were back in the car. They eased down the drive as Trina frantically waved goodbye in the rearview mirror.

"Trevor, you're a multimillionaire," Vanessa said. "You need to have a home befitting your status."

"I liked the house we looked at yesterday," Trevor said. Many of his teammates lived in a neighborhood near the Stallions's facility.

"It was a dump."

Trevor laughed abruptly. "A three-thousand-square-foot house is hardly a dump, Vanessa."

"It is when it's surrounded by thousands of identical three-thousand-square-foot houses, Trevor. But *that*," she pointed over her shoulder to the estate, "is a one-of-a-kind home that makes a statement."

Trevor released a typical sigh of surrender. What difference did it make? He had more money than he could possibly spend, and if Vanessa loved this house, he could buy it just as easily as any other house.

"I'll call Trina and tell her we want to make an offer," Vanessa said with finality. To her chagrin, Trevor had purchased their automobiles months earlier without consulting her. She'd clucked her tongue when he came home telling about the deal he'd negotiated on a three-year old Range Rover for himself, but she'd nearly had a heart attack the next day when he'd presented her with a used Mercedes Benz. Vanessa didn't see any reason for them to drive other people's hand-me-down cars.

■ ■ ■

They'd first met a year and a half earlier in a criminal justice class. Vanessa Patterson had purposely sat next to Trevor Deale and smiled invitingly whenever their eyes met, but Trevor rarely smiled back. He always averted his eyes the moment they met hers.

The smile would slip quickly from Vanessa's pretty face. Her carefully styled hair hung down to her shoulder blades. She liked to run her hands through her mane, roughing it up casually and feeling sexy doing it. Vanessa kept a close watch on Trevor, but as far as she could tell, she had no effect on him.

But she was not deterred. Vanessa had many weapons in her arsenal, and she was prepared to use all of them on Trevor Deale. Before the next class, she stood in front of the mirror with her hair pulled up in a loose tangle and decided that she looked vulnerable with her delicate neck exposed. *Yes*, Vanessa thought as she primped, *I look like a damsel who needs to be rescued, and that might be just the right bait.* But during fifty minutes of class, Trevor didn't appear to glance her way. Vanessa stormed out of the room crafting yet another plan. She came to class in tight jeans, then in a mini-skirt and finally in a pair of fabulously short shorts that revealed the bottom curve of her firm cheeks and caught the attention of every man in the room—hell, every man on campus—except Trevor Deale.

What Vanessa didn't know was that Trevor had noticed her in the same way he noticed defensive linemen on the football field. He kept his eyes downfield, yet he knew when to step up to avoid the rush and when to flee a collapsing pocket. Trevor saw Vanessa, but he had no idea what to do about her.

Vanessa came to class in tiny hip-hugger slacks and tight pullovers with plunging necklines that revealed the sort of miracle most women needed bras to create. She tried six different brands of perfume and four different hairstyles. She'd sit one row over from Trevor and one seat up, so she'd be in his line of sight if he wanted to mentally undress her. She'd flip her hair, cross her legs, show as much thigh as possible and lean down to retrieve items from her purse, giving him a bird's-eye view of her cleavage.

She even tried a trick she'd read in *Cosmopolitan*: she yawned openly, then waited a second or two and turned to see Trevor's reaction. The magazine had pointed out that yawns were contagious, and if a girl wanted to know if a particular boy was checking her out, she should let her mouth gape. Vanessa looked around, and every man in the class was yawning, including the professor, half the women had their hands over their mouths, but Trevor's mouth carved a thin unflinching line across his face. It seemed that whenever Vanessa turned to look at Trevor—discreetly at first, more blatantly later—she found him staring out the window or taking notes, seemingly oblivious to the spectacle she was creating.

Finally, Vanessa grew weary of waiting. She scribbled a message and slipped it onto his desk, watching him hopefully with her sexiest smile at the ready.

Trevor looked down at the note, surprised and a little embarrassed. Half the class was watching to see what would happen next, and Trevor felt little of the confidence he possessed on the football field. He didn't have much practice at asking beautiful women out on dates, and he wasn't sure what to do. He picked up the note and stuffed it into his pocket. He'd read it when he returned to his dorm room.

Across the aisle, Vanessa was fuming. She was throwing herself at Trevor Deale—she'd never thrown herself at anyone!—and he seemed unfazed. She leaned over and jabbed him hard with two sharp fingernails.

"You could at least read it, you jerk!" she said in a fierce whisper.

Now she really had the attention of everyone in the room. Trevor looked at her and smiled. He had a nice, sincere smile, Vanessa thought. It surprised her.

"I will," he said.

She waited, expecting him to pull the piece of paper out of his pocket, but he didn't move. They looked at each other, and Vanessa settled down, happy to have his attention. She eased the angry look off her face and showed him her teeth.

When the class ended, Trevor walked away without saying a word. Vanessa shook her head and watched him go. She wanted to follow him to see if he tore the note out of his pocket the moment he reached the hallway, but a sudden, uncomfortable fear struck her—*what if he didn't reach for the note?*

Vanessa was waiting at the door when Trevor arrived for class two days later.

"Hi there," she said. She had a notebook cradled in one arm; it pressed against her bulging breasts. Her jeans hugged her legs like paint.

"Hello," Trevor said.

"So what do you think?"

Trevor thought she might want an appraisal of her outfit. "About what?"

Vanessa cocked her head and narrowed her pretty eyes. "About the note I gave you, silly."

"Oh," Trevor said. "I thought it was nice."

"And?"

Trevor chuckled. "I think you should just tell me what you want."

Vanessa studied him for a moment. "My note wasn't clear enough?"

Trevor shook his head. "Your note was very clear, but I have a feeling it has nothing to do with what you really want."

"It said," Vanessa repeated from memory, "'Trevor, give me a call if you'd like to study together sometime,' and then there was my phone number."

"That's what it said."

"So do you want to study together?"

"Why don't we save some time and you just tell me where this is headed?"

He has very calm eyes, Vanessa thought. She felt her own gaze skitter out of focus. "Let me think about it for a few minutes," she said.

They walked into the room together and took their seats. Vanessa spent most of the class agonizing about what she could safely reveal to

Trevor. Now that she had his attention, she didn't want to lose it. At the end of class she put her hand on his arm—her soft delicate hand spoke to Trevor more powerfully than her voice ever could—and said, "I think I want you to be my boyfriend."

Trevor swallowed hard. "And someday your husband?"

Vanessa's pulse quickened. "If it comes to that."

Trevor nodded. "Must have heard I'm gonna be rich."

Vanessa didn't know if she should deny that. "I've heard a thing or two."

"So you figure we fit the classic formula. Athlete with fame and fortune marries beautiful girl who wants to share it."

"We'd make a cute couple," Vanessa said, smiling.

And they did.

For the next year, Trevor Deale and Vanessa Patterson could be found walking hand-in-hand across campus, chatting quietly in the cafeteria, standing in a corner at fraternity parties, or sitting outside reading on warm spring days. They had an easy rhythm together, and everyone who knew them was convinced that they would get married and become a celebrity power couple.

5

Jonathan Kinneson eased a silver Rolls-Royce Bentley up to the gate at the Stallions' workout facility and extended a manicured hand to enter the security code. A three-quarters moon illuminated the midnight sky, and purple clouds painted shadows on the asphalt. The gate opened with a low, efficient rumble, and he drove to his reserved space. After Jonathan Kinneson purchased the team in February, the grounds crew had removed the previous owner's name and stenciled the word KINNESON on the curb. When he arrived at the facility for his first day of work, Kinneson stormed into the building and demanded that the receptionist tell him who was responsible for the parking lot.

"*Responsible* for the parking lot?" she echoed. She shook her head. "I'm not sure I understand the question. Who are you with?"

"Who am I *with*?" Jonathan Kinneson bellowed. He leaned over the desk, spittle dancing on his lips. "You'll find out who I'm with when you're on the street looking for a job, you stupid bitch! Now tell me who painted the fucking curb!"

The receptionist inched back from the desk. "Probably the grounds crew," she said weakly.

"Where?"

She pointed toward the floor. A tear leaked down her cheek. "The basement."

Jonathan Kinneson yanked open the door marked STAIRS and marched down to the basement, where a young man named Jose stood over a barrel mixing fertilizer and grass seed into a spreader. Kinneson grabbed Jose by the front of his work shirt.

"Come here." He dragged the worker across the room, up the stairs, past the receptionist—who had called 911—and out into the parking lot where he jabbed a finger at the curb and screamed, "My name is not Kinneson!"

"My name," Jonathan Kinneson said, pulling Jose close and glaring down at him, "is *Mister* Kinneson! You got that?"

Jose got it. And so did everyone else at the Stallions Center, who from the very first day knew to maintain a safe distance from the irrational, mercurial temper of Jonathan Kinneson. The stencil was changed to read MISTER KINNESON! The grounds crew had been afraid to abbreviate the title, and the exclamation mark was Kinneson's idea; everyone in the building quietly agreed.

Now, in the middle of the night with the parking lot empty, Jonathan Kinneson shuffled toward the front door fumbling with a set of keys he rarely used. Ordinarily a building manager arrived at 6 A.M. each day to prepare the building for the rest of the employees, but Kinneson had the hardware to open the front door. He had alarm codes scribbled on a slip of paper in his wallet just in case he ever needed them, which until now, he'd used only once when he met a pretty young lady who'd wanted a private tour of the Stallions headquarters, and Kinneson agreed, believing it was the perfect opportunity for him to get a private tour of her.

The facility spanned nearly half a million square feet and included a small museum celebrating the brief history of the San Antonio Stallions. The main floor included a weight room big enough for all fifty-three players to work out at the same time. There was a training room with eighteen treatment tables, three offices, ten taping stations, two living-room-sized hot tubs, four two-man cold tubs, and a work-out room for players rehabbing from injuries. The long rectangle of the players' locker room had stalls along the perimeter and waist-high Gatorade coolers down the middle. A media room with twenty-four workstations sat just behind the reception area. Digital portals had been hard-wired into the walls so television crews could plug in their cameras and send live signals straight back to their stations via satellite dishes on the roof.

The Stallions Center had an equipment room holding an impressive arsenal of shoulder pads, helmets, thigh and knee pads, jock straps, cleats, neck braces, and other protective gear. The facility had a digital editing room that dwarfed the capacity of most of the local television stations, and included a library of videotapes of the Stallions past games, tapes of upcoming opponents, and, of course, every practice the Stallions had held since the beginning of training camp. Every meeting room in the facility was equipped with a Betamax projector that was connected to a mainframe in the basement. Coaches and players could call up a play by typing an order into a computer as if it were an Internet search engine. During his first week of work, Kinneson had typed the words, "Priest Holmes toss right." The computer had produced a list of twenty-eight plays, each showing the Kansas City running back accepting a pitch to the right side of the formation.

The key turned in the lock, but the front door didn't open when Kinneson pushed against it. Then he remembered the deadbolt that kept the glass door in its frame. He bent down to slide a different key into the lock at the bottom of the door, and the glass swung in easily. Kinneson stood with a groan, dusting off his knee. The security system bleated insistently as he entered, and he turned on the overhead light before walking to the wall to disarm it. The sound—an annoying *beep-BEEEEP! beep-BEEEEP!*—put Kinneson on edge as he yanked his wallet out of his back pocket. He realized with a grunt that he should have retrieved the code before he got inside.

Now time was working against him. How long did he have? Thirty seconds? A minute? If the alarm went off, the police would respond, which would be a hassle and an embarrassment (*beep-BEEEEP!*). Where was it? He recalled that the six-digit code was written on the back of a business card, but as he checked the nooks and crannies of his wallet, he didn't see it. The alarm's rhythmic pattern seemed to become shriller by the moment (*beep-BEEEEP!*). How long had it been? Finally, he found the card and punched the numbers into the keypad. The alarm stopped at once and he was plunged into blessed silence. He let out a breath and turned to face the room. A portrait mural of himself—another exclamation point—towered up behind the receptionist's desk. He loved this lobby.

Photos of great players of the past and former coaches were hung down the hallway; Kinneson decided that once he fired Max Starnes, the coach's picture would never adorn these walls. It would become a trivia question that would survive for decades: Which former coach of the San Antonio Stallions never had his picture posted on the walls of the team's facility? Kinneson smiled at the thought.

A trophy case stood off to the right side of the lobby bearing division championship iron; there was plenty of room for a couple of Lombardi trophies.

Jonathan Kinneson took the elevator to his suite on the third floor, where more pictures of himself graced the walls of his outer office. In the photos he stood with movie stars, politicians and other famous people. He walked into the inner office and closed the door behind him. Angular, modern furniture stood in clusters like guests at an exclusive party. A leopard-skin rug was stretched between two couches, abstract artwork hung on the walls, and a long, flat, polished cherry desk, shaped like a teardrop, held center court.

Kinneson pulled a bottle of Scotch out of a low cabinet and poured himself a drink. He dropped to one knee, flipped the dial of his floor safe, and grumbled as he extracted the small card Gasca had given him. He glared at the card and took a swallow of Scotch. The mere thought of Michael Gasca and his big thug made Jonathan Kinneson shudder with rage. The humiliation he'd endured! He gulped down the last of the fiery liquid in his tumbler and smacked the bottom of the glass on top of his desk. They would not escape without punishment. Kinneson believed that everything was negotiable—*everything!* He'd pay the million dollars due immediately, but they would never get eleven million. Getting rid of Max Starnes was the first priority. After that, Kinneson would renegotiate the contract.

Michael Gasca's five-step wiring instructions were typed in small print. Kinneson logged on to his computer and transferred $999,000 into Gasca's account—he'd subtracted the thousand dollars Roscoe Evans had forcibly removed at the country club.

6

Tui Acondaca could read people. He could sense their moods, feel their ambitions, and understand their motivations. Within ten seconds of meeting a person, Tui knew if he was nice or mean, scared or happy, angry or sad. Tui's ability made him very good at his job as a bodyguard for the rich and famous; of course, standing six-foot-five and carrying an athletic three hundred pounds helped a little, too. In more than a decade on the job, Tui had reacted with calm efficiency on those rare occasions when someone pulled a knife or a gun, and he'd been firm but pleasant with overzealous fans, angry lovers, paparazzi and even other celebrities who tried to get too close.

But tonight it wasn't a weapon or an overaggressive person that had him spooked—it was a tone of voice. Tui knew that tonight he'd have to betray the boss. And betrayal just wasn't part of his disposition. He threw another worried glance at the rearview mirror. He'd never seen the boss in such a state. Caleb Alexander was fidgeting in the back of the limo, sighing, leaning his head against the seat, then slumping forward limply. His cell phone rang continuously, but he didn't answer it. Tui looked up at the mirror again. They stared at each other for a couple of seconds.

"Everything okay, boss?" Tui said. He got no response. He'd been Caleb Alexander's limo driver for three years, and he'd never seen his employer in a mood like this. Caleb seemed so disappointed, so desperate, so alone. Tui scowled and wondered if he should call Michael Gasca.

"Caleb received some very bad news," Gasca had said when he talked to Tui earlier in the day, "and I have a feeling that very soon he's going to be ripe to hear a proposal I'd like to make. You understand what I'm saying?"

"Yes, sir," Tui had said. He'd met Michael Gasca on several occasions, and though Gasca seemed to be a nice, nonviolent businessman, Tui sensed a vicious undercurrent that told him he should never get on the wrong side of the man.

"I could call Caleb right now," Michael Gasca said. "And he might be receptive to my proposal. But I'd rather call him after the bad news has really sunk in. I want to be able to talk to him when he's really feeling desperate. I need you to be my eyes and ears."

"Mr. Gasca," Tui said slowly, "with all due respect, I've been working for Caleb for three years, and he's been real good to me. He—"

"No, hang on, Tui," Gasca said. "I can appreciate loyalty. I can respect that. I would never ask you to turn on him. All I need you to do is make a phone call. You call me when the time is right. I won't put you in a bad spot."

"I appreciate that, Mr. Gasca."

"But Tui. If I don't hear from you tonight, I'm gonna take it as a personal insult."

There was that tone again.

"Yes, sir," Tui had said. "I understand."

Tui watched Caleb Alexander shuffle a stack of fifty-dollar bills from hand to hand. He didn't appear to be counting the money, just taking pleasure from the touch the way a man might find comfort in rubbing rosary beads.

"You okay, boss?" Tui repeated.

Still Caleb didn't answer, but he looked up with eyes so haunted that Tui was afraid to interrupt again. Twenty-four hours ago, no one could have convinced Tui Acondaca that the boss would ever look the way that he looked now, but he appeared defeated, like a man who'd been fired from a job or dumped by a woman or...Tui wondered what had happened. Caleb had money, he had women, he had an NFL career, he had talent, he had a decadent life. He had everything a man could want, but as the sleek Mercedes limousine turned onto Alamo Street, Caleb stared out the window as if he were searching for something. The limo eased down the block slowly, like a parade float. Pedestrians turned to point and gawk; everyone knew the occupant of the vehicle because Caleb Alexander's limo was as famous on the party scene as he was. His cell phone rang again, but still

Caleb didn't answer. He found it hard to believe that just this morning he'd been laughing, planning a recreational jaunt with his homeboys.

Caleb, Jimmy, and Keith had been chomping on Cheerios while they worked out the logistics for a trip to Vegas. Jimmy was in charge of finding the girls, Keith was making the hotel arrangements, and Caleb was lining up a charter plane. Jimmy had just dialed his cell phone and said, "Young delicious Veronica! You up for a trip to Sin City?" But he had accidentally dialed his girlfriend, Lisa, and she wanted to know who the hell Veronica was, and why was he taking her to Las Vegas? Jimmy pulled the phone away from his ear and swore, then got back on the line and stumbled over himself.

Keith rolled his eyes. "How stupid do you have to be to not recognize your girlfriend's voice when she answers the phone?" Then he whispered: "Hey, tell her you were reading Archie and Jughead and just called her Veronica as a joke."

Jimmy nodded vigorously, then said, "Honey, no...hang on...listen...she's a friend of Caleb's...no, no...he asked me to call her...honey, I'm so in love with you that...look...see, out of force of habit, I dialed your...no, honey...didn't say delicious...said...um...wait, you remember Archie and Jughead?"

Caleb laughed and answered his jingling cell phone.

"Gasca baby," he said, "glad you called. Check it out, you gotta get a Westwind 'cause me and Keith got a trip to Vegas planned." He winked at Keith. "Jimmy was gonna go too, but looks like he might be on house arrest for a while." That brought another long peal of laughter.

"Actually, that's why I was calling you," Michael Gasca said. He'd first met Caleb Alexander five years ago when the Eagles drafted him. Gasca didn't have much face-to-face contact with him—relationships between known crime family members and NFL players were strictly forbidden—but after hearing about Caleb Alexander's early spending habits, Michael Gasca had found a way to make himself the kid's discreet contact for chartered planes.

"Yeah?" Caleb said. "You turnin' psychic on me?"

"I was calling to let you know that you can't afford any more chartered jets."

That caught Caleb off-guard. His lexicon didn't include the words "can't afford." He had many phrases to describe his finances, and they all started with I've-got-more-money-than. The moment he signed his first NFL contract, affordability had ceased being the arbiter of Caleb's purchasing decisions.

"Hush your mouth," Caleb laughed. "I've got more money than Tiger Woods. Just book the plane and quit trying to mother me." Caleb had pocketed a then–NFL record thirty-three-million-dollar signing bonus his rookie year, and he'd earned nearly three million a season since then.

"Caleb," Gasca said with a long-suffering sigh, "I've never been able to protect you from yourself. Can't say I haven't tried though. I've done everything I could to help you, but it's been a fruitless effort. You've ignored my advice…laughed at me…ridiculed me, and you've spent your money in the most irresponsible manner possible. Now, you're just about broke."

For the first time in years, Caleb's confidence stuttered. "Wait a minute…come on…what do you mean?" He got up from the couch and walked into the kitchen, throwing a cautious smile at Keith.

It was Michael Gasca's turn to laugh. "Frankly, you've been the stupidest, most short-sighted person I've ever met. I mean…Caleb…help me out here." Gasca winked at Roscoe and continued. "When I tried to talk you out of paying a quarter million for a Ferrari, did you listen to me? Of course not. Three months later when you were tired of the car, you sold it at a fifty-thousand-dollar loss. Did that teach you a lesson? No. A week later you dropped three hundred grand on a Rolls-Royce, and eventually sold that at a huge loss. You've owned twenty-eight cars in five years—including that limousine you love so much—and twenty-two of them had price tags in excess of a hundred grand. The money you lost on those cars—not the money you spent, just the money you *lost*—could have supported the average family of four for two decades."

"I don't care how much money I've lost," Caleb said, pouring a glass of orange juice. Criticism of his spending habits never affected him. "You're wasting your breath, Gasca. I've got more money than the Pope, so I don't have to watch my pennies."

"Where you stand, Caleb, you're less than a hundred and fifty thousand dollars ahead of your debt service."

Caleb raised his free hand in the air. "Debt service? What the hell are you talking about?"

"You're broke is what I'm talking about."

"Shut up," Caleb said. But it wasn't a command—it was a question.

"Right now, you've got," Gasca flipped open a file and pulled out Caleb's most recent bank statement, "$146,420 in your account. And that's after we used your last check of the season to pay all your bills current, and set aside enough to cover your bills through March. That's it, Caleb. I don't know what else to tell you. You're probably going to have to declare bankruptcy before next season."

Over the past five years, Michael Gasca had attained a strangle hold over Caleb's life. It had started with the charter planes. Then Gasca had recommended an investment broker, accountant, financial planner, lawyer, and agent, all of whom Caleb accepted and all of whom reported to Michael Gasca. The league would never have allowed any of this if it was aware of the situation, but Gasca had been careful to keep a low profile.

"But I've got more money than Wyoming," Caleb said. It was a plea.

"Past tense, Caleb…you had…told you to save some money, but you refused to listen. It boggles the mind, Caleb. Even after taxes and commissions, you had nearly twenty million in cold, hard cash when you were twenty-two years old. For the average person, twenty million is an unconquerable sum. They couldn't spend it in five years if they worked at it. Plus, you've made another fifteen million in salary. It just doesn't seem possible that you could be broke."

"You got that right," Caleb said, relieved.

"But you've done it," Gasca continued. "I told you the mansion in Miami was a bad idea. I told you that the resale market for a ten-million-dollar estate was pretty small, didn't I? The house has been on the block for nearly four years, but there have been no takers. You're making mortgage payments of fifty-eight thousand a month on an estate no one is using. Meanwhile, you bought a five-million-dollar home in San Francisco, and a three-million-dollar apartment in New York."

Caleb pressed the phone tight against his ear. He didn't want to hear another word, but he couldn't stop listening.

"Then," Gasca said with a flourish, "we come to the matter at hand: your obsession with chartered planes. Do you know it costs you a minimum of twenty thousand dollars every time you want a plane? You would have been better off buying first-class commercial tickets for you and your friends, but that was never good enough. You fell in love with the 'Israel Aircraft Westwind,' and you had to have it for every trip. You've spent more than three million on chartered planes alone. And I don't even want to talk about the wild parties in Las Vegas, except to say that it's especially ironic that at the exact moment I called to tell you that you're out of money, you were planning another trip to Vegas."

Caleb had heard enough. "Isn't there anything we can—"

"Nope," Gasca interrupted. "You're broke."

■ ■ ■

In the back seat of the limousine, Caleb stared down again at the stack of fifty-dollar bills in his hands and the memories of the morning's conversation brought a sudden rush of panic bursting from his lips, which sounded like a cross between a cough, a laugh, and a scream.

Tui's eyes jumped to the mirror again, and Caleb stared back. His mouth curved into a terrified smile.

"Something in my throat," Caleb explained desperately. Tui tore his eyes away and didn't look back again.

Caleb had made a flurry of phone calls after the conversation with Michael Gasca. He'd pulled out bank statements that he'd never bothered to check and called the numbers listed. He had several accounts in addition to his main brokerage account, but the answer was the same no matter where he called—he didn't have any money.

Three parking attendants at Club Trixadelphia raced from their posts to remove cones set up in front of the building. Every club in town had a space reserved for Caleb Alexander; no one knew when he might stop by, but everyone wanted to be ready when he did. The head valet—wearing a black T-shirt imprinted with the club's logo "Turnin' Trix"—had his hand on the limo's back door before the vehicle came to a stop.

A line of patrons stretched down the block waiting to get into the club, and many of them smiled and waved. Caleb waved back as he stepped out of the vehicle. He had a fifty-dollar bill in his hand for the valet, who said, "Good evening, C.A. It's always good to see you."

Caleb wore a loose cream-colored silk shirt under a leopard-print coat and a matching leopard hat with a long brim shading one eye. In nature, the dappled camouflage of a leopard's spots allowed it to creep undetected toward a herd. Caleb liked the outfit for the exact opposite reason—it drew everyone's attention. The bouncers at the door greeted Caleb with smiles; he palmed a fifty into each of their hands.

Trixadelphia was teeming with beautiful young bodies. A deejay pumped urban funk out of the speakers, and half-naked, gyrating bodies packed the dance floor. Trixadelphia had become the hottest Friday night hangout, and Caleb always found a way to put himself in the middle of it. The valet called the deejay booth, and before Caleb was five steps into the building, the deejay's voiced boomed over the music:

"LADIES AND GENTLEMEN! FREAKS AND FRIZZETTES! OUR MAN CALEB ALEXANDER IS IN DA HEEZEE FO SHEEZEE!"

A roar of applause and cheers rose up from the club.

"WELCOME BACK, C.A.!"

As Caleb worked his way down the steps, women rushed to his side. He was six-foot-two and a solid two hundred thirty pounds, with muscles rippling under his light brown skin. Women had found him attractive most of his life, but fame and wealth had made him irresistible. They came in all shapes and sizes, easing toward him with inviting smiles, running their hands over his powerful frame. When Caleb walked into a room, he filled the space around him with women as easily as a farmer drawing water from a well. Caleb handed a fifty-dollar bill to a cocktail waitress who edged through the throng, but shook his head from side to side telling her he didn't need anything at the moment. He continued forward, looking down at each of the women in turn, openly evaluating them. They never knew what he would want. Sometimes he picked women with tight, athletic bodies; other times, voluptuous women with thick waists, thicker busts, and even thicker bottoms. Sometimes he liked blondes, sometimes brunettes, sometimes redheads—sometimes all three at once.

Tonight Caleb ignored the women who approached him. He was searching for a *sweet* girl, and he'd know her when he saw her. The club manager pushed his way through the throng to put a hand on Caleb's shoulder.

"Hi, C.A. Tom Banks. It's good to see you again. Can I get you anything?" He had to yell to be heard over the music.

Caleb barely glanced at the man, but slipped him a fifty.

It didn't take long to find her. She stood at the edge of the dance floor with two girlfriends. She was about five-foot-five with short black hair and a trim, athletic body. She wore a too-tight shirt that stopped short of a small gold hoop in her belly button. Black stretchy pants revealed the curve of her toned legs. She had dressed to attract attention, and though she hadn't yet realized it, she'd been spotted by the most aggressive predator in the club. Caleb knew she was sweet because she didn't respond to him. When Caleb Alexander walked into a room, every head turned in his direction; the face that didn't turn was like a domino that didn't fall.

Caleb walked up to her and slid a hand around her waist as he leaned in close. "I'll give you a grand if you come home with me tonight."

She scowled and pushed him away.

"How about fifteen hundred?" He eased the wad of fifties out of his pocket.

She studied him for a moment and looked down at the cash. "Is this your technique?" she said with an edge. "You find a girl, walk up to her, show her a few bucks like every woman is a prostitute and you're gonna buy her?"

Caleb shrugged. "I don't like to waste time."

She crossed her arms. "Well, I'm not for sale."

Caleb smiled. That's what made her sweet. She didn't yet know she could be bought. Once she knew he was a multi-millionaire, she'd do anything he wanted.

"You could do a lot with fifteen hundred dollars."

She stared levelly.

"You change your mind," Caleb said. "I'll be here a while."

■   ■   ■

Heather Kirksey turned to her friends with a look of disgust. She expected praise for blowing off the megalomaniac jerk, but her friends had other thoughts.

"Do you know who that is?…that's Caleb Alexander…you know, the guy who plays for the Stallions?…he's got more money than Oprah…every woman in here is after him…if he had asked me, I would have gone home with him in a heartbeat…fifteen hundred bucks?…you could probably talk him into giving you twenty-five hundred and cover your rent next semester…look at him, he's a total hottie…I'd do him just because he's cute…if he wanted to give me some cash, that's just a bonus…my friend Melanie went to a party at his house, and she said he was walking around handing out hundred-dollar bills. By the time she left, she had more than three grand."

They told Heather about Caleb's mansion, his Mercedes limousine and his Lamborghini Diablo. They told her about the jets he chartered, the trips he took, the beautiful women he dated, the lavish gifts he dispensed, and his legendary spending sprees. Heather insisted that none of that stuff mattered to her, but her conviction was slipping. She watched Caleb from a distance and saw the surge of people moving toward him. She saw the women competing for his attention. She wondered if she'd been too hasty. If everyone was so eager to be near him, he must not be that bad, and he was sort of cute, she decided, in his funny leopard hat and silky shirt. The more Heather thought about it, the less insulted she felt. She could use fifteen hundred dollars, and she felt oddly flattered that someone would pay so much just to have sex with her.

"What do you need?" the bartender yelled to Caleb, throwing down a napkin.

"Budweiser!" Caleb yelled back. He slipped the man a fifty and a credit card. "And a round for five minutes."

The bartender nodded knowingly, raising an arm and circling it several times, then held up five fingers toward the stage. The deejay's voice boomed over the music,

"LISTEN UP PLAYERS AND HUSTLERS, FREAKS AND FRIZZETTES! OUR MAN CALEB ALEXANDER HAS DONE IT AGAIN! FOR THE NEXT FIVE MINUTES, YOU CAN GET YOUR DRINK ON COURTESY OF THE LATEST AND GREATEST AND STILL-REIGNING HEAVYWEIGHT KING OF THE SAN ANTONIO STALLIONS…CALEB ALEXANDER!"

The crowd roared back : "CEE-AYY, ALWAYS COMES TO PLAY!"

"YA CAIN'T LOSE WITH FREE BOOZE," the deejay continued. "AND JUST SO YOU KNOWS HOW THE TIME GOES, I GOT FIVE MINUTES THAT PHAT PHREAKY PHUNK. WHEN THE MUSIC STOPS, SO DO THE DRINKS. YOU'RE ON THE CLOCK, FREAKS. GET IT ON!"

Later, as Caleb headed toward the door, Heather Kirksey squeezed in beside him. He looked down at her, smiling, knowing that she'd been educated.

"Am I still invited?" she said. Her lips were close to his ear; the soft caress of her breath tickled his skin.

"You're not offended anymore?" Caleb asked.

"I didn't know who you were."

"Now you know?"

"Yeah."

Caleb reached down and adjusted his rigid erection. A sweet girl was exactly what he needed. Heather snuggled a little closer into his armpit, looking viciously at a dark-haired girl who'd eased in on the other side of him. Heather leaned into his ear and tried to keep the plea out of her voice.

"I thought I was the one for tonight," she said.

Caleb smiled down at her. "Oh...you're definitely a winner, but so is Elizabeth...if that's all right with you."

Heather frowned.

"Now, don't getting all pouty on me," Caleb warned. "If it's not you and Elizabeth, it'll be two other girls. Elizabeth's ready to play, aren't you darlin'?"

"I'm down for whatever," Elizabeth sighed. She dragged her tongue along Caleb's neck.

"So you in or you out?" Caleb asked Heather.

An odd desperation tugged at Heather's heart. She looked around. Women were everywhere. They seemed ready to pounce on Caleb, yet here he was again choosing her. She didn't want to lose her opportunity. She wanted to be the one.

"I'm in," she said softly, leaning up to kiss his lips.

"No, darlin'," Caleb said. "It's not me you gotta make up with. It's Elizabeth. Why don't you give her a kiss, tell her you're sorry for being so selfish."

Heather hesitated as Elizabeth leaned across Caleb's body. Heather had never kissed a woman, and she wasn't sure what to expect. Their lips touched lightly, then their tongues met, and Heather closed her eyes. She was surprised at how soft the other woman's lips felt. Elizabeth's hand came up to Heather's breast, caressing it through the fabric of her shirt, and though Heather was shocked, she couldn't help moaning.

"Good girls," Caleb said, when they broke the kiss. He had a woman on each arm as he strutted out of the club.

Tui was relieved when he saw the boss. The smile was back along with the cocky swagger. Caleb threw fifty-dollar bills at the bouncers and valets and waved at the line of people waiting to enter the club.

They tumbled into the limo, and Elizabeth and Heather had their shirts off before Tui pulled away from the curb. They caressed each other as they tugged at Caleb's clothing, and he smiled contentedly, kissing each woman in turn. This, Caleb mused, was just what he needed. Heather kissed him aggressively as if she had something to prove, Elizabeth dragged down his boxers and took him into her mouth. Tui couldn't keep his eyes off the mirror.

Suddenly Elizabeth sat up, scowling. "Don't you want me?" she said. She wiggled his limp penis back and forth. "Hello? Hello? Does this thing work?"

"You're not doing it right!" Caleb snapped. His face was hot as he slapped her hand away.

"Look, this isn't my fault," Elizabeth said. She sat on her haunches staring at his flaccid member.

"I don't know what's going on," Caleb said, covering his penis with both hands. "This has never happened before." His eyes danced back and forth between the two women calculating how far this news would travel.

"I still get two grand even if you can't get it up, right?" Elizabeth said.

Heather slid away from Caleb. Suddenly, the fifteen hundred dollars she'd been promised seemed like an insult. "She's getting two grand?"

"Tui, stop the car!" Caleb dug into his clothes on the floor, pulling out the wad of fifties. He peeled off a handful and threw the money out the open door, pushing the girls out after it.

Elizabeth laughed. "Maybe you should spend some of that cash on a penis pump!"

He tossed their clothes out and screamed for Tui to speed away.

The driver sneaked another glance at the mirror. Caleb sat naked from the waist down with his face in his hands. Tui raised the glass between the two compartments and eased a cell phone out of his pocket.

"I think it's time," Tui whispered to Michael Gasca.

"What's he doing?"

"He had two girls, but he couldn't...perform, so now—"

"He couldn't get it up?"

"Yeah, and now it looks like he's crying."

"Hand him the phone."

Tui paused. "Sir...if I give him the phone, he's gonna know I'm involved in this. You could call his cell—"

"Hand him the phone, Tui."

"Mr. Gasca, I'm begging you. You said you were gonna leave me outta this."

"Are you arguing with me, Tui?"

There was that tone again.

"No sir." Tui said quickly. He lowered the glass. "Boss, there's someone wants to talk to you."

Caleb shook his head. "Not right now."

"It's Michael Gasca," Tui said. He couldn't meet the boss's eye.

Caleb took the phone.

"So your dick's on the fritz, eh?" Gasca said.

Caleb scowled at Tui.

"Well," Gasca continued, "that's the bad news. The good news is that you might not be as broke as we thought."

"Yeah?" Caleb asked desperately.

"I've found five hundred thousand."

Caleb was starting to get hard again. Maybe he'd go back and pick up the girls. "That's great!"

"But you've gotta work for it."

"No problem." He would definitely go back for the girls. They'd probably still be getting dressed. Tui could go back and pick them up before they found another ride. Yeah, they'd be pissed, but Caleb would offer them a few more bucks and they'd be good to go.

"What do I have to do?"

"Something you've done by accident many times in the past, Caleb. Only this time, you're going to do it on purpose. On Sunday, the first time you get the ball inside the red zone, I want you to fumble. You do that, you get five hundred grand."

Silence stretched between the two men; Michael Gasca let it grow.

Caleb had been a highly paid flop most of his career, but Sunday would be his first start in two seasons.

"I can't...fumble."

"Sure you can, you've done it quite a few times in your career. I'd say you're prolific at it."

Caleb's erection faded. "But if I lose another ball…"

"If you don't want the money…"

Caleb licked his lips. "Where's it coming from?"

"It's yours."

"No, I mean, who's putting it up?"

"You are," Gasca said.

Caleb frowned. "I don't get it."

"Three years ago I started skimming from your paychecks, and I've deposited that money in a bank in the Cayman Islands. You've got, nearly one million in the account," Gasca shuffled some more papers, "$993,047, to be exact. I'll give you a little more than half of it."

"You stole my money?"

"I didn't steal anything, Caleb. The account is in your name, so it's still your money, but without me, you don't have access to it."

"I could start calling banks," Caleb said. His dick was hard again. Just knowing that he had money made him lightheaded with delight. "I could find the account myself."

"Don't be stupid, Caleb. You don't know the name of the bank, the account numbers or the access codes. What are you gonna do, get out the Yellow Pages and ask them if they have an account in your name?"

Caleb considered his options.

"Tell you what," Michael Gasca said. "Sleep on it. Sunday, the first time you get the ball inside the twenty, you fumble it. You do that; you'll have your money. You don't come through for me, you're still broke."

Gasca hung up the phone and turned to Roscoe Evans with a smile. "I think we'll be okay."

"You shouldn't have hung Tui out like that," Roscoe admonished.

"Had to do it," Michael Gasca shrugged.

"You could have called Caleb on his own cell phone and left Tui out of it."

"Roscoe, believe me, I like Tui and I didn't want to put him in a bad spot, but I needed Caleb to know that he didn't have anyone on his side. He's completely isolated, and the only one who can help him is me. So that meant I had to burn Tui a little bit. He'll get over it."

Roscoe shook his head. "I've been watching you for three weeks now," he said. "You've been setting things up, havin' meetings, and I've heard every word, but I still don't get it. Who cares if Caleb Alexander fumbles once on Sunday? There are fumbles in every game. How is him fumblin' once gonna fix things so that the coach don't get the win he needs?"

"See Roscoe, it's like the old days when we were kids. Remember when I hired those two high school kids who roughed up your cousin?"

"Welton."

"Welton Levenger. Kid owed me a few bucks and wouldn't pay. So I sent a couple of high school boys after him. But you took care of both of them."

"Got 'em with my little brother's bat," Roscoe said with pride.

"This is the same game on a different level, Roscoe. Uncle Nick gave me five million in seed money, and I've promised him that I can turn that into a thirty million by the end of the season."

"You gamblin' with Uncle Nick's money?" Roscoe said with arched eyebrows. "I thought he was opposed to gamblin' no way, no how? He always says, 'we're bookmakers, not gamblers.'"

"That's true," Gasca said, "but I convinced him that this was worth the risk."

"But how is getting Caleb to fumble gonna help?"

"It's like leaning on a guy who owes you something," Gasca said. "You don't want to break him. You just gotta give him a little nudge in the right direction then sit back and wait and see what happens."

"So you're givin' this game a nudge?"

Gasca nodded. "A couple of years ago, I was reading the box scores, and I started seeing some patterns. I realized that if I worked at it, I could manipulate any game I wanted without arousing the suspicion of the league."

"Okay," Roscoe Evans rumbled. "So how's it work?"

"In this case," Gasca said cryptically, "it works if Caleb Alexander fumbles once in the red zone."

7

Roscoe Evans pulled up next to a pay phone at the edge of a gas station parking lot and thought life just couldn't get any better. The phone stood four feet high and didn't have any obstructions around it. Roscoe could ease up next to it and dial a number without squeezing out of the rented Town Car. Although he would never admit it to Michael Gasca, Roscoe hated the effort it took to climb in and out of the car.

At the moment, he needed to place a bet, and he couldn't do that with any of the bookies in San Antonio. Gasca had told him he had to keep a low profile in Texas, and so far Roscoe thought it had been the most boring assignment of his life. They spent most of their time sitting in the turn-of-the-century house they'd rented. It was a formidable old home that Roscoe thought was a little too creepy. The hardwood floors creaked under his feet, the crown molding looked as though it belonged in a scary movie, and hidden in the cellar was a secret room about the size of a freight elevator.

The property manager had told the advance team that the house had been a speakeasy during the Prohibition, and moonshine was shuttled in and out through a tunnel that had long ago collapsed.

"Maybe we should nail the entrance shut," Roscoe had said nervously, when Gasca first showed him the secret room.

"Roscoe," Michael Gasca had said, smiling with real surprise, "are you scared?"

Roscoe had shrugged his meaty shoulders self-consciously. "I just don't like old houses," he'd grumbled.

"We could head up to Austin," Roscoe had suggested recently. "I hear there's good live music up there."

"Yeah?" Gasca said. "And what do we do when word gets out that there's a three-hundred-twenty-pound black guy in Texas who looks a lot like the infamous Roscoe Evans from Philadelphia?"

Roscoe scowled, which to Gasca was like watching a face on Mt. Rushmore change expressions. "Nobody down here knows who I am."

"Everyone knows who you are, Roscoe." Which was no exaggeration. Everyone in the organized crime world knew of the tandem of Roscoe Evans and Michael Gasca. Even people who had never met them would recognize them on sight because of Roscoe.

"You look like Shaq's big brother," Gasca observed.

"*Big* brother? He's older and bigger than me."

"Yeah, but it's a context thing," Gasca had said. "To most people, Shaq doesn't seem so big because the only time they see him is when he's on the basketball court surrounded by other big men. But you spend all your time around regular folks so when people see you on the street, you look twice as big as Shaq."

Roscoe snatched the pay phone off its hook and stabbed the buttons with a meaty index finger.

"Hello?" The guy on the other end sounded surprised, as if he didn't receive many calls.

"Is this Mickey?" Roscoe boomed.

"Yeah. Who's this?" Mickey Uso was not yet nineteen years old; he'd been taking bets for a little over a year.

A tractor-trailer rumbled into the parking lot. Roscoe shouted to be heard over the noise. "This is Big Daddy! You know who I am?"

Mickey perked up immediately. "Yes, sir!"

Roscoe's calls to young bookies were legendary. The FBI tended to tap the phones of major players in the crime world, so Roscoe skirted their surveillance by simply avoiding the big bookies. He had a cell phone sitting on the center console of the Town Car, but it wasn't an encrypted line like Michael Gasca's, so he knew better than to use it for business.

"I want you to take some stuff down for me," Roscoe told Mickey. "What's the line on the Stallions–Packers game?"

"I got 'em at…Stallions…minus three and a half."

"Perfect. Gimme ten dimes on the Packers." Ten thousand dollars was a typical bet for Roscoe. He loved to gamble, always had. If anyone had asked—for instance, the IRS—Roscoe couldn't have provided even a rough estimate of his annual income. He didn't receive a W-2 from an employer, and he had never filed an accurate tax return. Gasca gave Roscoe fifteen thousand dollars a month in cash for general maintenance. On top of that, Roscoe earned twenty percent commission on collections, plus whatever he managed to rustle up on his own. Jewelry, cars, drugs, women, and booze tended to float into Roscoe's life as gifts— sometimes surrendered under great duress—from people who wanted to keep him happy. Roscoe didn't know how much money Gasca earned each year, but he knew it was seven figures. Michael Gasca was barely twenty-six years old, and he was rolling in it.

"All right Mr....uh...Big Daddy," Mickey Uso said. He didn't know what to call Roscoe. Young bookies were always shocked when Roscoe called. Ten thousand dollars! Mickey did the math in his head. He had no idea where he would lay off this big bet.

"But," Roscoe said, "I need you to keep this real quiet."

Even at his young age, Mickey Uso understood exactly what the term *real quiet* meant. If it was *quiet* it was a secret; if it was *real quiet* it never happened. If word of this transaction got out, Mickey would be real quiet for the rest of his life.

"You cool with that?" Roscoe asked.

"Yes, sir," Mickey croaked. How could he possibly lay off this bet without telling anyone who had placed it?

"You know how to do it?" Roscoe said.

"No, sir," Mickey admitted.

"You call nine guys. Young guys. And tell them that you want to lay off some action. You don't tell them about me. You tell them whatever you need to tell them. Maybe it's a group bet by a bunch of yuppies that threw down some money. I don't care what you say, but you don't mention my name. You understand that?"

"Yes, sir."

"You give them a thousand each. I'll call you next week. If I win, you collect the money from the other nine guys and get it to me. If I lose, I'll pay you and you'll distribute it to the other guys. You understand that?"

"Yes, sir."

"I'll talk to you next week."

8

"You need to be more social," Vanessa Patterson admonished. She whipped the Mercedes around a Dodge minivan cruising too slow in the fast lane and threw a withering glance at the driver as she sped past. She darted back into the left lane, nearly clipping the van's front bumper. The driver honked his horn and raised his fist. Vanessa smiled at him in the rearview mirror and stomped on the accelerator; the Mercedes shot forward with a low diesel rumble.

"I'm social," Trevor Deale said. The San Antonio Airport was just ahead, and the Stallions charter plane was scheduled to depart in an hour to take the team to Green Bay.

"Only with Martin, Robo, and Caleb," Vanessa said. They'd been fighting for several days over little things that didn't amount to much, but were magnified because they were living together for the first time. She was annoyed about the way he left his clothes on the floor, squeezed the toothpaste tube from the middle and watched sports every hour of the day. Trevor was upset with her continual spending. They had already committed two hundred thousand dollars to an interior decorator, but Vanessa kept adding things and changing her mind, so the price was creeping up to three hundred thousand.

"I could buy six houses like my mother's for what we're spending on decoration," Trevor had complained.

Vanessa had waved him off. "It needs to look a certain way," she'd said.

Now, as they cruised toward the airport, Vanessa said, "There are a lot of other players on the team that you should get to know."

"I know all my teammates."

"Not just *know* them," Vanessa clarified. "Spend time with them. Like the Petersons, the Smiths, and the Everetts. They've been in the league a long time, and they know a lot of other famous people."

"Mmmm."

"Did you know that Dexter Peterson is a good friend of Tiger Woods?" Vanessa looked over at Trevor to see if he was impressed. "Sometimes during the off-season, they go golfing together. Did you know that?"

"No, I didn't."

"We should get to know them better. Maybe we'll get to meet Tiger." Vanessa had a lot of big plans, and she was infuriated by Trevor's apparent indifference. "There are businesspeople and politicians that you need to know. If you get in good with the politicians you could be set."

"Vanessa."

She looked over at him with an exasperated expression that told him she was serious.

"We don't have to have a game plan for everything. We'll make friends with whoever we make friends with, and we don't have to use anyone to meet someone else."

Vanessa closed her eyes at the wheel, but didn't take her foot off the accelerator. After a moment, she opened them and blared the horn at a car that appeared to be weaving into her lane. She screeched to a stop as cars queued up in the departure area.

"You need to position yourself for the future," she said.

Trevor kissed her on the cheek and climbed out of the car. "We'll talk about it later," he said.

"See ya, sweetie." She blew him a kiss. "And Trevor—"

"Yes?" He leaned down to look at her through the open window.

"You need to get rid of that jacket."

Trevor smiled and ran his thumbs under his lapels. He thought his tweed sports coat looked dapper. His teammates teased him about it good-naturedly, but Vanessa absolutely hated it. Every time she saw it she threatened to throw it away.

Trevor walked into the crowded airport without drawing much attention. He was still relatively new to San Antonio, so few people recognized him out of uniform. His best friend on the team, Martin McNeil, could never have walked down the concourse unmolested. In fact, Martin was the only player on the team permitted to circumvent the security checkpoint. For every road game, Martin reported to a special room where authorities searched him away from the public before loading him on to a cart and driving him through basement corridors to board the plane by way of a cleaning crews' platform. It had taken a lot of negotiation with the FAA to work out this exemption, but after seeing the mobs that rushed Martin McNeil and the delays they caused, the FAA had approved the special procedures. One day, Trevor might warrant the same exemption, but for now, he could still travel in relative anonymity.

On the plane, linebacker Michael Robinson stood near the front inspecting his teammates one by one as they boarded. Everyone—including his mother—had called him "Robo" for as long as he could remember. He stood just under six-foot-four, weighed two hundred thirty-five pounds with barely five percent body fat. He wore black alligator shoes and a custom-tailored black pinstriped suit with wide shoulders and a narrow waist. Diamond cuff links twinkled at his wrists, matching the diamond stud in one ear, the diamonds on his Rolex watch and the diamonds in his pinkie ring. All together, Robo was wearing more than seventy thousand dollars in clothing and jewelry. He was easily the best-dressed man on every Stallions road trip, and he felt it was his duty to provide fashion advice for his teammates.

"Trevor, Trevor, Trevor," Robo said, shaking his head wearily. "Haven't we talked about this jacket of yours? As much money as you make...that thing looks like someone pulled the blanket off a horse and put arms on it."

"It's my lucky jacket."

"More like your *fucky* jacket."

"If it makes you feel any better, Vanessa wants me to throw it away."

"And insult the garbage man?" Robo said. "Hell no, kid, you need to burn that thing."

Trevor smiled and moved down the aisle past his teammates, who were shoving their bags into the overhead compartments. It was a charter flight so no tickets were issued with printed seat assignments. Instead, each seat bore a hello-my-name-is tag with a player's name written in calligraphy. Trevor found his name and plopped into the aisle seat. Martin McNeil smiled at him from the window seat.

"What's up, kid?" Martin said.

"Not too much."

"See you're wearing tweed again."

"Yep." Trevor smiled wickedly. "Drives Vanessa crazy."

Martin laughed. "Then it's not completely without value." Martin leaned in close and whispered, "I heard a rumor about Coach Starnes."

"Yeah?"

"He might get fired if we don't win this weekend."

"Who told you that?"

"David Costanzo. Columnist over at the *San Antonio Light*."

"You think he really knows anything?"

Martin shrugged and looked around to see if anyone was listening. "Costanzo's convinced something is gonna happen this weekend."

"You know," Trevor said, having a sudden recollection, "I went by Mr. Kinneson's office a couple days ago to talk to him about a charity event. Neither of his secretaries was there, but I could hear him in his office. So I started to peek in, just to let him know I was there, and I heard him talking about a meeting he was going to. I remember him saying something about Starnes and this being the most important weekend."

"Really? When was that?"

"Wednesday, I think, maybe Thursday. It didn't sound like a big deal to me at the time, but now that you tell me about this rumor, it makes sense."

"I wouldn't be surprised if Mr. Kinneson was rooting against us this weekend," Martin said.

"But we'll beat Green Bay."

"Probably," Martin agreed. "But what if we don't?"

"You really think Mr. Kinneson would fire Starnes in the middle of the season?"

"It's not really the middle. It's still close enough to the beginning for a new coach to make a difference."

"Who would take over?"

"One of the coordinators, probably. If it were up to me, I'd give it to Coach Plantier. He knows the offense, and he's been a head coach before. He could handle it."

"I guess," Trevor said.

Up at the front of the plane there was a sudden clamor.

"Oh, shit! Will you look at this!" Robo had found a serious fashion faux pas. "T.D. Cox is wearing a choke chain."

"It's not a choke chain," Cox said. He was an offensive lineman with a thick neck and a thicker body.

"Come on, man," Robo said. "The chain should hang down near your collarbone. It shouldn't be all up in your Adam's apple looking like a boa constrictor."

"Leave my chain alone." T.D. muscled past, but Robo followed him down the aisle.

"Look, y'all. He's got a twenty-inch neck and an *eighteen-inch* chain. Veins bulging out. You know you can barely breathe."

"I told you to leave my chain alone. My mother gave it to me."

"Don't your mama know your size?" Robo asked. "When you're dead, she's gonna be laying on top of your casket sobbing 'Why…didn't…he…exchange…it?' You gotta have some common sense, T.D."

"I'm warning you."

"All right, I'll leave your chain alone because I want to talk about this gray belt you're always wearing."

"You like this belt, don't you?" T.D. said with a smile. An elk was engraved on the oval buckle. "Oughta get you something like this to go with your banker's suit."

"I'm tired of seeing that same belt every day," Robo said. "You wear it on the plane, you wear it to work every day, you probably wear it at home when you're hanging out in nothing but boxer shorts. Got the belt pulled on tight so you don't show no butt crack when you bend over to get another beer out of the fridge."

"Screw you."

"I'm serious. Did your mama give you that belt too, cause it's looking a little tight. Look y'all," Robo said, "he's got this thing pulled all the way to the last hole. This belt is just barely hanging on, but he won't let it go 'cause it was a gift. You're making nearly a million dollars a year and you're wearing a fifteen-dollar convenience-store belt. What's it made of, anyway?"

"This is high-grade Texas leather." T.D. smiled with pride.

"It looks like dried rat skin."

Robo turned and saw offensive lineman Anthony Stewart watching him.

"What are you looking at, you fucking runaway slave?" Robo asked.

Stewart laughed and shook his head. He knew enough to stay mute when Robo got rolling. If Stewart tried to defend himself, it would just give Robo more ammunition.

"Hey, did y'all see Anthony last week when he picked up that squib kick at the end of the first half?" Robo said. With under a minute left, the Indianapolis Colts had kicked the ball on the ground to keep the Stallions from having a good return. "He picked that thing up and started running. Who'd you think you were, O.J. Simpson?"

Anthony Stewart didn't respond.

"'Cause you looked more like *Homer* Simpson," Robo continued. "Then you saw a guy coming and tried to lower your shoulder, but that was a mistake. You ran up into a bees nest. Got hit by four guys at once. WHAP! WHAP! WHAP! WHAP! You went down like a hooker on a john. What were you thinking?"

"I didn't realize they were so fast," Stewart confessed with a chuckle.

"They had a forty-yard running start, of course they're fast. And you," Robo paused to stare dramatically at Anthony Stewart. "*You* are slow. Watching you run is like watching three rounds of boxing—your body parts are all fighting with each other. And you can't take a hit," Robo continued. "You might be big, but when them fools hit you, you collapsed like a plastic cup getting stepped on."

"Remember," Dante Thompson interjected from two rows up, "we asked him if he knew where he was?"

"And this idiot," Robo hooked a thumb at Anthony Stewart, "said, 'Yeah, I'm in the kitchen. Tell mama to pass me the syrup.'"

"All right, man," Stewart said. "Everyone knows that I got tagged."

"*Tagged?*" Robo said. "Animals on the Discovery Channel get tagged. What you got was damn near killed. Next time, leave the running to the professionals."

Robo pushed his way back up to the front of the plane to find another target. "Oh, shit! Paisley!" he exclaimed. "Y'all check it out. John is wearing a paisley shirt. Don't you know that paisley hasn't been in style for years? *People* magazine May 1989 said paisley was hot. *People* magazine January 1990 said throw away all your paisley. But look at you. Must have thought you looked good getting dressed this morning."

"I look smooth," John Friedman said.

"Smooth out of style." Robo looked at the next player boarding the plane and laughed. "Few minutes ago, we had a guy get on in a nice mink, but now you show up in an alley-cat coat." Robo squeezed his nose between two fingers and said, "Move along."

Ed Jackson, a wide receiver, came out of the bathroom just then.

Robo said, "Damn, Ed, your breath is kickin'."

"Really?" Ed cupped a hand and breathed into it.

"You're gonna need more than a mint to tame that shit. Go see if the trainers can put you on a Listerine IV."

Ed waved off the criticism. "Ha-ha, funny guy."

"I ain't joking," Robo insisted. "It smelled so bad out here, I thought you were in the bathroom taking a shit, but now I think you were just in there breathing."

9

Michael Gasca could have been good at anything. Tucked under his short dark hair, behind sharp blue eyes, atop a lean runner's body, lived a brain with such clarity of intent that it could cut right to the core of any problem and fashion a quick remedy. His I.Q. had never been tested, but if it had, he surely would have been declared a genius of the highest order and paraded around as a jewel of the scientific world. He could have been a mathematician dancing in the heady realm of theoretical numbers or a physicist or an inventor or a scientist exploring the outer reaches of human understanding. Michael Gasca could have been good at anything; it was only by blind chance that he became a bookie.

Michael Gasca was born in Philadelphia to an unwed mother who would not keep him for fear of the shame she would bring upon her Catholic family. She abandoned him with teary-eyed conviction just inside the front door of St. Agnes Medical Center. There Michael Gasca began his unlikely journey into a world where his magnificent mind would create order in complex systems and generate tens of millions of dollars for himself and his benefactors.

From an early age, his quick intelligence impressed everyone who met him. By age four, he could effortlessly add, subtract, divide, and multiply large numbers in his head. As he grew older, he picked up languages and accents, learning to speak English and Italian and a little bit of the street Puerto Rican he heard around him. He devoured books, played chess in the park, and understood blackjack on a professional level. Michael Gasca mastered anything that required mental precision, which was why he was so good at escape. He ran away from more foster homes and orphanages than the state of Pennsylvania could count. No matter what precautions were taken to keep him in, he found a way out. During one of these sojourns, he met the man who would change his life forever: Dominic Sarcassi, the patriarch of the Sarcassi crime family.

Michael Gasca spent most of this young life on the streets, following the men who worked the neighborhoods in Philadelphia. He loved their suits, cars, power, intensity, and money. And the men treated him like part of the family. It was hard not to like a kid who knew so much. They'd hire him as a lookout one day and an errand boy the next.

Michael Gasca met Dominic Sarcassi as the old man was walking out of Umberto's Pizzeria on 52nd Street. Sarcassi had five guys walking with him, surveying the street like Secret Service agents. Gasca happened to be coming around the corner after escaping from yet another foster home when he recognized the old man.

"Mr. Sarcassi!" he screamed, trying to shove off the hand of one of the bodyguards. "I know I'm just a kid, but one day I'm gonna be the best damn bookie in the whole city!"

Dominic Sarcassi smiled down at Michael Gasca's confident young face. "Oh yeah?"

"Yes, sir." Gasca had a fierce, determined look. "And I'm looking for a job right now, so if you wanted to hire me, you could get me cheap."

Sarcassi patted his bodyguard on the shoulder and allowed the boy to approach. "How old are you, son?" Dominic Sarcassi had heard about young Michael Gasca.

"I'm nine years old, and I'm a real good lookout, and I run errands for people, and I'm pretty good at figuring things out."

"Where's your mama and papa?" Sarcassi asked, even though he already knew the answer.

"I don't have any parents," Michael Gasca said. "And I just ran away from another stupid foster home. I can take care of myself."

"Where you gonna sleep tonight?"

"I'll find a place."

Dominic Sarcassi thought about this for a moment. His entourage fidgeted. He'd been standing still for too long. "You want a job?"

"Yes, sir!"

"Come along then." Dominic Sarcassi draped an arm over Michael Gasca's narrow shoulders and they marched off to Sarcassi's Georgian mansion. A stone fence encircled the house, and there were never fewer than six men and two dogs on security duty. Dominic Sarcassi had fought his way to the top, and he knew many men wanted to kill him and lay claim to his empire.

Dominic Sarcassi took in Michael Gasca in an informal adoption that the state would have called a kidnapping if officials had known where to find the boy. He told Michael Gasca to call him Uncle Nick. He had only three rules: Gasca had to attend school every day, he could never engage in petty criminal activities such as theft or vandalism, and he could never attempt to escape from his new home.

"What do I get out of it?" Michael Gasca had countered.

Uncle Nick had smiled. The kid was a born negotiator. "You get room and board, my protection on the streets, and you get me as your personal tutor in the bookmaking industry. You wanna be the best bookie in Philly? Your lessons start today."

Sarcassi called the kid Little Mikey and generally treated him better than his own children and grandchildren. From the start, Uncle Nick knew Little Mikey was a comer—a child prodigy with a criminal mind.

"If everything worked perfectly, we would never take a risk," Uncle Nick said, trying to explain bookmaking in language the kid could understand.

"How do you not take risks if you run a gambling operation?" Mikey asked.

Uncle Nick chuckled hoarsely; his laugh turned into a cough that racked his whole body. After a few minutes, his coughing subsided and he puffed on a cigar. That's what he loved about Mikey. The kid got it right off the bat.

"Mikey," Uncle Nick said, patting the boy on the arm. "That's the most important question you could ask me. We run a bookmaking operation for gamblers, but we are not gamblers ourselves. We like to get half the people betting on one side and half on the other side so we can sit right in the middle."

"That's still a gamble," Mikey insisted. "You might get too many people betting on one team and not the other team."

Uncle Nick nodded at this shrewd young friend. Nine years old, and already he knew the system better than half the mooks on the payroll.

"That's why we have a point spread."

"So we can predict who's gonna win the game?" Mikey said.

"Not quite," Uncle Nick said. "We're not trying to predict the outcome of the game. We're trying to predict what people *think* the outcome will be. You understand the difference?"

"I think so."

"Look at it this way," Uncle Nick suggested. "The weather man on TV says it's gonna rain tomorrow, so I set up shop outside an apartment building with one hundred people inside. I've got a bunch of gamblers ready to put down money on the number of people who are gonna walk out of that building with umbrellas. It's an over/under bet, and I set my line at twenty, because I want half of my gamblers to bet that more than twenty people will have umbrellas and half will bet that it'll be less than twenty. My line has nothing to do with whether it's actually gonna rain. Just whether people think it's gonna rain. You get it?"

"Yeah," Mikey said. "I'd bet the under."

"Oh yeah? Why's that?"

"Because I bet half the people in the building didn't watch the news, so they don't know what the weather's supposed to be like."

"That might be true," Uncle Nick conceded, "but you're not betting in this one. You're the bookie, and you're just trying to stay in the middle."

"So if I have too many people betting the 'over,' you could bump the line up to twenty-five to get more people to bet the 'under,' right?"

"In this example that would be fine, but when you're taking bets on NFL games, you'd never make a big jump from twenty to twenty-five. If you've got your line set right to begin with, then moving half a point or a full point should even things out. The NFL is different than other sports, so once the line comes out of Vegas, it's almost never gonna move much."

"What makes the NFL so different?"

"A lot of things." Uncle Nick took a moment to relight his cigar. The air around his head went hazy with smoke. "The NFL gets the most action of any wagering sport," Uncle Nick said, extending his index finger to mark the first point, "and that means there's a lot of focus on the games and gambling." Another finger shot out from his gnarled hand. "Second, each team plays only sixteen games per season—which is nothing compared to basketball, baseball, and hockey." A third finger. "And there's a week between each set of games. So there's plenty of time for people to get information, study the teams, watch the news, and place their bets." A fourth finger. "The format of the point spread is easy for people to understand, so they lay down more cash than they do on something like baseball, where there is no point spread and you're betting against a money line that's too complicated for the average person to follow."

"What if I move the line," Mikey said, "and I still can't get enough people to bet the other side to get balanced out?"

"In that case, you're no longer a bookie," Uncle Nick said. "You're a gambler."

During these long conversations, Uncle Nick taught Michael Gasca everything he knew about the money wagered in Nevada—the only state with legalized sports gambling—and everything he knew about illegal bookmaking. Each year, Las Vegas handled a little more than two billion dollars in bets on all sports, with college and pro football accounting for nearly half of that.

That was the legal world. No one knew for sure how much money changed hands illegally each year, but Michael Gasca had read that among Americans twelve and older, seventy percent reported at least a casual interest in football and twenty-six percent described themselves as fanatics. And experts estimated that roughly forty million Americans wagered more than six billion dollars annually on sports, and the Sarcassi clan, controlling more than eight hundred bookies throughout the Northeast handled just over one billion a year.

"It's the most stable game out there with the most information," Uncle Nick said. "See, gamblers aren't all stupid micks just trying to throw their money away. If you want to get a guy to lay down a bet, you gotta give him a lot of information. He'll read the papers, watch *SportsCenter*, listen to talk radio, read *Sports Illustrated* and *Pro Football Weekly*, watch *NFL Tonight* and *NFL Countdown*. Then he thinks he knows something, and he doesn't feel like he's gambling. He thinks he's making an investment and it's gonna pay off on Sunday. It's hard to do that with baseball, basketball, hockey, and horse racing because there are so many games, so many races, sometimes the games are played on consecutive nights. It's tough to keep track of everything. But football is nice and neat. You got one set of games per week."

As a general rule, the Sarcassi bookies were not gamblers. They took their profits on a modest ten percent commission on the losers, and a hefty vig on outstanding debts, and they also issued loans to gamblers who couldn't afford to pay their tabs.

"You loan a guy your own money so he can pay back his gambling losses to you?" Mikey asked. Even to a nine-year-old that sounded ridiculous.

"Yeah, Mikey," Uncle Nick said with a dry chuckle. "That's how we build our business. Take bets from a guy long enough and eventually he loses more than he can afford to lose. So we loan him ten grand at forty-five percent. We let him run for a little bit, and then we take over his business. Maybe not all of it. We might ask for twenty, thirty percent of his cement company or his garbage company. That's how we get warehouses, trucking companies, fish markets. Little bit of everything."

10

No one spoke to Caleb Alexander, and he preferred it that way.

He sat on a folding metal chair in front of his locker stuffing his knee and thigh pads into mesh pockets that lined the inside of his game pants. Rough gray carpet tickled the bottoms of his bare feet. The crowded locker room buzzed with the murmur of low voices and the sound of the early game on CBS.

Caleb turned toward the room and watched his teammates prepare. Everyone had his own routine. Martin McNeil was crouched in the corner doing yoga poses—stretching in odd positions and breathing in exaggerated patterns. His teammates had teased him about it when he first came in as a rookie, but after seeing his performance on the field, three other players had joined him. Now everyone called them Martin and the Grasshoppers, but no one disrupted their pre-game ritual. Michael Bishop's lips were moving as he studied his playbook. It was rumored that Bishop was the flat-out dumbest player ever to trot onto an NFL field—which was quite a statement given some of the idiots Caleb had met—but he compensated for his lack of intellect by having great study habits. Bishop claimed that he suffered from a long-term memory problem. He rarely could recall anything for more than half an hour, so he studied his playbook right up until kickoff and had one of the equipment managers keep his book on the sideline during the game so that he could continue to review. He had been in the league seven years, so his technique appeared to be working.

The team seemed relaxed, but an undercurrent of anxiety coursed through the locker room. Caleb reached up to a simple gold cross hanging from his neck. He'd worn it since his mother gave it to him for his 14th birthday. He brought it to his lips for a gentle kiss.

Equipment managers rushed about the locker room making last-minute adjustments. Coaches paced back and forth, stopping every now and then to stare at their laminated game-plan sheets.

Caleb Alexander walked into the training room, where he waited in line while a defensive lineman got a tape job that was so thick and stiff that he couldn't flex his ankles when he got off the table. He hobbled away saying, "my toes are falling asleep," but he sounded happy about it, as if numbness was exactly what he wanted. Two trainers were working on the knee of linebacker Michael Robinson, applying tape in a pattern that would have made an engineer proud.

"Need you to run the hell outta that thing today, kid," Robo said in a rare moment of sincerity. His voice sounded surprisingly soft when he wasn't making wisecracks and jokes. It took Caleb a moment to realize that the words were directed at him. He waited for the punchline. But when Robo didn't laugh, Caleb worried that the linebacker might suspect something.

"You got it," Caleb said, moving past the linebacker to a taping table a few feet away. The social confidence Caleb felt in the nightclub scene always slipped away from him when he entered the locker room. Young partygoers treated him like a crown prince, but most of his teammates resented him for the fat paychecks he collected despite delivering so little performance on the field. He climbed on to the table and asked for a fifty-fifty with no lock—a minimal tape job that offered slightly more support than wearing two pairs of socks.

He continued to watch the trainers working on Robo's knee. Caleb had never seen a knee taped for stability; the process reminded him of a crew constructing a bridge. The trainers talked to each other continuously, sometimes stopping each other, one guy adding another piece of tape before allowing his partner to continue. Long strips started on the outside of Robo's thigh and snaked diagonally across his leg to a point just under the knee on the inside of his calf. Thick rounds of tape at the top and bottom served as anchors. It took another ten minutes to complete the work, and when it was done, the two trainers stood back staring like artists admiring a painting.

"Thanks," Robo said, flexing the knee a few times. "Feels good." He looked up at Caleb. "I hate wearing a knee brace 'cause it's too heavy," he explained. "This gives me the support without having the weight or restriction of a brace. Gotta be fast out there, my brotha!"

Caleb nodded.

Robo leaned forward and grabbed Caleb's arm. "Gotta smurf that thang man! Ain't that right, y'all?" Robo said to the room. "When you get that smurf in your hands, you gotta smurf it like a smurfamatic smurfing machine. And when those smurfs try to smurf you, you gotta give 'em a smurf-arm, juke 'em with a smurf-move, and then smurf your ass into the smurf-zone. You hear me, playa?"

"I hear you," Caleb laughed.

"Can I get a witness?"

"A-men!" said someone on the other side of the training room.

"And Lord we pray that when the smurfin' is done, and all smurfs have turned in for the night, smurfing in their beds, having smurf-dreams, that you would reward us for our loyal smurfalty by giving each of us a Smurfette of our own—"

"Or three!" someone suggested.

"A Smurfette or three," Robo corrected, "to smurf us all night long until we can't smurf no more. Can I get a witness?"

"A-smurf!"

Robo gave Caleb's arm a final squeeze. "Play like you're about to lose your smurfing mind," he said, then turned and walked out of the training room. Caleb felt tears sting his eyes. He was only twenty-seven years old, but already he'd had a long, pitiful career. He appreciated Robo's encouragement.

Back at his locker, Caleb slowly wound thin strips of tape around each knuckle of his left hand, and with every rotation his resolve grew stronger. He wouldn't fumble. He *couldn't* fumble! He absolutely *would not* fumble! His stomach churned with fear, but he knew that if he did Michael Gasca's bidding, he couldn't live with himself. Caleb Alexander had never planned for anything other than pro football, and his career thus far had been a crushing disappointment. He'd been an all-state running back in high school, amassing more than nine thousand career rushing yards, setting a state record in Florida. He'd been recruited all over the nation before finally choosing the University of Nebraska. No one who'd followed his exploits in high school expected him to stay long in college, and he didn't. He left Nebraska after two record-breaking seasons and entered the NFL as the Philadelphia Eagles' first-round draft pick.

Caleb finished taping the fingers in his left hand and moved on to his right hand. Despite his bright beginnings and the monster signing bonus, his professional career had been marred by injury and ineffectiveness. Four games into his rookie season his anterior cruciate ligament snapped on a simple two-yard run in the first quarter. The injury knocked him out for the season, into surgery, then rehab, then back to training camp the next year, but he never regained his previous intensity. The knee had healed, but his confidence had not. He got beaten out for the starting job and played only sparingly in his second year.

Before Caleb's third season, the Eagles traded him to San Francisco. The Forty-Niners traded him to San Diego, who released him after half a season. Caleb signed with Atlanta, who traded him to Baltimore, who cut him. Cleveland signed him, then traded him to Cincinatti, who traded him to Detroit on a one-year contract. The Lions did not renew his contract, and Caleb signed with San Antonio as a free agent. Caleb had played for nine teams in his short career, never staying long with any of them, but always earning a big paycheck. He possessed such enormous talent that teams were willing to gamble on him, but once he arrived, most coaches were stunned by how little he actually had to offer.

Caleb joined the Stallions halfway through training camp after the team suffered a plague of injuries in the backfield. But even then he didn't play. He was an emergency backup, earning a paycheck but never performing on game day. Last Sunday, Lester McCallen pulled a hamstring, and finally Caleb got the starting nod.

Caleb took a deep breath and pulled his game pants up. He was determined to have a good game. He would run hard, block well, and, above all, hold on to the football. As he laced up the front of his pants, running backs coach Frankie Johnson put a hand on his shoulder.

"Come here," the coach said, walking toward the showers.

Caleb followed him through the curtain and into the expansive tiled shower room. He figured the coach wanted to go over formations and assignments to make sure Caleb knew everything he needed to know.

Frankie Johnson closed the curtain and stood close to Caleb. A little too close, Caleb thought.

"Look," the coach said, pausing to wipe the back of his hand across his forehead. For some reason, his black skin glistened with sweat despite the frigid weather outside. "I didn't want to sign your ass 'cause I don't think you're worth a shit." Johnson paused for a moment as if he expected a response. "But we had to have somebody and you were the only guy available. Today you're gonna start. So when you go out there, I want you to keep it simple. No showboating, no trying to be a superstar. Just don't screw up. You got me?"

Caleb nodded.

"We can't afford to lose this game, and I'll be damned if I'm going to let some punk like you mess it up for us." A sharp crease formed between Johnson's eyebrows. The square black rims of his glasses bobbed up and down as his spoke. "Squeeze the ball tight," he said, demonstrating with his own arm, bent at the elbow, pressed against his ribs. "There shouldn't be any daylight between the ball and your body. You got me?"

Caleb nodded.

"I want to see both hands on the ball when you're in traffic. I don't want you fighting for extra yards. I don't want to see you stretching the ball out trying to get a first down. I want it tucked in nice and tight. You got me?"

Caleb nodded.

"You got more talent inside you than half the guys on this team put together, but you're a goddamn waste of time. I watch you play and the effort you put out is not good enough for you," Johnson stabbed a hard finger against Caleb's chest. "It's not good enough for me," hooked a thumb at himself, "it's not good enough for us," twirling a hand around to encompass the entire team. "It's not good enough to feed my four kids." Johnson paused to lick his lips, as if the thought of feeding his kids had sparked hunger pains. "I'll tell you what it is," he said, glaring at Caleb as if he wanted to throttle the player. "It's just good enough to get your little ass fired. You got me?"

Caleb nodded.

"I've been coaching a long time, and I'll still be coaching long after you've been kicked out of the league, spent all your money, and are living back in your mother's basement. So don't screw up. You got me?"

Caleb nodded again. He wanted to tell the coach that he'd made up his mind. He absolutely would not fumble. He would not hurt his team. He would have a good game. He would earn his keep and help the Stallions win. The coach stormed through the curtain, leaving Caleb staring blankly at the wall. He'd heard it all before. No one seemed to like him. They all felt that he was an overrated under-performer, and they didn't trust him.

■ ■ ■

The roar rose feebly into the cold October air, carrying the chattering voices of thousands of spectators. The sun was parked three quarters of the way across the clear blue sky, spilling so much light on to the stadium that most of the people on the east side had their hands raised to block the glare, but the day, for all its beauty, was frigid in Green Bay, Wisconsin.

An official stamped his feet and blew a frosty breath between clenched fingers. He stole a glance at his watch, marking the seconds until the television time out ended.

Caleb Alexander stood motionless on the field with bare arms below his shoulder pads in apparent indifference to the single-digit temperature. Inside a fever burned. His team had scored seventeen points, but Caleb hadn't yet had the ball inside the twenty-yard line, and if he never had the ball in the red zone, he wouldn't have to worry about Michael Gasca's request. He wondered what would happen to the money in that case. He'd had a decent game so far with eighteen carries for seventy-three yards. He'd caught a couple of passes and blocked well against the blitz.

"Huddle up! Huddle up!" screamed Trevor Deale. The fourth quarter had just begun and the Stallions led the Packers by three points. Martin McNeil had hauled in a thirty-yard strike to give them 1st-and-goal at the four-yard line. On first down, they'd run a play-action pass to the tight end that had fallen incomplete. It was second down.

"Let's get it in the zone," the quarterback said, nodding to Caleb with confidence. "Strong right slot Z disco 34 bend, on two, on two, ready?"

Ten voices said, "Break" in unison. Caleb would have been the 11th, but he couldn't open his mouth. He moved slowly into position, seven yards behind the line of scrimmage, and surveyed the defense as the quarterback ran through his cadence. Caleb felt determined. He'd had a great game thus far; there had been no fumbles. No missed assignments, no bad reads. And now the Stallions stood at the goal line and the coach was entrusting Caleb with the ball. He hadn't scored a touchdown in three years. If he scored here, he'd be a hero. The Packers crowd would boo, but all his teammates would jump on his back and slap his helmet. The coaches would congratulate him as he came off the field. He could have a new beginning and possibly salvage his career. Surely, Caleb thought, Michael Gasca would understand that. Surely, he'd understand that Caleb was an athlete, and a true athlete always worked hard for his teammates. Caleb set his jaw as he studied the defense.

"Hut! Hut!" Trevor screamed. The center snapped the ball. Caleb took a step to his right and rolled downhill. He saw a hole developing behind the center's block. The nose guard was fighting over the top, and the backside defensive tackle was collapsing on a cut block. Caleb's body took over, reacting automatically to the information his eyes provided. He felt like his old self again, lowering his shoulders, racing through the small opening in the defensive front.

The "Will"—weak side—linebacker scraped over the top and barreled into the hole. He met Caleb at full speed. Caleb felt him coming at the last second and spun his body slightly to the right, taking the blow at an angle. The linebacker knocked him sideways, but Caleb kept his feet. He twisted toward the end zone, and suddenly the free safety drove his helmet into Caleb's chin, taking him off his feet. But even as he fell, Caleb stretched toward the goal line. He was determined to make the big play, but it was clear that he did not have enough for a touchdown. Caleb would have been down at the one-yard line, where it would have been 3rd-and-goal, and he might have had another shot at scoring—but he lost the ball. The safety's hit dislodged the football, and Caleb's heart galloped as it slid down his body. He snatched at it with both hands, but the ball hit the ground and bounced into the end zone. Another linebacker, hustling toward the play, recovered the loose football, and Caleb could do nothing but sit on the ground and watch as the Packers celebrated and the crowd roared its approval.

All day he'd agonized over Michael Gasca's instructions. After finally deciding that he simply could not fumble on purpose, he'd accidentally lost the ball, and that felt worse than anything Caleb could imagine. He realized too late that it would have been easier if he'd done it on purpose. His teammates might have hated him, the coaches might have yelled at him, but deep down he would always know that he had fumbled on purpose. No matter what everyone else thought about him, he would know the truth.

This legitimate fumble was much worse. It proved that even when Caleb wanted to do the right thing, he couldn't be trusted.

Trevor Deale walked over to him and extended a hand. Caleb Alexander got up slowly.

"Don't sweat it, man," Trevor said. "You'll get a another chance to punch it into the zone."

Caleb looked at Trevor blankly and walked to the sideline where running backs coach Frankie Johnson was fuming.

11

The Stallions's locker room was filled with sound as players, coaches, trainers, equipment men, reporters, friends, security personnel, and countless other people milled around talking. The players stripped away their uniforms in a synchronized ceremony they'd performed after every practice and every game since they were kids. Each man had a travel bag at his feet into which he stuffed his helmet, shoulder pads, shoes, and leg pads. The players zipped their bags and tossed them into the middle of the room—with little warning to the people standing in the way—where several equipment managers scooped them up and carried them outside to the truck. Socks, jocks, T-shirts, wristbands, and any other undergarments were stuffed into small mesh bags and sealed at the top with oversized safety pins. When the bags went into the washing machine, everything would get clean, but all of a particular player's undergarments would stay together. Jerseys and game pants were tossed into separate piles in the middle of the room, where they would be gathered up by another equipment manager, counted to ensure that they were all there, and then loaded into a bin and packed on the truck. Each jersey would be washed and examined for wear; any damage would be repaired before next week's game.

A third of the players found their way into the training room to get treatment for injuries. They emerged with ice wrapped on their shoulders, knees, elbows, hands, hamstrings and ankles. The trainers dispensed pain medication and made note of each new injury. Any player hurt badly enough to miss practice on Wednesday would be ordered to report for treatment on Monday and Tuesday. If he failed to show up for treatment and then was unable to practice on Wednesday, he'd have to pay a two-thousand-dollar fine.

Each player had a small blue towel wrap hanging from a hook in his locker that he could use to cover himself while walking to the showers. A curtain shielded the showers from the main locker room. The wrap and shower curtain had become standard fare shortly after female reporters were permitted in the locker room, but most players weren't modest enough to use the wraps. They'd strip naked, conduct interviews, and walk to the showers still naked.

A crowd of reporters gathered at Trevor Deale's locker. It didn't matter whether the Stallions won or lost, or whether Trevor played well or poorly. He was the quarterback and the star player on the team. Therefore, the media wanted to hear his thoughts.

"What happened out there, Trevor?" a television reporter asked. Six cameras and about the same number of radio microphones were pointed at him. The newspaper reporters crowded in close, trying to keep pace with their notepads.

"They just outplayed us today," Trevor said. He knew it didn't have to be that way. If Coach Starnes would give him more freedom to call audibles, the offense would be a lot more productive. But Trevor was a rookie quarterback, and he didn't want to be too presumptuous. He'd had problems with his college coach when he tried to assert himself too soon, so he thought he'd be a little more patient in the pros.

"We made too many mistakes," Trevor said to the reporters, speaking by rote. "We didn't take advantage of opportunities, and it cost us."

"You guys are 2–3 now. Do you think this loss puts you out of the race for the playoffs?"

Trevor said, "We've got a lot of games to play, so we're just gonna have to regain our focus and play hard."

"Trevor," said Brian Boling, the host of *The Beat*, a sports talk radio show in San Antonio, "we're live right now during our post-game show, and many of our listeners have only one thing on their minds. And that's this: You get paid a lot of money to make big plays, but on that last third down when the team really needed you, you dumped it to the fullback for a three-yard gain. Do you think you're worth the millions the team is paying you?" An aggressive sneer formed on Brian's face. He stood with his legs spread apart, as if bracing himself for impact.

Trevor smiled patiently and used a towel to remove eye-black from his cheeks. "Brian, I appreciate your asking me that question on behalf of your listeners. By the way, I listen to your show, and I really enjoy it." The compliment caught Brian off guard. His stance shifted slightly, and he looked around to see if the other media members had heard that. Trevor Deale liked his show. "And since I know you're very well-schooled in football strategy, let me run it by you and see what you think."

"Okay," Brian said with hesitation. He liked to *ask* questions, not *answer* them, but what could he say? They were live. If Trevor Deale (*who liked his show!*) wanted to ask Brian's opinion, who was Brian to argue?

"It was third-and-six," Trevor continued, "and the call in the huddle was I-right slot close, z right, fake 34 bend Y hook. So the tight end was the primary receiver, but the Packers lined up in a brown, four-three under with cover four over the top. That put the Sam linebacker in trail position on the tight end. I'm sure you're well aware that a hook, a curl, and generally an out-route are all useless if the defender is playing trail coverage."

Trevor paused, and Brian quickly filled the space. "Of course," he said in a knowing way. "Trail coverage kills it." He didn't know what trail coverage was.

Trevor continued, "The front gave us a protection problem in the formation we were in, so we couldn't audible into something else. The Z had a drag route and the X had a post, neither of which was any good against cover four. The Packers didn't know the play we were going to run, and we didn't know what coverage they'd be in, but in this case, they guessed right. They had the perfect defense for the play we called. But I'm glad you asked the question, because it gives all of us a chance to learn from your expertise. What would have you done if you were the quarterback?"

Brian's face bloomed pink. "What I would have done is not the point," he sputtered. "I'm not a quarterback, and—"

"Hey, we agree on that," Trevor said. The other reporters chuckled.

"It's your job to know these things," Brian said.

"We agree again."

"I'm asking you why you didn't do something."

"Brian, you have to remember that the other guys get paid, too; sometimes they're gonna beat us on a particular play or on a particular afternoon. When they win, we move on to the next play. On that third down, they outfoxed us. The next time, we'll get them."

"That's Trevor Deale," Brian said, yanking back the microphone. He wanted to move on. "We're in the locker room, where the Stallions have suffered another humiliating loss in a season that may have been lost before it ever began. We'll take a quick timeout and bring you more from the locker room in a moment. This is Sports Radio—"

"Hey Brian," Robo interrupted, leaning into the microphone, "are we on the air?"

"Hey Robo," Brian said, a little annoyed, but unable to do anything now that the audience had heard Michael Robinson's distinctive voice. "Well, ladies and gentleman, before we go to our commercial break, we have a special guest: linebacker Michael Robinson. You want to tell us what happened out there, Robo?"

"Who are you supposed to be?" Robo said, looking Brian up and down carefully. "Are you an anchor on the news?"

"Well, sort of," Brian preened. "I'm a radio talk show host, and that's sort of like—"

"'Cause you look more like the anchor on a *ship*," Robo said, "all cruddy and ugly and no use to anybody until we've stopped for the day and all the work's done." Robo walked away. Brian stood speechless while the reporters in the area laughed so hard that several of them had to sit down.

"Are there any other questions?" Trevor said over the laughter.

When he completed the interviews, Trevor shucked off the last of his clothing and hustled into the showers. The big open space had spigots mounted every three feet along the walls, but there only twelve showerheads, and forty-six players who needed them, so they had to double up or wait for other players to finish. Trevor walked over to Caleb Alexander, who stood motionless with his head under the spray of water.

"You mind if I share this with you?" Trevor said.

Caleb looked up slowly, then shrugged and moved aside.

Trevor stepped under the water, grabbed the soap off the tray, and rubbed his hands together quickly to lather up.

"You doing okay?" he said.

"No." Despite being six-two, two hundred thirty pounds, Caleb looked like a little boy. He had a pouty bottom lip and he was slumped forward with eyes at half-mast.

"Anyone can fumble," Trevor said quietly to Caleb. "That's the nature of the game."

Caleb shook his head. "You don't understand."

"You think I don't have regrets about the interception I threw in the second quarter? Or the sack I took in the fourth? I just had Brian from *The Beat* out there saying—again—that I don't deserve my salary because I failed to convert on our last third down. You've gotta have a short memory and live in a continuous present. The only thing that matters is what you're doing right now."

"I lost the game." Caleb's voice cracked.

"You personally?"

"Yes."

"Your ego might be getting a little big if you think the success or failure of the team rests on your shoulders alone. Let me get back under the water." Trevor stepped forward and rinsed the soap off his body, wincing as the water sluiced over cuts and abrasions on his elbows and along his flanks.

"Nobody asked any of the other players to make mistakes," Caleb whispered.

That confused Trevor. He wiped water off his face. "Of course nobody asked us, but we still did it."

"I wasn't gonna do it. But now I'll get the money because they think I did it on purpose."

Trevor suddenly realized what Caleb was saying. In a hushed voice he said, "Caleb, don't talk about this here, okay?"

Caleb shrugged, but didn't raise his head.

"Seriously, Caleb," Trevor whispered. "I don't know exactly what's going on, but I'm gonna help you. You just have to keep quiet about this until we get back to San Antonio."

Caleb looked up and nodded with what looked like relief coloring his face.

"Don't tell anyone else what you just told me," Trevor instructed.

"Okay," Caleb said.

"Is Tui gonna pick you up in the limo?"

"Yeah."

"You can give me a ride home tell me about it in the car."

12

Jonathan Kinneson hated riddles. He didn't like having doubts, and he didn't like having to figure things out. He pushed his supple first-class seat back to the full reclining position and sipped his Scotch from a thick tumbler. The glass belonged to the airline; the Scotch was from Kinneson's private collection. In the distance, the sky was bursting with color as the sun crept below the horizon, ending a day that had started for the team with a pre-game breakfast at 7 A.M., followed by kickoff at 11 A.M., and the final seconds ticking off the clock at 2:33 P.M. It took an hour for the players to get off the field, do post-game interviews, remove their equipment, get showered, changed, and loaded on to the buses. The equipment managers and trainers spent another half hour loading their bags, boxes and carts into the back of a rented U-Haul truck. Then the caravan—a limo for Kinneson, four buses, and the U-Haul—set off for the airport. They loaded the plane, and the wheels lifted off the runway on time at 5:27 P.M.—another perfect logistical performance by the Stallions director of operations. Of course, no one noticed. That was the life of the operations manager. A delay would have caught everyone's attention; perfection was unremarkable.

In seat 1A, Jonathan Kinneson replayed the game in his mind, trying to make sense of what he had seen. Michael Gasca had told him to watch Caleb Alexander, which Kinneson had done. Caleb had turned in an unremarkable performance, including a fumble that hadn't seemed manufactured. Kinneson had watched Caleb carefully on the Jumbotron screen as the camera zoomed in. Caleb didn't look like a player who had pulled off a contracted mistake. The owner saw real disappointment in the player's face. Was the fumble the play Gasca had engineered? Ultimately, the Stallions had lost the game, which is what Kinneson wanted, but the defeat hadn't seemed to hinge on any action by Caleb Alexander, for which Kinneson was paying $1 million. He took another slow sip and looked across the aisle at his soon-to-be-former head coach.

Kinneson decided that he should say nothing to Starnes. He'd just call a press conference in the morning, make the announcement that he was firing his coach, and let Starnes find out about it when reporters called him for his comments. Kinneson smiled at the thought of coach Max Starnes suddenly unemployed and caught off guard by the media.

But if he did that, Kinneson wouldn't get the satisfaction of giving Starnes the news face-to-face. No, he definitely wanted to see the coach's reaction when the end came. He'd call him into the office first thing in the morning—*and make him wait an hour!* Kinneson thought with a wicked grin—then fire him. That had a certain appeal too, but that was private. Public embarrassment was even more enticing.

Jonathan Kinneson shook his glass three times, rattling the melting cubes; the flight attendant responded immediately, taking the tumbler out of his hand and giving him a fresh one. She smiled at him, but he didn't look at her. He never looked at her—at least not her face.

Kinneson didn't always travel on the team charter. He had a private jet with two pilots and a flight attendant standing at the ready, but sometimes it was nice to fly with his troops.

He shook his glass again, and the flight attendant was at his side with a fresh one. He didn't know how many he'd had, but it wasn't yet enough.

All the coaches were sitting in the first-class section of the chartered 747; the players were spread out in the back, two athletes per row with plenty of room for their card games. During their return flights, the players always had the same youthful exuberance whether they won or lost. They'd been athletes their entire lives, and most of them had learned that they couldn't take the outcome of any game too seriously. They enjoyed victories and shrugged off defeats with apparent ease. The coaches, on the other hand, were as moody as preteen girls. After a victory, they smiled and glad-handed each other like politicians on the campaign trail, telling jokes, replaying funny moments in the game, contemplating the future of the season with just-how-good-are-we comparisons that invariably started with the phrase "when I was coaching at—" followed by a description of the best team, best players, best season they ever had and ending with "—and this team is *even better* than that." When the team won it was always "the most talented team" they'd ever coached. After a victory, the plane could go into a twenty-thousand–foot nosedive, and the coaches would keep smiling, convinced that under their leadership, the pilots would find a way to succeed.

When the team lost, the sadness the coaches felt was too profound for words. They'd sit quietly, staring at their game plans, replaying the game in their heads, wondering where things went wrong and whether they could be fixed. They worried that the team might slide too far, lose too many games and never recover. Most of them had been hired and fired half a dozen times, and every loss made them wonder if they'd be moving again soon. They bounced from high school to college to pro teams, moving more than military families. A great season would propel them to a better job in a bigger venue for more money. After a losing season, they'd pack up their offices and their houses and their families and trek across the country to a lesser job in a lesser venue for less money. They lived a continuous cycle of victory and defeat, job offer and dismissal. The players had youth and flexibility on their side, but the coaches had age and responsibility working against them. Their wives had endured too many changes of address, and their teenage children hated them for the social havoc they wrecked.

The loss to Green Bay dropped the Stallions to 2–3, which was a tough way to start the season. It took nine victories to make the playoffs in a low-tide year, ten wins in an average season, and twelve to be locked in when there was high tide. The Stallions had three losses in their first five games, and every coach on the plane understood their precarious position. High tide hit the 1985 playoffs when the AFC East delivered the Dolphins (12–4), Jets (11–5) and Patriots (11–5), the AFC Central produced the Browns (8–8), and in the AFC West the Raiders (12–4) and Broncos (11–5) led the pack. Back then, only five teams made the playoffs and the Broncos were the odd team out. Despite their lesser record, the Browns earned an automatic berth by winning their division, and the Jets and Patriots both had tie-breaking advantages over the Broncos, so even with eleven victories, Denver stayed home. A high-tide year was the worst fear of every NFL coach. Victories were hard to come by, and in a high-tide year it just took too many to get into the post season.

With three losses already, the Stallions had to count on being close to perfect for the remainder of the year or pray for the type of low tide that occurred in 1995 when the 49ers (13–3) and Cowboys (12–4) won far more games than everyone else in the NFC, and the other teams limped into the playoffs with mediocre records—Vikings (10–6), Packers (9–7), Lions (9–7) and Bears (9–7), which was the sort of record the Stallions were likely to have this season.

Right this second, Kinneson decided suddenly.

He killed the fresh glass of Scotch in one big swig. He stood up in the aisle and looked down at the coaches slumped in their seats. He glared at head coach Max Starnes, but the coach didn't return the look. The two men had adopted the habit of ignoring each other—even when they were sitting three feet apart on an airplane.

"Shitty game today, coach." Kinneson had just the slightest slur from the alcohol.

Starnes looked up at Kinneson impatiently, then returned to his playbook.

"Now we've got three losses." Kinneson pressed his palms against the overhead compartments to steady himself. "Two teams in the conference are still undefeated. Did you know that?"

Everyone knew that. Every coach on the plane was worried about that. Starnes continued to ignore the owner.

"Three other teams in the league have only got one loss. Did you know that?"

Max Starnes lowered his playbook into his lap, took a deep breath, and brought his eyes up to study Jonathan Kinneson.

"So now we've lost three games and the playoffs are looking like they might be out of reach." Jonathan Kinneson was working himself up to it.

"You might be prepared to give up on the team," Starnes said, "but I'm not. We still have a lot of games to play."

Jonathan Kinneson smiled then, and that surprised Coach Starnes. "Actually," the owner said with such uncharacteristic glee that Starnes realized he was absolutely drunk, "I'm not giving up on the team. I'm giving up on you."

That was no surprise to Starnes. He and Kinneson had never developed any rapport. He shrugged and picked up his playbook. They'd had this conversation on many occasions, but Starnes knew that Kinneson couldn't fire him without paying a substantial penalty, so he didn't worry about the owner's bluster.

"I have waited for a long time to say these words to you," Kinneson said. He cupped his hands around his mouth as if to shout, but then spoke in a stage whisper: "You're fired!"

Coach Max Starnes again lowered his playbook. "Well, hallelujah."

Kinneson was practically dancing in the aisle. "That's right. You...are...eff-eye-erred! Effective immediately, no need to report for work tomorrow."

"You're gonna pay to get rid of me?"

"Don't have to, 'cause you lost today."

"It doesn't matter if I lost today. I'm in the fifth year of my guarantee. You can't fire me unless we're mathematically eliminated from the playoffs."

Jonathan Kinneson continued to dance as he reached into the overhead compartment and retrieved his briefcase. He snapped it open with a flourish and pulled out a document. "You know what this is?"

Starnes shrugged. He wasn't interested in guessing games.

"It's your contract. You know what it says?"

Coach Starnes waited.

"Paragraph seventeen says that you have a five-year guarantee, but after year three, your cumulative record has to stay above .500. If I fire you while the team is below .500, then I only have to pay you one hundred thousand dollars in severance, which I will gladly do."

Starnes reached for the contract and flipped through the pages. He read paragraph seventeen carefully. He'd forgotten about this part of the contract, and although he didn't have a clear memory of it even now, the words were printed right there on paper. He checked the back page and saw his signature. He'd would check his own copy when he got home, but it appeared that Kinneson had done his homework.

"Well, at least somebody on this plane is happy we lost today," Starnes said ruefully.

"You got that right." Kinneson fell back into his seat and signaled for another Scotch.

13

"Can you believe Mr. Kinneson fired Coach Starnes like that?" Caleb Alexander asked. "Right there on the plane in front of everybody?"

Trevor Deale shook his head. "It was pretty surprising." But not nearly as surprising as it might have been. Trevor reflected on the conversation he'd overheard outside Kinneson's office and realized that this must have been the owner's plan all along. When Caleb revealed in the showers that someone had pressured him to fumble, Trevor guessed that Kinneson must have manipulated the outcome of the contest. But the quarterback had spent the long flight home thinking about it, and he still couldn't understand how Caleb's fumble could have made enough of a difference to guarantee a Stallions loss.

They sat side by side in the back of Caleb's plush Mercedes limousine. Tui Acondaca raised the privacy partition and drove toward Trevor's house at a leisurely pace. The air had been a little tense between Tui and Caleb after Michael Gasca's call, but eventually Caleb forgave his driver. He knew how persuasive Gasca could be; he knew Tui had been put in a tough position.

A row of lights mounted just below the ceiling illuminated the cabin. A TV was perched in the corner above a DVD player, a videogame console, and a fully stocked bar.

"Tell me what happened," Trevor said.

Caleb let out a long slow breath. "There's a guy in Philly who helped me get Westwinds to hit Vegas, L.A., or the Bahamas—"

"A Westwind?"

"It's a type of Leer jet. Israel Aircraft Westwind. Plush, fast, and sleek. It's my favorite. Well, over the years, this guy started helping me out with some other things like cars, houses, and jewelry. The man's got mad skills 'cause there ain't never been nothing he couldn't get for me."

Trevor nodded.

"He called me the other day," Caleb continued, "and said that I was just about out of money, but he would give me some cash if I fumbled the ball."

Just about out of money? That shocked Trevor, although it shouldn't have, given what he knew about Caleb's spending habits.

"What does 'just about out of money' mean?" In the most literal sense, it might mean that Caleb had spent through his entire fortune. But for a man who had tens of millions, the phrase "just about out of money" could mean that he was down to a few million.

"I've got less than a hundred and fifty grand," Caleb said quietly.

Whoa! "But that's really not true," Trevor said after a moment. "You've got a lot of stuff, Caleb. You can sell some of it, get rid of some debt, and you'll be okay. Put the money in the bank, settle down a little bit. If you play this out right, you'll be fine."

"You think so?" Caleb said hopefully.

"I know so. But tell me more about this guy."

"His name is Michael Gasca."

"How did you first get in contact with him?"

"I really don't remember. I think my agent put me in touch with him my rookie year when I was trying to get a plane."

"And a few days ago he told you that you were broke?"

"Yeah."

"How would he know?"

"He handles a lot of my money."

"He has *control* over your money?" Trevor tried, without much success, to keep the reproach out of his voice.

"It's not exactly like that," Caleb said defensively. "I have a broker, a lawyer, an accountant, and a financial planner; they're all connected somehow, and they share information. I never worried about it, because letting them talk to each other made it a lot easier for me. If I wanted a plane, Gasca would charter it and then Phil, my financial guy, would send him the payment. It was all worked out between them."

"How did you hire all these people?"

"My agent recommended them."

"First thing we have to do is get you a new agent," Trevor said. "Then you have to get your finances moved over to someone else, and get this Michael Gasca person out of your life."

"Okay," Caleb said gratefully. He'd never developed friendships with any of his teammates, and all the people he partied with were just milking him for the free ride. Trevor seemed to really care about him.

"So now, when Michael Gasca called, exactly what did he tell you to do?"

"Fumble the first time I got the ball in the red zone, but I didn't want to do it. I made up my mind that I wasn't gonna do it. I wasn't gonna let everyone down. I was gonna hold on to the ball, but then I got hit and I fumbled for real. I didn't mean to do it." Caleb was nearly in tears.

"I know you didn't," Trevor said uncomfortably. He didn't know how to respond to Caleb's sudden emotion. "I know you didn't," he said again.

They rode in silence for a few minutes. "How much money is he gonna pay you?" Trevor said.

"Five hundred grand."

"For *one* fumble?" Trevor didn't know how much gamblers typically paid to arrange a fix, but he knew it couldn't be half a million dollars. He wondered how Michael Gasca could make a profit on the game if he had to spend that much to buy the fix.

"It's my own money," Caleb said. "He said he's been skimming for the past few years, and put it into an account in the Cayman Islands. It's still my money, but I can't get to it without him."

"How much is in the account?"

"About a million."

"And he's giving you half of it?"

"Yeah."

"And all you had to do was fumble one time in the red zone?"

"Yeah."

"That's it?"

"That's all he told me."

"From that, he figured we'd lose the game?" That didn't make sense to Trevor. Any team could survive one fumble.

"That's what he told me to do."

"Maybe he got to some other players, too. Maybe there were three or four guys who made mistakes, and that's why we lost." But could Michael Gasca really have control over that many players? Had he been stealing money from all of them? Even if he had, how many of them were in the desperate financial situation Caleb was in? How many of them could be manipulated by the promise of getting back some of their own cash?

The limo pulled up to the gate leading into Trevor's housing area, and a uniformed guard approached the back window.

Trevor rolled down his window. "Hey Edward, how you doing?"

Edward Ortega had an autographed Trevor Deale football card taped to the wall in his booth. Most of the owners zoomed through the gate using their remote controls and never said a word to Edward unless they needed to put someone's name on the guest list, and then they spoke to him gruffly as if he existed solely to take their orders. Trevor Deale had actually stopped by to chat. Trevor knew that the guard had a wife and three kids, and he worked this job because it gave him time to do his homework. Edward was studying marketing at San Antonio College and someday hoped to have a career rather than a job.

"Hey, Trevor," Edward said. "Sorry about the loss today."

"You win some and you lose some," Trevor said.

"Let me get the gate for you."

"Thanks. Have a good night."

Tui eased through the neighborhood and pulled up to a second gate, which led up to Trevor's house. "It's two-seven-four-seven then pound," Trevor said when Tui lowered the privacy screen. Tui punched in the code and the gate slide open.

"Listen," Trevor said as the limo stopped in front of his house. "If he's giving you half the money now, he's probably going to ask for another favor down the road if you want to get the other half."

"I hadn't thought about that," Caleb said.

"When you talk to him again, let me know."

"I will."

"And Caleb?"

"Yeah?"

"Slow down. No more parties, no more jets, no more big spending. We'll get together later this week and start sorting through your finances and figure out how to get you out of this mess. Is that cool?"

"That sounds great," Caleb said. "Thanks, Trevor. I really appreciate it."

14

Jonathan Kinneson took great care to suppress his smile during the press conference to announce the firing of Coach Max Starnes.

"There were philosophical differences about how the team should be run," Kinneson said to the assembled media. He was positively radiant.

"Don't you think it's dangerous to fire a coach in the middle of a season?" a reporter asked.

"Yes," Kinneson agreed, "but I think it's more dangerous to keep the wrong man at the helm when you're hoping to win a championship. With Starnes I just didn't believe we'd make the playoffs, and I didn't want to throw away a year like this. We've got a talented pool of players and we need a coach who can maximize their potential. I felt it was better to make the change now, early in the season, when we've still got a chance to make a run."

"So who's your new coach?"

"I'm not going to announce that today, because we're still finalizing a couple of details, but tomorrow I'll name a successor."

"Is it someone on the current staff?"

"No."

"Mr. Kinneson, with all due respect, you're going to hire a new coach in the middle of the season who's not part of the current staff? A new coach working with the old staff and with the old system isn't going to be any better than Starnes, and probably a whole lot worse."

All of the reporters knew that a new coach bringing in a new staff would totally disrupt the Stallions' season. Would the new coach bring new offensive and defensive strategies with him? How would the players learn all of the new formations and plays when so much time had already been invested during training camp learning Starnes's system? Could the new coach step in and run Starnes's program? If so, how would he learn it so quickly?

"Believe me," Jonathan Kinneson said. "I've considered the potential problems. I'm bringing in just a head coach at the moment. He's going to keep most of the existing staff, and he'll be running Starnes's basic package. It wasn't the nuts and bolts that needed replacing; it was the overall leadership. The new coach will bring with him a level of aggressiveness that has been sorely lacking the past few years."

■ ■ ■

Roscoe Evans and Michael Gasca drove slowly through the red-leafed University of Oklahoma campus in Norman, Oklahoma, admiring the pretty young women who shuffled among the trees with backpacks slung over their shoulders.

"So you gonna tell me how you knew?" Roscoe rumbled.

"How I knew what?" Gasca said.

"That the Stallions would win if Caleb Alexander fumbled."

"Take a guess," Gasca said. "What percentage of NFL games do you think get decided by seven points or less?"

Roscoe considered this for a while. "Fifteen percent?"

"Higher."

"Twenty-five?"

"Higher."

"Come on, really? Thirty-five percent?"

"Higher."

Roscoe looked over at Gasca. "You gotta be shittin' me. Higher than thirty-five percent?"

"It's higher than forty-five percent," Gasca said. "I've been noticing over the past few years that there were a lot of close games, so I started paying attention. What I've found is that forty-nine percent of the games are decided by seven points or less."

"Almost fifty percent, huh?" Roscoe said. "That's pretty good."

"You find a way to put seven points on the board or take seven off, then you got a fifty-fifty shot of changing the outcome of the game," Gasca said.

"So you figured if Caleb fumbled once, that would be enough?"

"That would give us a shot, but it gets even better than that. There are a few really good teams every year, and a few really bad teams."

"Oh, I get it," said Roscoe. "You shave off the best and the worst to get a different average?"

"That's the basic idea, but it's actually even simpler than that. You don't have to take off the top and the bottom, just one of them. Which one do you think?"

"Hell, I don't know. The three worst."

"Why do you think that?"

Roscoe thought about it for a moment. "I bet the best teams win by a little bit, but the bad teams lose by a lot," he said. "Sort of like when you watch the sprinters in the Olympics. The guy at the front wins by just a step or two, but the guy in eighth place is always a long way back."

"Not bad," Gasca said. "That's a good theory, but it's exactly opposite of what happens in the NFL. The worst teams tend to lose a lot of close games, while the best teams win by big margins. So you take the three best teams out of the calculation and you know what you get?"

"A higher percentage?"

"That's right. Without the top two or three overachieving teams, sixty-five percent of the games are decided by less than seven points."

"Sixty-five percent!"

"That's why I thought Caleb's fumble would work," Gasca said. "If I could get him to fumble once in the red zone, that would take seven points from the Stallions and give a pretty solid push in the direction of losing the game. It's not a guarantee, but it's as close as we can get without raising suspicion."

"But what if he never got the ball in the red zone?" Roscoe wondered. "Or what if he fumbled but his own team recovered? Or what if he got hurt on the first play of the game?" All the variables were rolling around in Roscoe's head now. He didn't have Michael Gasca's brain power, but there seemed to be a lot of holes in this plan.

"You're right. There are a lot of things that could go wrong," Gasca conceded, "but you gotta play the odds. Remember what Uncle Nick taught us about collecting money? The thing he said was the most important part of the job?"

Roscoe chuckled as he recalled the lessons they'd learned from Dominic Sarcassi. "Sometimes you gotta give 'em a nudge."

"Just a nudge," Gasca agreed, smiling.

They were fifteen years old when Uncle Nick taught them that lesson. They'd been best friends and business partners since junior high school when Gasca started calling Roscoe, "My Heavens Roscoe Evans" and Roscoe called Gasca, "Michael Gasca the Masta." This was back when Gasca was climbing the ladder in the Sarcassi family and taking Roscoe along for the ride. Gasca would send Roscoe out to talk to a guy, and Roscoe would come back with cash, "like manna from Heaven," Gasca would say.

Nobody really understood their friendship. All the Italian guys called Roscoe a *totzone* or a *muli*. Roscoe knew those were bad words, but since he didn't speak Italian and no one ever called him a nigger in English, he didn't raise a fuss. They wanted to know why Gasca used a *totzone* for collections instead of somebody from the family, and Gasca never gave them an answer. He'd just smile and say, "My Heavens, it's Roscoe Evans," and both boys would laugh. Of course, Roscoe's people didn't like the way he called Gasca "Masta," but that was because they didn't get the joke. Roscoe didn't call Gasca master as if he were a slave owner. The nickname was short for "master control." Roscoe had never met anyone who was more in control than Michael Gasca.

They took their lessons straight from the mouth of Uncle Nick and on a balmy summer afternoon he taught them about nudges. They were standing near the end of a pier at the dockyards. Birds pinwheeled overhead, and ships slid smoothly into the bay. Uncle Nick was talking about collecting from deadbeats.

He said, "Guy doesn't pay you right away, you gotta give him a nudge."

"A nudge?" Gasca said.

"Yeah, you send Roscoe over to visit him. And when you get there, Roscoe, you don't threaten him, you don't hurt him. You just walk in and ask him how he's doing and when he's gonna pay. The more polite you are, the better."

"That's it?" Roscoe asked doubtfully. He preferred a little heavy lifting. Roscoe believed it was foolish to use diplomacy when you had physical superiority.

"You never want to do any more than is necessary," Uncle Nick said. "Most of the time, a little nudge is enough."

"I don't know, Uncle Nick," Roscoe said. "Some of these guys are knuckleheads who don't understand nothing but a knuckle to the head."

Uncle Nick nodded. He'd been in the business a long time. He knew how tough it could be. "How much you weigh, Roscoe?"

"About two-fifty." Roscoe could not keep the pride out of his voice. He was only fifteen, and still growing. Compared to the man-mountain he would become, at two hundred and fifty pounds, Roscoe was gangly.

"You think you could balance on that post?" Uncle Nick pointed to a round pylon jutting up at the end of the pier. It rose three feet above the main platform and served as a perch for seagulls watching the water below for fish.

"Piece of cake." Roscoe hopped up on the post like a graceful circus elephant, standing on one foot, then the other, turning in a circle. When he completed the turn, Uncle Nick was standing next to him, and before Roscoe could react, Uncle Nick pushed him. Roscoe gyrated for a couple of anxious seconds then tumbled off the pylon and into the murky water fifteen feet below.

"See," Uncle Nick yelled down, "most of the time, a nudge is all you need."

Roscoe and Gasca still laughed every time they thought about that day at the pier.

"Well," Gasca said, "all we can do is give the game a nudge. There are no guarantees, but Uncle Nick was right. A nudge usually gets the job done."

"So," Roscoe said, "Caleb's fumble cost them seven points, and that was enough of a nudge?"

"But the effect was a lot bigger than just that one play," Gasca said. "The Stallions lost the momentum and got a little demoralized by the fumble. For the Packers, that was a huge play. The defense created a turnover right on the goal line, so the crowd got back into it. Everyone on their sideline was high-fiving each other. It may not have seemed like much, but a nudge can be a powerful thing."

"So," Roscoe nodded, "while you're working on Trevor Deale—"

"You'll be out giving nudges."

Roscoe turned his attention back to the road. He pulled into the parking lot at the OU stadium and drove around to the football offices. They walked into the building, past the vacant secretary's desk, and caught Coach Joseph Repanshek in his office studying game tape. It was about 10 A.M., and most of Repanshek's players were either sitting in class or still sleeping in their girlfriends' dorm rooms. They'd report for meetings after lunch and then hit the field for practice.

Even Joseph Repanshek, who spent his days surrounded by large men, had to blink three or four times to take in the sheer bulk of Roscoe Evans. And the fact that Repanshek had seen Roscoe once before—in this office just a few months earlier—did little to mitigate the shock. A rhino stumbling into Repanshek's office a second time would have elicited the same alarm. Roscoe smiled as he ducked through the door, and Repanshek felt a little better. Roscoe had a nice, friendly grin that put people at ease.

Michael Gasca walked in behind him. "Coach, good to see you again."

"You too," Repanshek said carefully. He was a fifty-six-year-old alcoholic who'd landed the head-coaching job at Oklahoma after thirty years of trying. He'd lived all over the country, and his family had packed and moved so many times they'd finally quit—three wives and all six kids. Now he lived alone, but he was a head coach—at Oklahoma, by God!— and that was something. The walls in his office bore dozens of plaques honoring Repanshek's achievements. He had a few pictures of politicians and movie stars hanging among scores of pictures of football players with their powerful arms draped over Repanshek's shoulders. He always asked that of his players. "Put your arm around me," he'd say before the photographer snapped the picture. He liked the way it looked—as if the player would fall down if not for the support of his coach.

"You remember a few months ago when we talked about a possible NFL job?" Michael Gasca said.

"Of course," Repanshek said. There were many college coaches who had no desire to move up to the pro level. They enjoyed working on campus, dealing with an administration and helping to mold young men. Repanshek was not one of those coaches. He'd dreamed about being an NFL coach for most of his life.

"What we'd like you to do is take over the head position with the San Antonio Stallions and do with Trevor Deale what you did with him here."

"Right now?" Repanshek said, looking across the room. A mural of the Sooners' schedule dominated the far wall with home games painted red and away games in white. He couldn't abandon his team in the middle of the year, could he? He'd sat in the living rooms of every kid on the roster, and in front of their parents and siblings, he'd made solemn promises. He'd told them that he wouldn't leave the school during their tenure, that each of them would get a chance to start, that he'd make sure they graduated on time, and that he absolutely did not want to coach anywhere other than the University of Oklahoma. He'd sat in their living rooms, drank their coffee, admired their family portraits, and assured them that he would take the best possible care of them.

But now staring at an offer to coach in the NFL, he knew there was no way he could turn it down. He looked out the doorway of his office as if planning his escape.

"Right now," Michael Gasca said. "You'd make a million dollars a year, and there's a good chance that under your leadership the Stallions will make it to the Super Bowl. All you gotta do is coach Trevor."

That unsettled Repanshek. He'd worked with Trevor Deale for three seasons at Oklahoma, and he'd barely survived the experience. Coach Repanshek had lost his mind back then—along with his third marriage—and he believed Trevor was the main cause of his dementia. Repanshek thought back to one of the last conversations he'd had with Trevor Deale nearly a year ago, right here in this office.

"Come on in and sit down, son," Coach Repanshek had said gruffly.

Repanshek had never had a player with the size, speed and easy athleticism that Trevor possessed. Pro scouts had flown out to the school routinely since the boy's freshman year. They stood on the sideline during practice and whistled as Trevor launched balls sixty yards, hitting receivers in stride. They watched game tape and scribbled furiously, making note of his amazing talent.

Repanshek watched the scouts eyes fall greedily on Trevor's six-foot-four-inch frame, and he wanted to warn them: "He'll drive you insane!"

Coach Repanshek stared across his desk at Trevor Deale, who waited patiently for the lecture to begin. This was during Trevor's third season at OU, after being named a Kodak All-American the previous two years;

he'd carried the Sooners to two bowl berths, and he was the odds-on favorite to win the Heisman Trophy. Repanshek leaned back in his chair and let out a big breath.

"Son, I wish I didn't have to talk to you about this kind of stuff all the time."

"You don't," Trevor said.

Repanshek steepled his fingers in front of his mouth, pressing his hands together tightly, blowing hot air through his nose. "That attitude..." he warned, unable to finish the thought.

Trevor had a baseball cap pulled down over his eyes. He waited with no expression on his face.

"What I want to talk to you about is the god-awful things you said to the good folks at the booster club last night." Repanshek kept his eyes locked on Trevor's. Most players withered under the coach's glare, but Trevor didn't seem bothered.

"The booster club is the easiest audience you're ever gonna face," Repanshek continued. "They come to every game—home and away. They donate money to the school. These people love their Sooners, and when they show up on a Tuesday night to meet one of our players, they wanna leave feeling good." Repanshek ran a hand across his face and broke eye contact with Trevor. His eyes came back quickly, but suddenly, he felt uncomfortable under Trevor's unflinching stare.

The coach cleared his throat. "Last week," he continued, "Roland had 'em eating out of his hands. This kid ain't goin' pro, he might not even start next week, but they loved him. He told stories about growing up in Louisiana and about how exciting it was to run out on to that field every Saturday, and how honored he was to be a player at OU. That's what they wanna hear."

Coach Repanshek believed Trevor had some sort of social disorder. He was too self-contained, too impervious to things that other people were naturally emotional about. A couple of years earlier Repanshek had tried to talk to Trevor about leadership, and it was like punching a bag full of thumbtacks—only more painful.

The coach had said, "Trevor you're the quarterback, so the guys look to you for leadership. You've got to—"

"What's leadership?" Trevor had interrupted.

Back then, the question didn't annoy coach Repanshek, because it was still early in his relationship with Trevor Deale. But months later—years later—questions like that would bring angry tears to Repanshek's eyes and push him to the edge of his patience.

"Like last week," Repanshek had said, "when Mitchell dropped a pass you put right between the numbers. Something like that, I expect you to get on him a little bit when he comes back to the huddle."

"Get on him?"

"Let him know that just ain't acceptable."

"Of course it's acceptable."

Coach Joseph Repanshek had never coached a player like Trevor, and Lord willing, he'd never have another one.

"Trevor," he had said carefully, not quite believing that he had to explain this to a player of Trevor's caliber. "Mitchell ain't on scholarship to drop passes. He's here to catch 'em. Dropping passes is not acceptable."

"It has to be acceptable," Trevor said. "Dropping a *baby* is unacceptable. That's why parents don't play catch with their infants. But every time I throw the ball, I accept the possibility that it'll hit the ground or get intercepted. I could never succeed as a quarterback and Mitchell could never succeed as a receiver if we truly believed that an incomplete pass was unacceptable."

Coach Repanshek had paused numbly, not sure what to say. "Son," he said after a moment, "I think I understand what you're saying, and in a way you're right. But that's not the point I'm trying—"

"Do you 'get on' a guy who suffers a serious injury?" Trevor asked.

Coach Repanshek stopped again. "Of course not."

"Why not?"

Why not? Repanshek repeated silently. Why not was a typical Trevor question. He was always asking why not this and why not that.

"Because, Trevor," Repanshek said slowly. He always spoke slowly when he responded to Trevor's whys and why nots. "Injuries are accidents."

"Oh," Trevor said. "You think Mitchell dropped the pass on purpose?"

Eventually during Trevor's freshman year, Repanshek got so twisted up and frustrated that he quit speaking to his star quarterback. Trevor had too many questions. Too many off-putting arguments. Once on the sideline, Repanshek had called time-out on a critical third-down play in the second quarter.

"It's okay to punt, Coach," Trevor had said.

"What did you say?" Repanshek pulled his headphone off and stared hard at his young quarterback. Trevor was only eighteen then, playing in his fourth collegiate game.

"It's okay to punt."

"Trevor, we need eight yards for a first down and if we don't get it we *will* punt, but I don't ever want to hear you say anything like that ever again. You keep your focus on making plays, and I'll worry about whether we need to punt."

Trevor nodded. "You're probably going to call Three Jet Bingo Cross, and it's not going to be there. The Sam linebacker has been running with the tight end all day, and as soon as the Y makes his break, the safety's gonna jump the route. No matter how well I time it, and no matter how well I place the ball, at best they'll break up the pass, and at worse they'll pick it off. Unfortunately, the game plan we've got doesn't give us anything that'll get eight yards against the cover four zone they're most likely to play. So our best bet is to call something safe and punt on fourth down. Punting is not the worst thing in the world, coach."

Repanshek stared at Trevor Deale with bulging eyes and rigid veins standing on his forehead and neck. Not only had Trevor accurately dissected the precise play the coach planned to call, but he had done it in front of two assistant coaches and half the players on offensive. Now everyone was staring at the coach waiting for his response.

"I-Right Slot 34 Lead," Repanshek spit out finally. It was a handoff to the tailback. It gained only three yards, and the punt team jogged on to the field.

After the game, the coach didn't know what to say to Trevor Deale about his insubordination, so he'd avoided his quarterback.

Three weeks later, Trevor did it again.

It was late in the fourth quarter, and the Sooners needed only a few inches for a first down. Coach Repanshek called time out and told Trevor to run quarterback sneak.

"Stutter-Go would be a better call," Trevor said.

In all his years of coaching, Repanshek had never had a player argue with him on the sideline, and he wasn't going to let Trevor get away with it a second time.

"Son, you run what I tell you to run!"

Trevor pointed at the end zone clock, which displayed forty-seven seconds. "I run the sneak and get the first down, but they take their time getting off the pile and by the time everyone is set, and I spike the ball, we'll have thirty-five seconds, at best, to get into the end zone. They'll jump into a prevent defense, and we'll never score. But we've got an opportunity right now. They know we have to get a first down, so they're going to be aggressive to stop us on this play. They're going to pack the line of scrimmage and play man-free behind it. If we call Stutter-Go, we might have something."

"Stutter-Go is a terrible call," Repanshek interrupted, but Trevor continued as if the coach hadn't spoken.

"The cornerback on Ricky has had trouble all day, so the safety's cheating in his direction. The corner covering Mitchell has been playing bump-bail, and he's looking into the backfield. He's jumped the last two slant routes we've run, so when I pump at three steps, he's going to bite. When he does, Mitchell will run right by him, and we'll score a touchdown."

"Quarter...back...sneak!" Repanshek snapped barely holding it together.

"Okay," Trevor said without hesitation. He pulled his helmet on and trotted back to the huddle.

Coach Repanshek paced the sideline and watched with dismay as the defense lined up exactly as Trevor had predicted. The safety was cheating to the far side of the field. The cornerback on the near side was looking into the backfield playing bump-bail coverage. The center snapped the ball, and Trevor lunged forward for the first down. The referees scrambled in, and the Oklahoma players rushed back to their positions. Trevor barked the signals and spiked the ball, stopping the clock with thirty-three seconds. The defense jumped into prevent coverage, and the Sooners never got close to the end zone.

That afternoon marked the beginning of Repanshek's uneasy reliance on Trevor Deale. Coach Repanshek called the plays, but Trevor changed them whenever he saw an opportunity. Trevor understood football strategy as if he'd been studying the game for decades; he anticipated defenses as if the other team's coordinator were whispering in his ear. He knew when the opposition would blitz and when they would bluff and hang back. He knew when to audible into a better play and when to fake the audible to get the opponent to change defensive fronts.

During meetings and film study, Trevor asked a steady stream of questions. He spotted every inconsistency, every tendency, and every problem.

Once Trevor said: "That's an unsound blocking scheme. There's no one to pick up the strong safety if he blitzes, and I already have a hot read on that play." He was right.

Once Trevor said: "We have four plays in the game plan that each have their own unique formations. If our opponents are smart, they'll know exactly what we're doing with the ball the moment we line up. If we're smart, we'd have a couple new plays to run out of each of those formations." He was right.

Once Trevor said: "Instead of having Avery run a hook on the backside, why not put him on a shallow cross? That would make him the fourth receiver on the strong side. If they're in their two-deep zone coverage, there's no way they can account for a fourth receiver showing up in the flat late." He was right.

When Trevor raised his hand to ask a question, Repanshek shuddered silently knowing that he wouldn't have an answer. He should have been grateful. Thanks to Trevor, Coach Repanshek was enjoying the best seasons of his career, but he didn't feel grateful. He felt embarrassed. And when Joseph Repanshek got embarrassed, he got aggressive—just ask his ex-wives. He went on the offensive with Trevor, calling the quarterback into his office and taking him to task every time Trevor's "honesty problem" got him into trouble.

"Son, as smart as you are at football, there were chickens on my daddy's farm had more common sense than you got." Repanshek was staring across his desk at Trevor with a pen gripped tightly in one fist. "Last night at the booster club all you had to do was tell 'em what they wanted to hear."

"I answered their questions," Trevor said.

"But, my god, son, the things you said! Old Fred Conner asked you how bad we're gonna beat 'em on Saturday and all you had to say was '45 to nothing' and the whole place would have gone wild. But you went and said some fool thing about how we might not win the game."

"We probably won't."

"See!" coach Repanshek threw his hands in the air. "You say something like that people don't know what to think."

"Texas is better than we are," Trevor shrugged. The University of Texas was undefeated and ranked number three in the nation. "They'll probably beat us no matter what we do."

"Son, shut the hell up!" Repanshek spat. He closed his eyes and rubbed his temples. He always got a headache when he talked to Trevor Deale. "Can't you hear how bad that sounds? Sounds like you already gave up. Like you don't even want to win the game. You're not planning to lose on purpose, are you?"

"No."

"Then don't say things like that."

"So if I think Texas is better than we are, I shouldn't say that?"

"No!" the coach said. "You say," he took another deep breath. "You say that we're gonna stomp 'em."

"We're gonna stomp 'em?"

"That's right. Then everybody claps and cheers and everything is fine. What you did last night was like pouring ice-cold water on a couple of horny teenagers. You didn't just ruin the mood—you killed it. Them people gonna be mad for a week."

Trevor had walked out of the coach's office and back to the locker room. Repanshek had reached into the credenza behind him and pulled out a bottle of Jack Daniels, as was his custom after he talked to Trevor.

■ ■ ■

"You'll be coaching Trevor again," Michael Gasca said to Coach Repanshek, "and you'll be running Coach Starnes's offensive system, but that's not a problem because you just handle things the same way you did here. You call the plays, but Trevor will keep the offense out of trouble."

"He ain't gonna ask me any questions, is he?" Repanshek asked carefully.

"I can't promise you that, Coach," Gasca said. "You know how Trevor is."

Repanshek shuddered.

"But you know what Trevor can do on the field, and he needs a coach like you to give him free reign over the offense. You figured it out pretty quick here at Oklahoma. And that's what makes you a great coach. You saw what you had in Trevor Deale and you let him run with it."

Coach Repanshek nodded. "Do I get a full million for this season, or is it pro-rated for the games I've already missed?"

Michael Gasca and Roscoe Evans smiled at each other. "You get a full million, Coach," Gasca said. "Welcome to the team."

15

Steven Oquist called NFL Security's New York office as soon as he heard the news.

"You've got to send me to San Antonio," Oquist said to Ken Parsley.

The assistant director knew the Stallions had a new coach, but he didn't see any cause for alarm. "I'm still not convinced there's a problem."

"Not convinced?" Oquist pulled the phone away from his ear and stared at it for a moment. He took a breath and said, "You saw the tape of Michael Gasca talking about Trevor Deale and San Antonio. Now we see that the Stallions' coach has been fired in the middle of the season, and Trevor Deale's college coach is coming in to lead the team. Don't you think that's strange?"

"I'm not saying you're wrong," Ken Parsley said carefully. "I just don't think we should drop into San Antonio like storm troopers when we don't know what's happening. We have to be very careful about how we handle things."

"I know, I know," Oquist said.

"We can't have any media reports out there suggesting that we're investigating a team for possible gambling ties."

"I understand the need for discretion—"

"If we start sniffing around the Stallions too hard, and some reporter gets wind of it and writes a story…you understand the damage that would do to us? Mob figures linked to a team? I can't let you go in there half-cocked ready to blow up the world to find Michael Gasca."

"Believe me, I understand," Steven Oquist said. He'd heard this lecture many times. Every investigation conducted by NFL Security had to be handled with so much care that the targets of the case—usually play-ers, coaches, and front-office staff—generally never knew they'd been examined. Most importantly, the media never learned of it.

"I need you to make a soft landing," C.C. said, and Oquist realized that he was getting his wish.

"Soft as butter," he said eagerly.

"If I hear you're making a big splash, I'll pull you out of there," C.C. said.

"I understand." Oquist was all agreement now. "No big splash, no ruf-fled feathers, no cavalry. I'll be nice and quiet."

16

Roscoe Evans stepped off the elevator on the forty-fifth floor of the Tacoma Building in downtown San Antonio and tilted his head back to look all the way to the top of the enormous door at the entrance of Kinneson Corp.

"Now that's a door!" Roscoe boomed. The fortified entrance spanned twenty feet and rose more than forty feet toward the ceiling; it had thick, dark, ancient wood with tarnished metal plates racing across it. A small sign affixed to the wall explained that the door had been recovered from the ruins of a 12th century French castle, where it had served as a drawbridge. "A close inspection of the inside of the door," the sign read, "reveals faint semicircular indentations left by heavy armored horses that crossed the bridge." A camouflaged hydraulic motor ensured that even a small child could swing the door open with ease.

Roscoe Evans held the bridge open for Michael Gasca, and they approached a pretty receptionist sitting at a large mahogany desk answering a phone that never stopped ringing. Her mouth fell open when she saw Roscoe's towering frame. He smiled down at her, and she held up a nervous finger while she connected a call. She had a clean, rosy face with light freckles across the bridge of her nose. Curly red hair danced down to her shoulders.

"Welcome to Kinneson Corp.," the receptionist said. "How may I help you?"

"You have beautiful hair," Roscoe said.

"Oh…thank you," she blushed. She reached up and touched it lightly.

"Great cut and a wonderful color," Roscoe added. "What you think, Gasca? Is she the bomb or what?"

"Absolutely gorgeous," Michael Gasca agreed. Then he said doubtfully, "Your hair isn't naturally that curly, is it?"

"Yes," she nodded. "Sometimes I wish it weren't so curly."

"Mine's naturally curly too." Roscoe pointed at his bald head. "It's all tucked in right now."

"Like Moe, Larry, and Curly?" Gasca asked, grinning.

"Curlier," Roscoe said.

"Gentlemen," she said shyly, "How may I help you?"

"I'm sorry," Roscoe said. He put a hand over his heart. "I know you're busy. What's your name?"

"Tracy."

"Tracy, it's nice to meet you," he extended his hand. "I'm Roscoe Evans, and this is Michael Gasca. We have an eleven o'clock appointment with Mr. Kinneson."

"If you'll have a seat, I'll let Mr. Kinneson know you're here."

"Thank you, Tracy." They moved to a couch along the wall. There were seven other people in the waiting area all staring at Roscoe, but they looked away quickly when he turned in their direction. Michael Gasca checked his watch and made a note of the time, then picked up a magazine and got comfortable.

Roscoe was still smiling at Tracy, but out of the corner of his mouth he whispered, "How long you think we got?"

"It'll be a while," Gasca said.

Two hours later, they were still sitting on the couch. Tracy had apologized several times, to which Roscoe had replied, "No problem, Tracy. I'm sure Mr. Kinneson is a busy man." She'd offered them water, soft drinks, and even an orange that she'd brought from home. Gasca had said no thank you to everything, but Roscoe had accepted a single wedge of the orange, saying, "Nothing would brighten my day more than a little slice of Tracy's fruit." He winked; she winked back.

The wait stretched to nearly three hours before a young man in a blue suit came to fetch them. Tracy waved prettily as they left the lobby. The man in the suit, who never introduced himself, led them through a labyrinth of cubicles before finally reaching Kinneson's outer office. The secretary waiting there had gray streaks in her hair, crafty eyes, and a serious demeanor. She looked over her glasses and pointed to a pair of chairs without saying a word.

Roscoe dropped into the nearest seat and read the nameplate mounted on her desk.

"Good afternoon, Mrs. Moya," he said. "Must be tough being the gatekeeper for such an important guy."

Elizabeth Moya looked at him carefully. "It's not so tough," she said.

"Most guys must come back here pissed off that they had to wait a couple or three hours just to get to this point," Roscoe said. "Then you gotta deal with 'em, huh?"

She pulled her lips in tightly and went back to her paper work.

"I read in a magazine that the average wait to see Kinneson is three hours and twenty minutes," Roscoe said. "If you can get us into his office in the next ten minutes, that would be cool 'cause then we could say we just beat the average."

Mrs. Moya didn't know how to take that smile or the tone of voice. This giant in front of her seemed friendly enough, but what if he got angry? Who would stop him?

"Mr. Kinneson is a very busy man," she said.

"Oh, believe me, I know. And he's about to get a lot busier. That's why I don't mind waiting." After a moment Roscoe said, "You wouldn't happen to have any fruit, would you?"

Elizabeth Moya looked confused.

Both Roscoe and Gasca laughed. "Sorry," Roscoe said. "Inside joke."

They did not beat the average. It took more than three and a half hours to get into the billionaire's private chamber.

■ ■ ■

Jonathan Kinneson's long, rectangular office was arranged like a cathedral with tall windows at the end and banks of chairs, couches, and conference tables on either side of the aisle. Kinneson's desk was an enormous chunk of travertine marble that received a daily polish, and behind it Jonathan Kinneson looked like a preacher in a pulpit. He leaned forward with his arms spread and palms down on top of the desk.

"You look happy," Michael Gasca observed.

"I *am* happy," Kinneson said with gleaming teeth.

"Coach Starnes is gone."

"*Long* gone," Kinneson beamed.

"Coach Repanshek is on board."

"At the helm."

"So now we need to talk about getting you to the Super Bowl."

"Nope." Kinneson shook his head.

"You don't want to go to the Super Bowl?"

"We need to talk about how much money I'm going to pay you."

Roscoe smiled. "That's funny. We came here to talk about the same thing."

Kinneson smiled back. It was an angry smile. It was his business smile. It was his "My Time is More Important Than Your Time!" smile.

"Well, how fortuitous," he said.

"You've transferred one million so far," Gasca said, "and this week you've got another million due."

"I won't pay."

"No?" Gasca raised his eyebrows.

"That was no guarantee last weekend!"

"The Stallions lost the game," Gasca said.

"Yeah, but we had the lead when Caleb Alexander fumbled."

"But," Roscoe pointed out, "the Stallions didn't have the lead when the game ended."

"It was early in the fourth quarter," Kinneson protested. "What if the Packers hadn't scored? Or what if they did? There was still plenty of time for the Stallions to score again and win the game."

"But," Roscoe offered, "the Packers *did* score and the Stallions didn't score again so the Stallions lost, which was the plan."

"It could have gone the other way!"

Roscoe and Gasca looked at each other. "Mr. Kinneson," Gasca said, "you got what you wanted. The Stallions lost, Starnes got fired. What more were you expecting?"

"I was expecting a guarantee! That's what you promised me in that country club when your big thug," he pointed an accusing finger at Roscoe, "picked me up by my ankles and put me on my back. You sold me a guarantee, and Caleb's fumble on Sunday was no guarantee. There was a lot that could have gone wrong."

"It didn't," Roscoe said.

"It *could* have!"

Roscoe wondered how long they would dance around this point. "Mr. Kinneson, the sun could have exploded yesterday, but it didn't. You're upset about something that didn't happen, let's talk about something that could happen. I could drop you on the edge of something hard." Roscoe ran a finger along the curve of the marble desk.

Jonathan Kinneson stared at Roscoe Evans with far less fear than he'd had during their previous meeting. Kinneson had a gun strapped under his desk—put there just yesterday in anticipation of this reunion—and if Roscoe tried to come after him, the gun would come out, and then they'd see who felt the edge of something hard.

"You trying to back out of the deal, Mr. Kinneson?" Michael Gasca asked.

Kinneson shrugged. "I've got the players and the coach to make it work. Maybe I'll take my chances and see if they can make it to the Super Bowl the traditional way."

"They won't," Roscoe said.

"They might."

"Mr. Kinneson," Gasca said, "if you try to back out of this deal, I'm guaranteeing you that you won't make the Super Bowl."

"If that's anything like your guarantee last weekend, I'll take my chances."

"This one needs more than a nudge," Roscoe said. He thought he might squeeze Kinneson's head with his big paws and lift the Stallions' owner off the ground. Years ago, he'd picked up a guy named Vito Gragioli that way and held him for more than a minute. Afterward, Vito had babbled as if he'd been struck by lightning, and Roscoe never had a problem with him again.

"Last resort, Roscoe," Gasca said. "Last resort." To Kinneson, he said, "What I promised is that it would be subtle and it would be effective. Now, what I do is I find a way to influence the outcome of the game, but I do it quietly enough to stay under the NFL's radar. What were you expecting on Sunday? A play with a big neon sign blazing over it saying, 'Here's the play that was fixed'? You leave the manipulations to me, and make your payments on time because you really don't have any other choice."

"I'll report you to the league!" Kinneson said.

Roscoe laughed, filling up the room with so much sound that Kinneson covered his ears. "What are you gonna tell them?" He managed between guffaws. "The guy who was fixin' games for you has turned against you?"

"What you've got to worry about now is that *we'll* tell the league," Gasca said. "How long do you think you'll keep control of this team if the commissioner finds out that you hired some guys to fix games?"

"Tell him about the other thing," Roscoe said, smiling and clapping his hands.

Gasca nodded. "Roscoe needs a jet."

"So go buy one!" Kinneson spat.

"He's gonna have to do a lot of traveling to work on all these games, so he'll need to have access to your Lear jet."

"With all the money I'm paying you, you can get your own damned plane!"

"He has to go to Denver tomorrow," Gasca continued, "and then he'll need your jet every week through the end of the season."

"Fuck you!" Kinneson bellowed. "He can get his own jet!"

■ ■ ■

Roscoe Evans leaned back in the soft leather armchair of Jonathan Kinneson's plane and smiled contentedly. He had a beer in one hand and the remote control in the other, and he thought the satellite reception on the TV was remarkably good at forty-two thousand feet. Far below him, the suburbs of Denver appeared. The city sat at the end of a long plain nestled against snow-covered mountains rising in the west. The low murmur of the pilots' voices drifted back into the cabin as they got clearance to land at Centennial Airport.

On the tarmac, Roscoe had to take a deep breath and hold it to squeeze through the plane's small door. When he saw Vincent Agape waiting for him, he took another breath, deeper this time. It was going to be a long few days.

"Welcome to Denver, where the ground is a mile high and the sky reaches all the way to your feet," Vincent said. He sounded like a teacher Roscoe had hated in high school. The guy always took fifteen minutes to say something he could have spit out in thirty seconds. "I've got the entire scene scouted out. We've got the subject targeted and locked down. I know where he's gonna be tonight." Vincent Agape's age was the same as his waist measurement—fifty-three. Veins showed through his cheeks, and he had a bulbous red nose that leaked constantly. He paused every few seconds to wipe his upper lip with a handkerchief. "I figured we'd sneak in early in the morning and surprise him."

"Who?" Roscoe said, striding toward the car.

"He's a guy in a critical position who has an opportunity to help us further our goals. And I think we can lean on him with just the right pressure, and—"

"Vincent," Roscoe rumbled, "who is he?"

"He's a husband and a father of two, and he's got a little predilection that we've been following for a while now and we think he's ripe for a meeting with—"

Roscoe stopped walking. "How much longer are you gonna keep talking before you tell me the guy's name?"

Vincent stopped. He'd been referring to a page of sloppy handwritten notes. He looked over his glasses and dabbed his nose. "I'm getting to that, but I thought I'd tell you about him first."

"You've been telling me about him like you're introducing the goddamn keynote at a Rotary banquet," Roscoe said with uncharacteristic impatience. "It's just the two of us here, Vincent. You can be a little informal."

Vincent looked down at his notes and turned a couple of pages. "Well, I'm building up to that."

Roscoe looked around at the jets and Cesnas parked on the flight line. "How tall is he?"

Vincent stumbled for a moment. "I think...he's five...ten, maybe five-eleven."

"You think or you know?"

"I'm pretty sure. I can make a quick call and find out."

"See, that's what I'm talking about," Roscoe said. "Who the hell cares how tall he is?"

"You're the one who asked!"

"Only to show you that I don't need all these extra details. I'm outta patience here, Vincent. The next words out of your mouth better be this guy's name."

Vincent dabbed at his nose.

"Okay?" Roscoe said.

"All right."

"So what do we got down here?"

"Robert Maxwell."

"Was that so hard?" Roscoe said. Vincent didn't respond. "What's his deal?"

Vincent counted to five and looked off toward the clouds boiling over the mountains. "I'm gonna get to that too, but I'm trying to do this in a particular order if that's okay."

"What order is that?"

"The order I planned it!"

"Yeah, and sometime next week, you'll finish up. For God's sake man, I wanna know what his deal is!"

Vincent sighed and stuffed his notes into his pocket.

"Philanderer."

"Now we're getting somewhere. A serious philanderer?" Roscoe asked hopefully. He didn't want to deal with a guy who was a first-time offender. Roscoe had leaned on first-timers before, and it was always awkward. It was usually some straight arrow who got bent on a business trip. The guy would be a nervous wreck when Roscoe threatened to tell his wife. Once, a first-offender started crying so hard that Roscoe had to give the poor guy a hug and tell him everything would be okay. First-offenders were a pain in the ass. It was much easier to deal with someone who'd been keeping the secret for a while and had already thought through all the angles. Roscoe knew he could negotiate with a guy like that.

"Prolific," Vincent said. "We've turned up more than a dozen women just from the past two years."

"Good," Roscoe said. "Caught or uncaught?"

"Caught."

"Even better," Roscoe said. It would be easier to negotiate with a guy who'd already been busted by his wife once. "How do you wanna work it?"

Vincent reached back into his pocket for his notes. "Got a girl lined up to do a wake-up-and-smell-the-perfume."

Roscoe nodded. "You know, a wake-up always works better with two girls."

"Yeah?"

"You got time to get one more?"

"Of course."

"And make 'em blondes," Roscoe said.

▪ ▪ ▪

A thin patina of sweat covered Robert Maxwell's body as he tossed in his sleep. He mumbled an indecipherable complaint and rolled over, draping an arm over his wife's body. Angela muttered and snuggled closer to him.

Robert suffered through his regular recurring dream. It was a scary dream—not quite a nightmare, because nothing terrible ever happened—but it was close. His borderline nightmare always had the same progression. He'd come home to discover that Angela had packed up the house, loaded the boys into the car, and driven away while he was at work. It scared him because he knew it wasn't an idle fear. One more screwup and he might lose his family. That's why he had changed his ways. No more affairs. No more lies. No more secret life.

Over the years Robert had proven to be a very adept philanderer. He'd kept a string of girlfriends on the side when he and Angela were dating, and their wedding had only slowed him down for the ten days of their honeymoon. Angela had suspected him for years and had accused him on many occasions, but Robert always delivered a good story and there was never enough evidence to confirm her suspicions.

That changed about a year ago when Timmy, their youngest, misplaced his *SpongeBob SquarePants* action figure. Every attempt to distract the boy had failed, and he'd cried inconsolably all morning. Angela desperately searched the house for the toy, but found nothing. She rooted through her car, and then went into Robert's car. It was then, with her head down near the floor and her hand stuck under the seat, that she encountered a cell phone. She didn't recognize it, but clearly, it belonged to Robert. It was mounted in a special holder and set on "meeting" mode, presumably so that it wouldn't ring at inconvenient times. Angela stared at the phone for a long time before making up her mind. She scrolled through the memory and wrote down every number listed. The next day, she made an appointment with a private investigator. Once and for all, she was going to learn the truth.

That's how she happened to walk in on Robert and Courtney two months later while they were in the girl's bed, making loud passionate love on a Tuesday afternoon. The private investigator picked the lock and pushed the door open quietly. Angela walked down the hallway to the bedroom. She stood and watched with surprisingly little passion as Courtney straddled her husband. The girl's back was to the door, and Angela watched as her plump cheeks rose and fell. Robert's hands grabbed her ass, squeezing gently, guiding her. The movements were familiar. This was Robert's favorite position. Angela listened as Robert plunged fully inside of the girl and groaned his finale. Suddenly, she regretted hiring the investigator; she knew more than she wanted to know.

"You could have at least worn a condom," Angela said.

Robert and Courtney nearly leaped out of bed. But Angela held them in place with an outstretched palm. "Don't get up," she said.

That day, she had threatened to leave Robert. It wasn't just catching him in the act with Courtney. It wasn't a wild overreaction to a solitary indiscretion. She knew about Anice, Ann, Barbara, Cara, Erica, Jenny, Joslyn, Lynn, Megan, Rebecca, Sarah and Sue, and the breadth of her knowledge terrified Robert. He lay naked in his lover's bed with only a thin sheet to cover the tool of his betrayal. He listened raptly, too stunned to deny anything and too guilty to argue forgiveness. For the first time, he understood the true price of his affairs.

Angela kept talking and he listened desperately. He realized then that despite years of casual infidelities, he did not want to lose his wife—and he especially didn't want to lose the boys. He would do anything to keep his family.

Angela left that day, saying that they'd talk more when they got home. Robert had nodded numbly, finding hope in the fact that she'd said the word *home*. When he got back to the house, they sat across from each other at the dining room table, and she told him that she would stay with him, but she would keep the private investigator on retainer. Robert tried to make promises, but they tumbled from his lips feeble and ineffective.

That was nearly ten months ago, and he'd been completely faithful ever since. All along he'd known his actions were wrong, but somehow he'd always found a way to justify a little extramarital play. But now, he understood what it meant to be committed. Even though Angela didn't trust him, he was determined to prove that he was worth another chance. He would be faithful and that was that. He had broken up with his many girlfriends, thrown away his secret phone and started paying attention to his wife.

Despite his newfound fidelity, Robert had been haunted by the borderline nightmare of Angela leaving. It wasn't a true nightmare because she never actually left. Even in his dreams, Angela was faithful to him.

Robert mumbled in his sleep and turned back the other way, his arm falling across Angela's body. Robert sensed that something was wrong, but he couldn't focus his mind on it. In his dream, he was barreling through his neighborhood, screeching into the driveway, and rushing into the house, expecting everyone to be gone. But Angela was there in the living room, looking at him with a blank face. In his dream, she was where he expected her to be, but somehow, in the real world, Robert knew something wasn't right. He'd turned to his right and felt Angela. Then he'd turned to his left and felt Angela.

The phone rang, and his eyes fluttered as he came fully awake. Robert reached across his wife's body to answer it.

"Hello?" It was a couple minutes before eight. Somehow he'd slept through his wake-up call.

"Hi honey," Angela said. "I just wanted to make sure you're ready to go." Robert had worked a double shift the day before, and he slept at the hotel as he often did when he had worked a long day. "You remember we promised to take the boys to Water World?"

"Uh…yeah babe…I'm just getting up now." He looked at the woman beside him. Blonde, beautiful, naked. On his other side was another woman just like the first. "Where are you?" he asked Angela.

"I'm about ten minutes away," she said.

"I'll meet you in the lobby."

"We'll just come up," Angela said. "I promised the boys they could see the room." Robert stayed at the hotel twice a week, and when Angela was coming down to meet him, she always made an advance call because she didn't want to find any surprises. But she always came up to the room to give it a quick once-over just to be sure.

"Okay," Robert said.

"See you in a few."

He hung up and full panic set in. "What the hell is going on?"

One of the women smiled at him and the other ran a hand across his chest. "You don't remember last night?"

Last night? Robert wondered. He didn't have time for this. "You've got to get out of here," he said.

"That was your wife on the phone, huh?" the other woman said. She reached under the covers to rub his crotch. Robert was disappointed to feel himself rising to her touch.

"You have to go!"

"We can't leave until you talk to Mr. Evans."

"Who the hell is Mr. Evans?"

"I am," Roscoe said.

"Holy shit!" Robert said. It looked as if a tyrannosaurus rex had slipped through the door to the connecting room.

"I know we're short on time," the dinosaur said, smiling pleasantly, "so I'll make this quick. I need a favor."

Robert stared with an open mouth, stunned by the immensity of Roscoe.

"Nothing major," Roscoe said. "See these pills here?" Six tiny yellow capsules in a small plastic bag sat in the middle of Roscoe's meaty palm. "Want you to drop them into Antoine Kennedy's eggs Sunday morning."

"What?" Robert tried to get out of the bed, but the two naked women held him in place. He looked at the clock. How long had it been? "I can't do that."

"Nobody will notice," Roscoe promised. "You're the head chef here at the hotel, and you personally prepare Antoine's scrambled egg whites before every game. You put these in about thirty seconds before you take the eggs off the skillet and they'll just melt right in. He'll never taste 'em."

Robert took another glance at the clock. Had it been two minutes or eight?

"What are they?"

"Nothing serious," Roscoe promised. "Just something that's gonna make him feel pretty sick."

"I can't."

"Sure you can."

"For all I know, you're asking me to kill the man."

"Think about that for a minute," Roscoe said. Robert didn't want to think about it. He wanted to get this wrapped up and get everyone out of his room. But Roscoe took his time. "If this was something that was gonna kill him, then there'd be an autopsy wouldn't there? He's a healthy professional athlete. His death would raise a lot of inconvenient questions. You don't know why I need this to happen, but take my word for it, I don't want anyone to be suspicious."

"It'll look like food poisoning," Robert said suddenly alarmed. His professional pride was injured. He didn't want the newspapers to report that the Broncos' star running back had gotten food poisoning at his hotel.

"It won't be your problem," Roscoe said. "The symptoms he's gonna get will make it look like something he ate twenty-four hours ago, not at the pre-game meal."

"I can't," Robert said with another worried glance at the clock. Was his wife about to knock on the door?

Roscoe's phone jingled. He put it to his ear and listened for a moment. He hung up and said, "Your wife is in the lobby. If you won't help me, then I'm gonna step through the connecting door here, and you're gonna be left by yourself to explain why these two pretty little ladies are in your bed."

Robert didn't say anything.

"And their story," Roscoe continued. "is that they're flight attendants you met in the hotel bar last night."

Robert thought about his borderline nightmare. "He'll just get sick?"

Roscoe smiled. "Just a little sick." He handed the small bag of pills to Robert. The girls jumped out of bed and ran naked into the other room.

Robert climbed out of the bed too, pulling on his pants and looking around desperately for any sign of the women's belongings. Apparently they'd come into the room naked, so there was nothing to leave behind. Angela knocked on the door.

Roscoe stepped into the connecting room. He leaned back and whispered, "And just in case you change your mind before game time, this is a video tape I shot last night." He held up a VHS cassette. "We got an actor to stand in for you, but in the darkness, it sure looks like you getting freaky with these two fine ladies. And in the light of morning, there's no doubt that it's you sleeping between them. Your wife would be convinced."

Angela knocked again.

"I'll take care of it," Robert said quietly.

Roscoe winked and closed the door.

17

Roscoe Evans called Mickey Uso from a pay phone in the back of Don's Bar, tucked in a hard-to-reach corner just off Sixth Avenue in Denver. Roscoe knew he shouldn't be wandering around the city, but he'd been lured out of his hotel room by an ad for Brother's Barbecue. The prospect of a sinking his teeth into slab of soul-cooked ribs was too enticing to resist, so he snuck out. When he walked into the restaurant and learned that the brothers in question weren't *brothas*, but a pair of twenty-something white boys dressed like skateboarders, Roscoe felt that he'd been tricked. He turned to leave, but the aroma of food trapped him and he placed and order. When he finished his meal, Roscoe gave the chef a thumbs up as he backed out the door. Roscoe had to concede that though the brothers weren't *brothas*, they sure had soul. He wandered across the street to Don's, a dive bar with fluorescent lights in the front window and a battered pool table in the back. He pulled a chair over next to the pay phone and made his call.

"It's Big Daddy," he said to Mickey. "I want ten dimes on the Stallions." Roscoe liked Mickey. The kid was polite, could keep a secret (Roscoe had made some discreet inquiries after he placed the first bet), and handled the situation like a pro. Roscoe had decided that Mickey would be his go-to guy for the entire season. "What's the line?"

"Broncos minus five and a half."

"I'll take the Stallions to cover."

"Same stipulations as before?"

"Everything's the same," Roscoe said.

"I've got it."

"Talk to you next week."

18

Little Mikey Gasca was an apt pupil. He learned his lessons so well that by age ten—with Uncle Nick's permission, of course—he was running his own book at school. He took small bets; a dime here, a nickel there (these were literal nickels and dimes, not code for the larger denominations he would handle as an adult). He kept track of his bets, and every week set his line perfectly to keep himself right in the middle of the action. By the time his twelfth birthday arrived, Mikey was running bookies in eight schools and had a crew of muscled teens to beat down anyone who tried to compete with him. It was that year, in seventh grade, that he met Roscoe Evans, the hulking boy who would become his lifelong friend and business partner.

As a general rule, the black kids and the Italian kids at Roberto Clemente Middle School didn't mix. The blacks gathered in one corner of the lunchroom while the Italians staked out another corner. The two groups liked to glare at each other, but they rarely made contact.

One day during the fall semester, a black kid named Welton Emerson refused to pay a two-dollar gambling debt to Michael Gasca. There was a lot of posturing in the lunchroom for a few days, but Welton stood firm with a strong crew behind him. Gasca eased off for about a week to let things settle down. Then he hired a couple of high school students to send a message.

"Don't hurt him bad," Gasca had instructed. "Just scare him." The older boys had followed Welton home for nearly two weeks before they finally caught him alone. One guy held Welton in a full nelson while the other one reared back and brought an open palm across his face a dozen times. The teens took fifty cents from Welton's pockets—all he had—and told him he should deliver the balance to Michael Gasca first thing in the morning if he wanted to avoid another beating. The boy slumped to the ground with a busted lip and a black eye.

The next day, Welton did not deliver a payment to Michael Gasca as instructed, but he did walk home alone. The two high school boys spotted him and shook their heads at his stupidity. They fell in behind him, and began to mock him without ever thinking that Welton Emerson might be bait.

Roscoe Evans raced up behind the two teens with a miniature bat in his hands. It was his little brother's fourteen-inch toy, which Roscoe had hefted before he left the house and thought would deliver a nice sting. He stretched his arm back as he covered the last few feet, and aimed for the elbow of the Italian bully on the right. Roscoe swung the bat hard but missed the teenager's arm. The bat connected with the rib cage and a sharp crack echoed in the air. The boy clutched his elbow to his side and dropped to the ground as if he'd been shot. Roscoe knew immediately that he'd snapped one of the boy's ribs. It was the first of many bones that Roscoe would break in his career. The other Italian turned toward Roscoe with wide eyes, and Roscoe, feeling a little desperate now that he'd done real damage, figured he'd better not hold back. He swung the bat at the second boy's head, barely missing. The kid ducked out of range and sprinted up the street in terror.

The next day, the air in the cafeteria was thick with tension. Several kids reportedly had come to school armed with guns and knives. The students who were not involved had positioned themselves near the exits because they expected a full-scale massacre. Roscoe Evans, who towered over all of his classmates, stood with his palms facing out and strolled across the cafeteria to the Italian section. Every eye in the room followed him. The Italian kids rose from their seats and looked at him with hard faces, but Roscoe never took his eyes off Michael Gasca.

When he reached Gasca's table he said, "You mind if I sit down?"

Gasca nodded toward a chair.

Roscoe slid into it. "I came over to apologize for what happened yesterday. I didn't mean to break your friend's rib. I was aiming for his arm, and I missed."

"I appreciate the apology," Gasca said.

"Things have gotten pretty hot all over two dollars." Roscoe reached into his front pocket. "I've got the money to cover the debt. You already got fifty cents from Welton, and you can keep that for the delay."

Michael Gasca looked down at the cash and nodded. "I appreciate this, Roscoe, I really do."

"Let's make a deal," Roscoe continued. He pointed at the dark-haired boys standing near Gasca. "I don't want any of these Italians messing with my friends. If they mess with my friends, I'm gonna have to mess with them right back, 'cause that's just the way things are."

"That seems to be the case."

"Any of the black kids ever owe you money," Roscoe said. "You let me know. Don't send nobody from your crew over. You talk to me. I'll talk to my people, and we'll be cool."

Michael Gasca knew most of the other Italian kids wouldn't have taken this type of talk from a *totzone*, especially not one who'd beaten up one of his enforcers, but Gasca had always had a lot of respect for Roscoe Evans. And Gasca had learned his lessons well from Uncle Nick. Running a business wasn't about pride. It wasn't about racism. It wasn't about hurting people or sending messages. It was about collecting money. If Roscoe Evans was volunteering to be his collector among the black kids, that made Gasca's life easier.

The two boys shook hands and defused what might have been the deadliest day in the history of Roberto Clemente Middle School. They also forged an alliance that would carry them through high school and into adulthood.

As he grew older, Michael Gasca's responsibilities within the family increased. At fifteen, Uncle Nick put him in charge of the Felicci group on Philly's west side, which included twenty-five bookies handling about five million dollars annually.

"The past couple of years," Uncle Nick explained, "they've been sliding. Takin' bad bets, getting overloaded, just leaking more money all the time. I need you to straighten things out, get 'em back on track." Uncle Nick had made a personal trip over to Ignacio Felicci's house to introduce Gasca and ensure that everyone would show proper respect to the kid. Every day after school, Gasca took the bus over to Ignacio's house and examined the deals made that day and developed strategies for the following day. Michael Gasca was a magician. He knew where to set his point spreads, when to layoff a bet, when to ride out an overload and when to refuse a customer. But no matter how much good advice he gave, Gasca could not always control dumb bookies. He had problems with a bookie named Rico Salvotelli right off the bat.

"You're telling me you took three thousand dollars on the Eagles today, and only one person bet for the Cowboys?" Gasca asked Rico. He had all the bookies gathered in Ignacio's living room.

"Hey," Rico said, shrugging and sneering. "Everybody wanted the Eagles today. What can I tell you?"

"You can't tell me anything," Gasca said. "But I'll tell you something. You're on your own. I'm not taking the layoff, so you'd better go out tomorrow and find three grand on the other side."

Rico was thirty-four years old and had been working books since he was eighteen. He'd been overloaded many times in the past, but the family had always found a place for his layoffs.

He said, "You can't leave me on the hook for this."

"Rico," Gasca said. "The problem with you is that you're a stupid fuck. I don't think you're cut out to be a bookie, and if you can't find your way out of this hole, you'll prove my point."

After Michael Gasca left, Rico complained to Ignacio that the kid was being unreasonable.

"And he's always bringing that *totzone* Roscoe with him. Who does he think he is bringing that *muli* into your house?"

Ignacio didn't approve of the language. He shrugged his old shoulders and said, "Michael Gasca is Uncle Nick's boy."

So instead of working the streets the following day, Rico Salvotelli went to Uncle Nick and complained about the disrespectful treatment he'd received.

Dominic Sarcassi listened to the story and said, "Rico, 'stupid fuck' is the kindest thing anyone could say about you. And you've never been stupider than when you woke up this morning and thought that I wanted to hear you moan about Michael Gasca holding you responsible for losing my money. You tell your partners down there that Michael Gasca is running the show. You got a problem with him, you take it up with him.

I'll tell you one more thing, Rico." Sarcassi aimed a wrinkled finger at the young man in front of him. "Michael Gasca is doing you a favor. You keep going the way you're going, you might not be *breathing* at the end of the year."

Rico Salvotelli had backed out of Uncle Nick's study bowing deeply and apologizing with sweat glistening on his cheeks. That weekend, the Eagles won, but Rico didn't have the money to pay off his winners. His career as a bookie was over. Michael Gasca stepped in to cover his debts, but the lesson resonated through the whole Felicci clan: Michael Gasca was the new boss.

Over the next three years, Gasca turned the Felicci group into the most profitable operation in the entire Sarcassi stronghold. As a gift for his eighteenth birthday, Uncle Nick gave Gasca thirty-two more problem bookies and within a year he turned them into winners. Michael Gasca had a gift. He never forgot a spread or a name. He had a computer in his head that was always running full tilt, measuring the balances of bookies against each other.

Just last year, Gasca had a long private conversation with Uncle Nick about a scheme for making even more money. They were sitting in front of the fireplace in Uncle Nick's Philadelphia mansion with the lights turned down, talking quietly with long periods of comfortable silence.

"You know that's not how we run the business, Mikey," Uncle Nick had said, wagging a finger at his young protégé. "We're like conservative bankers. We run a nice quiet shop. We make our money, and we never get greedy. Greed is a gambler's problem."

"But what if we could make more money without gambling?"

"You're talking about taking bets on one side and not the other, but you're not calling it a gamble?" Uncle Nick asked doubtfully.

"Say a guy walked up to you and said, 'I'll bet you a hundred dollars the sun won't come up in the morning,'" Gasca said. "Would you take the bet or would you wait to see if you could get someone to bet the other side first?"

Uncle Nick contemplated this. The two men stared into the fire. After a few minutes the old man said with a sly look, "Depends on where I'm living."

Gasca hadn't expected this. "Come on, Uncle Nick, what difference does that make?"

"Say I'm living in Alaska the day before they start having that six months of darkness." He barked a hoarse dry laugh. "Then no, I wouldn't take that bet."

Michael Gasca laughed with him. He shook his head and thought about the three decades Uncle Nick had been at the top. He survived because he thought things through. He always calculated, always made sure he had all the angles covered.

"Okay," Gasca said, "say you're living right here in Philly and a guy wants to make that bet?"

"Hell, Mikey, of course I'd take it. I know damn well the sun's gonna come up tomorrow."

"That's all I'm saying, Uncle Nick. If we got a bunch of people who want to bet that the sun won't come up, then we're not gambling. We're just taking their money." Michael Gasca was on the edge of his seat. "We already get a lot of inside information. We've got relationships with owners, coaches, players, trainers, equipment managers, secretaries, and anyone else we can talk to—"

"But that's only so we can set an accurate point spread," Uncle Nick interrupted. "What's gonna happen if we start using their information to do something else? And what's gonna happen to our line if we start fixing games, because I know that's what you're thinking."

Michael Gasca considered those words. He understood the importance of protecting the relationships the family had in the league. The casinos and crime families didn't try to fix NFL games because it didn't serve their interest to do so. Most of the families—the smart ones—just wanted to get gamblers betting on both sides, so the information was most powerful when it was used to set an accurate point spread.

"Uncle Nick, I understand your concern, but let's think about this for a minute. If we fix a game and no one knows about it, how is anyone going to get hurt?"

"*We'll* get hurt, Mikey!"

"How?"

Uncle Nick held up a weathered hand, silencing Gasca. Over the years, there had been many men who wanted him to take more risks.

They always had new ideas. They always thought that the old way wasn't the best way. They didn't understand that it had all been tried before with bad results. Things were done a particular way because they'd been proven to work.

"Mikey," Uncle Nick said with more patience than he would have shown anyone else in the family, "think about how screwed up things would get if you started fixing games after we set the spread."

"Uncle Nick," Michael Gasca said slowly, "if no one knows about the fix, then it won't affect anything."

Uncle Nick puffed on a cigar. Over the years he'd learned to listen to Mikey's ideas no matter how outrageous they seemed at first blush. That was tough for Uncle Nick because he'd been around a long time and he'd watched the crime syndicates grow up alongside the professional leagues. Sports came before sports gambling, but they were like a set of twins born minutes apart. When the NFL got its start, the criminal networks immediately sought ways to increase their profits by manipulating the outcomes of the games. Eventually, they abandoned this course because they discovered that gamblers would lay down a lot more money if they thought the games were legitimate. An uneasy alliance developed between the NFL and the crime syndicates. The league wanted gamblers because betting helped fill stadiums and pump up television ratings, but they didn't want any illegal activity surrounding the games. The crime families feared fixed games because it would reduce their overall earnings, so both sides worked together to ensure the integrity of the NFL.

"Let's make the case with just one bookie," Gasca said, using an educational technique Uncle Nick often employed.

"All right," Uncle Nick replied patiently. "We've got a case study of one bookie."

"Let's say our bookie sets the perfect line. He's got twenty-thousand dollars on one side and twenty thousand on the other side."

"He's right down the middle."

"So now the game starts, and we've fixed the outcome. Team A *was* going to win, but because of our manipulations, Team B wins. What difference does it make to the bookie?"

Uncle Nick smiled. "I see what you mean, but you're forgetting something important."

"I know what you're gonna say, but I'm not forgetting it."

"You haven't mentioned unnatural money."

"That doesn't mean I've forgotten about it."

They both knew that unnatural money always accompanied a fix. The bookie set the line and then watched the bets come in. If he saw a sudden spike on one side or the other, he might adjust the line to even things out or layoff some action. But experience taught him the difference between natural and unnatural spikes. When someone fixed a game, they had to lay down a lot of money to make it pay off, but the extra cash in the market got them caught. If the bookie had suspicions, he'd refuse the bet, and he might take the game off his board. He'd get on the phone and call other bookies and word would spread quickly. In a matter of hours, no one in the country would accept wagers on the suspect game. Unnatural money tipped off the bookies long before kickoff, and it made fixes hard to pull off.

"So how do you account for the unnatural cash?" Uncle Nick asked.

"What if there was none?" Gasca said.

Uncle Nick shook his head. He'd been around a long time, and he'd seen guys pull a lot of stunts. "It doesn't matter how many beards you use to hide the bets or how much you try to spread it out. You lay down enough to make the fix worth the effort, and somebody's gonna smell it."

"I'm saying, what if there wasn't any unnatural money?"

Uncle Nick thought about it. This was new. If there was no unnatural money wagered on the game, why fix it? He tried to think it through the way Gasca must have, but he couldn't see the benefit.

"All right," Uncle Nick said, "you got me. Why wouldn't there be any unnatural money?"

"First, we find someone who needs a particular team to win, who will pay to make it happen. Second, it has to be someone who doesn't need to make his money back by putting bets down on the game. Who do you think fits that profile?"

Uncle Nick's eyes lit up. He could see it. "Everybody on the inside!" he exclaimed. "*Everybody* on the inside!" He laughed for a long time. "The owners want to win to get into the playoffs because they'll make more money. Coaches want to get into the post-season because it's good for their job security. Players have all sorts of performance bonuses in their contracts! You get close to the end of the year and somebody on a team with a tight, make-or-break game, might be willing to pay a hefty sum to get a guaranteed victory."

Michael Gasca laughed along with his benefactor. This was Uncle Nick at his best. The old guy didn't always see it coming, but once it arrived, he got it. He understood it and knew how to apply it.

"The third thing," Gasca said, "is that we're still basically in it to catch all those people who want to bet against the sun coming up in the morning. So we have to ask ourselves, what's the one time of the year that it's easiest to hide unnatural money?"

Uncle Nick smiled again and puffed contentedly on his cigar.

"The Super Bowl," he said.

The two men started to laugh. Their voices echoed in the quiet room.

19

Joseph Repanshek, the new head coach of the San Antonio Stallions, tapped a few keys on his computer and game tape appeared on the screen in front of him. He leaned back into his plush leather chair and reached for a smoldering cigar in a crystal ashtray. Soft classical music danced with the spiraling smoke. He looked around the room, still not quite believing that he'd finally made it to the NFL. His office had a formal sitting area, a private restroom with a shower, a 75-inch plasma screen, and a computer that could grab any play he wanted from the team's archives.

Repanshek wished his ex-wives could see him now. He'd spent the previous evening unpacking his boxes and decorating his office with thirty years of memorabilia, which gave the room a sense of history and a feeling of permanence. He looked over the items before him and thought it looked good. If someone walked in to meet him for the first time, it would appear that Repanshek had been with the team for decades rather than hours.

He took a long pull on the cigar and hit the rewind button on the remote control. The players on the screen moved backward to their original positions. Repanshek made a mental note that on running plays to the left, the Stallions right guard had a sloppy first step. He had to remember the players by their jersey numbers and positions rather than their names because he didn't know most of them. Repanshek had been a coach long enough to know that the key to success was identifying little problems and correcting them before they became big problems. He knew how to use praise to keep players moving in the right direction, and perhaps more importantly, he knew when to back off and let the athletes use their instincts. That's how he'd found success with Trevor Deale.

He puffed on his cigar and stared at Trevor Deale on the screen. The quarterback's mechanics as he dropped back to pass were perfect—shoulders perpendicular to the line of scrimmage, ball locked just under his chin, back elbow up, head scanning smoothly from playside to backside. Trevor delivered a strike to Martin McNeil that arrived shoulder high just as the receiver came out of his break. Repanshek hit the rewind button to watch the defense. Coach Repanshek let the play go forward and saw that the defense had come with a zone blitz, but the rush didn't appear to affect Trevor Deale at all. The quarterback took a five-step drop and delivered the ball on a quick parabola, twelve feet off the ground, arching over the outstretched hands of a linebacker, then sinking down to hit Martin McNeil between the numbers.

Repanshek shook his head in admiration. As frustrating as Trevor could be at times, there was no denying that the kid's composure in the pocket. Trevor Deale was the latest innovation in the offensive strategy.

NFL offenses and defenses had always fought a continuous arms race in which every new strategy on one side of the ball led to a specific improvement on the other side of the ball. Three wide receiver packages on offense led to the invention of the nickel package on defense—pulling a linebacker off the field and replacing him with a cornerback. When the offense put four receivers on the field, the defense brought on another cover guy and called the package "dime." Advantages sluiced back and forth and the latest and trickiest of these schemes was the zone blitz, which Coach Repanshek thought had an impact on football roughly equivalent to that of the computer on industrial society. It completely changed the game.

Repanshek rewound the tape again and watched three lineman and a linebacker rush the quarterback while a defensive end dropped into coverage. The zone blitz allowed any four members of the defense to blitz, while the remaining seven played a conservative zone behind it. When the quarterback and receivers saw a linebacker or a safety zipping across the line of scrimmage, it looked like a normal blitz to them. Over the years, offensive players had become adept at handling the blitz. Receivers ran their hot routes and quarterbacks threw them the ball immediately, getting rid of it before the blitz arrived. Hot routes and quick throws presumed man coverage, but were mostly ineffective against zone.

Coach Joseph Repanshek puffed on his cigar and decided that if the zone blitz was the computer, then Trevor Deale was the Internet—he was the next great innovation. Trevor saw right through the zone blitz by somehow counting the rushers as a set rather than as individuals. Coach Repanshek was the first person to understand Trevor's unusual talent, and he had explained it to OU boosters using eleven coins as a model.

At a booster club meeting, Coach Repanshek had asked for a volunteer; he wasn't halfway through the request before Stuart Weatherby limped to the front of the room. His knees creaked and his liver-spotted hands shook gently, but his sharp eyes were glowing with Sooner pride.

"Whatever you need, I gotcha covered," Weatherby said.

Coach Repanshek wore a wry smile. "What am I supposed to do about all these people that got their hands up?"

Stuart looked around the room. "Tell 'em to put 'em down."

Everyone had a good chuckle at that. Repanshek said, "Next time, you're gonna have to raise your hand like everyone else."

"I'm too old to raise my hand," Stuart said. "Figure if I'm gonna raise anything it might as well be my whole self."

"How's your eyesight, Mr. Weatherby?"

"You talkin' up close like seeing them little sailboats you got on your tie? Or off in the distance like the three inches of cleavage Ms. Talbot got showing in that beautiful blouse of hers?"

Everyone laughed except Ms. Talbot, who was quite proud of her cleavage—and who had worn that blouse because it displayed her bosom so spectacularly—but now felt obliged to button up so people wouldn't think she was being deliberately showy.

"I guess your eyesight's just fine," Coach Repanshek said. "All right, what I've got in my hands are eleven coins. They're all either quarters or pennies. I'm gonna throw 'em on the table here, and I want to see how fast you can tell me how many quarters there are."

"So there might be anywhere from one to eleven quarters in there?" Stuart asked.

"Actually, the range isn't that big. There may be as few as two quarters and as many as seven. The rest are pennies."

"Let her rip."

Repanshek opened his hands and the coins spilled out on to the table. Before they'd all come to a rest, Stuart Weatherby called out the correct answer: "Four!"

"All right," Repanshek said, picking up the coins. "Let's try again." He turned his back and made a few adjustments then dropped the money on to the table.

"Five!" Stuart Weatherby said without hesitation.

"Thank you, Mr. Weatherby. You can go sit down now."

"You brought me all the way up here for that?"

"You brought yourself up here, Mr. Weatherby."

Coach Repanshek almost expected the old man to *harrumph* like a cartoon character, but he turned and walked back to his seat.

"What Mr. Weatherby just demonstrated," Repanshek said, "is the talent that Trevor Deale has, and it's what makes him such a good quarterback. Trevor sees the rushers as a set. In Trevor's head rushers are quarters and everyone else is a penny. He doesn't sort them out one by one. He just sees them. During practice we'll do drills with the defense crowding the line of scrimmage, and I'll mix up all sorts of zone blitz combinations. Trevor makes his drop, and calls out the number of rushers before he throws the ball to an open receiver. His unusual ability allows him to effectively kill the zone blitz."

■   ■   ■

"Coach?" A female voice said through the intercom.

"Yes?" Repanshek said.

"You're due for your meeting with Mr. Kinneson in five minutes."

"Thank you. I'm on my way."

Coach Repanshek walked down a hallway lined with pictures of famous players and coaches of the past. There were former Pro Bowl players, Hall of Fame members, and some past hopefuls whose careers had been brilliant but short. He wondered what it would take to get his photograph on these walls.

Joseph Repanshek reported to Jonathan Kinneson's secretary, who invited him to have a seat. Nearly half an hour later, Repanshek entered the owner's office.

"Come on in, coach," Kinneson boomed. Repanshek walked into the expansive office and slid into a chair. This was the strangest coaching gig he'd ever had. He'd been hired without being interviewed. He hadn't met the general manager, the owner or any of the assistant coaches until the press conference two days ago, and then they barely spoke except to say congratulations before scurrying back to their offices.

"What makes you think you can coach on this level?" Jonathan Kinneson was all business, glaring across the desk, and Repanshek was immediately on edge. That was an interview question, not a first-meeting-with-my-new-head-coach question. Repanshek already had the job, didn't he?

"I've been coaching for more than thirty years. I understand the theory of football, and I have the practical knowledge of how to prepare a team to win on Sundays." Coach Repanshek had been hired, fired, resigned, and moved on from so many jobs that he could easily answer any question Mr. Kinneson chose to throw at him, but what he really wanted to know was why Kinneson was asking questions.

"That's nice," Kinneson said in a tone that suggested that he didn't think there was anything nice about it, "but you don't know anything about the NFL." He ticked off the points. "You've never worked through a sixteen-game schedule with the type of pressure and scrutiny that you're going to get here. You've never worked with a salary cap. You've never had to deal with players who make more money than you do. You've never had players whose instincts are so keen and talents so refined that they might be too advanced for you to teach them anything. You could be like a third-grade math teacher suddenly trying to teach high school calculus. You might be out of your element." Kinneson smiled wickedly, almost maniacally, Repanshek thought. "How will you get ready for the draft next April? None of your previous coaching experience has prepared you for the NFL."

Coach Repanshek was tempted to ask Mr. Kinneson what experience he'd had before he purchased the San Antonio Stallions a few months ago. If Joseph Repanshek lacked the qualifications to coach an NFL team, then Jonathan Kinneson surely lacked the qualifications to own one. But Repanshek kept that thought tucked away under the sudden icy fear that he did not have this job. He reviewed the events of the past week and wondered how that could be possible.

The Stallions' previous head coach, Max Starnes, had been fired. Michael Gasca had met with Repanshek and offered him the top spot with the team. Joseph Repanshek had accepted the offer then submitted his letter of resignation to the board of regents in a meeting packed with so much acrimony that Repanshek still wasn't sure how he survived it.

One of the board members was eighty-two-year-old Mel Bane, who hadn't missed a Sooners home game since 1953 and was so sickly that he could barely speak. Mel sat in the corner like an old oak dresser— surprisingly sturdy but quiet as a dead tree. It shocked everyone when Mel, after Repanshek finished reading his letter, burst into tears, crying unabashedly with heavy, heart-wrenching wails that stung Repanshek's heart. The emotion touched the coach so deeply that he nearly walked over and hugged the old man.

Coach Repanshek imagined hundreds of thousands of Sooner fans having a similar reaction when they heard the news, not because they loved Repanshek—although most of them did—but because they hated anyone who hurt the team. The coach took a closer look at Mel Bane, and realized that the tears streaming down the old man's face were not tears of sadness. Mel Bane's eyes glistened with homicidal rage, and his moans were born of the impotence of not being able to rise from his wheelchair and wrap his arthritic hands around of Coach Joseph Repanshek's throat. Repanshek was suddenly sure that if he rose to give Mel Bane a hug, it would be the last hug he ever gave. The meeting ended with screaming and name-calling and eventually the threat of a lawsuit, but Repanshek had calmly pointed out that his contract gave him the right to leave at any time to accept an NFL head-coaching job.

The next day he flew to San Antonio, where he stood next to Mr. Kinneson while the owner announced that Repanshek was the team's new head man. He flew back to Oklahoma to collect everything from his office—which had been dumped into two laundry bins and left on his front porch without a note—and to pack up his clothes. He wouldn't have time to move out of his house until after the Stallions's season ended. He flew back to San Antonio, checked into a hotel, and then settled into his new office. Clearly, he was the head coach of the Stallions—*though I haven't yet signed a contract*, he realized with a start. Yet, despite everything, Jonathan Kinneson was talking to him as if the matter was still in doubt.

"I *am* qualified for this job," Repanshek said a little defensively. "No, I've never coached a team through a sixteen-game schedule under NFL pressure, but I've been in big programs at Oklahoma and Florida, and believe me, every game counted at that level, too. The school, the fans, the alumni, and the media expected a lot from the team every Saturday. I led my teams to eight bowl games in ten years."

He paused to wipe a hand across his brow. "No, I've never had to work with a salary cap, or deal with players who made more money than me, but I've dealt with scholarship limitations and my share of egos over the years. I know how to keep the kids focused on their jobs. And if a player is such a great athlete that I can't do much to help him, then I know how to step back and let him be creative. That's what I did with Trevor at Oklahoma."

Coach Repanshek didn't mention the humiliation he'd endured over the years as it became apparent that Trevor was a better tactician than his coach. Those details would stay in the past where they belonged.

"And no, I've never conducted a draft, but I'm just taking over the staff that Coach Starnes has had for the past four years. They've done it before, so I'll rely on them to help me through the process. What I bring to the table is a fresh set of eyes. I know I'm qualified for the job because coaching is primarily about leadership, and I know how to lead."

Jonathan Kinneson studied Repanshek, calculating whether this was the right choice to get his team to the Super Bowl. Michael Gasca had insisted on Repanshek, and had forced Kinneson into the press conference before he'd ever had a sit-down conversation with the man. Gasca had said that every time they fixed a game, they'd create a trail for NFL Security to follow, so the best way to get to the Super Bowl was to take the old fashioned route—rack up legitimate victories. With Repanshek at the helm handling Trevor Deale, Michael Gasca believed that the Stallions would win most of the games they needed to win.

Coach Repanshek seemed competent, capable, and confident. "You'll report directly to me," Kinneson said finally. "Your weekly game plans and any player personnel decisions will be approved by me."

Repanshek was so relieved by the change in tone that he wasn't actually listening to the owner's words. But after a moment alarms started to clang.

"You'll approve *game plans?*" Repanshek asked.

"That's right. And hiring and firing of players, coaches, scouts, and other football personnel. And, of course, I approve all contracts."

Although Repanshek had never coached in the NFL, he'd dealt with his share of athletic directors, university presidents, and boards of regents. He knew that he had to have the final word on everything related to the action on the field. Repanshek, not Kinneson, should decide which players started and which didn't. The coach had to make the call on what the off-season workout program should be, whether to go for it on fourth down, call an onside kick, run the ball, or pass it. Coach Repanshek was the one who would get blamed for anything that went wrong on the field, so he needed to have control over the decision-making. He could not surrender approval of game plans to the owner.

"Mr. Kinneson," Repanshek said cautiously, "I've got to have the freedom to manage the team the way I see fit. Of course, I'll be happy to keep you in the loop, but for informational purposes only. Not for input."

Jonathan Kinneson and Joseph Repanshek stared at each other across the desk, and Kinneson considered everything that needed to happen to get his team into the Super Bowl. Somehow, Michael Gasca was convinced that this was the man for the job and had left Kinneson no choice in the matter.

"You report to me," Kinneson said finally. "No one else. Not the general manager, not the media, not anyone. Just me." The owner leaned forward across the desk and extended his hand. "I'm telling you, Coach, we've got all the ingredients this year. It could be the best season of your life."

"I'm looking forward to it."

Kinneson pressed a button on his phone and glanced at his watch. It was nearly 11 A.M. "Linda? Send in my ten o'clock."

20

The game plan for the week had been constructed before Coach Joseph Repanshek had come on board. As usual, the offensive and defensive coaches had arrived at 7 AM on Monday to review Sunday's game, hand out grade sheets to the players, and go through the tape, play-by-play, position-by-position, praising the things the players had done well and correcting their mistakes. Afterward, the players went home to relax for the remainder of the day. They had another full day of recovery on Tuesday. However, there was no rest for the coaching staff. They went straight from the Monday film review into game-plan preparation for the Denver Broncos, the next team on the schedule.

For the coaches, Monday was the longest day of the week—they rarely got home before midnight. They returned to the Stallions Center at 7 AM Tuesday to create the playbook for the week. The process was arduous, but necessary, because on Wednesday the position coaches would have to explain in detail what each player was expected to do on every play out of each formation against every possible defensive front or blitz.

Tuesday was another long day, though not quite as long as Monday—the coaches usually got home in time to watch Jay Leno.

At 8 AM Wednesday, the players filled up the team meeting room to begin preparation for the upcoming game. Coach Repanshek hadn't been hired until Wednesday, so he'd had no role in creating the game plan. It was now Thursday.

The coaches generally worked through lunch, sitting in their offices studying tapes or reviewing their game plans, but today, Repanshek asked all of the offensive staff to join him. They got their food in the cafeteria, then filed into his office silently and took their places around his conference table. Repanshek could feel their nervousness. They were acutely aware that when a new coach arrived, he typically fired all of the previous staff members.

"The first thing I wanted to tell you," Repanshek said, "is that none of you will lose your jobs right now. After the season, I'll sit down with each of you individually, and we'll talk candidly about what's going to happen next year."

The men around the table looked visibly relieved.

"The real reason for this meeting," Repanshek continued, "is that I want to add a package to this week's game plan."

Ernie Plantier, the quarterback's coach, shook his head. "We're too far into the week to add packages."

"I'm aware of that," Repanshek said.

"The players learn things on a particular schedule every week," Plantier continued. "It's not smart to upset their rhythm."

The other coaches nodded as they chewed on their sandwiches. Never upset the flow. That's what they believed. If Coach Repanshek had a special package to put in, he could do it next Monday.

"I think we can do this one without much problem," Repanshek persisted. "It only involves Trevor Deale calling more audibles at the line of scrimmage."

Again, Plantier spoke for the group, and Repanshek realized that Plantier had hoped that he would be the new head coach. "This isn't a good week for an audible package. We're on the road in Denver, and that's a loud stadium. But next week, we're at home against Detroit, and we can put in a full audible package if you want."

"I know it's tough to audible on the road," Repanshek said. "But I'm assuming you use audibles in your two-minute package?"

"Yes," Plantier said, "but those are all married to hand signals, so even if the receivers can't hear, they can *see* the call."

"What I envision," Repanshek said, "is that Trevor will use the hand signals from the two-minute package to call audibles in other situations." Repanshek knew this was unorthodox and flat wouldn't work with most quarterbacks, but he believed Trevor could handle it.

"Can't do it," Plantier said. "Our two-minute package is four wide receivers and a running back. Everyone lines up in the same formation every time, so the plays are designed to work only from that formation. Those hand signals just aren't going to be any good if we've got two running backs, a tight end and a Z receiver going in motion. They're not in the right positions, so they can't possibly run the routes the way they're drawn up."

"You're right," Repanshek conceded.

Ernie Plantier sat back in his chair clearly pleased that his more-knowledgeable opinion had been accepted.

"But," Repanshek continued, "you're forgetting one important point."

Ernie Plantier couldn't think of anything he had forgotten. He knew this offense better than anyone, and he knew that you couldn't use two-minute audible signals in normal game situations.

"What's that?" he asked cynically.

"Some of those players *are* lined up in their two-minute positions."

The coaches stopped eating as they considered this.

Finally, Plantier said, "Maybe one or two of them."

Repanshek said, "We can pretty well guarantee that no matter what formation we get into, at least one receiver and/or running back is going to be lined up exactly as he would if it were two-minute. The package I want to install would allow Trevor to use the two-minute signals, and whichever players were lined up in their two-minute positions would run the routes that he's called."

"What would the other guys do?" Plantier said.

"Run the play called in the huddle."

The room grew quiet. The coaches were experienced at sorting through new ideas because they engaged in this sort of mental exercise every Monday and Tuesday. One coach would have an idea and the other coaches would test it with questions and scenarios, trying to think up the worst possibilities to see if the play could handle everything the defense threw at it. So they thought about Repanshek's idea for a long time. Some of them drew up formations on their notepads and considered the implications.

"Won't work," said David Schwartz, the receivers' coach. "All the pass routes are coordinated. The problem with your idea," he said, not unkindly, "is that we'll have one or two receivers running one play while the rest run another play. It could be a train wreck out there."

"Or what if we have a running play called when Trevor audibles to a pass?" Plantier said. "The offensive linemen are blocking for the run, and they have no idea that Trevor audibled. So he throws the ball, and it gets called back for having an illegal man down field."

"That's all true," Repanshek said again. "For all the reasons you mentioned, this would be a terrible idea if we were talking about any quarterback in the league except Trevor Deale. I coached this kid for three years at Oklahoma, and I'm telling you, he has the most amazing football mind I've ever seen. I'm sure you guys get a glimpse of it every now and then, but I believe Coach Starnes's play calling system was too rigid for Trevor."

"What if he calls a play that looks good, but we're not in the right formation for it?" Plantier insisted. "Or we don't have the right personnel on the field?"

"Trevor won't call the wrong play," Repanshek said confidently.

"This ain't college," said running backs coach Frankie Johnson. "This is the NFL. You got me? It's complicated. Trevor might have been able to call his own plays at Oklahoma, but he ain't gonna be able to do it here."

"Trevor can handle it," Repanshek said. "The only thing we need is a special call for the offensive line that will take them off a run and put them into basic pass protection."

Coach Repanshek looked around the room, and he could see that none of the coaches shared his confidence in Trevor Deale. They'd been working with the quarterback since early June, and while they saw tremendous talent, they didn't see genius. They didn't believe Trevor could keep all of the plays and all the routes in his head, survey the defense, and then find a play that would match his formation and personnel all within the twenty-five to thirty seconds he'd have at the line of scrimmage. It was too much to ask of any athlete.

"Gentlemen," Coach Repanshek said, "I appreciate your input, and I'll always expect you to speak candidly with me, but on the matter of Trevor Deale and his capabilities, I think you're gonna have to see it to believe it. This kid will make us unstoppable."

21

An abstract arrangement of red, brown, and green splotches stained the front of Robert Maxwell's white chef's uniform, evidence of past culinary creations. He marched through the crowded kitchen, barking orders at his staff. Pre-game meal for the Denver Broncos was an important contract for the hotel, and Robert worked hard to make sure everyone on the team was well-fed. A full buffet of scrambled eggs, hash browns, toast, bacon, sausage, spaghetti, meatballs, steaks, baked potatoes, broccoli, carrots, spinach, and dinner rolls sat in the dining area.

A server came into the kitchen. "Antoine is here."

Robert immediately started preparing Antoine Kennedy's meal of six scrambled egg whites, three slices of dry wheat toast, four strips of crisp turkey bacon, and a MET-RX shake.

Robert licked his lips, breaking eggs over a bowl, shuffling the yolks between the halves, letting the whites slide out while stopping the yolks from falling. Back and forth the yolks traveled, and Robert watched them hypnotically, wondering if he had the courage to do what he was supposed to do.

He put the eggs into the pan and stirred them slowly. The tiny yellow pills sat in the front pocket of his jacket. The ogre in the hotel room, whose name Robert couldn't remember, had said that they should just be dropped in thirty seconds before he took the eggs off the heat.

When the eggs were just about done, Robert reached into his pocket and pulled out the small plastic bag. He studied the pills. He liked Antoine. He was a good player, and he seemed like a nice guy. It didn't seem right to do this to him. But Robert knew that if he didn't do this, his wife would get the videotape from the hotel. He could try to explain to her that it wasn't what it appeared to be, but he knew she wouldn't believe him. His track record would validate the tape, and Angela surely would leave him this time. He'd lose his boys. He'd lose the house. He'd lose his wife. He'd lose everything.

Robert threw a quick glance over his shoulder, but no one was paying any attention to him. He dumped the pills into the pan, and they sat on top of the eggs like decorative sprinkles. Robert chewed the inside of his cheek. He could still scoop them out. Slowly, the pills began to melt, losing their oblong shape, merging with the eggs. After a few seconds, Robert could no longer see them. He stirred the eggs quickly and scooped them on to a plate.

He grabbed toast out of the toaster, and turkey bacon from the oven where he'd kept it warm. He took the plate and strode out of the kitchen and into the conference room, which had been converted into a dining hall. Players and coaches sat around the room, eating quietly, watching the television in the corner or reading newspapers. Robert weaved through the tables trying to not think too much about what he was doing.

"Here you go, Antoine." He set the plate down in front of the running back.

"Thanks," Antoine said. "How's life in the kitchen?" It was the same question he asked every week.

"Hot." It was the same answer Robert gave every week.

"Stay cool," Antoine said.

"I will." They never had any more conversation than that. Robert turned away and walked back into the kitchen.

Antoine Kennedy dug into his eggs.

22

Michael Gasca and Roscoe Evans were sitting on the dusty old couch in the living room of their rented home. Pictures of the past tenants hung on the walls, and the ancient furniture creaked ominously whenever Roscoe sat down. He'd found the house somewhat fascinating when they'd first moved in, but now Roscoe just thought the place was creepy.

His eyes darted toward the doorway leading into the dining room. He could have sworn that he'd seen something move.

"How much longer are we gonna stay here?" Roscoe asked.

"Until we're done," Michael Gasca replied. He didn't seem the least unnerved by the strange noises that echoed through the house during the night. "It's an old house," Gasca had said on several occasions. "The walls are just settling."

"Settling on what?" Roscoe had asked. He wondered if the ghosts were settling on whom they wanted to kill first.

Michael Gasca and Roscoe Evans had been sleeping on separate beds in the same room since they first arrived; Roscoe refused to sleep alone.

"As big as you are, what's a ghost gonna do to you?" Michael Gasca had asked.

"I don't wanna find out," Roscoe had said. He'd dragged his bed into Gasca's room, locked the door and turned on a lamp in the corner. He had a gun in top drawer of the nightstand.

On the television, the Stallions starting offensive lineup was being introduced at Invesco Field at Mile High. The commentators had spent most of their pre-game analysis talking about Jonathan

Kinneson's surprising decision to hire a new coach rather than promote someone already on staff, and now they were reporting that Denver star running back, Antoine Kennedy, was not on the field. The CBS sideline reporter was trying to find out what was wrong.

Gasca and Roscoe smiled at each other. Robert Maxwell had come through for them. The league's leading rusher hadn't been more than five feet from a toilet in more than an hour.

"Just gave him a bad case of the runs?" Roscoe wondered.

"The pills were a hopped-up diuretic," Michael Gasca said. "He's got the worst case of diarrhea he'll ever have this side of the Mexican border. Even if the shitting stops, he will have lost so much water that he'll be too dehydrated to play. Without him, the Broncos don't have a chance."

Fans filled every seat, as they had for every Denver home game since 1970. It was late in the third quarter, and the Stallions were leading 35–17; Trevor Deale was having the best game of his brief professional career.

"What I don't understand," Roscoe said, "is why Trevor wasn't playing this good a few weeks ago."

"The main problem was Coach Starnes," Gasca explained. "He wouldn't let Trevor change the play at the line of scrimmage."

"I never heard of an NFL team that didn't audible," Roscoe grumbled.

"Well, there were some audibles, but they were all pre-ordained, left-right, or run-pass options."

"What the hell does that mean?"

Michael Gasca thought for a moment. "If the play was a running play to the right, he could switch it to the left side if it looks better that way. Or he might call a running play and a passing play in the huddle, and at the line of scrimmage he tells the offense which one they're going to run."

"That sure sounds like audibles to me," Roscoe said. "I thought you said Starnes wouldn't let him do that."

"That's *all* Coach Starnes would let him do. Just those few pre-ordained audibles."

"That sounds stupid."

"Honestly, that's what most teams do. It used to be that quarterbacks called all the plays at the line of scrimmage, but that was before all these substitutions, formations and complications were invented. Now offenses have so many personnel groupings and formations that it's impossible for a quarterback to keep it all straight in his head."

"So maybe Coach Starnes was right. He didn't let Trevor call audibles, because it's not possible to call audibles."

"With most quarterbacks he would have been right," Michael Gasca said. "But with Trevor he was wrong. The kid can handle it."

■ ■ ■

Trevor took in a deep breath of mile-high air and thought again about what a strange week it had been. He'd been surprised when Coach Repanshek was hired, and his first meeting with his old coach had been interesting. The coach had offered no criticism and no mention of Trevor's "honesty problem." Repanshek had explained to Trevor, privately first, then in front of the entire offense, that he would call audibles during the game. Any play he wanted to run was fine. If the crowd was quiet, he could call out the play. If the crowd was loud, he'd use the hand signals for the two-minute plays, and only those receivers lined up in their two-minute positions would run those routes. It had sounded terribly complicated when Coach Repanshek explained it to the offense, but once they hit the field for practice on Friday, Trevor had used an audible about every fourth play, and it went more smoothly than anyone expected.

He surveyed the Denver defense. The Stallions were in I-left slot formation, and the Broncos free safety was cheating two or three steps toward the slot receiver. Trevor glanced to his right and saw that his receivers were facing bump coverage. As Trevor bent under center, the safety took another step up and over. Trevor looked at the defensive line. The tackle to Trevor's left had a lot of weight forward in his stance, but the defensive end was light—his hand was barely bearing any weight. Suddenly, Trevor could see the defensive scheme as easily as if it were illuminated on the stadium's DiamondVision board. The cornerback over the slot receiver was going to blitz, and the safety was cheating so he could take over the corner's coverage responsibility. The defensive tackle was going to bull rush straight ahead, and the end was going to loop around him.

"Blue 35!" Trevor audibled. Blue was the team's live color. The play was 35 Oskie, a handoff to the tailback. Trevor had picked a play out of the playbook, matched it to the personnel and formation and called it at the line.

"Blue 35!...Set-Hut!"

The center snapped the ball, and Trevor turned to his left and delivered it to Caleb Alexander, who angled toward the outside leg of the offensive tackle. The defense ran its stunt, which would have worked well if the Stallions had a pass play called. Instead, the bull rusher got double-teamed into a stalemate at the line of scrimmage, and the end looped inside and got caught in traffic. Caleb carried the ball right through the space vacated by the looping end. In a normal situation, the free safety would have come up for weak side run support and made the tackle after just a few yards, but he'd taken five or six steps toward the uncovered receiver before he recognized that it was a run play. He was out of position, which allowed Caleb Alexander to scamper seventeen yards before the defense caught up with him.

23

NFL Security officer Jerry Powers met Steven Oquist in the baggage claim area at the San Antonio Airport. They'd known each other nearly a decade, first with the FBI and later with the league, and they had a great deal of mutual respect. Oquist scanned the crowd with practiced ease as he came down the escalator. He'd learned over the years to see everything without appearing to look at anything. He and Powers spotted each other about the same time and exchanged barely perceptible nods.

Oquist studied Jerry Powers from a distance. Powers was a sixty-year-old former district attorney who'd gone to work for the FBI in his late thirties and then came to the NFL about six years ago. He was built like an apple tree in full bloom—his legs, when he stood with his feet together, looked like a skinny trunk leading up to the perfectly round canopy of his stomach. When Jerry Powers had first hit the streets with NFL Security, a bookie had described him as a dickey-do, which was a term Powers had never heard. When he'd asked what it meant, the bookie had laughed and patted the agent's prodigious stomach.

"Wherever you go and whatever you do, your belly gets there before your dickey do."

"How you doing, Jerry?" Oquist said, extending his hand. Jerry Powers was a good man and a great investigator.

"How's life treatin' ya?" Powers asked.

"I've been good," Oquist said. "You?"

"Damn fine," Powers said. He stood just under six feet tall in cowboy boots, Wrangler jeans, a plaid shirt, a bolo tie, and a wide silver belt buckle that somehow fought against the pressure of his stomach to stay upright. Oquist looked his friend up and down and wondered whether Powers was now a full-fledged Texan or just masquerading as one.

"Where's your cowboy hat?" Oquist asked facetiously.

If Jerry Powers sensed that Oquist was teasing him, he showed no sign. "It's in the truck," he said.

When they got outside, Oquist learned that the truck was a full-on, cowboy-style, load-hauling Ford F-350 Dually with a tool box bolted in the bed, a crew cab to seat five, and a gun rack.

Steven Oquist didn't say a word.

They drove through sweltering city streets. "If it's this hot in October, when the hell does it cool down?" Oquist said.

"Starts to settle a spell 'round No-vim-ber, Dee-cim-ber, but winter ain't all that long 'round here," Powers said.

Oquist wondered how a man who had lived his entire life on the East Coast could have a Texas accent after just six years. Jerry Powers talked as if he'd been born in a saddle.

"You wanna go to the hotel first, git checked in?" Power twanged.

Oquist shook his head. He didn't want to waste time. "Let's go straight to the street, see if anyone in town has seen Roscoe Evans."

"I've been pokin' around a bit," Powers said, "but nobody's spotted anything."

"I'm sure you've got it covered, Jerry, but I just want to talk to some of these people myself. Look 'em in the eye and see what they're all about."

They went to see Victor Romano, who ran a book out of a bar called Sadie's. Victor stood only five-foot-six, and weighed maybe one hundred and thirty pounds, but he had vicious eyes.

"Jerry Powers!" he exclaimed with a smile that softened up his features. "It's always good to see you."

"Howdy, Victor," Powers said.

"You NFL Security too?" Victor asked Oquist.

"Yeah," Oquist said, "out of Philly."

Victor climbed up onto a bar stool. "You're a long way from home."

"This is where the action is."

"Is it?" Victor rapped his knuckles on the bar, and the bartender delivered a glass of water.

"I'm looking for a guy."

"Aren't we all?" Victor said. He gulped down half the water. "What's his name?"

Oquist knew that if he mentioned Michael Gasca and Roscoe Evans, the entire crime world would turn its attention to San Antonio. "I don't know his name."

Victor looked from Oquist to Powers and back again. He smiled, and his eyes glittered with mischief. "You guys need some drinks?"

"Naw. We fine," Powers drawled.

"'Cause it could take a while to track down a guy whose name you don't know, but who you followed all the way down here from Philadelphia, and who you know must be in San Antonio, even though you haven't seen him and you don't know his name. You might get pretty thirsty on that kinda mission."

"We're checking a lot of cities," Oquist said. "What I need to know is if you've heard anything about someone on the streets here in San Antonio who might be doing some unusual stuff."

"Who's watching Philly while you're away?" Victor knew that each NFL city had only one NFL Security officer.

"It's still Thomas Pimm. I'm a regional administrator."

"Oh. A big wig," Victor said, arching his eyebrows.

"Sort of."

"How many cities you checking?"

"Have you seen or heard anything strange?" Oquist asked.

Victor brought the glass back to his lips and drank until it was empty. "You mean strange like Michael Gasca and Roscoe Evans strange?"

Oquist's heart quickened.

"Look, let's just shoot straight here," Victor said. He wiped his mouth with the back of his hand. "I haven't heard anything from anybody. But the buzz on the street the past month is that Michael Gasca and Roscoe Evans have disappeared. There's a lot of places they could go, and in our business, somebody goes underground doesn't always mean he's up to something. But they're the biggest names in Philly, and no one has seen them for a while. Now you're down here from Philly asking if there's been anyone strange on the street. So I put two and two together."

Oquist nodded. "All right. Are they here?"

"Nope."

Steven Oquist looked at Jerry Powers to see what he thought. Victor had no reason to lie to them, but Powers knew the man better than Oquist did.

"You sure you ain't heard nothin', Victor?" Powers said. "You know what we're all about. We ain't out to bust nobody. We just gotta make sure the game is legit."

"I'm being straight with you," Victor said. "As far as I know, they ain't here, and if I don't know about it, then chances are, they ain't here. There are no solo projects in this industry. If you're gonna leave your hometown to go work in some faraway city, you better have a man on the street to help you out, show you around, and introduce you to people. If Michael Gasca and Roscoe Evans had come to town, I would have heard about it. You might as well move on to the next city on your list."

▪ ▪ ▪

When Steven Oquist and Jerry Powers finally reached the office, Oquist pulled the file on Trevor Deale. Like all NFL Security officers, Jerry kept detailed records about players, coaches, and other team staff. The star players drew more scrutiny than the backups, but everyone had a file. Most of it came from public records—real estate transactions, marriage licenses, divorce decrees, legal judgments, etc. Oquist read about Trevor's new mansion, including a backgrounder on the realtor. He saw the cars registered in Trevor's name and the dates and details of the purchases. Most of the players used the team's travel agency to book their personal flights, and all that information was quietly turned over to NFL Security. There was nothing unusual in Trevor's life. He had a girlfriend, Vanessa. They'd been together a year and a half and would probably get married. His father had abandoned the family years ago, and his sister and mother still lived in Lamesa, Texas. Trevor's agent, accountant, lawyer, and financial advisor all checked out clean.

Oquist knew Michael Gasca had targeted Trevor Deale, but he just didn't know exactly when, where, or how the contact would be made. He could set up surveillance on Trevor and wait for Gasca to make his move, but that would be costly and probably impossible. Trevor lived in an exclusive neighborhood. There was no way to do it right without Trevor's cooperation, and assistant director Ken Parsley would never approve of that.

Oquist could hear the questions Ken would ask: What are you going to tell Trevor? That he should be alert because the mob might be after him? What if that news affects his performance on the field? What are you going to tell Jonathan Kinneson about how our investigation undermined the concentration of his star player?

Even though NFL Security operated in the open, traveling with the team and offering information to any player who requested it, its efforts at policing gambling were a closely guarded secret. At the beginning of each season, the league held meetings in every NFL city, during which the players were reminded of the rules about contact with members of the gambling community, and they were introduced—reintroduced in many cases—to their local NFL security officers, who urged the players to call if they ever had any problems. Oquist had learned over the years that the players *did* call. Mostly it was after they'd landed in trouble, tried to handle it themselves, and realized that they couldn't. He'd received countless calls from players who had learned that a girlfriend was pregnant. Some of the players were angry because they didn't believe they were the fathers—a paternity test would settle the claims—but most contacted NFL Security out of desperation—they were married, and they needed to keep their wives from finding out about the affairs.

Steven Oquist always offered the same three pieces of advice. The first was, "Tell your wife." If the guy confessed, then everything was out in the open and the girlfriend lost her leverage. But most players didn't want to deal with the marital consequences of their infidelities. They'd rather spend the money to get rid of the girlfriend, even—and this always tickled Oquist—if it became clear that the woman was *not* pregnant.

The second piece of advice Oquist offered—usually when players were arrested for domestic violence, drunken driving, disturbing the peace, etc.—was "Get a lawyer," which, surprisingly, many players did not do. Too often, they'd start blabbing to the cops, thinking that if they just told the authorities what had happened everything would be okay. Most of them didn't realize until too late that they had offered up the words that would be used against them at trial.

Which led to the third piece of advice Oquist gave to players—"Don't talk to the cops." Dealing with those types of situation was not Steven Oquist's primary responsibility, but his job was to monitor anything that might be used as leverage against a player.

A recent addition to the annual security meeting was a twenty-minute video that the players really enjoyed. The NFL had commissioned a Hollywood production crew to create a movie-quality video with professional actors, screenwriters, sound engineers, and one of the best directors in the country.

On the screen, a young black man with rippled muscles and the trendy clothing of wealth was standing in a club chatting with a buxom woman in a tiny black dress. She had long dark hair, caramel-colored skin, a tiny waist, and a bulging bust line. The athlete said something, and she laughed, throwing her head back, laying a hand on his chest. He pulled a wad of cash out of his pocket and signaled to the bartender. She leaned in to whisper in his ear, her loose top fell away from her skin revealing more cleavage. The NFL players watching the video sang a chorus of *oohs* and *ahhs*. They recognized themselves. They were just like the athlete on the screen, rolling into a club, picking up the finest woman in the place, winning her over with their charm, good looks, and wealth.

The woman on the screen looked over the player's shoulder and beckoned a friend to join them. The player turned, and a second woman appeared. She had tanned skin, green eyes, close-cropped hair, and she wore a skin-tight dress that revealed a body that would have made God blush.

"Gawd damn!" said one of the players, standing up and raising his arms to the screen. Everyone laughed with him. They all had the same thought—*where could they find her?*

On the screen both women laughed at something the player had said. They stroked his muscular arms and whispered in his ears. The three of them left the nightclub together, kissing in a cab and walking into the lobby of a luxurious hotel, where the clerk gave the player a knowing nod. They moved into the elevator where the women kissed him aggressively. The players watching the tape burst into applause.

"Take care of yo bidness!" someone shouted.

"That's how I be workin' it!" said another voice.

The threesome on the screen stumbled into a dimly lit hotel room, ripping off their clothes, grinding against each other, falling onto the bed. A dim lamp in the corner provided just enough light to illuminate every sordid detail. When the women's dresses hit the floor, several players in the audience stood up and applauded; one guy raced to the front of the room as if he were going to jump into the action.

Giggles and moans filled the hotel room. The video wasn't soft-core, cable-style porn, which suggested penetration rather than revealing it. The tape was hardcore, graphic XXX. When the dark-haired woman climbed on top of the player, everyone in the meeting room watched transfixed as the camera zoomed in as she slowly impaled herself on him. She rode up and down, shuddering and moaning. The other woman slipped out of bed but returned a moment later, nudging her partner with a gentle hand. The dark-haired woman moved off his penis, sliding up his body and dropping her breasts into his face. The white woman took him into her mouth, slurping up and down as he writhed and moaned.

The camera zoomed in again. The short-haired woman's face had changed subtly. Her nose was a slightly different shape, her hair a slightly different length. Her Adam's apple a little larger.

"Oh shit!" someone in the audience said. "That's a man!"

The camera drifted from the player's face contorted in ecstasy, down to his crotch where it was clearly a man giving him a blowjob. He climaxed, and the unknown man swallowed every drop.

The exuberance of the audience had disappeared. The players sat in stunned silence watching the man slip out of the bed. The pretty, short-haired woman returned. The stud on the screen didn't know what had happened. He snuggled with the two women with a smile on his face as if he had just conquered the world. The players in the audience yelled at him, angry about the deception, disgusted by the perversion.

The video delivered NFL Security's message in a way that resonated with the players.

"Be careful," officers in every NFL city said after showing the video. "There are a lot of people who will try to set you up to get money out of you or to get a favor. You may not realize what's happening until they show up a few days later with a videotape. But don't be afraid to call NFL Security. No matter what the situation, we can help get you out of the mess."

24

Trevor Deale's younger sister, Mandy, walked through the historic downtown of Lamesa, Texas, hand-in-hand with her boyfriend, William Stoughton. She'd lived in Lamesa her whole life, but seeing the town fresh through William's eyes reminded her of just how small and insignificant her home was. William was a prison consultant from Detroit who traveled down about once a month to work at the Preston E. Smith State Penitentiary. They'd met nearly nine months ago and had quickly fallen in love.

They stopped at a bench near the courthouse and Mandy studied him for a moment. He was a perfect gentleman and a perfect lover. He was affectionate and patient and nicer than she'd ever believed a man could be.

"I feel so lucky to have you in my life," she said.

"I'm the lucky one," William said, kissing her hand. Mandy had long legs and simple country grace. She wasn't classically beautiful, but William thought her sincerity and warmth more than made up for it. He had been smitten almost at first sight.

"Mandy," he said. She turned toward him fully; her heart warmed at hearing her name come out of his mouth. "I know we're still getting to know each other, but I want you to think about something."

"Anything."

"One of these days I might ask you to move to Detroit with me. Do you think you could ever leave Lamesa?"

Mandy flushed. "Oh my."

"I'm not asking you now," William said quickly. "I'm just saying that if we're gonna keep seeing each other, we'd better find out where we stand on stuff like this."

"Well…guess I'd have to think about that." She bit her bottom lip. "There's no way you could move down to Texas?"

"It's possible," William said cautiously. Mandy held one of his hands in both of hers. "I could probably get a job in Houston or Dallas, but, for sure, I'd never find work in a small town like Lamesa."

"No, of course not." Mandy knew Lamesa offered few prospects. She had often wondered if she would ever leave this little town. "I'd be far away from my family."

"Yeah, I thought about that too." William leaned back against the bench. "Tell you what. Let's not worry about it right now. Like I said, I was just trying to get a feel for what's what."

Mandy gripped his hand more tightly and put her head on his shoulder. It felt nice to have a man in her life trying to figure out how to spend more time with her. She didn't know where they were headed, but she was enjoying the ride. She looked at her watch and saw that it was creeping up on 3 P.M.

"We could go back to the house," Mandy said, giving him her most wicked look. "Mom won't be home for a couple of hours and the rest of 'em won't get here until 7." Trevor and Vanessa were on their way up from San Antonio, and her Uncle Jim and Aunt Nancy were driving down from Amarillo for the weekend.

The first time she and William had made love, her mother had called just as they finished. Mandy had answered the phone breathless and stumbled about for an answer to her mother's question. "Oh…just finished…washing the dishes." Since then, household chores had been their euphemism for lovemaking.

"Oh yeah?" William said. "What could we do in two hours?"

Mandy shrugged. "We could wash the dishes."

"Sounds sexy."

"Or fold the clothes."

"Ooh …tell me more." William pulled her to her feet.

"Mop the floors."

"Hubba hubba." They walked toward the car.

"Scrub the windows."

"I might lose control and ravish you right here in the street."

"Mow the lawn."

"You had to mention the lawn, you naughty little girl," William grinned. He opened her car door. She watched him as he walked around the front of the car to the driver's side.

"I could vacuum."

William leaned over and kissed her passionately holding her head in both hands.

"I need to get you home," he said.

"Hurry."

■ ■ ■

It was a long drive from San Antonio to Lamesa, and the Stallions' bye week had been Trevor's first chance to get back home since signing with the Stallions in June. Trevor and Vanessa had left San Antonio about 10 AM Thursday and hoped to arrive in time for dinner. Vanessa wore a sundress with her shoes kicked off. Her beautiful bronzed legs were stretched onto the dashboard and her seat was reclined. The dress slid back along her legs almost to the top of her thighs, creating a tantalizing view for Trevor—and every trucker they passed. She wore sunglasses and when Trevor glanced over, she appeared to be asleep.

"We should have flown," she said gruffly. She wasn't asleep, he realized. She was sulking.

"I thought a road trip would be fun."

"You thought wrong."

"Hmm." Trevor wasn't in the mood to argue.

"Why couldn't your mom come see us instead?"

"Because I wanted to get out of town."

"If you wanted to get out of town, we should have gone to the Bahamas."

"My mother doesn't live in the Bahamas, Vanessa. She lives in Lamesa, and I want to see her new house. I thought you might be interested in seeing the place I grew up."

"You ever heard of pictures?"

Trevor shook his head. Vanessa got into these moods at times during which she complained about everything. He'd learned to just stop arguing with her and let her anger dissipate.

"You should buy your own plane," Vanessa said after a few minutes.

Trevor laughed. It never stopped.

"Trevor, you've got a gazillion dollars sitting in the bank. It's okay to spend a little money every now and then. Jesus! You act like such a damn monk."

A monk? He was sitting at the wheel of a Range Rover, wearing nice clothes, and paying the mortgage on a six-million-dollar Mediterranean estate, but in Vanessa's eyes, he wasn't spending enough money. Trevor knew her rage was misplaced. What she was really angry about was that he had not yet proposed marriage. Trevor was confused about that himself. Most men would have killed to have a girlfriend like Vanessa, and they'd do more than that to have her as a wife.

Trevor loved her, but he wasn't sure he could marry her. The tension between them had been worse lately because Vanessa had asked him for a ring point-blank, and he still hadn't pulled the trigger.

The week Coach Repanshek was hired, Vanessa had thrown a party to celebrate the beginning of a new era. That evening they'd had more than three million dollars in automobiles parked in front of their Mediterranean mansion. The lineup included a Lamborghini, a Ferrari, three Porsches, four Mercedes, two Range Rovers, a Rolls-Royce, and a host of cars bearing the symbols of BMW, Cadillac, and Audi.

Vanessa had glided through the house laughing at a joke here, touching an arm there, reveling in her reign as belle of the ball. The final bill for the interior decorator had been more than three hundred and fifty thousand dollars, but Vanessa thought it had been worth every penny. No one on the team had a home like theirs.

"I love what you've done here, Vanessa," said the wife of one of the players. "It's so elegant."

"Yes, isn't it?" Vanessa said. She didn't stop moving. The woman's husband was a backup linebacker who rarely touched the field. Vanessa didn't waste her time talking to someone so far beneath her.

Everyone on the team, including a few coaches, was there. Vanessa had sent out an email to all the wives and girlfriends at the last minute, and of course they had all accepted her invitation.

Vanessa inclined her head toward five women standing in the corner. At the center of this clique stood Andrea Peterson, wife of defensive end Dexter Peterson. Andrea was the leader of the wives and girlfriends. Until Vanessa's arrival, Andrea was the only person who could put a party together on two days' notice and have everyone attend. Andrea could ensure the success or failure of any party with just a few words of praise or condemnation. She headed up the annual Stallions's Wives Food Drive, and it was to Andrea that the wives turned when they had questions to ask, gossip to share, or concerns to broach. Many a wife had lived with regret after running afoul of Andrea Peterson.

The five women stared at Vanessa with open contempt. She smiled at them and twinkled her fingers in a delicate wave. At first, none of them responded, then Andrea Peterson raised her left hand and extended a finger. At first Vanessa thought the older woman was flipping her the bird, but then she realized it was Andrea's ring finger; Andrea was showing off her diamond-encrusted wedding band and four-carat engagement ring.

Vanessa scowled and turned away quickly. She shouldn't have invited that bitch. She marched down to the basement, where Trevor stood off near the bar with Martin and Robo. As usual, Robo was perfectly turned out in a khaki Kani jacket with matching Kani jeans and designer combat boots. A few of their teammates were shooting nine ball on the pool table and shouting insults at each other while wagering five hundred dollars a game.

"Hi Martin," Vanessa said.

"How you doing, girl?" Martin kissed her cheek.

"Couldn't be better." She looked at Robo. "Did you get enough to eat?"

"Yeah, that brisket was kickin'."

"Did you try the chicken?"

"I sure did," Robo said. He jokingly referred to his dates as a chickenheads, so the question had a double meaning. "And by the time I was done, the breasts were *flushed* and the thighs were *quivering!*" Robo laughed and raised a hand to Martin for a high-five.

Vanessa didn't have time for that. She turned to Trevor. "I need to talk to you."

"Oh yeah?"

"In private." She grabbed his hand and led him away from the noise into a small guest room at the far end of the basement. "I just got humiliated by Dexter's wife," Vanessa said when the door closed. Veins were showing near her temples, and Trevor knew that she was absolutely pissed. "Andrea showed me her diamond ring, and looked at me like I was a piece of toilet paper stuck to your heel, and you'd get rid of me the first chance you got."

Trevor shook his head, baffled. "What are you talking about?"

"I'm not going to tiptoe around it any more," Vanessa said. "I can't continue to just be your girlfriend. I need a ring."

Trevor was speechless.

"You know why there are so many fancy cars parked in front of our house tonight?" Vanessa continued.

"Because we have a lot of guests?" Trevor offered.

"No, it's because a fancy car is the way people tell the world that they're rich. And if you can afford it, a beautiful ring is how you tell the world that you love your woman. If you love me, what are you waiting for?"

"Maybe I'm waiting to be ready for marriage."

"Trevor, it's not that complicated. Either you love me or you don't. If you don't, you should let me know so I can move on. But if you do love me, then you should pop the question already."

Trevor had known that Vanessa wanted to get married, but he'd never expected her to be so aggressive. He said, "Marriage is not something you just jump into. We need to think about it, talk about it and make sure we're ready."

"What do you want to talk about?" Vanessa had her arms crossed, her naked ring finger on display at the crook of her elbow.

"Nothing right this second."

"It's hard to build friendships with women who've got their engagement rings and wedding bands as a constant reminder that I'm not one of them." The veins at her temples were even more pronounced. "I can't talk to you right now," Vanessa said, throwing up her hands.

She ripped open the door and stormed across the basement and up the stairs. Trevor came out of the room slowly with a dazed look on his face. His teammates erupted in laughter. They hadn't heard the conversation, but they knew from the steam coming off Vanessa that Trevor was in big trouble.

"What was that all about?" Martin asked.

"She wants a ring."

"Oh shit!" Robo said. "He got the ring speech!"

"It was bound to happen one day," said Caleb Alexander. "I'm just glad it happened when you were among friends."

"Imagine if he'd been alone," Robo shuddered.

"Here's what you do," Caleb said. "You call Joshua over at Isotel's Jewelry. He'll get you something pretty spectacular."

"But what if I'm not ready to get married?"

"Doesn't matter," said Mike Griffin, a tight end. "Got my fiancee a fifty-thousand-dollar engagement ring a couple of years ago and I haven't heard a peep out her since. We don't have a date, and whenever she tries to force me to commit to a wedding date, I start getting all agitated like I'm gonna break up and fight to get the ring back. She shuts up real quick."

"Bottom line," Caleb said, "is that you have to get her a ring, but you don't have to marry her. The ring is your way of keeping her at bay until you figure out what you want to do."

"Trevor, if you don't get her a ring," said Robo, "then she's gonna be...say it with me fellas..."

A chorus of voices sang, "embarrassed around her friends."

"And a woman ain't like a man, Trevor," Robo continued. "When a man gets embarrassed, he starts a fight. When a woman gets embarrassed, you wake up in the middle of the night with your jimmy whacked off."

25

A pitted and scarred pickup truck rumbled down a dirt drive, kicking up a fog of dust that rose into the cloudless sky like a miniature sand storm. Trevor's mother, Kathy Deale, stood on the front porch with one hand resting on her hip and the other shading her blue eyes in an imprecise salute. She wore blue jeans and a green button-up shirt. Her hair was tied up in a light green strip of ribbon.

Mandy and William stood just behind her holding hands. Mandy's face was still flushed from all the *housework* she and William had done before her mother came home. She looked over at him and smiled.

"Glad we finished up before anyone got here," William whispered.

"We could duck in the house and squeeze in another thirty seconds," Mandy whispered back.

"I can hear you love birds back there," Kathy said, turning toward them with a stern glare. Then she broke into a smile. It made her heart sing to see her baby girl in love.

Kathy stepped out into the drive as the truck, which seemed exhausted after the hundred-and-eighty-mile trip from Amarillo, settled with an audible groan; the engine continued to rattle.

Her brother-in-law, Jim, slid out from behind the steering wheel. Kathy looked at the drooping front bumper of the old vehicle and said, without a hint of sarcasm, "New truck?"

"Well, thank ya for noticin'," Jim said. He hitched up his jeans with honest-to-God pride. He ran a delicate hand over the rusting front fender. "I forget how far out here y'all are." Jim looked back the way he'd come as if calculating the distance. "Let me get to the younguns first," he said, giving Kathy a quick peck on the cheek. "You must be Willie," Jim said. "I hear you're a good man."

"Well…hope so," William said nervously. He wanted to add that he preferred to be called William—not Willie—but he didn't want to create any tension.

"Now here's my honey." Jim grabbed Mandy and squeezed her tight. "You're so grown up, I can hardly stand it. I wanna shrink you back into a little girl and swing ya around by your arms."

Mandy hugged him back, smiling. "I've missed you, Uncle Jim."

"I've missed you too, cutie pie. But you know who I missed most of all? Your young mother over there."

He looked Kathy up and down. "Shoot, if I'd've remember how sexy you were, I'd've left the ol' ball and chain back in Amarillo." He jerked a thumb at his wife, Nancy, who was climbing out of the truck after straightening her hair in the mirror.

Nancy clucked her tongue. "Sounds exciting, huh Kath?" She had a friendly weathered face with deep laugh lines around her eyes and mouth. "You bed down with this old fart, it'd be the best two minutes of sex you ever had."

"Hell, woman!" Jim protested. "I'd last damn near twice that long."

The women shared a long hug. "It's so good to see you," Kathy said. "It's been a long time."

"Too long," Nancy said.

"Hey, don't I get some of that action?" Jim had his arms spread wide.

Kathy smiled. She'd forgotten how much she missed him. "Oh, I suppose I could give an old man a thrill."

Jim picked her up and swung her around. "It's good to see ya, kid. How've ya been?"

"Everything's been good around here." Kathy held Jim's hand and led him toward the house. "How've you been?"

"Oh, you know me, handsome, healthy, and thirsty as heck. You got any beer?"

"In the fridge." Kathy held the screen door open.

"This is beautiful!" Nancy exclaimed, stepping into the air conditioning. All the furniture and appliances were new.

"I've been takin' all the pictures out of the albums and putting them in new frames so I can decorate the house with pictures of my babies." Kathy said.

"Let me know when you're ready for a new picture of me and my truck," Jim said. "Might look good up on the mantle there."

William laughed, but stopped when Jim said, "What's so funny?"

"We've been shoppin' every day," Mandy said. "We threw away just about everything from the old house."

Trevor had given his mother and sister carte blanche. They could have anything they wanted, but the two women could not escape their frugal past. They still shopped at garage sales and discount stores and had spent less than five thousand dollars for all the furnishings and decorations in the house.

Nancy settled on to the couch. Jim marched back into the room from the kitchen with a beer in each hand. He tossed one to William. "Heads up, Will!"

"Maybe Trevor will get you a new truck," William offered, again ignoring the shortening of his name.

"He already did." Jim nodded toward the front of the house. "That's how I got that."

"It's…nice," William said cautiously.

"Hell, man, you ain't gotta dance around it. It's a piece of shit! Plain and simple. But I couldn't drive one of them new-fangled trucks. I need a vehicle that's got a little character. I need something with a carburetor and a little bit of rust I gotta watch out for. What the hell would I do with my time if I didn't have any trouble with my truck?"

"You might pay more attention to your wife," Nancy said.

"Woman," Jim said with a dismissive wave of his hand, "the only time I wanna spend with you is when you're just steppin' outta your dress at the end of the day, like that sexy little number you wore to church last Sunday."

"There wasn't nothing *sexy* about anything I wore to the Lord's house."

"I was ready to ravage ya!"

Nancy waved him off. "Y'all don't pay him no mind. He's just an old fool who's drank too many beers in his life. What I want to know about is you kids. How long have y'all been dating?"

Mandy looked at William with an intimate smile. "About nine months."

"How'd ya meet? Gimme the juicy scoop!"

Another smile. "He came into the store—"

"You still workin' at the supermarket?" Jim interrupted.

"Yes, and William came in to buy a few things."

"I was staying over at the Cotton Gin Inn," William said, "And since I was gonna be in town about a week, I wanted some snacks for the room."

"He had a whole cart full of stuff like he was gonna be here for a whole month!" Mandy exclaimed.

"I got a little carried away," William confessed. "I filled up my cart, so it would take her longer to ring me up."

"But he hardly said a word! We stood there like two dummies and didn't say anything to each other. At the end, he paid me and then walked out the door."

"So how did you actually meet?" Nancy said.

"Yeah," said Jim with a loud beer belch. "Cut to the goddamn chase."

"Watch your mouth!" Nancy said.

Jim rolled his eyes.

"He came back in about half an hour later with a bouquet of flowers," Mandy said. She reached over and put her hand on top of William's. "We just couldn't stop smiling at each other."

"And you're still smiling," Nancy cooed.

"Well, that's downright sweet," Jim said. "I gotta get me another beer. You want one, W?"

"No, I'm okay." He hesitated for a moment. "And Jim…it's William. I don't mean to be a stick in the mud, but I really do prefer William."

Jim looked confused. He didn't get the distinction. "All right, Willie. I got it." He turned and walked into the kitchen.

Suddenly, Kathy heard a vehicle out on the gravel drive and clapped her hands. "Trevor!"

"Well I'll be damned," Jim said, looking through the window. "He's got one of them fancy SUVs!"

Kathy had a smile as big as the interstate. She raced out on to the porch and into the driveway. She jumped into Trevor's arms before he stepped fully out of the truck.

"Hello there, Mr. Football Player!" She kissed both his cheeks and squeezed him so hard he thought she might break his neck. But Trevor was happy to endure the pressure. Until that moment, Trevor hadn't realized just how much he had missed his mother.

"It's so good to see you, honey," she said softly.

"You too, Mom."

Vanessa stepped out of the truck and both Jim and William's jaws dropped.

Jim didn't waste any time. "Vanessa? I'm your Uncle Jim."

She extended her hand, but Jim ignored it, moving in to give her a tight hug, which Vanessa returned with a look of discomfort. Jim hugged her longer than was prudent and would have continued if his wife hadn't smacked the back of his head.

Jim flinched. "Oww!"

"Leave the poor girl alone, you pervert!" Nancy shook her head. "Vanessa, please don't mind him. He's harmless." She gave Vanessa a hug. "Welcome to Lamesa."

"Thank you," Vanessa said.

"Oh, so it's okay for you to hug her, but not me?" Jim sounded truly wounded.

"There's a difference between affection and assault, and you were dancin' on that line," Nancy said.

"Well, I was just trying to be affectionate."

"It's okay," Vanessa said, sounding more generous than she felt.

"Maybe I should try again," Jim suggested. "See if I can get it right."

"Don't you touch her," Nancy snapped.

Jim glared at his wife but stepped back on to the porch to wait.

Vanessa took in the scene. Kathy's dilapidated, clapboard house stood off to the left, surrounded by flat, desolate farmland. The porch on the old house sagged at the corners like a frown and a family of wayward white-throated swifts were roosting in the chimney. The new house stood directly in front of them, gleaming like a beetle in a fresh pile of dung.

Kathy came around the truck and gave Vanessa a hug. "It's nice to see you again," she said. She wished she meant it. She'd met Vanessa once while Trevor was in college, and she had tried, without much success, to like the girl. "Trevor, I don't think you could have found a more beautiful girlfriend." And that was true. No matter what Kathy thought about Vanessa's personality, she could not deny the girl's beauty.

"And it looks like Mandy couldn't have found a nicer man," Trevor said, shaking William's hand.

"I think," Kathy said, opening the screen door and ushering everyone into the house, "it's time we got some food in our bellies."

"What about our bags?" Vanessa said, looking around nervously as if she thought someone might steal them.

"We'll send the boys out for 'em after supper."

Once they were all inside, Kathy gave them an update on all the local gossip. Lamesa was a very small town, so there was a lot to talk about. Her report took them all the way through setting the dining table with plates, glasses, and silverware, ferrying in the salad, roast beef, corn on the cob, mashed potatoes, and green beans from the kitchen and getting seated. While they got their drinks and salads, Kathy told them about the weather in Lamesa and the effect it had had on the cotton crop. All the way through dinner, Kathy told them about the controversies and fights that had erupted in the small town. It was a virtual monologue because they all knew that Kathy Deale rarely had this sort of audience.

"You still got Trevor's ol' tire hangin' out back?" Jim asked during a lull.

"Of course," Kathy exclaimed, as if she were offended at the suggestion that she might have taken it down. "Every time I look at that old tire, I think about Trevor out there for hours and hours throwing his football. Now when I see him on the TV, I can believe it's the same little boy."

"He ain't little anymore!" Jim said. "You think you could tackle this big guy, Willie?"

"Heck no."

Trevor blushed. "So what else has been happening around town, Mom?"

Kathy thought for a moment. "One of the inmates out at the prison took some hostages."

"Really?" said Nancy.

"He was getting treatment for somethin' or other, and guards turned their backs for just a second. He grabbed two nurses and locked himself in a room with them."

"Did he have a weapon?" William asked. He had heard about the situation, but he didn't know any of the details.

"I don't know, but he raped those poor women a bunch of times before the other guards could get in there and bust 'em free."

"That's horrible," William said.

"They oughta castrate that guy, huh Willie?" Jim said.

"It's William."

"Just snip his nuts right off!"

"Watch your language!" Nancy said.

"You want me to watch my language when I'm talking about a rapist?" Jim said indignantly. "That's the worst kinda human being there is next to a child mo-lester, and you're upset about me sayin' they oughta get their nuts cut off?"

"You don't have to say it at the table."

"Then pretend I didn't say it at the table," Jim said. "Pretend I said it two hours ago, and you're just rememberin' it at the table."

"Anybody want some desert?" Kathy sang. "We've got pecan pie and ice cream."

"That sounds great, Mom," Trevor said.

"I'll help you," Mandy said, grabbing dirty plates off the table.

"William?" Kathy said.

"Yes ma'am! I'll have a slice."

"Vanessa?" Kathy said.

"I'd better not." Vanessa patted her flat stomach. "I'm on a diet." Kathy rolled her eyes.

"You ain't gonna say anything about all this?" Jim asked his wife.

"About what?"

"You got on me for talkin' about nuts at the table, but you don't say anything when they're goin' on and on about pee-can pie."

Nancy stood up to help clear off the table. "I'm through talking to you."

Jim shrugged his shoulder and elbowed William. "Willie, you're my witness. Is there or ain't there nuts in pee-can pie?"

■　■　■

"Your mother doesn't like me," Vanessa said. It was nearly midnight. She was sitting on the edge of the bed brushing her hair in long slow strokes. Her short silk nightgown hung delicately on her body, and she had one beautiful leg tucked under the other.

"She likes you," Trevor said. He pulled his shirt over his head and unbuckled his pants. "You just have to get to know her better."

"She gives me these looks like I'm a bimbo."

"You're not a bimbo," Trevor said. It was moments like these when he truly loved Vanessa. She could be a pain in the ass at times, but deep down he knew she was just a sensitive, insecure girl who desperately wanted to be liked.

"I try to be nice to her," Vanessa said quietly.

The sincerity in her voice touched Trevor. He kissed her on the forehead.

"My mother is very old-fashioned," he said, trailing kisses down the side of Vanessa's neck. She giggled and turned her head to give him easier access. "She wants what's best for her only son." Trevor kissed his way to Vanessa's mouth; she kissed him back with her soft lips slightly parted. "But the important thing is that I love you, especially at moments like these, when you're so sweet and nice. If I love you, then my mother is going to love you because she wants me to be happy."

"Mmm-hmm," Vanessa moaned. "Then I'd better make sure that you're very, very happy."

"You're making a good start."

■ ■ ■

Vanessa woke from a light sleep and listened to the darkness around her. She heard nothing. There were no city sounds, not even animal noises in the middle of this tract of farmland. Trevor was snoring softly. It was about three hours since they'd made love, and Vanessa still felt good. Whatever problems she and Trevor might have, sexual chemistry wasn't one of them. She got up slowly and used the moonlight to admire her reflection in the mirror. She had a slim, athletic frame. Her legs were muscular without being bulky. Her stomach was flat and her breasts were so high and firm that even women with silicone implants couldn't compete.

She slipped on her silk robe and eased out of the room. She walked down the hallway to the bathroom. She pushed the door shut, put down the lid on the toilet and sat down to wait. She didn't need to pee. Five minutes later, she heard footsteps on the carpet and a light tap on the door. She stood and opened it; Michael Gasca walked into the bathroom.

"William Stoughton?" she said with a smirk. "Where did you come up with that ridiculous name?"

Michael Gasca smiled back. "A name is a name is a name, right?"

They spoke in whispers pausing every few moment to listen to the silent house. "Whatever you say, boss."

Michael Gasca had hired Vanessa for this job nearly two years earlier with simple instructions: Make Trevor Deale fall in love. Gasca had flown Vanessa down to Oklahoma, set her up in an apartment, bought her a car, and with help from a local contact, got her enrolled as a part-time student at the University of Oklahoma. She joined Trevor's criminal justice class three days into the semester.

Michael Gasca had had reservations about choosing Vanessa for this task and even Roscoe had worried that it might backfire.

"She's a bitch," Roscoe had warned.

"I know," Gasca agreed.

"I mean a first-class, to-the-core bitch," Roscoe explained, as if Michael Gasca had forgotten the personality of a woman they'd known most of their lives. Vanessa had been twenty-five at the time, a couple of years older than Gasca and Roscoe, but she was easily young enough to pass as a college student.

"I know she's a bitch," Gasca said. "But she's also off-the-charts beautiful."

Roscoe couldn't argue with that. Vanessa was the most physically attractive woman he'd ever seen. But he also knew that she was walking proof of the aphorism, beauty is only skin deep. For Roscoe, the rotten-ness that lived just below the surface completely spoiled Vanessa's looks.

"She's pretty," Roscoe said shaking his head, "but I don't know. . ."

"How many times have we worked with her?" Gasca had asked.

Roscoe let out a weary breath. Again, he couldn't argue with her track record. They'd used Vanessa half a dozen times, and she always delivered. She'd get close to a guy, show him some cleavage, hang on his arm, have sex with him, and within a week control him as if the blowjob she'd given had sucked the brain right out of his head.

"Those were all gamblers," Roscoe argued. "This kid's a different target."

"That's why we're gonna develop a Plan B, just in case," Michael Gasca had said. Plan A was a kidnapping scheme. Vanessa Patterson would earn a hundred and fifty thousand dollars to become Trevor Deale's girlfriend, then fiancée, then wife. When the time was right, Vanessa would leave her superstar husband and make a phone call. She'd tell him that she'd been kidnapped. Gasca would snatch the phone out of her hand and tell Trevor what he wanted while Vanessa screamed in the background as if she were being tortured.

"The brilliance of this plan," Gasca had explained to Roscoe, "is that if we pull the trigger at the right time, Trevor will be completely at our mercy. He'll do whatever he needs to do to save his beautiful wife, and we'll avoid the logistical and legal risks of staging an actual kidnapping."

Michael Gasca had never been to prison, and he had no desire to ever live behind bars. He'd planned his move on the NFL cautiously, taking careful measure of the laws he would break. If he got caught, he wanted to negotiate with the FBI, not some local district attorney. He believed he'd fare better with federal authorities.

"You don't have a ring," he said quietly, holding Vanessa's hand.

Vanessa looked guilty. "Believe me, I've been trying, but he's resisting me."

"You were supposed to have control of him by now."

"I do." Vanessa had never met a man like Trevor Deale. With most men, the hard work was done the moment she gave them her full attention, but somehow Trevor seemed immune to her charms. "I'll come through when the time is right."

"This is important," Michael Gasca said. "I need you to be honest with me. If you feel like he's slipping away, you need to let me know. We can't have him falling out of love with you at the wrong time."

"He's not slipping away," Vanessa said. "I've got him."

Michael Gasca studied her for a long moment then stepped forward and pressed his mouth against hers. He untied her robe and leaned back to admire her. "Very nice."

"Why thank you." Vanessa took his hand and put it on her breast. They kissed passionately for three or four minutes. Finally, Gasca broke it off.

Vanessa pouted. "No fair."

"Stay focused," Michael Gasca said. "We're almost there." He opened the door and walked back to his bedroom.

Vanessa checked herself in the mirror. She waited a few minutes, then opened the bathroom door and move down the hall toward the kitchen. A small bulb over the stove gave her enough light to maneuver. She opened the refrigerator, hoping to find some bottled water; she didn't know if it was safe to drink from the local supply. She found only sodas and beer in the fridge. Vanessa sighed. She opened a few cabinet doors and filled a glass from the tap. She turned on the overhead light and held the glass up in front of her, studying the water. She bought it up to her nose and took a sniff.

"The water's fine," Kathy Deale said from the doorway.

Vanessa nearly dropped the glass. She collected herself as Trevor's mother walked out of the darkened living room. Kathy had a thick cotton robe cinched around her.

"I know," Vanessa said finally, taking a small sip. She wondered if Kathy Deale had seen or heard her and Michael Gasca while they were in the bathroom. "It was just dark, and I wasn't sure if...you know..."

Kathy smiled patiently. "You didn't grow up out in the country?"

"No," Vanessa said. "I'm a city girl."

Kathy opened the cabinet, pulled down another glass, and glanced at Vanessa briefly before turning on the faucet. The girl was clearly naked under the thin silk robe, and Kathy thought Jim might have a heart attack if he saw her like this.

"Would you like some hot tea?" Kathy said.

Vanessa thought boiling was just what the water needed, but filling a pot and waiting for it would take time, and she didn't want to be stuck in the kitchen with Trevor's mother.

"No, I just wanted to get a quick sip and get back to bed." She stretched and yawned theatrically as if to prove her fatigue.

"Listen," Kathy said, stepping forward and laying a maternal hand on Vanessa's arm, "I don't think you and I got off to the best start."

"No, I guess not," Vanessa agreed. She was still holding the water, but after the first obligatory sip, which had tasted like the sockets on a nine-volt battery, she hadn't taken another. She wanted to set the glass on the counter and run back to her room.

"Do you mind if I ask you a question?" Kathy said.

Vanessa minded very much, but what could she say? "Sure."

"Why are you with Trevor?" They both knew that Trevor was not the sort of man who would ordinarily attract a woman like Vanessa.

"Because I love him."

"Really?" There was so much sarcasm wrapped up in that word that Vanessa was tempted to slap Kathy across the face.

"I truly love him," Vanessa said, barely containing her anger, "ever since I first met him." She realized with a start that she was telling the truth. She'd taken this assignment at the request of Michael Gasca, but as she'd gotten to know Trevor Deale, she'd fallen for him. She'd never known a man who was quite as decent as Trevor.

Kathy set her glass on the counter and crossed her arms, and Vanessa watched her carefully, wondering if she might be preparing to fight, then realizing, with great relief, that she could follow Kathy's lead and set down her glass as well. But before she got it to the counter, Kathy asked another question.

"What do you love about him?"

That caught Vanessa off guard. She thought for a moment, then raised the glass to her lips and took a big swallow. She was suddenly quite thirsty, and the water, coppery or not, was needed to lubricate the words that would come out of her mouth next. "Well," she started. She didn't know what to say. She'd served up so much criticism about Trevor's looks, habits, personality quirks, and, most of all, his refusal to propose marriage, that it took a moment to recall his good qualities. "He's a very kind man," she said finally. "And very talented."

"He's also nice and rich," Kathy said with a knowing grin.

"Yes."

"Somehow I just don't see you sticking with a guy just because he's nice and talented."

Vanessa crossed her arms. "Why do you think your son is with someone like me?"

"Because you're beautiful, you have a perfect body, and you're probably great in the sack."

"Do you think he loves me?"

Kathy took her time answering. "He probably thinks he does."

"You know why he chose me?"

"Why?"

"Because he *could*." Vanessa let that sit between them for a good long while. "Trevor isn't out looking for some dowdy, delicate wallflower who grew up in the country like he did. He's a talented, famous, rich football player so he can catch prettier girls. But just because he can get someone prettier doesn't mean he's not sincere about loving her. He can love a pretty girl just as easily as he can love an average-looking girl."

"I suppose so," Kathy conceded.

"And I can love a rich man just as easily as I can love a poor man. I know you think I'm just using him for his money, and I won't argue about that. Of course his wealth is part of the attraction, but at the same time we both know that my beauty is part of his attraction to me. There's nothing wrong with that, but it's not all we have. We laugh together, and play together, and when we make love it's truly beautiful. When he's out on the field throwing the ball, I feel so proud because I know he's worked really hard to get where he is."

"I know," Kathy said softly, "I feel the same way when I watch him. It's hard to believe my little boy has turned into a man." They stood in comfortable silence for a long while. "Vanessa," Kathy said eventually, "I'm sorry. It's not my place to stick my nose into your relationship. You shouldn't have to explain yourself to me."

Vanessa smiled. "That's okay. I can understand why you're protective of him. He's lucky to have a mother like you."

The two women shared a long hug.

"Thank you," Kathy said.

"Is the tea offer is still open?" Vanessa asked. "I'd love a cup."

26

Trevor woke just as the sun touched the blinds. He stretched and turned his head to the side, cracking his neck. Vanessa snored delicately beside him. He kissed her on the forehead and climbed out of bed. It was a couple of minutes before 6 AM. He pulled on a pair of jeans and a T-shirt and slipped out of the room. He grabbed an apple as he passed through the kitchen and eased out the back door. The sun was cresting the horizon, spilling reddish golden rays over the farmland. He stood on the back porch, took a deep breath, and stared at his former home. The old shack sat behind and to the left of the new house; the two structures were positioned like a pair of planes flying in formation.

The shack was still standing because his mother had refused to let the construction crew destroy it.

"That's where we come from!" she had exclaimed. "I'll be damned if we're gonna forget!"

Trevor knew that letting go of the old house would be like letting go of an old friend. For all its failings, that dilapidated shack had protected them for many years. When the time was right, they'd have a farewell party and lovingly pull the house apart, board by board.

Trevor walked across the yard and pushed open the front door, which didn't creak despite its age. The wood floors were bare, and Trevor thought the living room looked smaller without furniture. He took three strides into the room and purposely stepped on a spot in the floor that had always produced a squeal. As expected, the wood sang, and Trevor smiled. This was his home. Every nook and cranny held a memory. He understood his mother's attachment.

Though it looked like a wreck, the house was solid. When the contractor applied for the permit on the new house, Hank Peterson from the county had questioned the prudence of leaving the old structure in place.

"It'll be an eyesore," he'd complained.

"It's been an eyesore for twenty years, Hank," Kathy Deale replied. "What the hell difference does it make now?"

"But then it was necessary. You don't need it anymore. It oughta get leveled before some kids come out here and get hurt."

"It ain't coming down, Hank."

She stared at him until he walked back to his car and drove away.

Hank checked with the zoning board and discovered that no rules prohibited having two houses on Kathy's plot, and since the shack passed an inspection by an engineer, there was nothing Hank could do.

Standing inside watching sunlight creep through tiny cracks in the walls and roof, Trevor wondered how long the house would last. Being empty seemed to have accelerated the aging process. He sat down facing an empty corner in the living room and recalled one of his most vivid memories in the house: Christmas when he was ten years old.

That year, Trevor, Mandy, and his mother had huddled in front of the tree wearing three layers of clothing with every blanket they owned thrown on top of them. Kathy Deale sat on one side; Trevor sat on the other, and they squeezed Mandy between them to keep her warm. Trevor looked out the window and saw snow drifting down. He knew that soon the moisture would worm through the roof, collect in the attic, and drip through tiny cracks in the ceiling. They'd get out all of their pots, pans, and buckets and position them on the wood floor, but they had a couple of hours; the snow had just started.

Mandy's teeth chattered and small plumes of smoke marked her breath. She was six going on seven, but she didn't look that old. She had a frail, thin frame and a neck that barely looked strong enough to hold up her head. Her cheeks were sunken, her teeth had gaps and her eyes seemed too large for her face. Trevor pulled the top blanket a little closer to her chin, and she smiled up at him with twinkling eyes.

"Thank you, Mr. Blanket Puller Upper!" She giggled; her voice echoed off the cold walls.

Trevor couldn't help giggling with her. She jabbed him in the side, and he moaned in mock agony and jabbed her back—but gently. She seemed too fragile for jabbing.

Trevor remembered his mother smiling at them, sniffling and wiping her nose with a handkerchief. That winter, she'd been sick for months, but she couldn't go to the doctor. They'd had neither insurance nor money. Trevor had a feeling that his mother was suffering the effects of malnutrition. Every time they sat down to eat, she pushed all the food to her kids. She'd nibble off Mandy's plate because the girl always left a bite or two as if she understood, even at her young age, how desperately they lived. Trevor always planned to save some food for his mother. He'd look at his plate of runny stew and think that he'd take just a few bites then let his mother have the rest, but when the first spoonful hit his lips, he'd forget his promise and eat with an urgency that embarrassed him once the plate stood empty.

"Did you get enough?" his mother always asked when he finished. She'd look at him with so much love in her eyes that he almost allowed himself to believe that she wasn't hungry. Some nights Trevor's stomach growled and he wanted to tell her that no, he hadn't had enough, because he knew she would let him have whatever remained on Amanda's plate.

On those nights, Trevor stared at the small heap of food in front of his little sister, and his stomach lurched with real shame.

"I'm stuffed," he'd say. He tried not to watch as Amanda pushed her plate over to his mother.

Only one present was under the tree that year. Trevor had wrapped it in newspaper and put it there just a few hours earlier. The holidays always hit them hard because Amanda still believed in Santa Claus. They had a battered black-and-white television in the corner, and Kathy Deale encouraged her kids to watch it every day. She wanted them to see what the world had to offer. She wanted them to understand that the squalor around them shouldn't constrict their dreams.

"You can be doctors or lawyers and live in big houses and drive fancy cars," she often said. "You can travel to the places you see on TV. You can do anything you want to do."

Ironically, the bruised television was the source of Mandy's Christmas angst. She knew they were poor, but the TV had taught her that

Christmas brought magic. On Christmas Eve, Santa Claus visited every home, delivered presents to every child, and lifted even the poorest families out of their meager lives for a day. Trevor thought God was playing a cruel joke on his little sister. He tried to explain to her that there was no Santa Claus, but she held on to the belief with such desperation that he never brought it up again.

Instead, he and his mother explained that Santa Claus couldn't get into their house because their chimney was blocked. Kathy Deale promised to get it cleaned out as soon as she had the money, and Mandy seemed to accept this.

She knew the present under the tree was for her her, and she knew that Trevor had made it.

"Maybe next year we'll get the chimney cleaned out," Mandy said.

"Yep," Trevor coughed. The optimism in her voice made him shake with rage. "Maybe next year."

"Can I open my gift now?" she said, looking up at her mother with wide eyes.

Her mother sniffled and said, "Of course, honey."

"What could it be? What could it be?" She gripped it with both hands and shook it. The newspaper wrapping crinkled, but nothing inside moved. She smelled it and put it to her ear. "It's wooden," she whispered, looking at Trevor with mischievous eyes.

He nodded and smiled at her. He'd whittled a figurine. It hadn't started off as a gift for his sister. At first, hacking at a stick helped to vent his frustrations. When their well heaved its last load, Trevor didn't panic. He just sat on the back porch and jabbed his blade into the flesh of the wood and sliced away big chunks until he felt better. When the power company shut down their heat at the start of winter, he spent hours tugging his knife through the wood. Eventually, he decided to carve an angel in a long robe staring up at the heavens and give it to Mandy for Christmas. But he had little talent as an artist, and when he finished, the strip of wood didn't look like an angel. It had a thick bottom, a narrow top and two oddly shaped lumps on its back. He almost didn't give it to her because he thought it was ridiculous. It looked more like a salt shaker than an angel. But she had it in her hands now, hidden beneath a yellowed sheet of newsprint.

Mandy unwrapped the present with care, revealing it an inch at a time. She stared at the figurine for a long time. Trevor wanted to snatch it out of her hands and throw it into the snow. At ten years old, he knew the hard pain of impotence. He could do nothing to improve their situation and even his attempt to bring a little joy by carving a gift for his six-year-old sister had failed.

"It's an angel," Amanda said.

Trevor started crying. Heavy, heaving sobs pushed out of his chest and tears ran down his cheeks. He was so angry and so happy and so sad all at the same time. Kathy Deale reached over and hugged him tight.

Amanda kissed him on the cheek and raised the angel to his lips so that he could give it a kiss.

▪ ▪ ▪

Trevor wiped the memory from his moist eyes and rose from the floor. He walked across the living room and out in the sunlight. He shut the door and stood a hand pressed against it for a long time.

"Good-bye, old house," he said solemnly.

The smell of bacon drifted out of new house and Trevor's empty stomach grumbled. He looked at his watch and was surprised to see that it was nearly 8:30. He'd been daydreaming for more than two and a half hours. He walked across the yard and stood at the back door for a moment watching Kathy, Mandy, Nancy, and Vanessa hustle about the kitchen. The four women he loved most in the world were all together.

"Smells good in here," he said.

"Well there you are," Kathy Deale said, raising her cheek to accept his kiss. "I figured you went for a walk."

"I was just out back," Trevor said. He moved on to kiss his Aunt Nancy's cheek before doing the same with his little sister.

"Remembering?" Mandy said.

"Yeah," Trevor said.

Kathy used a fork to turn the bacon. "There are some good memories out there."

"And some bad ones," Nancy said.

"Yeah," Trevor agreed. "Some bad ones, too."

"But they're our memories," Kathy said. "Good and bad, they're all part of who we are."

"But now we've got eggs, hash browns, bacon, sausage, biscuits, and pancakes to make some new memories," Vanessa said. Trevor leaned down to kiss her on the lips. Her eyes glittered with real excitement, and Trevor smiled at her wondering what had happened to put her in such a good mood.

"You ladies need any help in here?" he said.

"The person who needs help," Nancy said, nodding toward the living room, "is William."

"The boys are too terrified to come into the kitchen," Kathy said. "They think they'll grow breasts if they help us prepare a meal."

"Jim's out there," Nancy said, "with a beer in his hand this early in the morning like some kind of alcoholic, and he's talking William's ears off. You might outta go save the poor boy."

27

Roscoe Evans thought Michael Gasca had gone too far this time. Gasca had sent Roscoe to Missouri in Mr. Kinneson's jet with very specific instructions, which Roscoe had followed to the letter despite his personal misgivings. Roscoe trailed Walter Darrow, a wide receiver and punt returner for the Kansas City Chiefs.

Walter Darrow pulled into the parking structure at the Missouri National Bank, and Roscoe followed him in, muttering angrily under his breath.

"What if I don't wanna do that?" Roscoe had said when Gasca told him the assignment.

"You have to."

"But what if I don't want to?"

Michael Gasca had looked at his life-long friend carefully. "You've never been squeamish before."

"You've never asked me to do anything like this before," Roscoe rumbled.

Gasca had sighed. "Believe me, if there was any other way to make it work, then we'd do that, but you know how carefully I study these situations. I know this is the only way to properly motivate Walter Darrow. So as much as you dislike it, I need you to do exactly what I've asked you to do."

Roscoe had reluctantly boarded the plane to Missouri and checked into a nondescript hotel in the heart of the city. He had called the number Gasca had given him and met with a guy who had a camera, a case full of film, and no questions. For three days, Roscoe and the little cameraman had sneaked from place to place snapping photos. Afterward, Roscoe tailed Walter Darrow waiting for an opportunity to ask a favor.

Walter Darrow climbed out of his Mercedes and walked across the parking structure into the bank. Roscoe drove past him, up one level, then muscled his way out of the Town Car slowly. He walked back down the ramp and leaned against a concrete pillar. While he waited for Darrow to exit the bank, Roscoe considered the wide array of offenses he'd committed over the years. He'd broken fingers, cracked ribs, choked people, jabbed his meaty fingers into sensitive places, and held men under water. He'd shot one guy in the foot, thrown another off a roof with a rope tied around his ankles, which didn't kill him, but tore a chunk out of his face when he crashed against the side of the building. The most serious injury Roscoe had ever inflicted came when he used a vise to slowly break both bones in a guy's arm. Roscoe had never killed anyone, but he was still young. He assumed that before his career ended, he'd have a long list of homicides to his credit. He didn't look forward to it, but he knew it was inevitable. But his current assignment? Roscoe didn't have the stomach for this kind of work. He'd much rather beat a guy up.

Walter was halfway back to his car when Roscoe stepped out between a Ford Explorer and a Jeep Cherokee and nearly bumped into him.

"Oh shit!" Walter said, jumping back. He looked Roscoe up and down and smiled. "Excuse me brotha, you scared me for a second."

"Sorry about that," Roscoe said, smiling with him. They continued to walk toward Walter's car.

Walter gave Roscoe a top to bottom appraisal. "Man, I gotta tell you, you are one big brotha!"

"Yeah, I know."

"How much you weigh?"

"About three-twenty."

Walter shook his head as if he couldn't believe it. "But you wear it well, man. You ain't sloppy like the Fridge. Remember the Fridge?"

"William 'The Refrigerator' Perry. Of course I remember him."

"He could play ball, but he was sloppy," Walter said. "But you look good, man. Big, solid guy. We could use you on the D-line."

Roscoe smiled. "That's nice of you to say, but I think I'll leave that to the professionals."

"All right man." Walter had reached his car. "Take it easy."

"Actually, I needed to talk to you real quick."

"Oh yeah?" Walter peeked at his watch.

"It's about the game this weekend."

"Yeah?"

"I need you to drop a punt."

Walter studied Roscoe. "You need what?"

"I need you to drop a punt."

Walter got the joke then and laughed. "Man, you're a piece of work!" He was still laughing as he opened his car door.

Roscoe laughed along with him. His voice echoed off the concrete walls. Then Roscoe did what Gasca had asked him to do. He handed Walter a manila envelope.

"What's this?"

Roscoe shrugged. He'd prefer to give the guy a too-tight bear hug or grab him real hard where his chest met his underarm and not let go until Walter agreed to do what he'd been asked to do. Now that he was looking at Walter, Roscoe was convinced that a little physical persuasion might go a long way. But Gasca's instructions had been very specific. Walter Darrow had to get the envelope.

"Something for you to see," Roscoe said.

"Maybe I don't wanna see it."

Roscoe thought this might turn out okay. If Walter refused to open the envelope, he could tell Gasca he tried, but it didn't work. But Roscoe knew he couldn't give up until he gave it a good solid effort.

Reluctantly, he said, "Open it. I promise, it's something you want to see."

Walter eased open the top of the envelope and pulled out a stack of photos. "What the hell?" he said. His legs wouldn't hold him anymore. He sank into the driver's seat.

"The first time you go back inside your own twenty, you need to drop the punt," Roscoe said quietly. "Don't make it obvious. Just take your eyes off it, let it hit your chest and then the ground."

"Stay away from her!" Walter said. His eyes filled with tears.

"Listen Walter, this ain't my style," Roscoe said. "I don't want to hurt your daughter, but the guy I work for wants this pretty bad, and I gotta do what he tells me to do. That means, if you want to protect her, you need to drop one this weekend."

Walter slowly shuffled through the photos again. There was a shot of his wife and his four-year-old daughter, Mykayla, at a grocery store with Roscoe standing in line behind them. There was a picture of Mykayla at home on the front porch with Roscoe walking toward her. And the final picture—the most obscene picture—showed Mykayla asleep in her bed with Roscoe looking down at her peaceful face.

"What have you done to her?" Walter was crying openly now. How could he protect his family if a guy like Roscoe could waltz into his daughter's bedroom without attracting the attention of the neighborhood rent-a-cops, setting off the home security system or waking his two Rotweilers?

"We haven't done anything to her," Roscoe assured him, gently pulling the photos out of his hands. "Mykayla's just fine, and she'll stay that way if you come through for me on Sunday. I know you'll do the right thing." Roscoe walked away then, leaving Walter sitting in his car crying pitifully.

■　■　■

"You do it?" Michael Gasca asked when Roscoe called.

"Yeah, but I'm telling you we didn't need to do it that way. I looked this cat in the eye. There's a lot of things I could have done to persuade him."

"It had to be done, Roscoe. When you see the game on Sunday you'll understand why."

"Yeah?" Roscoe didn't sound convinced.

28

Steven Oquist turned to Jerry Powers on the Stallions' sideline and raised his eyebrows theatrically. Jerry nodded; his big cowboy hat bobbed back and forth. The NFL Security officers knew that they finally might have something to work with. The Chiefs' punt returner, Walter Darrow, was standing on his own fifteen-yard line trying to field a punt, but when the ball arrived, it went right between his arms, careened awkwardly into a crowd of players. The play looked so foolish it would certainly make its way onto an NFL bloopers reel, but for Steven Oquist it was a signal that Walter Darrow was ripe for an NFL Security investigation.

It might have been an innocent miscue, but there had been an awful lot of miscues that had benefited the Stallions lately. When Oquist saw Darrow's face on the Jumbotron, he saw the expression of a man hoping his performance was good enough to satisfy someone.

Finally, Oquist had something to work with. He'd present everything he had to Ken Parsley in New York. Surely the Corpulent Copulator would have to authorize contact with Darrow to get a feel for what had happened. Oquist could do it soft. Just go in and talk to the guy, make sure everything was okay without spooking him. If someone had made threats against him, Darrow might be happy that NFL Security had noticed his performance and sought him out.

Later in the first half, Walter Darrow dropped another punt, this one clanging gracelessly off his facemask and skittering toward his own goal line. Oquist let out a sigh. This didn't look good. He knew Michael Gasca's style, and he knew that whatever Gasca did to manipulate the outcomes of these games was subtle. He kept it nice and quiet by compelling guys to make routine errors in routine situations. Two pitifully botched punts in one game was not subtle. The commentators in the booth were surely talking about Walter Darrow; they probably had their stat guys trying to figure out how many times Darrow has done this in the past. ESPN would show these lowlights on *SportsCenter*, and the big ballsy voice of HBO's *Inside the NFL* would intone that the Chiefs watched their playoff hopes ricochet into a stampede of Stallions. Two dropped punts were worse for Kansas City than one, but Oquist knew he'd have a tougher time selling two fumbles to C.C.

When Walter Darrow muffed a third punt in the second half, Oquist released a long, weary sigh. The Chiefs' coaches took Darrow out of the game. For the final two punts of the contest, the Chiefs played without a return man, putting eleven men on the line of scrimmage and letting the ball roll to a stop.

"It looked like we might've had something there in the first quarter," Powers drawled.

"Yeah, it looked good," he agreed. Everyone at NFL Security knew that players worked under tremendous pressure, and many of them suffered from high levels of performance anxiety. The players all managed their nerves in different ways. Some had pre-game rituals to chase away the demons, others used their faith in God and others had overlarge egos that insulated them from their own humanity. Most players used a combination of all three to handle the money, scrutiny, expectations, and judgment that came with the job. They loved the praise that followed their great plays. For many players, seeing themselves on *SportsCenter* was better than sex.

But they all feared the scrutiny that chased down their mistakes. A dropped pass would be replayed over and over in slow motion. Analysts would use telestrators to reveal to the audience the embarrassing details of every miscue. The play would be broadcast on *SportsCenter* every hour from 3 AM to 10 AM then again at 5 PM and 6 PM, again at 10 PM, 11 PM, and midnight. All the other cable programs would take a shot—*Inside the NFL, NFL Today, NFL Tonight, NFL Countdown*, the *Jim Rome Show*, the *Best Damn Sports Show Period*, etc., etc., etc. The mistake would be the subject of talk radio programs where every wannabe jock in the city would weigh in with his assessment of the player and why the team ought to trade him for someone who could actually play.

Roughly twenty percent of the players in the NFL relied on sports psychologists to help them handle the pressure. NFL Security had learned over the years that most players feared being embarrassed on the field more than they feared death.

"Think about it in terms of impotence," a lecturing psychologist had explained during an NFL Security training session. "Every man at some point in his life suffers temporary impotence. Imagine you're a twenty-two-year-old stud, and you're in bed for the first time with a particular beautiful woman. But no matter what you do, you cannot get an erection. It's bad enough when it happens with a long-term girlfriend or your wife, but the feeling is the worst when it happens the very first time you sleep with a woman. It can cause psychological impotence that can last for years. That's the kind of embarrassment that many players feel on the field. They'll do anything to avoid that humiliation."

These lectures provided important information for NFL Security officers. There were several barriers standing in the way of anyone who wanted to fix an NFL game. First, the players made so much money it was difficult to entice them with cash. Second, the threat of being caught and kicked out of the league would keep most players from taking a chance even if the money was right, and third, the fear of embarrassment was generally too profound to overcome. A player wouldn't purposely make a mistake on the field any more than a young man would purposely make himself lose his erection.

Oquist watched Walter Darrow and thought the thing that separated the great players from the average players was mental toughness. The great ones bounced back from their mistakes. Darrow dropped a punt and couldn't forget about it, so he ended up having the worst day of his career.

Roscoe Evans pointed a meaty finger at the television screen. "That ain't subtle," he complained, "That's three muffed punts in one game."

"Yep," Gasca agreed.

"So now the Stallions are up by twenty-four points and the league's gonna know something's up."

"Probably not," Gasca said. "Everyone has a shitty day, Roscoe."

"Yeah, but when it's that bad, the league has to investigate, right?"

"I doubt it," Gasca said. "No one would expect a fix to be that obvious."

Suddenly, Roscoe understood it. "This is what you were expecting all along."

"Of course, Roscoe. The man's four-year-old daughter was threatened; that's gotta take the shine right off his focus. That's why I made you give him the pictures. I know you didn't like it, and frankly, neither did I. But we needed a little bit more than a nudge. We needed a guarantee, and Walter Darrow having a horrible day was just the ticket."

29

Every NFL football team arranged itself into a loose hierarchy of players formed on the axes of age, ability, salary, position, and race; the San Antonio Stallions were no different. Trevor Deale, Martin McNeil, and Michael Robinson had become great friends during training camp by virtue of their talent (they got the most air time on *SportsCenter*), their contracts (a combined thirty million dollars per season was nearly half of the Stallions salary cap), and their celebrity (they were in the ranks of the Kobe Bryants, Jeff Gordons, and Ken Griffey Juniors of the sports world). They hung out together because they had more in common with each other than they had with anyone else on the Stallions roster. Recently, Trevor had moved Caleb Alexander into the guesthouse on his estate, and he'd brought the embattled running back into their clique.

After the Green Bay game, Trevor had virtually adopted Caleb Alexander. Michael Gasca had wired five hundred thousand dollars into Caleb's account as promised, and Trevor had called his various managers—attorney, agent, broker, and financial planner—and put them to work taming Caleb's complex financial situation. They immediately sold off the automobiles, real estate, artwork, furniture, and jewelry. They reduced Caleb's physical assets to his clothing and a BMW 528i. He lost money on many of the sales, but the combined agreement of the various experts was that the quick losses were ultimately less expensive than the cash flow drain Caleb would endure if he held on to the property. He was a millionaire again, recovering nearly seven hundred thousand dollars in cash to go with the half million Michael Gasca had returned. He moved into Trevor's guesthouse, which was by far the smallest home he'd lived in since signing his first NFL contract, but he appreciated the space.

It shouldn't have surprised Caleb—it did—but his friends slid away as easily as his assets. He'd had an entourage of eight to twenty people partying with him, laughing at his jokes, treating him like a king. But as he scaled back his spending, his entourage shrank until it no longer existed. Trevor Deale's commitment meant more to Caleb than he could express.

Martin and Robo had accepted Caleb into their small group with little comment. They'd never actively disliked Caleb; they had simply never known him.

"Just don't come around us smelling like ten gallons of get-back," Robo had said. When Caleb looked confused, Robo explained, "That means wash your ass every day. Take a shower, brush your teeth, don't be smelling like no crack ho."

The four players were sitting in a small boat bobbing gently on Medina Lake about two hundred yards from shore and about half a mile from the nearest other fishermen. Robo was dressed as if he were a model in an outdoorsman's fashion show—albeit the hip-hop version of the outdoorsman. He wore designer combat fatigues, a crewneck sweater, a vest by Tommy Hilfiger, and a Kangol hat with fishing hooks and lures artfully embedded in it.

"You know who was at my house last night?" Robo said.

"Who?" Caleb asked.

Martin said, "Don't you get tired of being with so many different women?" Martin had been married seven years, and he couldn't imagine living the single life again. Robo's dating schedule sounded exhausting.

"Tired?" Robo said. "Nigga is you crazy?"

"Who was at your house last night?" Caleb asked again.

"Marguerite."

"The Luscious Latin Lady?"

"Triple L. That's the one."

"What were y'all doing?" Caleb asked with a wink.

"Playing Trivial Pursuit."

"Come on."

"Seriously." Robo nudged Caleb. "Pants are trivial. Shirts are trivial. Bras are trivial. Panties are trivial. . ."

"You're crazy," Martin laughed.

"But you know what the best part is?"

"What's that?" Trevor asked, smiling.

"She always wants to gamble for sexual favors."

"Sounds nice," Caleb said.

"But I don't let her off easy. Last night we were watching this movie and I said the black dude was gonna get killed first. She didn't believe me, so I made a bet with her for ten you-daddys."

"Don't tell me you got her saying 'you-daddys'?" Caleb said enviously.

"She didn't know what it was at first, but then I explained it, and she just laughed and said okay. But she had no idea what she was getting into."

"Did you win?" Caleb asked.

"Of course I won. That nigga dropped before they finished the opening credits."

"When did you make her pay up?" Martin said.

"I used the first one on the elevator coming down this morning." Robo lived in a swanky loft apartment. "There were three people on the elevator with us, and I said, 'Who rocked your world last night, girl?' All three of them looked at us and then looked away fast. One guy started smiling. Marguerite was embarrassed and she shook her head like she wasn't gonna deliver. But I just gave her that look, and she knew she had to pay up. So all soft and sexy she said, '*You, daddy.*' Boy, I nearly lost my mind!"

Caleb and Martin high-fived each other, laughing hard; Trevor smiled. "Then," Robo continued, "when I dropped her at her apartment, she was walking into the building and there were a bunch of people cruising by on the sidewalk. I lowered the window and yelled at her, 'Who's the *man*?' and everyone on the sidewalk looked over at me. She smiled this time, then said it all sweet, dragging it out, singing it, '*Youuuu, daddddy.*'"

"Boy, I can just see her saying it." Caleb shook his head. "That girl is too damned fine."

"So you still got eight left?" Martin said.

"She's gonna be you-daddying me all over the city."

"You gonna deliver you-mamas to her if she ever beats you at something?" Trevor asked.

"She'll never beat me at anything," Robo said. "We only bet on TV stuff, and I'm the master of TV. Speaking of which, Caleb, I coulda sworn I saw you mom on the tube last night."

"Oh yeah?" Caleb said doubtfully.

"She was doing a Strychnine commercial, talking about 'just a pinch between my cheek and gums gives me great poison taste.'"

"Screw you," Caleb said with good humor.

"Man, this is great," said Martin. "I haven't been fishing since I was a kid." In fact, the last time Martin had been in or around any body of water he was twelve years old and he'd nearly drowned in the Cantarka River. He had reluctantly accepted the invitation to go fishing with the boys, and he was pleasantly surprised to discover that he wasn't scared.

"Everything is great right now," said Robo, "and that's what's got me nervous. It's almost too damn good. We're 11–3, heading for the playoffs and we haven't lost a game since Repanshek took over."

"You're unbelievable," said Martin. "When we were kids didn't we all dream about being in the NFL, playing for a winning team, getting into the playoffs, and winning the Super Bowl? Well, here we are. We're living extremely large."

"Hey, don't get me wrong," said Robo. "I ain't exactly crying myself to sleep at night. It just seems unreal to me that things could be going so well for us this season."

"You're trippin', man," Martin said.

"It does seem a little strange, doesn't it?" Trevor said after a moment. He shared a meaningful look with Caleb. He and Caleb had talked about this a few days before, and Trevor thought it was time to bring Martin and Robo up to speed.

"*You* seem strange to me, QB," Martin said.

"Seriously," Trevor said. "It almost seems as if we've been steered through the season."

"You mean like predestination?" said Robo.

"Sort of."

"So what are you saying?" Martin asked. "That we're like meat puppets? Someone's pulling our strings and we're just doing a cosmic jitterbug? We end up wherever the strings take us?"

"Let Miss Cleo tell ya what she tinks ya got comin'," said Robo, affecting a Jamaican accent. "Me tinks dat if ya call dis numba now, and pays me tree-ninety-nine a minute, I tell ya if you gonna win da sooper bowl."

The four men laughed.

"It just seems that every now and then we're a little luckier than we should be," Trevor said.

"Better to be lucky than good," Martin said.

"True dat," said Robo.

"Actually," Trevor said, "Martin, remember the conversation we had on the plane before the Green Bay game?"

Martin shook his head. "Nope."

"That Mr. Kinneson might fire Coach Starnes that weekend."

"Oh, yeah, yeah. I remember."

"Well, after the game, Caleb told me that someone had pressured him to fumble."

They all looked at Caleb.

"Who?" said Robo.

"A guy named Michael Gasca," Caleb said. "He was my hookup for charter planes and other stuff that I needed—"

"Wanted," Trevor corrected.

"Right. Other things that I wanted." Caleb had been seeing a psychologist who helped him understand the difference between his wants and needs. "But he'd skimmed off a bunch of my money and put it into an account in the Cayman Islands. He said that if I wanted to get it back, I'd have to drop the ball."

"I remember that fumble," Martin said. "I never would have guessed that it wasn't legit."

"It was legit," Caleb said desperately. "I'd made up my mind that I wasn't going to fumble, but then when I got hit, I dropped it on accident." The ironic shame of it still burned inside of him.

"So let me get this straight," Robo said with his characteristic smirk. "The Stallions are paying you a lot of money to hold on to the football, and this other guy offered you some money to fumble it. You didn't purposely deliver for either side, yet you got paid by both?"

"Yes," Caleb said quietly.

Robo shook his head. "That's a hell of a racket, kid."

"I didn't mean to fumble."

"What's your slippery ass made of, Olestra?" Robo asked.

"The point is," Trevor said, "that Michael Gasca wanted him to fumble so that Coach Starnes could be fired, which he was."

"That was some show," Robo said, grinning. "Kinneson standing up in the aisle, leaning drunkenly from side to side. 'Hey Starnes,'" Robo said, imitating Kinneson's voice, "'you ain't got to go home, but you gotta get the hell up out of here. Carry yo ass! You're fired!'"

"They said in the paper that Starnes's contract allowed him to be fired because he was below .500," Martin said.

"And I heard Mr. Kinneson talking on the phone to someone about that earlier in the week before that game," Trevor said.

"I remember you saying that," Martin said.

"So you think this same guy has been helping us win during the season?" Robo said.

"Yes," Trevor said. "And I think Mr. Kinneson is involved in it."

"Who else knows about this?" Robo said.

"Just the four of us," Trevor said.

"Maybe we should tell your mom," Robo said to Trevor. "She could chase down the bad guy and bite him on the leg with her sharp little bat teeth. Seriously y'all, I saw Trevor's mom on an infomercial the other night. She was racing against a guy with a circular saw to see who could cut through a block of wood the fastest. All she had was her teeth, but she beat him by four seconds."

Trevor ignored Robo.

Martin said, "Do you think we should tell someone?"

"I think the league already knows something isn't right," Trevor said.

"What makes you say that?" Martin asked.

"Who's our NFL Security officer?"

"Jerry Powers," Trevor's three friends said in unison.

"The overweight cowboy," Robo added, "who terrifies every horse in the county."

"So who's the dude that's been hanging with Jerry the past few weeks?"

They didn't know the answer.

"I think he's a security officer from some other city," Trevor said. "Somehow they know what's going on."

"Have you talked to them about your fumble?" Martin asked

Caleb shook his head. "I was afraid to."

"What I think we should do for the moment," Trevor said, "is keep our eyes open. We're eventually gonna talk to them, but not until the right time. I want to try to understand what's happening here. In the meantime, we're winning games, so there's no real hurry."

Martin said, "So we just keep playing and keep assuming that we're just getting lucky?"

"If we didn't have luck," Robo said, "we could end up in a rowboat out in the middle of a fishless lake in the middle of the great state of Texas. Oh my God! That's where we are! Does that mean our luck has run out?" Robo stood up in the boat and raised his arms toward the heavens. "Yes, Miss Cleo, I hear you. It's all very clear to me now. I see that I was meant to be here! It was foretold, by she who has foretold everything for tree-ninety-nine a minute!"

"Sit down," Martin urged. "You're rocking the boat."

"Miss Cleo! Should I go along for the ride or should I rock da boat?"

"Sit your ass down," Caleb said. He reached up to grab Robo.

"Miss Cleo tells me that we're all meant to be here." He swayed from side to side. "We were cast upon the great sea of life to answer one, and only one, great cosmic question. What's the question, Miss Cleo?…what's that?…she says…and I can just barely hear her…but the question is…will ya sink…or…will ya…swim?" He tipped the boat over, and all four men spilled into the lake whooping and hollering as their gear tumbled in after them.

"We're swimming!" Robo said. "Thank God Almighty, we're swimming!"

"Not for long," Martin said. "Let's drown this jerk."

30

"Good thing they don't have to win 'em all," Roscoe Evans said over lunch at Pappadeaux's. He was working his way through a huge bowl of gumbo.

"Who?" Michael Gasca asked.

"The Stallions." Roscoe slurped down another big bite.

"Why is that a good thing?" Gasca said. He cut into a big slab of salmon. They were both famished, because they'd missed breakfast and hadn't had time for lunch until well into the afternoon.

"Ain't no way the Stallions can beat the Raiders this weekend, even if they have your help."

"I've got a plan."

"Any plan you come up with that would work," Roscoe paused to shove a piece of cornbread into his mouth, "would be too obvious. And if it was too..." he searched for the right word.

"Subtle?" Gasca offered.

"Yeah, if it's too subtle then it ain't gonna work. They need something dramatic this week."

"I think I can make it happen."

"Not this time."

"What do you want to put on it?"

"I got the usual hundred bucks."

"Naw. I'm tired of taking your money."

"What then?"

Michael Gasca thought about it for a while as they continued to gulp down their food. It was nearly 4 P.M. and the restaurant had drifted into a lull of activity with a full staff of servers milling around with little work to do. A couple in the corner giggled as they fed each other dessert. They both were wearing wedding bands, and Gasca assumed they were having an affair; it would be nice if husbands and wives met in the middle of the afternoon to flirt, but he knew that was unlikely. A bartender was washing glasses, filling the ice container and restocking the coolers with beer. Servers in matching green and black uniforms wiped down tables and hovered in the back, waiting for the dinner rush.

"I tell you what," Gasca said, "if the Stallions win—"

"They won't."

"But if they do, then you gotta spend one whole day next week dressed in full team regalia."

"Regalia?"

"You know. Hat, jersey, jacket, pennant. The works."

"What team?" Roscoe was an Eagles fan down to the bottom of his oversized feet. He'd happily wear their gear.

"The Stallions, you idiot."

"I'd have to wear a Stallions jersey?" Roscoe's face screwed up as if he smelled something bad.

"Not just a jersey. Everything. As much Stallions stuff as we can get on your body."

Roscoe thought about it for a minute, then shrugged. "Which day?"

"I don't know yet, but I get to pick it."

Roscoe figured it didn't matter. The Stallions were seventeen-point underdogs to the Raiders. Michael Gasca couldn't possibly work his magic on this one. "Gonna take a lot more than a nudge," he warned.

"Maybe," Gasca said.

"What do I get if the Stallions lose?" Roscoe wondered.

"What do you want?"

"Only thing that interests me is cash."

"How much?"

"Ten grand."

"That's a lot of cash."

"I'm real interested."

Gasca shrugged. "All right."

Roscoe rubbed his hands together. "How you gonna do it?"

"You ever heard of Nathan Campbell?"

"Offensive guard for the Raiders?"

"That's the one."

"What about him?"

"He's how I'm gonna do it," Michael Gasca said.

31

Nathan Campbell sucked bourbon straight from the bottle. His disheveled black hair hung down in front of his eyes, but the blur in his vision was mostly from the booze. Flames licked the air in the fireplace, providing the only light in the darkened house. A nickel-plated nine-millimeter pistol lay on the table in front of him.

Nathan considered his options. When the guy came to the door, Nathan could open it and start shooting, blowing the hell out of the guy before he had a chance to react. But that would be complicated. The neighbors would hear the shots and call the police. When the cops arrived, there would be a dead man on his front porch, and Nathan would be standing there with a gun in his hand. He'd go to prison for murder.

Maybe Nathan should let the guy come in and then shoot him. Whomever they sent would definitely have a gun on him. So someone would hear the shots and call the cops, but when they arrived, Nathan could claim that it had been self-defense.

Nathan took another sip of bourbon. He held the bottle up and looked at it for a long moment. He didn't want to drink too much. He needed to think straight and shoot straight—if it came to that. No, he realized, self-defense wouldn't work either. Whoever they sent over to talk to him was connected to a whole lot of other people. Even if the cops cleared him, there would be someone else coming to kill him. He'd be dead by the end of the week.

He stared at the gun on the table. He could put the barrel in his mouth and pull the trigger. It would be painless, over in an instant. No one would miss him.

Most of the world thought Nathan Campbell had it made. He had a moderately handsome face with dark features and a crooked, boyish grin. His bulky two-hundred-and-eighty-pound frame looked good in a suit, and his job as an undersized twelve-year lineman in the NFL had to be the easiest gig in America.

He hadn't touched the field on offense since early last season when the Raiders' starting right guard, Mark Andrews, went down with a sprained knee. After a couple of weeks of action, Andrews was healthy, and Nathan was back on the sideline, where he could collect his fat paycheck without fear of injury.

But someone was coming over to talk to him about his gambling problem, which had first blossomed when he signed his rookie contract in the NFL a dozen years ago. From the start, Nathan had loved going to Vegas and throwing down big money. He liked the way people looked at him. At first, he had played mostly blackjack, but then he'd graduated to craps, then poker, then sports of all types. He bet on college football and basketball, NBA basketball, NHL hockey, MLB baseball, but he stayed away from the NFL.

"That's where they'd get me," Nathan had often told himself. "Bet on the league, and they'll get you." He'd lived with this prohibition for most of his career, but the temptation eventually proved to be too great. Seven years ago he'd met a guy in San Francisco who acted as a middleman for his NFL wagers.

Predictably, a couple of years ago, things had turned bad for Nathan. He'd run up a tab in Las Vegas that was too large for even his hefty NFL paychecks to cover. He was earning more than seven hundred and fifty thousand dollars a year with the Raiders, but it wouldn't cover everything he owed the casinos. So he had borrowed money to repay the gambling debt. A home equity loan and cash advances on his credit cards got him to the top of the mountain. He had walked into the various casinos in Las Vegas, and in each a security guard met him before he was a hundred feet into the building. He was led past grandmothers sitting hypnotized in front of brightly lit slot machines, past somber players at blackjack tables, past ebullient rollers crowded around high-walled craps pits, past the false enthusiasm of croupiers raking in money from the foolish and the dumb, past the crowds at the buffet, past the smoke-filled bars, past the sports books, past the cash machines where losers went to forage for more luck, past the money cage, past everything that Nathan had enjoyed so many times in the past, through a barely marked door to a meeting room, where frowning men in designer suits waited for him.

In each casino, Nathan pulled a cashier's check out of his pocket and presented it with a flourish. Weeks ago, the debt had seemed insurmountable, but he'd found a solution to the problem, and he landed back in good standing with the casinos.

The men in dark suits had smiled then. They had clapped him on the back, said they'd been worried about him. They offered him drinks, and invited him to sit down. Before Nathan left each casino, they had thanked him for repaying the debt and, as a show of appreciation, they restored his rating. He frequented five casinos and each promised him comped airfare, suites and drinks, and each gave him a one-hundred-thousand-dollar credit limit. Nathan Campbell had walked out of the casinos, past the common people at the common tables, with the firm assurance that he was anything but common. He was a special player and a special man, and he was back on top. Nathan planned to use the casinos' credit against them. He'd win some serious cash, and then they'd be the ones scrambling to find a way to repay *him*. He'd show them. Nathan had flown back to Oakland in first class—an upgrade compliments of one of the casinos.

It didn't take long to get back to where he started. Soon Nathan owed more money than he could pay, but this time he could not borrow the money. Nathan had called his contact in San Francisco for advice, and had been connected to a man who would loan him some money without demanding any payments until the following season when Nathan had income again. So Nathan Campbell repaid the casinos, and in another show of gratitude, they upped his credit limit once again. But Nathan stayed away from Las Vegas, because he knew that he couldn't stiff the man who had loaned him the money. He had to keep things under control and wait until he repaid the debt. Unfortunately, that commitment didn't last. He had used his casino credit to finance back-room poker, and lost even more money. When football season rolled around, Nathan Campbell couldn't repay the money he'd borrowed. So the loan was sold to another guy, who sold it to yet another guy; and it was the last guy who was now on his way to the house.

Nathan knew enough about these people to know that they were like prehistoric creatures—handy with tools, but not so good at talking. The last time someone had come to visit him it was an entourage of six men. They had wrestled Nathan into a chair and tied him up. They knew they couldn't do too much physical damage because Nathan still had to be able to play on Sunday. But one of the guys took a syringe loaded with heroin and injected it into Nathan's arm.

"This is gonna leave traces in your system for a couple of weeks," the man with the needle said. "If you get pegged for a random drug test, you'll be screwed. You'll come up positive and get a four-game suspension."

The NFL urinalysis program could not be beaten. The league used the best possible procedures, starting with random selection. Every player and every coach got tested once a year during training camp, and that became a baseline sample. Once the season started, a computer in the league's front office randomly selected five names per team each week.

Some players got picked five or six times in a season, others only two or three times, but a player never knew when his turn would come. He'd walk into the building one day and the drug-test doctor would call him into a room and demand a sample on the spot. The procedure did not allow a time lag between notification and delivery. The player would drop his shorts and pee into a cup, and the doctor would sit in a chair two feet in front of him watching intently to ensure that the urine came directly out of his body. A bag of someone else's piss strapped to a player's groin wouldn't work because the doctor would spot it. Even someone else's piss injected directly into the player's bladder wouldn't work because the player never knew when he would be tested. If he injected clean urine into his bladder but didn't get tapped for the test until hours later, dirty urine would mix with the clean stuff and ruin it. Upon notification, the player had to fill a six-ounce cup, but the doctor would take whatever he could produce on the spot. If it was less than six ounces, the player could go drink some water and come back in an hour to finish it, but then he'd be peeing into a fresh cup, and once the samples reached the lab, the contents of the two cups would be compared. Any difference between the two would be interpreted as a positive test.

If the player couldn't deliver even a partial sample, then he was not permitted to leave the room until he could. If he refused to wait, he'd get slapped with a positive test.

"If you're late making a payment again," the men said after untying Nathan and letting him slump to the floor in the initial stages of heroin-induced euphoria, "we're gonna pump you full of something that'll stay in your system a lot longer and guarantee that you get caught and suspended. If you don't pay us after that, we'll OD your ass."

Nathan thought they were crazy. Playing in the NFL was the only way he could make the money to repay the loan, yet they were willing to put his football career in jeopardy. But despite the risk they were taking, the men weren't stupid. They knew they had to threaten something important to Nathan, and they knew that football was the only thing he cared about.

Nathan looked at his watch and sipped bourbon. Maybe he'd shoot whoever came to the door, then commit suicide. He'd get the satisfaction of showing them that they couldn't mess with him, but he wouldn't have to endure prison or retribution.

■ ■ ■

"You think we should knock on the front door?" Roscoe Evans asked. His voice resonated with low timbre in the Town Car. He had the seat pushed back as far as it would go, and he was leaning on the center armrest as if it were a mean dog that had to be held down.

"Might get shot," Michael Gasca said. He was using the map light to study the directions to Nathan Campbell's house. "Guy's probably feeling desperate."

Roscoe fiddled with the radio, but it wouldn't hold a signal. "Second floor window's probably the best way to go," he said after a few minutes.

"Oh yeah? How are you gonna get up there?"

Roscoe took notice of that *you*. If somebody had to climb up a rain gutter to get to an upstairs window, it was going to be Roscoe—all seven feet, three hundred and twenty pounds of him.

"I picked up a ladder today."

Gasca looked in the backseat and didn't see anything. If it fit in the trunk, it couldn't be much more than a small stepladder. "Did you bring it with you?"

"It's collapsible. It's in the trunk."

Michael Gasca sat back and thought about the collapsible ladder in the trunk. "Is it a rope ladder?"

"Metal."

"There's a collapsible *metal* ladder in the trunk?"

"Yep."

"And it's strong enough to hold up your big ass?"

Michael Gasca wanted to make sure that no technicality—like a weight limit—would turn him into the guinea pig going up the ladder.

"The salesman said it was good up to four hundred pounds."

"Oh," Gasca said, relieved. "But you might make too much noise going up the side of a house on a folding ladder. What if the thing starts to collapse while you're on it?"

"I might make a little noise, but it won't be enough to worry about."

"When have you ever made a *little* noise?"

"I'll make a *little* noise when I squeeze your skull in my hand," Roscoe rumbled.

They drove in silence for a while. Finally, Gasca said, "You're not gonna go easy on this guy just because you don't want to lose the bet, are you?"

"You think I wanna get shot?"

"I don't know. You're pretty competitive, Roscoe. You might take a bullet or two if it means you'll win the bet."

"I ain't never been shot, and I don't intend to get shot tonight."

"I'm just saying…"

"Well, say no more."

They parked three blocks from Nathan Campbell's house and stepped out of the Town Car. It was a clear, cloudless night, with bright stars glittering overhead. Roscoe walked to the back of the vehicle and opened the trunk.

"You got two of them?" Michael Gasca said. A pair of ladders sat side by side, and each looked like a giant metal billfold. Hinges stuck out at the top of each rail, and the top halves lay folded down on the bottom halves.

"It's two, but it's really one," Roscoe said. "You unfold them they snap together." Fully extended, the two halves stretched to eighteen feet, but in the folded position, each was only four-and-a-half feet long. They walked casually down the street; Roscoe carried one half of the ladder easily in his right hand. Michael Gasca had both arms wrapped around the other half. Every few feet he stopped to change positions. The ladder clanged like a buoy in choppy waters.

"You're gonna wake up the whole neighborhood," Roscoe said. "You want me to help you with that?"

"I've got it," Michael Gasca said through gritted teeth. He adjusted his hands; the ladder clanged again.

Roscoe shook his head and started walking; he wore a small, victorious smile. They went to the back of Nathan's house and Gasca sat down on the grass to watch as Roscoe carefully unfolded the ladder and snap the two halves together. When it was fully extended, Roscoe laid it gently against the side of the house.

"You wanna go first?" Roscoe whispered.

Michael Gasca had an *are-you-crazy* look on his face. He still didn't believe the ladder would hold up.

"I don't know how to open the window."

"It's pretty simple. I could tell you how to do it."

"Roscoe…"

"Yeah?" All innocent.

"Get your ass up there."

They both smiled then, and Roscoe put a meaty foot on the bottom rung.

"Hold it steady," he said. Roscoe brought his other foot off the ground. Now his full weight was on the ladder. It seemed fine. He took another cautious step up with his right foot and brought his left up to meet it. On each rung, he paused and felt the ladder beneath him. It took more than three minutes to go halfway.

"You sure are slow," Gasca whispered.

Roscoe stopped climbing and looked down. "I'm trying to be quiet," he whispered back.

Eventually, Roscoe had climbed as high as he dared to go. There were three more rungs, but if he stepped up again, he wouldn't have anything to hold on to. He pulled a retractable razor blade out of his pocket and stretched his arm high above him to cut the screen along the edges. The big rectangle fell out of its frame and drifted silently to the lawn below. He reached back into his pocket and came out with a suction-cup mounted glasscutter. To do this part, he'd have to go higher on the ladder. He looked down at Gasca. Roscoe's whisper wouldn't carry that far, so he pointed upward; Gasca nodded and firmed his grip.

Roscoe brought his right foot up and the ladder groaned. He stood still for a long moment, and then moved his left foot up. He brought his left hand across his body and hooked his fingers along the rim of the frame that held the screen. With his right hand, he affixed the suction cup to the window about a foot below the lock. He slowly turned a crank in a complete circle around the suction cup. Roscoe pressed in, and a circle of glass broke free with a light clinking sound. He pushed up his sleeve and carefully reached through the hole and unlocked the window. He pushed the glass up, then when he was sure he had a firm grip on the frame, he took the last two steps up the ladder and muscled himself through the window. He eased softly onto the carpeted floor of a guest room. Roscoe looked back out the window and saw Michael Gasca making his way up the ladder. Once Gasca neared the top, Roscoe reached down and pulled him into the room.

They went to the top of the stairs, listened for a minute and started down. Roscoe took the lead, and Gasca followed close behind. The stairs dropped them near the kitchen. They stood still and listened, then moved toward the front of the house. Roscoe had a gun in his hand.

■　■　■

Nathan Campbell looked at his watch. They'd said they'd be coming by between 9 PM and 1 AM Gave him a window, like they were the cable company. It was nearly 11, and still no one had pulled up in front of his house. He took another long pull from the bourbon. He thought about turning on some music, but he decided that would be a bad idea. He needed silence so he could hear them. He needed darkness to give him the advantage. Only the fireplace illuminated the living room. He still didn't know what he would do, but he knew he couldn't sit by and let them hurt him.

■ ■ ■

Roscoe Evans peeked around a corner and saw Nathan in the living room. The player was facing the front door. A gun sat on the table in front of him. Roscoe made a careful survey of the room looking for mirrors, windows, or a glass on a table. Anything that might throw a reflection and give Nathan advance warning. The bottle of liquor on the table might give off a glint, but Roscoe didn't expect too much trouble.

He walked around the corner. In just a few steps, he had the muzzle of his gun jammed into the crook of Nathan Campbell's neck.

Nathan jumped and screamed, but Roscoe held him firmly in place.

"We're here," Roscoe said.

Michael Gasca walked around in front of Nathan and picked up the gun on the table. He sat down in a chair on the other side of the room.

"Hi, Nathan," he said.

Nathan was hyperventilating.

Roscoe removed the gun from his neck, walked around the couch, and sat down next to Nathan with the gun pointed at him.

"Let's not waste time," Gasca said.

Nathan's breathing slowed down, but his heart continued to race. He knew they had come to cause him pain, and he didn't see the need to rush right to it.

"You've been betting on NFL games," Michael Gasca said.

Whoa! Nathan's mouth fell open. He didn't think anyone knew about that.

Michael Gasca had known about Nathan Campbell's gambling habits for a few years, but there hadn't been any use for the information due to Uncle Nick's prohibition on fixing games. Now it was time to ask a favor.

Nathan reached for the bourbon, and Roscoe let him go for it. He tipped the bottom toward the ceiling and sucked for a long time; the fiery liquid scalded his throat. Finally, he lowered the bottle and wiped his mouth. "I promise I'll get you the money if I can just have a little bit more time." He wondered if they would leave his gun when they left. He might just shoot himself after all.

Michael Gasca seemed to consider this for a while. Nathan waited anxiously as the silence grew. Finally, Gasca said to Roscoe, "What do you think? Is he being straight with us?"

Roscoe looked at Nathan and shook his head. "He lied before. Only reason we're here is 'cause he lied."

"That's true," Gasca said.

"But I'm not lying this time," Nathan pleaded. He looked over at Roscoe again; the sheer power of the man scared him. "I swear I can get the money."

"How you gonna get it?" Gasca asked.

"I gotta lot of rich teammates who might—"

"Nobody's gonna loan you what you need because they all know that you're a gambling junkie," Gasca said. "You might get someone to loan you ten or twenty grand, but you owe hundreds of thousands. Who's gonna loan you that much cash?"

"I can round it up," Nathan said with false conviction. "I promise you."

Roscoe shook his head. "We might as well kill him while we're here. If we gotta come back, it's just gonna be harder."

Michael Gasca nodded.

"I swear," Nathan begged.

"You wouldn't fall for the second-floor window thing again, would you?" Roscoe asked.

Nathan didn't know how to answer that.

"Next time, we'd have to come in the front door, and we'd be dead before we rang the doorbell," Roscoe said.

"No," Nathan said, "I wouldn't do that. I just had the gun for protection. To feel better. I wasn't actually planning to use it."

Michael Gasca said, "How much time do you need?"

Air dumped out of Nathan's mouth in a thick cough. He didn't realize that he'd been holding his breath. "Two weeks."

"You'll have all the money in two weeks?"

"Well…not all of it, but enough to catch up."

Gasca pulled a slip of paper out of his pocket looked at it for a moment. "That's twenty-five thousand today. In two weeks you're gonna be up to forty thousand. You think you can come up with forty grand by then?"

"I can do that," Nathan insisted. "I can definitely do that."

Roscoe shook his head. "The man ain't gonna raise the money."

"He might," Gasca said.

"If he doesn't, you're climbin' the ladder."

Michael Gasca paused. "If I give you a break, Nathan, will you do me a favor?"

"Anything!"

"Can you spray the ball around on Sunday?"

The sudden turn in the conversation surprised Nathan. "When you say spray it around, you mean—"

"How long have you been a deep snapper?"

"All my life," Nathan said. "Started in junior high school, then high school, college, and now the NFL."

"So you've delivered the ball to a lot of punters and holders for field goals?"

"Yes."

"So you know what they hate. You know the hardest spots for them."

"Yes, I do," Nathan said eagerly. He saw how he could help them; he saw his way out of this mess.

"So on Sunday, you could spray it around. Don't make it obvious. I don't want someone sitting in the stands to look and say, 'Damn, that Nathan sure is having a bad game,' but I want your kickers to be talking to you on the sideline. You can screw them up without anyone ever knowing what's happening, can't you?"

"The coaches will know when they watch the film," Nathan warned.

"Yeah, but they won't really know, will they? You've had games where you were a little off target, so they'll just chalk it up as another bad day."

"Right," Nathan said. "Just a bad day."

"Not a horrible day," Michael Gasca reminded him. "Nothing too extreme."

"Just a little off the mark," Nathan winked. He was having a good time now. "When I come on the field it'll be 4th and fixed."

Roscoe laughed and turned to Michael Gasca. "We should have talked to Nathan a long time ago."

"I'll be watching," Gasca said. "If I like what I see, then we'll be back to talk to you in a couple of weeks. If I don't like what I see…" He left the threat hanging.

"No worries, man," Nathan said. "I'll take care of it."

Roscoe Evans and Michael Gasca walked out the front door; they took Nathan's gun with them.

■ ■ ■

The Raiders' first punt came midway through the first quarter. Nathan Campbell trotted on to the field with the rest of the special teams unit and took his position over the ball. He'd survived as a backup offensive lineman making three-quarters of a million dollars per season because he was one of the best deep snappers in the league. He delivered the ball with the precision of a machine. When a center looks between his legs at a punter, he has to throw the ball fifteen yards behind him. Years of practical experience—and thousands of blocked punts—had taught NFL teams that the ball had to leave the punter's foot less than two seconds after the center snapped it. Scouts with stopwatches timed the snap-to-kick of every punter in the league. If a team creeped up to two-point-two seconds, the scouts calculated that every fifth punt would get blocked, and more than eighty percent of those blocked punts would lead to points for the other team.

Nathan Campbell was a much-coveted deep snapper because he consumed only seven-tenths of a second throwing the ball back to the punter. Roughly eighteen times out of twenty, he put the ball in the sweet spot—hip high on the kicking-leg side of the punter. On the other two times out of twenty, he missed that mark by only a fraction. On field goals, his accuracy was even better. The snap had to cover only half the distance—seven-and-a-half yards—and virtually every time, Nathan gave the ball exactly six and a half rotations, delivering it twelve inches off the ground directly over the "spot" with the laces pointed up. Day after day, week after week, month after month, year after year, Nathan snapped with unerring consistency. If the wind blew hard from one side, he'd purposely aim slightly outside the target and let the ball drift back in. Into a headwind, he put more velocity on the snap, and he took pace off when he had the wind at his back. He snapped with the subtle finesse of a great baseball pitcher gently guiding the ball to different parts of the strike zone.

The Raiders punter, Roberto Mejia, was a second-year player out of Clemson. He had grown up in Guadalajara, Mexico, where his passion for soccer had developed into a talent for kicking a football. He'd played with many deep snappers over the years, but none had the refined talent of Nathan Campbell.

After the cadence was called for the first punt of the game, Nathan tensed his fingers and fired the ball back between his legs with a grunt. Instead of placing his right hand on the laces, as he normally would, Nathan had rotated the ball slightly so his fingers lay on the flat part of the ball. Instead of the zippy seven-tenths of a second the snap normally took, the ball lumbered back to Roberto with an elapsed time of just over a second. Roberto reacted like a batter swinging too early at a change-up. He started striding forward before he caught the ball, which threw off his rhythm and forced him to shorten his second step, which meant he dropped the ball a little too close to his body and had to compensate as he swung his foot up to meet it. The ball arched into the air with a severe wobble. The punt returner raced forward for the low kick and advanced the ball another ten yards before the Raiders coverage unit tackled him.

Roberto muttered as he walked off the field. On the sideline he charged up to Nathan. "What happened?"

"What do you mean?" Nathan asked innocently.

"Why was the snap so slow?"

"Was it slow?"

"It was slower than a damn mule!"

"My bad. I'll put some more zip on it next time." Nathan walked away to the Gatorade table, suppressing a smile.

■ ■ ■

"Well, that didn't work," Roscoe said. As usual they were sitting on their rented couch watching the game on their rented television.

226 ■ Reggie Rivers

"It worked perfectly," Gasca replied.

"Not if you were expecting the punt to get blocked."

"I wasn't expecting the punt to get blocked."

"So what were you expecting?"

"I was expecting Roberto to have a bad punt. The kick went only thirty-two yards."

"Thirty-two yards is still a long way."

"Yeah, but Roberto has been averaging nearly forty-seven yards a punt with five seconds of hang time and little or no return yards."

"Forty-seven or thirty-two, it ain't gonna be enough of a difference for the Stallions to beat the Raiders."

"We shaved fifteen yards off the punt, plus the returner gained ten, so the net was only twenty-two yards of field position. What Nathan has done has given the Stallions a better chance to score."

■ ■ ■

Every kicker, holder, and snapper knows that field goals are all about the laces. Yes, the kicker had to have a strong leg, and yes, the holder had to get the ball on the right spot, but the laces pointed in the wrong direction could ruin a perfect kick. When the kicker nodded his head, the holder flashed his hand, and the center shot the ball back. The kicker started forward at the moment of the snap, knowing that the ball would be caught and placed just a hair before his foot swung through the contact area. When executed correctly, the entire exercise took between 1.25 and 1.35 seconds—any faster than that and the kick would be too rushed to be routinely accurate; any slower and it would get blocked. The laces affected the flight of the football in the same way that laces affected the flight of a baseball. A pitcher could make a baseball curve, slide, wobble, or just zoom straight depending on how the laces left his fingers. A kicked football tended to taper in the direction of the laces, so the holder took great care to point the laces at the target.

In addition to his duties as punter, Roberto Mejia was the Raiders' holder for field goals. He trotted onto the field sweating more than he normally did during a game. He'd punted three times thus far, and each snap had been an adventure. After the first lethargic ball, Nathan sent the second snap smoking as if it had been shot out of a cannon. The young punter had handled it, but screamed with wide-eyed anger when he saw Nathan on the sideline. The snap had scared him, but more frightening was Nathan's apparent indifference. On the third punt, Roberto prepared for the worst, and Nathan didn't disappoint. He put the ball about a foot to Roberto's left—no-man's land for a right-footed punter. Roberto had to jump to his left to catch the snap, then reset himself to get the ball off. It resulted in his worst punt of the day—a twenty-seven-yard shank off the side of his foot that bounced back toward him when it hit the ground.

Now, as the Raiders lined up for a forty-two-yard field goal attempt, Roberto crouched on one knee and looked at Nathan with pure terror in his eyes. Nathan looked back between his legs and winked. Roberto flashed his hand, and Nathan shot the ball to the worst possible location. It came straight at Roberto's right ear. In order to control the laces, the holder needed to see the ball as it came into his hands. A snap, high and right, brought Roberto's left arm up across his face to make the catch, blocking his view of the ball as it traveled the final few inches into his hand. It also twisted him a little too far to the right, which meant he had to hustle to get the ball back around and hope that he was close to the spot. Roberto muscled the ball down, but he spotted the ball about three inches too far forward, and he didn't spin the laces to the front. Both he and the kicker watched as the ball sailed into the air and passed six feet outside the right upright. Nathan's errant snap had cost the Raiders three points, but to the television audience, it looked as if the kicker just pushed it wide right.

"What the hell are you doing?" Roberto demanded on the sideline.

Nathan shrugged. "I just don't have it today, man. I'm sorry."

"You're doing it on purpose!"

"I've had some bad snaps, man. It happens."

Roberto stormed away, but he kept a careful eye on Nathan for the rest of the afternoon.

32

Michael Gasca smiled at his friend in the driver's seat and decided that his entire life had been leading up to this moment.

"It just doesn't get any better than this," Gasca laughed.

Roscoe Evans looked at himself in the rearview mirror and grimaced. He was wearing a green San Antonio Stallions baseball cap, a XXXL Stallions Starter jacket with the team's name and logo emblazoned on the back, Stallions sweatpants, Stallions wristbands, Stallions socks, and a couple of Stallions logo stickers on his enormous tennis shoes. Roscoe frowned as he wheeled the Town Car through the streets of San Antonio.

Gasca chuckled. "You look like the Jolly Green Giant with a sponsorship deal." With the help of Nathan Campbell, the Stallions had beaten the Oakland Raiders 24–20, and Gasca was taking great delight in collecting his winnings.

Roscoe snorted.

Gasca patted him on the shoulder and said, "Relax. It's just for one day."

Roscoe wondered why he continued to make bets with Gasca when he never seemed to win.

"It's a sign of addiction," Gasca had said once. "When you keep doing something that brings you nothing but bad fortune, it means you're an addict."

They weaved through a maze of construction zones in San Antonio. It seemed that every street in the city was under repair.

"You gonna drink that?" Roscoe asked.

Michael Gasca was holding a latte from Starbucks in front of him as if it were nitroglycerin. "You purposely trying to hit every pothole?"

"Now you're blaming me for the roads?" Roscoe whipped the wheel to avoid a particularly bad wound in the pavement. The Town Car responded quickly, dancing around the obstacle as if the car were an extension of Roscoe.

"I'm just saying you could take a little more care," Gasca said. "I've got a hot drink in my hand."

"Should be drinking Dr. Pepper like me." Roscoe twisted the cap off of his soda and took a long swig. "Ah, that's good." He put the cap back on. "Looks like it's smooth for the next little stretch, you could get a sip in."

Michael Gasca eased the cup up to his lips but just as he started to drink, Roscoe turned the wheel sharply to the left. Coffee spilled out of the little hole in the lid, soaking through the front of Gasca's shirt and scalding his skin.

"Goddammit, Roscoe!"

The big man laughed, filling the car with his low rumble. "Remember," Roscoe said between guffaws, "senior year in high school and you spilled that Big Gulp?"

"That wasn't a spill." Gasca laughed with him. "Your clumsy ass reached over to grab it and accidentally knocked it out of my hand."

"That wasn't an accident."

"You kidding me?" Michael Gasca looked over at his friend and was reminded again that Roscoe was just a big, playful teddy bear.

Roscoe laughed even harder as he confessed to a crime committed more than seven years ago.

"All this time, I gave you the benefit of the doubt and never tried to retaliate."

"It was pretty funny."

"It was pretty *cold.*" Gasca used a napkin to wipe coffee off his shirt. "Now you got me with something hot too, so you've covered all the bases. No need to get me anymore."

Roscoe weaved around rough spots in the road. "So what do we have next?"

"Well," Gasca said, "for a little while, we have to be careful, because I saw Steven Oquist the other day."

"The guy who was always chasin' you in Philly?"

"Yeah, he's been hanging around the Stallions facility quite a bit."

"You think he knows we're fixing the games?" Roscoe said.

Gasca nodded thoughtfully. "He probably knows something's not right, but he can't figure it out yet, 'cause we're not doing the one thing the league expects us to do."

"One thing, huh?"

"Yep."

"What's that?"

"We're not making money off the games."

Roscoe hadn't told Gasca about the bets he'd been placing with the young bookies back in Philly. Roscoe Evans was a frequent gambler, and Gasca knew that. The big man didn't know why his instincts told him to keep his bets on the Stallions a secret, but somehow he knew that Michael Gasca would disapprove. Now Gasca had pointedly stated that the league hadn't caught them because they weren't making money off the games, and Roscoe worried that he might have ruined something.

"So if we were making money off these games what would happen?" He tried to make it sound like a hypothetical rather than a confession.

"That's what Oquist is waiting for."

"Really?" Roscoe had made nearly seventy thousand dollars so far.

"You've heard of the Securities Exchange Commission, the organization that monitors the stock market and catches people for insider trading and other forms of stock manipulation?" Gasca asked.

"Yeah."

"They watch everybody in the market to make sure no one is cheating the system."

"They didn't catch them dudes at Enron," Roscoe pointed out.

Michael Gasca chuckled. "That's actually a perfect example. The SEC can't stop Enron from overvaluing its stock. The SEC can't stop Enron executives from telling their employees that they aren't allowed to sell stock in their 401(k) accounts. They can't stop those same executives from selling off millions of shares of their own stock. But once the company goes bankrupt, the first thing the SEC does is follow the money. They're looking for everyone who cashed in before the company went under. They follow the money, and the money leads them to the perpetrators. NFL Security works the same way. They can't stop someone from trying to fix a game, but they follow the money. If you have a big payday betting on an NFL game, you can be sure that the league, the casinos, and possibly the FBI will take a close look at you. They learn everything they can about you. They find out if you have any connection to the players, coaches, or front-office staff of either team. Was there a particular play, series of plays, officiating calls, or other suspicious circumstances that influenced the outcome of the game? The league asks a lot of questions and generally finds answers. The casino won't pay out until the investigation is completed, so you get a microscope up your ass and chances are you're never gonna get your money."

"So we're keeping the league off our back by not putting down any money on the games?" Roscoe said. Sweat rolled down his face.

"That's right," Gasca said. "We've got a bigger mission to pursue. We're gonna make eleven million dollars off Kinneson, and then we'll have a big pay day by betting on the Super Bowl."

"Listen," Roscoe said, embarrassed. "I might have made a little mistake."

Michael Gasca turned to get a better look at his big friend. "Oh yeah?"

"See, I didn't know we weren't supposed to put anything on these games, so I've been laying down a little bit."

"Serious?"

"Not a lot." Roscoe tried to minimize the damage. "Ten grand a game. I've spread out through a bunch of young bookies."

"How many?"

"How many games or how many bookies?"

Michael Gasca was working hard to keep his patience. "How many bookies?"

"Ten guys each time. I'd get one guy and tell him to spread it around. A thousand bucks apiece."

"Who's the contact?"

"Mickey Uso. You know the kid? Just got started last year, thought I'd give him a shot."

Gasca wondered if this would hurt them. He hadn't told Roscoe not to put any bets down on these games; he had just assumed that his friend would know better. Ordinarily, Michael Gasca was aware of everything that happened in the Philadelphia gambling scene, so he would have discovered Roscoe's bets. But he'd been in San Antonio on this special mission and out of contact. If it was just ten thousand dollars a game, Gasca wouldn't worry, but he didn't know how much extra action Roscoe might have caused. If Roscoe gave a young bookie a thousand dollars on a game, the bookie might think it's a hot tip and put down two or three hundred dollars of his own money. He tells his father or his uncle or a friend about the game, and they throw a few bucks at it too. Pretty soon, there's an extra twenty or thirty thousand chasing all of Roscoe's bets, which would create a tide of unnatural money that someone was bound to notice.

"Did Mickey tell you anything about the action on these games?" Gasca said.

Roscoe shook his head. "I told him this had to be *real quiet*."

That was good, assuming Mickey was scared enough to keep his mouth shut. Gasca worked through it in his head. If the action on one of the games had been off, surely Uncle Nick would have called to alert them. Dominic Sarcassi was the only person in Philadelphia who knew about Gasca's special project. Gasca thought again about Steven Oquist. Something must have drawn the NFL Security officer down to San Antonio.

"Roscoe. . ."

"You don't even have to say it," Roscoe said. "I won't be laying down any more action."

"Good."

33

Steven Oquist knew that he could not continue to obey the Corpulent Copulator's instructions. He'd been chasing Michael Gasca for more than fifteen years, and now, finally, he knew for certain that Gasca and Roscoe Evans were manipulating NFL games. If he could catch them in the act, he would be vindicated. It would prove that he'd been right all along. No one else at NFL Security understood the risk Michael Gasca posed. They all thought Oquist was an obsessed idiot who only had eyes for one threat, and though he'd been promoted to Regional Director, few of his subordinates had respect for him. Oquist knew that would change when he caught Michael Gasca.

But Oquist had been in San Antonio for weeks, and so far, he'd found no direct evidence to implicate Gasca. At the moment, he was standing in the corner of the team's locker room, studying Trevor Deale from a distance. There were more than three dozen reporters, marketing personnel, and front-office staff members milling around, and during the past few weeks, Oquist had become just another face in the crowd. He entered the locker room every day with Jerry Powers, and the two of them chatted together quietly, sometimes joking with a player or two, but Steven Oquist never took his eyes off Trevor Deale. He wanted to talk to the quarterback and find out if anyone had approached him.

But if Oquist spoke to Trevor, and Trevor later called NFL Security to report the conversation, Oquist could lose his job. The Corpulent Copulator's instructions had been very clear. Oquist had no authority to talk to players about potentially fixed games. But Steven Oquist had been ignoring the advice of his superiors for many years, and he wasn't going to let the threat of unemployment keep him from catching Michael Gasca.

Oquist planned to wait until the locker room cleared of all media members before approaching the quarterback, and if that turned out to be too late, then Oquist might lose his opportunity. But he definitely couldn't allow anyone in the media to overhear the conversation.

The minutes ticked by, and Trevor sat in his locker studying his playbook. Occasionally, a reporter interrupted with a quick question to ask on camera. Trevor responded to these requests with something less than typical rookie enthusiasm, but with little of the hostility exhibited by cynical veterans. The director of media relations gave a two-minute warning to the reporters, then counted aloud from thirty seconds—"Thirty seconds! All media must be out in thirty seconds!"—down to zero, by which time all of the reporters had escaped. Oquist walked slowly to Trevor Deale's locker.

"Trevor," he said quietly.

The quarterback looked up and studied Steven Oquist with more interest that the NFL Security officer had expected.

"I'm sorry to bother you while you're studying, but I wanted to talk to you for a minute if I could."

Trevor set his playbook aside. "You've been hanging with Jerry Powers the past few weeks."

"Yes," Oquist said, surprised that Trevor had noticed. "I'm a regional administrator with NFL Security."

"Is Jerry in trouble?"

"No, no. He's doing a great job." Oquist could see the wheels turning in Trevor's head.

"Then the Stallions must be in trouble."

God, this kid was quick, Oquist thought.

"No trouble," Oquist lied.

"How many regional administrators are there?"

"Actually, just one. I just oversee the Northeast Region where the workload is a little heavier."

"You're a long way from the Northeast," Trevor observed.

"True."

"So what's going on?"

Oquist had spent all morning thinking about this conversation, but now that he was standing in front of Trevor Deale he didn't know exactly how to phrase it. Would he panic the quarterback if he told him he thought the kid was in danger? Would he impact Trevor's performance on the field if he told him that members of a crime family might ask him to do something? Would Trevor tell anyone about this conversation? Would word get back to C.C. in New York?

"What I need to talk to you about is a very sensitive matter," Oquist said.

"Does this sensitive matter have something to do with Michael Gasca manipulating our games?"

Steven Oquist blinked a dozen times and didn't breath for a full ten seconds. Finally he said, "I could lose my job for talking to you about this."

Trevor nodded as if he already knew that. "I won't say a word."

"Has Michael Gasca approached you?"

"No." Trevor knew that Michael Gasca had pressured Caleb Alexander to fumble in the Green Bay game, but he didn't expect Gasca to contact him. The criminal seemed to be helping the Stallions win, which meant there was no reason to approach Trevor.

Oquist shrugged. "Your name came up a couple of months ago in a conversation he was having in Philadelphia. Wait a second," Oquist looked around the room and lowered his voice, "if Gasca hasn't contacted you, then how do you know his name? And how do you know that he's manipulating your games?"

"I can't tell you that right now," Trevor said. He didn't want to get Caleb in trouble.

"But Gasca hasn't talked to you?"

"No."

"Is he here in San Antonio?"

"I don't know."

Oquist's heart was racing. This was the closest he'd ever come to direct evidence against Michael Gasca. He pulled a business card out of his pocket and handed it to Trevor.

"If he contacts you," Oquist said, "will you call me?"

Trevor studied the card. It had a Philadelphia address and presumably a Philadelphia phone number. But a local number had been written in ink on the front of the card. Trevor tucked it into his wallet.

"I might know something that could get you pointed in the right direction," Trevor said.

"Yeah?"

Trevor looked around the room, then said quietly: "Jonathan Kinneson."

Steven Oquist scowled and waited for more, but Trevor lowered his eyes back to his playbook.

34

Steven Oquist and Jerry Powers were both dumbfounded. They hadn't even considered the possibility that Jonathan Kinneson had manipulated the games, but if it were true, that would answer some of their questions about the absence of unnatural money. But exactly what did Kinneson stand to gain in all this? Was he really trying to buy a Super Bowl victory?

"We need to figure out how much Kinneson would make if the team went all the way," Oquist said. "We need everything from the gate for each of the playoff games, the value of his local media contracts, bonus structure within the franchise—"

"Plus, he's hoping to get a stadium vote on the ballot for May," Powers said, "and winning the Super Bowl would push that along."

"You check on the numbers, and I'm gonna try to find out if Kinneson has had any contact with Michael Gasca."

■ ■ ■

Steven Oquist walked casually into the lobby of the Tacoma Building. He took the elevator up to the forty-fifth floor, where he encountered the former castle drawbridge that served as the front door to Kinneson Corp. Oquist didn't go into the office; he just checked the corridor for surveillance cameras. Finding none, he let the elevator doors close and returned to the lobby. He asked the woman at the information desk to direct him to the building manager.

The manager of the Tacoma Building was a small pudgy man who worked in a basement office with his name—Clayton Beamon—posted on the door. Clayton took calls about overflowing toilets, burned-out light bulbs, full trashcans, malfunctioning security cards, and anything else a tenant could think of that may or may not actually be Clayton Beamon's responsibility.

Steven Oquist walked into the cramped office, where Clayton was eating a sandwich from a brown paper bag.

"Mr. Beamon?"

"That's me." Clayton didn't stand up or offer his hand. He continued to wolf down his lunch.

"I'm Steven Oquist with NFL Security." He laid a business card on the desk. Beamon looked at it dispassionately, but Oquist could sense a measure of relief overtaking the man. This wasn't a complaint visit. "As you know," Oquist continued, "Jonathan Kinneson is both the president of Kinneson Corp. on your top two floors and the owner of the San Antonio Stallions."

"Yep." Clayton perked up a bit. If this had to do with Mr. Kinneson, he'd take extra care. He didn't want to upset that psychopath.

"Recently, Mr. Kinneson has been threatened by a couple of individuals, and we're trying to determine exactly who they are and who they're affiliated with."

Clayton took a sip of Coke. It all sounded very exciting.

"I was wondering how long you keep the tape from the surveillance cameras in the lobby?"

"It's a continuous loop, two-week system. After that it starts to record over itself. Anything we need to keep longer goes into a safe where it can be stored indefinitely."

"Are the tapes in the building?"

"The two weeks' worth, yes. The indefinite stuff, no. That's with a separate company."

Oquist nodded. "How are the tapes recorded? In real time?"

Beamon shook his head. "Yes and no. They record in real time, but the way it lays down on tape, it's not possible to play it back in real time. It plays back in fast forward."

"So if I wanted to watch a full day's worth of tape it would take me—"

"About an hour."

"How many cameras are there?"

"Four."

"All recording onto different tapes?"

"They all feed onto one tape. On the screen you see quadrants."

"Where do you keep all this?"

"Video room down the hall."

"Could you set me up to review the last couple of weeks of tape?"

"You gotta watch everything?" That sounded like an assignment worse than trying to fill cracks in the molding on the sixteenth floor, which Clayton had to do later that afternoon. "Doesn't Mr. Kinneson know what day they came in?"

"You'd think," Oquist said with a shake of his head as if to say *Mr. Kinneson isn't as smart as everyone thinks*, and Clayton responded with a shake of his own head as if to say, *amen brother*. "The problem is that Kinneson didn't meet with them. They left a note, and Kinneson didn't get it until several days later. The receptionist doesn't remember which day it was either. She just knows it was last week sometime."

"Better get some coffee," Clayton Beamon warned. He led the way down to the small video room, and set Oquist up with a playback monitor.

Steven Oquist watched with a trained eye as the images raced across the screen at high speed. He'd done this with the FBI, studying airport or train station security tapes searching for a suspect in the heavy throng of travelers. The trick, he'd learned, was to know what he was looking for and ignore everything else. His instructor at Quantico had compared it to searching for a set of car keys in a messy house.

"Suppose you're running late," the instructor had said, "and you can't find your keys. When your brain is in that mode, it ignores dishes, towels, knick-knacks, furniture, family members, pets, and anything else that doesn't look like a set of car keys. You're not picking up computer disks and looking at them carefully to see if they might be what you're looking for. You only notice keys. Studying surveillance tape requires that sort of specific concentration. When you know what you're looking for, everything else fades into the background."

Steven Oquist was optimistic that these tapes would yield clues. Years of study in Philadelphia had acquainted him with Michael Gasca's M.O., and he guessed that any meeting Gasca had with Jonathan Kinneson would have happened at his downtown Kinneson Corp. office.

Oquist believed Michael Gasca would have used the location to further reduce Kinneson's options. He knew Gasca would never be foolish enough to go to the Stallions Center, because that would be too overt, and he probably wouldn't go to Kinneson's house, because that would be too private. But the downtown office was crawling with people and security cameras. For Kinneson, inviting Michael Gasca was like hosting a drug deal in his living room. But Steven Oquist suspected that the owner was ignorant of the risk he was taking, and Michael Gasca would have used that to his advantage.

Steven Oquist spotted them in his third hour of study. Six days ago, Michael Gasca and Roscoe Evans had walked right through the lobby, and the crowd had parted in front of them as everyone turned to stare up at Roscoe. They boarded elevator number four, spent half an hour upstairs, then walked back out through the lobby. Unfortunately, there were no cameras on the upper floors, but Oquist knew exactly what to do next. He grabbed the tape out of the recorder, dropped it into a plastic bag, and put it into his briefcase. Clayton Beamon was not in his office when Oquist poked his head in, so he scribbled a quick note of thanks and left it on his desk. He didn't mention that he had taken the tape.

He took the elevator back up to the forty-fifth floor and walked through the oversized door, which swung open with surprising ease. A receptionist with curly red hair greeted him from behind a mahogany desk.

"Welcome to Kinneson Corp.," she said in a crisp, clear, young voice. "How may I help you?" Steven Oquist felt old. She was undoubtedly in her twenties, but she looked about twelve.

"I just have a quick question," Oquist said, handing her one of his business cards. "I'm with NFL Security, and I work for Mr. Kinneson," which was technically a lie but imbued with enough truth to pass. The structure of NFL Security put the officers under the umbrella of the league, so security officers were not employed by the franchises that they investigated; they had loyalty to the *game* not a particular *team*. "What I need to know," Oquist continued, "is if an incredibly large black man has been here recently. This guy would be bigger than anyone you've ever seen."

The receptionist was nodding before he finished the question. "You mean Roscoe?"

Incredible. Oquist looked around. He wondered if he were on a hidden camera show. "Yes, Roscoe Evans."

"He's been here three or four times." She smiled as if Roscoe was a good friend.

"What's your name?" Oquist asked.

"Tracy Watkins." Then she held up a finger and pushed a button on the console in front of her. "Thank you for calling Kinneson Corp. How may I direct your call?" she hesitated a moment, then punched three keys and turned her attention back to Oquist.

"Do you happen to remember the last time he was here, Tracy?" Oquist asked.

"Sure, last week." She reached up and turned the sign-in book to face her and flipped through the pages quickly. She scowled when she didn't see Roscoe's name.

"Maybe the guy who was with him signed in," Oquist suggested.

"That's right," Tracy said. Now that he mentioned it, Roscoe always arrived with another man, who was cute, but honestly, Tracy was so caught up in Roscoe that she couldn't remember his friend's name.

"You mind if I take a look?" Oquist asked.

"Help yourself." Tracy broke away to handle another call.

Steven Oquist turned the pages slowly, running his finger down the names as he went. Ten pages back he found "Michael Gasca." He folded the corner of the page down, and flipped farther back in the book until he discovered three more entries for Michael Gasca.

"They set him up," Oquist realized. "Left us a trail like a neon sign." He shook his head. Michael Gasca must have disliked Jonathan Kinneson just about as much as everyone else who met the owner.

"Tracy," Oquist said after the receptionist connected another call, "do you have a copy machine?"

35

Jerry Powers ambled into the cluttered basement office of Keith Ramsey, a hacker who freelanced for the FBI and a host of other government agencies. Ramsey was reputed to be among the top ten most cunning hackers in the nation, but his ranking couldn't be confirmed because the agencies always had to assume that a few hackers were so talented that no one knew they existed. Keith Ramsey had started young—they all did—and his technique had only gotten more sophisticated when the government decided to pay him to break into places he was forbidden to enter.

"Mornin'," Powers said, his spurs jingling softly as he stepped over paper, food wrappers, and assorted computer parts littering the floor.

"Yes it is," Ramsey said. "What do you need this time?" Ramsey prodded the NSA's server, trying to get past a firewall that had kicked him out after three attempts and sent a nasty little worm out to find him. But he operated through several cutouts and defensive software; the worm couldn't track him down. If it did, a team of agents would kick in his door and race into his basement with guns drawn, and he'd have to explain to them—again—that he was only doing his job and that if they called a particular guy in a particular Washington office, then he'd tell them to put their guns away. The man in Washington would tell them that Keith Ramsey had authorization to breach the server and the only reason the gun-toting officers weren't aware of it was because they weren't authorized to know. Then he'd call a company to come fix his door, and he'd send the bill to the usual address in Washington.

So far Keith Ramsey had learned that the NSA's system was pretty tight, but he knew he'd eventually crack it. When he'd first started working for the government—before they knew just how good he was—they paid him only for breaches. Get in, they said, and we'll pay you to show us how you did it. After he'd burned through the firewalls of an entire alphabet soup of agencies, they'd put him on retainer to spend as much time as he wished trying to penetrate their security. He got paid whether he made it through or not.

"If I needed to see what a particular guy had on his personal computer," Jerry Powers asked, "would you be able to find it?"

Keith Ramsey didn't look up, but he wondered why, after all that he'd done, the spooks always came to him with a fatalistic tone as if they were asking him to fly to the moon and back before lunch.

"You want me to break into one guy's personal computer, and you're wondering if I can do it?"

"He might have two or three computers," Powers said apologetically.

"Oh," Ramsey said with wide eyes. "Well, why didn't you just say so? You had me thinking this was going to be easy."

"So you don't think you can do it?"

"Sit your fat ass down."

Jerry Powers looked around and pushed a stack of files off a chair onto the floor. After he was seated, Keith Ramsey said, "Who are we going after?"

"Jonathan Kinneson."

"Stallions owner?"

"Yeah."

"You breaking me in or am I going in through a phone line?"

"Phone line."

"T-1 connection at the office and dial-up at home?"

"Probably."

"Any other locations?"

"Well, he might have two offices, one at Kinneson Corp. and one at the Stallions Center," Jerry Powers said.

"I'll get everything on the hard drives."

"You can do that?"

Keith Ramsey wondered what Powers thought he was going to do. "Yes, Jerry. I can do that."

"How will you get into his computers?"

Years ago, Keith Ramsey might have refused to explain his strategy, not because he was afraid that someone would steal his techniques, but because he didn't want to waste his time explaining things to people who would never get it. But as he'd grown older—Ramsey was twenty-three now—he'd learned that some of the agency people needed to have the process explained to them so they could explain it to their bosses, which ultimately meant that Keith Ramsey would continue to get paid.

"I'll get on the net and track down all of his addresses, then I'll break into the phone company's computer to find all of his numbers. Then it's just a question of dialing up and crawling in."

"But he might have passwords?"

When he was younger, Keith Ramsey might have kicked out an agent who made a statement like that, but he'd learned patience over the years. "Let me ask you something. You've got a computer at home, don't you?" Ramsey's fingers flew over his keyboard.

"Yes."

"You got a password?" He clicked on the keyboard.

"Yes."

"Is it a family name? A wedding date? A random string of numbers?"

Powers said, "I'm not going to tell you."

"Is your password *Bobbisox3*?"

"Yes!" Powers said, amazed. "How did you know that?"

Keith Ramsey swiveled the screen so that Powers could see the desktop of his home computer. "Is Bobbisox the name of a family pet?"

Powers shook his head. "The first part is my daughter Rebecca's nickname. The second part is name of a cat my mother used to have, and the three is the number of kids I have. How in the hell did you figure that out?"

"Jerry, what you've got to understand is that the NSA has a security system like a bank vault. By comparison, you've got a security system like a peanut shell. I wrote a program that will run through every variation of every word in the English, Spanish, or French languages in less than a minute and a half, including human names, pet names, dates and every conceivable combination. You thought Bobbisox3 was clever, but in the time that you've been sitting here, I broke into the phone company, called your home computer, *and* learned your password."

"So you think you can get into Jonathan Kinneson's computer that easy?"

Keith Ramsey thought Jerry Powers might have suffered a brain injury.

"Is this stuff gonna be used in court or is it just for curiosity?" Ramsey often performed what the FBI called sneak-and-peek searches. He'd break into a guy's computer to take a peek at his schedule or a letter, memo, note, spreadsheet, money program, or anything that would give the feds an idea of what he was up to. Then they'd hope that information would lead them to something they could "discover" legally so that a judge would feel compelled to issue a warrant to search the guy's house, car, or computer where they could legally rediscover all the stuff they'd peeked at. The trick to doing a sneak-and-peek was to make sure that there was no evidence someone could use—for example, the suspect's attorney—to prove that the government had broken the law.

"Strictly curiosity," Jerry Powers said. He wasn't worried about spoiling any evidence for court because this case would never go to trial. The league would handle Jonathan Kinneson.

"That makes it easier," Ramsey said. "What are we looking for?"

"We think he's hired someone to fix some of the Stallions's football games—"

"So we want correspondence, records, wire transfers, that kind of stuff."

"That's right."

"Give me a couple of hours; I'll have a full report."

"Thanks, Ramsey."

"Who do I bill for this?"

"Send it to the usual New York address."

■ ■ ■

Jerry Powers walked back in Keith Ramsey's basement two hours later.

"I've got everything there was to get," Ramsey said. "I got into his computer, pulled up his browser and searched through his history. Most browsers keep about three weeks worth of stuff lined up so parents can check on the sites their kids are surfing, but with a little brute force, you can track down the history from as much as nine months or a year ago. First thing I did was check out all the sites that looked like email providers. He's got two accounts, one with *Yahoo!* and one with *kinnesoncorp.com*. No messages that looked suspicious related to fixing games, but he's got a couple of exchanges with a ticket broker in D.C."

"Really?" Jerry Powers said. That could be worth investigating.

"I cracked the broker's computer and Kinneson is moving about a thousand Super Bowl tickets at two grand apiece."

"Hmpfh," Powers grunted. San Antonio was the host city for the Super Bowl, so Jonathan Kinneson would control eight percent of the total tickets even if his team didn't make the big game.

"In case you're interested, Kinneson's password is *Kilamanjaro*. Nothing really exciting at any of the sites he frequents, but he goes to his investment account quite a bit, which piqued my interest because you wouldn't expect a guy like him to be a day trader. On closer inspection, I discovered that he wasn't trading; he was transferring—so far, six million dollars into an account in the Cayman Islands."

"Who owns the account down there?"

"That I don't know, and we may never know. If I worked at it, I'm sure I could get past the bank's security, but it might not tell us anything. These are numbered accounts and the only information they keep on file is stuff that allows people to access their money. The account holder doesn't give the bank any identifying information. No drivers licenses, no social security numbers, no passports. You want an account? They'll give you a sixteen-digit account number, a fifteen-digit authentication code, and a nine-digit password. As long as you have those numbers, then you're the owner of the account. No names are ever recorded."

"So we don't know who he's sending the money to."

"He could be transferring it to himself," Keith Ramsey said. "But that's unlikely. Usually, if you're hiding money in an offshore account, you find a way to get it there before you pay taxes on it. You don't do what Kinneson is doing, which is transfer it from your regular account where the bank is required to report it to the IRS. So he's not trying to shield the money from taxes. He's just paying someone, but he's not sophisticated enough to disguise the transfers. He clearly hasn't gotten his financial guys involved, so this is personal. And for six million dollars, it must be worth a lot to him."

"Anything else in there?"

"That's it."

"Thanks, Ramsey."

"You want me to keep an eye on him?"

"Kinneson? Yeah. Do you have time to check in on him every few days?"

"Piece of cake. I put the Green Lantern on him."

Powers shook his head. "What's that?"

"Key-stroke recognition program. It'll track every character he types. It doesn't matter if he later deletes the file because the program is recording him in real time as he types. We'll know everything he writes and everything he even thought about but deleted. If he's doing anything, we'll see it."

36

Trevor Deale drove his Range Rover slowly down San Pedro Avenue, taking more time than normal as a silent protest. Vanessa was tempted to comment on his conservative driving, but instead she pursed her lips and waited him out. They were on their way to the Northstar Mall, and Vanessa didn't want to start a fight in the car when they were so close.

"How long are we gonna stay?" Trevor asked, as he pulled into the parking lot.

"Until we're done," Vanessa said, purposefully vague. She refused to put a time limit on her shopping trips.

"How many stores do you want to visit?"

"I don't know, Trevor. However many it takes."

"What are we getting?"

"Something for your sister's birthday and my parents' anniversary."

"Why didn't we just pick something up when we got their Christmas presents a few weeks ago?" Trevor asked. He said *we* as if he had participated in the Christmas shopping, when they both knew that Vanessa had handled those purchases pretty much on her own. *Which is all the more reason*, Trevor thought, *why I don't need to be here now.*

"I didn't have time to get their other presents then," Vanessa said impatiently.

Trevor climbed out of the truck. "You're not shopping for yourself, are you?" He didn't want to spend the day watching Vanessa try on clothes. He'd done that before, and he'd vowed he would never suffer through that torture again.

Vanessa studied her nails, and thought that it was about time for another manicure. "If I happen to see something that's cute. . ." She left the threat hanging.

"I'm not gonna stay here all day," Trevor warned.

"We won't be here all day."

"I'm staying a couple of hours, tops."

"It won't take us much longer than that," Vanessa agreed.

Trevor, acting under his own will, would never have driven to the mall during the pre- and post-Christmas rush, but Vanessa had insisted. He lumbered through the crowded retail center, watching the ebb and flow of energetic shoppers with mute fatigue. Vanessa walked ahead of him. Tight butt in tight jeans. Hips rolling in characteristic sashay as she pushed through the throng. She had no tolerance for window shoppers, children, old people or anyone moving slower than her. She shoved through the crowd impatiently.

Her hair was French-braided, and she wore Ann Klein shoes with a matching belt. A Chanel purse swung from her shoulder and discreet diamond studs twinkled in each ear. She still had no engagement ring, but she was working on that.

Vanessa attacked each store's inventory and sales staff. She complained about the poor quality of the merchandise, the small variety in sizes, the predictable colors and the inadequate designs.

"What do you think of this for Mandy?" Vanessa said, holding up a light blue, cropped shirt.

"It's nice," Trevor said with little feeling.

Vanessa snorted and threw the shirt at the rack. The hanger missed the rod, and the shirt fell onto the floor. Vanessa moved on.

They marched in and out of stores, looked at racks full of clothing, jewelry, trinkets and artwork. Trevor looked at his watch. It had been nearly an hour and a half, and they still hadn't purchased a single item.

"Are you ready to go?" he asked.

Vanessa's eyes went wide. "No! I need to look in Foley's." But all at once she looked tired, as though the weight of dragging Trevor from store to store was too much for her. "Why don't you sit here for a few minutes?" She pointed at benches in the middle of the mall.

Trevor sat down and let out a long frustrated breath. He wanted to get out of there.

A young woman of about twenty-five approached the bench and hovered for a moment. The center of the mall was crowded with harried mothers, impatient fathers and weary children. The young woman stood still and Trevor noticed that she was trying to gather up the courage to sit in the small space next to him. She was about to walk away, when he scooted over a bit. She smiled politely, then eased onto the bench, taking care to not bump her neighbors.

Though they were on the downhill side of mid-January, the mall was still bedecked with the trimmings of Christmas. Trevor stared up at the enormous tree that stretched toward the vaulted ceiling. Its fat branches sagged with hundreds of ornaments and a flood of tinsel. Trevor recalled the dismal Christmas mornings he'd shared with his mother and little sister, and felt familiar anger rising in his throat. For most of his life, he'd endured the holiday season with a smoldering rage that threatened to consume him if he didn't keep it in check. In fifth grade, Mrs. Markosky had asked all the kids to make greetings cards to exchange with each other, but Trevor had quietly refused. He sat motionless with his hands folded on his desk and his eyes forward. Mrs. Markosky had asked him what was wrong, and Trevor had told her that he didn't believe in Christmas. The teacher had pinched her brow. *Didn't believe in Christmas?* She was speechless for a moment, but eventually she told Trevor that he could work on something else if he wished. That was Trevor's first step in abandoning a Christmas tradition that had abandoned his family years before.

"Christmas always makes me sad," said a small voice, nearly inaudible in the throng of shoppers, but loud enough to convey a desperate longing that Trevor knew intimately. He looked at the young woman sitting next to him. She stared up at the ridiculously decorated tree, shepherd to all those presents, icon of joy and happiness. Her face creased with familiar pain. She turned and looked at Trevor with a tight apologetic smile. She had moist eyes, and her lips quivered slightly. She was cute, Trevor thought. She had a petite frame in khaki pants and a polo shirt. Her auburn hair was pulled back in a barrette. She sat with her legs pressed together and her fingers clasped forming a corral around her small, black purse.

"I'm sorry," she sniffed. "I just get really sad at this time of year." She turned back to the tree. Trevor squinted slightly, but didn't say a word.

He too stared at the tree, having scooted fractionally closer to the young woman with whom he now shared a small pocket of silence in the teeming mall.

Vanessa came back a few minutes later. "Have you had enough time to catch your breath?" she asked, as if his fatigue were an indictment of his athletic ability. "We need to go to Neiman's." She glanced at her watch and started to walk away.

Trevor didn't move.

She turned back. "Are you coming?"

"I'll wait here."

Vanessa clucked her tongue and stared at Trevor. His resistance infuriated her. She was tired of always having to push to get what she wanted. It would have been easier if he argued back. Then they could have a fair fight, and she knew she could win a fair fight. But he'd sit there like a stupid animal, acting as if he didn't understand her words.

Vanessa threw up her hands. "I'll be back."

■ ■ ■

"Do you ever feel like nobody listens to you?" The young woman was speaking again. Her voice somehow found its way clearly to Trevor's ear. Her tears had dried up. She had a gentle mouth and dainty cheekbones, but strong eyes. "Like what you think isn't as important as what everyone else wants you to think?"

Trevor looked at the girl and nodded.

"I told my roommate that I didn't want to come to the mall, but she acted like she didn't hear me, like she always does." She looked up at Trevor with hazel eyes. "I'm sorry. I don't mean to bother you."

"No," Trevor said. He felt unsettled by this strange and lovely girl. "I don't want to be here either." The words stunned him. Trevor couldn't recall the last time he'd done something that he didn't want to do. He hadn't been that fatalistic about life since he was a child. He'd learned that everything was a choice, and his life was governed by his own personal decisions. But he'd just confessed that he didn't want to be in the mall, yet he was sitting the middle of the shopping center. *Why am I here?* he wondered. *Am I really here against my will? Did Vanessa really drag me here? Or did I choose to come?*

The girl nodded as if she understood perfectly.

"My. . . friend," Trevor said (why not *girlfriend?*), "insisted that I come even though she knows I hate the mall." Trevor smiled. "And I hate Christmas too," he added this as if he were a patron at a secret club giving a code to a bouncer.

She nodded. "Welcome to the Mall- and Christmas-Haters' bench." She extended her hand. "I'm Jennifer."

"Hello Jennifer. My name is Trevor." Their hands touched and held just a bit longer than necessary. Trevor felt something inside him stir.

"Looks like friend at two o'clock," Jennifer said quietly as she turned back to the tree.

"What?" Trevor said.

Vanessa clarified a moment later. "Okay, let's pop into Dillard's real quick."

Trevor stood quickly, feeling not quite like himself. "I thought we were leaving."

"We *are* leaving! I just want to look in there real quick."

Trevor sighed. He glanced back toward Jennifer. She would understand the battle he was fighting. She was a kindred soul. But when he turned toward her, she was gone.

Trevor scanned the area, his heart pounded with surprising urgency, but he didn't see her.

"What are you looking for?" Vanessa said. Her purse dangled from one hand. Her free arm was akimbo, fist pressed against cocked hip.

Trevor turned back toward her with steel in his eyes. "You said you wanted to stay at the mall for a couple of hours."

Vanessa took a step back. "I never said two hours!"

"Wait a second," Trevor said. "I said, 'I'll only stay for two hours,' and you said, 'it won't take more than that.'"

They stood a few feet from the huge Christmas tree.

"No," Vanessa corrected. "I said it won't take *much more* than that!"

They glared at each other, and it was the first time Vanessa had ever seen open hostility in Trevor's face.

"I can't believe you're being like this," she said.

"Like what?" Trevor said.

"Such a jerk!"

"I'm ready to go."

"We'll leave in a few minutes," Vanessa said. "I just want to look in Victoria's Secret real quick."

Trevor smiled. "You said Dillard's a minute ago."

"Well, Dillard's first, then Victoria's." She shrugged as if it didn't matter.

Trevor took the car keys out of his pocket and shook them dramatically. "I'm going to the car. When I get there, I'm going to start the car and drive home. If you want a ride, you should plan to be in the car."

37

A shadow settled behind Vanessa's eyes. Trevor didn't normally push things this way. He was quieter, more in control of his emotions. *I'm the one*, Vanessa thought, *who issues ultimatums and makes demands.* She watched him carefully as she contemplated her next step. She was seeing a side of her boyfriend that she'd never seen. He'd never been angry, demanding, or out of control. Vanessa thought it would have been more Trevor's style to hand her the car keys and leave without saying a word. He'd call a cab and when she returned to the mansion, she'd find him sitting in front of the TV as if nothing had happened. If she tried to argue, she knew it wouldn't go anywhere. He'd say, "I wasn't having fun at the mall, so I left. Did you have a good time?" And no matter what she said or did, she wouldn't be able to make him understand that she had wanted him to stay with her.

But, for some reason, today he was truly upset. Instead of just leaving, he'd issued the first ultimatum of their relationship—perhaps the first of his life. Vanessa studied him carefully and saw a hint of uncertainty in his eyes. Trevor opened his mouth, and she thought he was about to apologize.

"If you're not in the car when I get there," he said, "you can walk home for all I fucking care."

Vanessa's mouth fell open. That was the first profane word she'd ever heard him speak.

Trevor turned and strode away with measured steps.

Vanessa followed him in disbelief. Trevor didn't look back once. He walked straight down the mall and out the door into the bright sunshine.

Vanessa stopped at the glass door and watched him. She simply could not believe that he would leave her.

Despite the confidence of his stride, Trevor felt unsteady. When he reached the car, he climbed in and sat motionless for a long time. Vanessa, watching from the doorway, smiled triumphantly. After a couple of minutes she went back to her shopping, confident that he would still be waiting when she finished. For the first time in their relationship, Vanessa felt that she truly had the upper hand. She intended to teach Trevor Deale a lesson.

A few minutes stretched into half an hour and still Vanessa had not emerged from the mall. Trevor sighed and opened his door. He'd go back inside and try to find her. He'd only taken a couple of steps when he saw Jennifer walk by with another woman.

"Jennifer!" Trevor yelled across a row of cars.

"Hi," she said, looking up and smiling.

Trevor smiled back and walked closer. "I had to get out of there," he said.

Jennifer nodded. "I know."

"I was planning to go get some ice cream," Trevor said. "Would you like to join me?"

Jennifer's roommate, Gabrielle, shot a glance at her friend, trying by telepathy to tell her that she absolutely could not leave with a strange man she'd met at the mall.

"I'd love some," Jennifer said, quickly before Gabrielle could argue.

Trevor walked her back to his Range Rover and held open the passenger door.

"Nice car," Jennifer said. She had an easy confidence about her. Shy, but strong. Plain, but interesting. She pushed a loose strand of hair behind her ear and smiled at him. Trevor liked her smile.

"I've got a taste for some cookies and cream," Trevor said.

"That sounds yummy."

They drove out of the parking lot and turned onto Alamo Street.

"That was my girlfriend," Trevor said suddenly.

"Yeah," Jennifer said. "I thought so."

"I just abandoned her at the mall." He sounded ashamed.

Jennifer put a hand on his arm. "Maybe you should go back?"

"Probably." They drove in silence for a while.

"If you want to head back, that's okay. We could get together another time."

"No," Trevor said, shaking his head.

After a moment, Jennifer said, "How will she get home?"

Trevor shrugged. "She can call one of her friends."

She nodded. "It might be an embarrassing thing to have to explain to a friend."

"Yeah."

"Maybe she can call a cab. They won't ask her any questions."

Trevor looked over at Jennifer. "Why don't we stop talking about her."

"Okay."

"Let's talk about ice cream."

"Dairy products," Jennifer laughed. "That's always a safe topic."

■ ■ ■

Vanessa walked back to the window to check on Trevor. She'd visited three stores since he'd marched out of the mall, and she thought he'd probably learned his lesson by now. Either he would come back in to find her, or she'd walk out and climb into the truck; either way the point would have been made—Vanessa was in control, not Trevor. She stood just inside the entrance and looked down the row of cars. She didn't see the Range Rover. Maybe that's not the right row, she thought. But no, she remembered standing right in that spot watching Trevor as he had walked away. He'd gone about halfway down, and she'd seen his head as he sat in the truck waiting for her. He was no longer there. Maybe he'd moved. She looked as far as she could to the right and left, scanning the parking lot, looking for a black Range Rover. She pushed the door open and walked out, carrying two bags. She walked along the sidewalk, looking down row after row. Surely he hadn't left. Vanessa plucked her cell phone out of her purse and hit the speed dial.

Trevor looked down at his caller ID. "Excuse me for a minute, Jennifer." He walked out of Baskin-Robbins and answered the phone.

"Where are you?" Vanessa snapped.

Dozens of people were streaming past Trevor on the sidewalk. Some of them recognized him. Trevor kept his voice down. "I've gone for ice cream."

"Oh yeah?" Vanessa growled. "Get me some Rocky Road." People were walking past Vanessa too, but she spoke loudly, as if she were alone.

"I came here with a friend."

"Who?" Vanessa said sharply. Two women walking out of the mall looked over, but kept walking.

"You don't know her."

Her? Vanessa had thought he might have been with one of his teammates, not with some woman. Many players on the Stallions roster were cheating on their wives or girlfriends, but Trevor wasn't one of them. Vanessa was certain of that.

"Who, Trevor?"

"Her name is Jennifer."

"Todd Crosby's wife?" Vanessa exclaimed. Jennifer Crosby was a beautiful, statuesque blonde. Vanessa knew Trevor would like her, but would he really mess with the wife of one of his teammates?

"No, it's not Todd Crosby's wife. It's a girl I met at the mall today."

When did Trevor have time to meet someone at the mall? *While he was sitting on the bench*, Vanessa realized. She left him there, and some little bitch made her move.

"Trevor, you mean to tell me that you left me at the mall without a ride so that you could go on an ice cream date with some strange woman you just met?"

"That's not the reason I left, but yes, that's what happened." A woman and her son stood next to Trevor. The boy looked about nine years old. He was lanky with feet far too big for his body. He was wearing a Stallions jersey, and they'd been waiting for Trevor for more than a minute. "Hang on a second, Vanessa." Trevor moved the phone away from his ear. "How are you doing?"

"We're sorry to bother you," the woman said, "but my son wondered if you'd sign his jersey?"

"Sure, do you have a pen?"

"Oh." She hadn't planned ahead. She reached into her purse. "I thought you might carry one with you."

Trevor shook his head. "Maybe they'll have one inside."

"I'll check," the woman said. She went inside the shop, but her son stayed outside watching Trevor.

"Sorry about that, Vanessa."

"Is that bitch sitting right there listening to our conversation?"

"Who? The woman who wants the autograph?"

"No, the fucking bitch you went on a date with!" Vanessa still could not understand how this could happen. Sure, Trevor might have met someone while he was sitting on the bench, but Vanessa had watched him get into the car. He didn't have anyone with him then.

"No, she's inside, and I'm outside."

"Does she know you have a girlfriend?"

"Yes."

Well that was a good start, Vanessa thought. "When are you coming back to pick me up?"

"I'm not."

"What do you mean you're not? How am I supposed to get home?"

"You could call a cab."

"Trevor, you'd better get your ass back over here right now!"

"Call a cab, Vanessa." He hung up the phone and turned off the power.

"Trevor?" Vanessa screamed at the dead line. "*Trevor!*" People stared as they walked past cautiously. Vanessa threw her shopping bags down with a furious thump and nearly threw her cell phone through the glass door behind her, but stopped herself at the last moment.

"Is everything okay, Miss?"

Vanessa looked up at a young man in his mid-twenties looking at her the way most men looked at her—lustfully.

"I need a ride," she said.

"Sure," he said. "Where to?"

"The Estates at Dominion."

A rich girl! But she didn't have a ring on her finger. It would take half an hour to get there, and he would enjoy the time.

"I can give you a ride."

They marched off toward his pickup truck. "By the way, my name is Mark."

Vanessa didn't care what his stupid name was.

"Vanessa," she said with barely contained impatience.

"So how did you end up here at the mall without a ride home?"

Vanessa stopped walking. "Listen, Mark. I need to make some phone calls, so I won't have time for a lot of chitchat. Is that going to be a problem? Should I get a ride with someone else?"

"No, no problem at all," Mark said quickly. "You make your calls, and I'll get you there."

Vanessa called Trevor a dozen times, but he didn't answer. She left him a series of messages that grew progressively more venomous. Mark's curiosity was answered as he listened to her rant. Her boyfriend had left her at the mall and apparently had gone out for ice cream with another woman. Mark couldn't recall ever hearing anyone as angry as Vanessa.

When she stabbed the END button after one vitriolic message, Mark said, "Excuse me." He didn't want to disturb her, but he thought he understood what had happened. Vanessa glared at him with such malevolence that Mark suddenly understood why she'd been abandoned.

"You're calling Trevor Deale, aren't you?" he said with childish excitement.

When Vanessa nodded wearily, Mark said, "Do you think he'd give me an autograph?"

Vanessa unleashed an ear-piercing wail of raw, primal rage that stretched on for ten seconds and made Mark regret ever offering her a ride home. They covered the remaining distance in silence.

When she got home, Vanessa collapsed on the sofa. She quit calling Trevor's cell phone and focused her attention on how she should handle this situation when he returned. Should she scream and yell or should she just act hurt and betrayed? Would tears help? Would anger be better?

It was nearly 10 P.M. when Trevor finally walked in the door.

Vanessa was sitting in the darkened living room. She hadn't moved in hours.

"Welcome home," Vanessa said with as much sincerity as she could muster. "I was worried about you." Which was true.

"Put your shoes on," Trevor said. "I want to take you somewhere."

Vanessa wasn't sure how to play this. Should she ask where they were going, or just go along with him? Was this a good sign or a bad sign? She decided to let him lead. She got off the couch, grabbed her purse, and walked into the garage. He had the keys to her Mercedes in his hand. He opened the passenger door for her, then got behind the wheel. Usually they took his Range Rover, but it was not unprecedented for them to take her car. Vanessa decided not to ask about it.

"Where did you go?" she said as they drove.

"I went to get ice cream."

"I know. You said that earlier, but after that."

"I needed some time to think."

"What did you think about?"

"Us."

She waited for him to say more, but he seemed to be done. After a few minutes, she said, "What about us?"

"I'm not sure there is an us anymore, Vanessa."

Her heart dropped. "Trevor," she said carefully, "we got into a fight. It's not that big a deal."

"It's not just this fight. It's everything."

They were headed toward downtown. "What do you mean, *everything?*"

"I mean our whole relationship. We fight a lot, and I've realized over the past few months that I'm just not in love with you anymore."

Vanessa hadn't shed genuine tears since she was a little girl, but she was on the verge now. She was worried about how Michael Gasca would react to this development, but she was surprised to realize that she was truly sad to be losing Trevor.

"Is it because of this other woman?" she asked.

"No, it's not *because* of her." Trevor had dropped Jennifer at her apartment hours earlier.

"Do you love her?"

"Of course I don't love her, Vanessa. I just met her."

They drove in silence or a while. "Where are we going?"

"The Westin City Center."

"What are we going to do there?"

He didn't answer. He concentrated on the road, and he seemed so deep in thought that Vanessa wondered if he'd forgotten that she was there. She knew this was an important moment. Trevor had made up his mind. He'd obviously planned his course of action, so it wouldn't do any good to argue with him. She should go along and let him cool down; they could work on their relationship again tomorrow or the next day. Give him a little time to breathe. Let him miss her, and then she'd get back in. She couldn't lose him. She absolutely *could not* lose him.

They pulled up to the Westin. Trevor handed the keys to the valet.

"Staying for the night, sir?" the valet said.

"Yes."

Joy sprang into Vanessa's heart. Maybe she had misread the situation. Maybe Trevor felt guilty for leaving her at the mall, going on a date with another woman, and ignoring her calls for more than six hours. Maybe the spontaneous night at the Westin was a romantic balm for their ailments. But then Vanessa realized that Trevor was talking about the car, not himself. The valet wanted to know if he should leave the Mercedes up front or put it in the garage. Vanessa would be staying overnight; therefore, the car would stay overnight.

They walked inside to the reception desk, where an efficient manager stepped forward to greet them.

"I'd like your penthouse suite," Trevor said, pulling his wallet out of his back pocket.

The manager, whose nametag bore the name Russo, preened as he glanced from Trevor's athletic frame to Vanessa's unnerving beauty. They had no bags, and they weren't dressed for dinner. Russo suspected that Trevor was stepping out on his wife with this stunning creature. But as he studied the couple, he realized there was a storm brewing between them. Trevor's face bore a blank focus that in other circumstances might have prompted Russo to ask something silly like "Why the long face?" but under that flat look lived a current of angry tension that Russo didn't want to provoke. Vanessa's eyes glistened with despair, and Russo realized that they weren't new lovers—they were quite the opposite. He was standing in the cool shadow of their decaying relationship.

"The LBJ suite is certainly available," Russo said, trying to project as much optimism as he could. "Just last month, our penthouse was named best stable by *Texas Farm & Ranch* magazine." He clicked away at his keyboard. "I haven't seen the magazine myself, but I've heard that the story was quite impressive."

"How much is it?" Trevor said.

"Oh, I imagine the magazine's just three or four dollars at the news-stands," Russo said.

"The *suite*." Trevor sounded strained even to himself.

"Oh. The suite. Of course. How silly of me. The rate is two thousand dollars a night, but because you're local, I can give you a ten percent discount. We like to let people know that they don't have to be from out of town to treat themselves to a night on the town."

"Let me have a week." He laid a platinum American Express card on the counter.

Trevor and Vanessa didn't say a word in the elevator. Russo had attempted to escort them to the room, but Trevor had refused the offer, politely at first, then a bit more firmly. He stepped off the elevator, opened the door of the fifteen-hundred-square-foot suite and handed Vanessa the room key plus an envelope containing five thousand dollars.

"Someone will bring your clothes, jewelry, makeup, and toiletries first thing in the morning. I'm paying for this suite for one week, so you should use the time to find an apartment. I'll pay your rent for the next six months, and I'll give you thirty thousand dollars for furniture and anything else you need to get set up. The Mercedes is yours to keep, as is the jewelry, clothes, and everything else that'll come in the morning. After six months, you're on your own." Trevor stepped back into the hallway and pressed the down button on the elevator.

Vanessa pleaded with teary eyes. "Trevor, I'm sorry."

"Me too." He stepped onto the elevator and rode out of her life.

■ ■ ■

"She lost him," Roscoe said.

"You think?" Gasca said. He'd just finished listening to Vanessa's voice message. She sounded calm, but she said she needed to talk.

"Wouldn't be calling you if there wasn't a problem," Roscoe rumbled.

"We'll see." Gasca dialed her cell phone. "What's up, girl?"

Vanessa was sitting in the living room of the LBJ suite looking up at a portrait of the former president.

"There's been a little setback," she said, putting it mildly.

"You're not calling me from the house, are you?" Michael Gasca asked. He didn't want to have this conversation if Trevor might walk in at any moment.

"I'm in a safe place." She almost told him she was at the Westin, but thought better of it. Michael Gasca might send Roscoe over to pick her up, and then…well, she didn't want to know what might happen.

"Did you lose him?"

"I'm not sure," she lied. Somehow she'd miscalculated. Trevor had dumped her—completely and unexpectedly.

"We were shopping," she said to Michael Gasca, "and after a little argument, he left me at the mall."

"What was the fight about?"

"Nothing, really. He didn't want to be there."

"And then he just left? No warning? One minute he was there, the next minute he was gone?"

Vanessa had to speak carefully. The simple facts might be damning to her, but she couldn't lie either. They were close to the endgame, so Michael Gasca might have had people watching her.

"No," she said. "He warned me. He said he was going to the car and I'd better go with him if I wanted a ride home."

"But you didn't go with him?"

"No, I didn't," Vanessa said defensively. "This was the game we played." But that wasn't entirely true. Throughout their relationship, Vanessa had pushed and dragged, but Trevor had never really pushed back. The minute he walked away from her, she should have known something was wrong. He'd broken from his normal routine, but she didn't read it. She had thought it was a test, and she had planned to pass with flying colors.

"It was a power struggle," she said, "and I had to make sure I had control of him." Surely Michael Gasca wouldn't fault her for that. She had tried to do her job.

"So are you still at the mall?"

"No, I got a ride home."

"I thought you said you weren't at home right now."

"I'm not. Trevor drove me to a hotel."

"Where is he now?"

He'd better not be out with that little home-wrecking bitch! Vanessa thought. "Probably at the house."

"So go home and make up."

"I don't think he'd open the door for me. I've never seen him like this."

"You only had one job to do, Vanessa," Michael Gasca admonished, "and that was get control of Trevor Deale. Now you've lost him at the worst possible time."

"Maybe I can call him tomorrow," Vanessa said nervously. She knew there was no hope of reconnecting with Trevor. She'd seen the finality in his eyes and felt it in his tone, but she couldn't confess that to Michael Gasca.

"Where are you now?"

The question scared Vanessa. "Please, Michael," she said.

"What's wrong?" Gasca said innocently.

"Please," she said. Her eyes misted.

"Let me know where you are, and I'll send Roscoe over to pick you up. We can talk in person."

Vanessa pushed the END button with so much force that the phone skittered out of her hand. She covered her mouth and stared at the phone for a long time. She looked around the room and moaned.

"Gotta go, gotta go, gotta go." She called the valet and asked him to bring her car to the front. She'd leave San Antonio immediately. She couldn't stay at the Westin, because Trevor was planning to send her belongings over in the morning. Roscoe would undoubtedly follow the delivery.

She'd drive tonight, get out of town, maybe get all the way up to Dallas. She felt a pang of regret about the jewelry, clothing, and thirty thousand dollars in cash she was leaving behind, but nothing at Trevor's house was worth risking her life over.

Michael Gasca said, "Well, she definitely lost him, and now she's going to run."

"Where's she gonna go?" Roscoe wondered.

"Don't know. But she's scared."

"I guess that's better for us if she's out of the picture, huh?" Roscoe said. "I mean, now that we put Jennifer in play."

Jennifer Winesett, their high school friend and waitress at Lenny's Grill in Philadelphia, was sitting on the couch between them. She'd flown down to San Antonio a week earlier at Michael Gasca's request.

"Having her leave town probably isn't the best thing for us," Gasca said. He dialed Vanessa's cell phone number again. "Vanessa," he said to her voice mail, "I know you're nervous right now, but I want to assure you that I don't plan to do anything to harm you. Of course, I don't expect you to take my word for that, so you go ahead and take off if you wish, but I need you to do me one favor. Tomorrow, you need to call Trevor with a story. I don't care what it is. Tell him you're going to visit your mother. You're leaving the country to clear your head. Anything. I just can't afford to have him calling the police to file a missing person's report because his girlfriend disappeared off the face of the earth. Your help with this will be greatly appreciated."

He hung up the phone and said, "Well, it's up to you now, Jennifer. Do you think you can handle him?"

She shrugged her petite shoulders. "He's awfully nice."

"I gotta admit, man," Roscoe rumbled, "when you first told me this idea, I didn't think it would work."

Roscoe and Jennifer had kept a loose tab on Trevor for several days, waiting for the right moment to approach him. The visit to the mall presented the perfect opportunity, and using the lines Michael Gasca had told her to use, Jennifer easily captured Trevor's attention.

"How did you know this would work?" Roscoe asked. "I mean no disrespect, Jennifer, 'cause you're a pretty girl, but Vanessa looks like a damn supermodel. I just didn't think you'd be able to steal Trevor away from her."

"I know what you mean," Jennifer said. "I didn't think it would work either."

"I had a feeling," Michael Gasca said. His feelings were legendary. When he had a feeling, it usually meant the Sarcassi family was about to make a truckload of money. "I've been dating his sister for nearly a year, and I've visited his mother's house. After meeting Trevor in Lamesa a few weeks ago, I could see that Vanessa was miscast for the role. She was the wrong look, wrong attitude, and wrong personality. She tried hard, but she just didn't fit."

"I told you she was too bitchy," Roscoe said. It was one of the few times in his life he could say that he'd been right and Michael Gasca had been wrong.

"Yes you did," Gasca agreed. "So now I figured we'd throw Jennifer out there and give Trevor someone else to think about. If he chose to stay with Vanessa, then maybe we would have helped affirm his love for her. But he left, so maybe we pulled the trigger at exactly the right time, because he might have been planning to dump her anyway."

"But you could have screwed it up," Roscoe said. "Vanessa was on the inside. Throwing Jennifer in just muddies the water. He might not ever call her again."

"You think he's going to call you?" Gasca asked Jennifer.

"I hope so," Jennifer said, meaning it. Connecting with Trevor was just a job to her, but she liked him. She'd expected the quarterback to be a typical dumb jock who would hit on her and try to get her into bed as quickly as possible. But she'd discovered that Trevor was quiet, sensitive, and interesting. They'd chatted about a million things, and she was actually looking forward to seeing him again.

"All I need you to do is keep an eye on him," Michael Gasca said. "We're shifting to Plan B, and I need to know how he reacts to it."

"I don't like Plan B," Roscoe grunted.

"Me neither," Gasca said, "but we don't have a choice."

38

Jonathan Kinneson's financial life was falling apart. Though he'd owned the San Antonio Stallions less than twelve months, he desperately needed to sell the team. The value of Kinneson Corp. stock had plummeted, taking his multi-billion dollar net worth with it; he was losing control of the company to an increasingly hostile board of directors, and there were rumors that he soon might be voted out as president. But before the predictions of his naysayers came true, he planned to right the ship by winning the Super Bowl, getting approval for a new stadium and selling the team for a one- to two-hundred-million–dollar profit. He'd get his cash back, and then some, start buying up Kinneson Corp. stock, regain control of the company, and then figure out how to get rid of as many of the disloyal, conniving board members as he could.

When he'd first contacted Michael Gasca, Kinneson had wanted to get rid of his irksome head coach and win the Super Bowl. His motivation was primarily ego, though he'd never have stated it that way. Leading his team to a world championship would prove his business acumen to all the so-called pundits who had panned his NFL purchase.

Jonathan Kinneson had planned to pay just one to two million to Michael Gasca for his services, but the criminal had demanded an outrageous eleven million, and though Kinneson had dragged his feet on making payments, he'd thus far been stumped on how to reduce the price.

And the more Jonathan Kinneson learned about the cash flow of an NFL franchise, the more exorbitant Gasca's fee became. Kinneson used to watch television cameras zoom in on owners in their luxury boxes biting their nails as they prayed for their teams to win. He'd always assumed that owners got rich on post-season games. He'd read newspaper stories about sixty-second Super Bowl commercials selling for two million dollars a pop and he thought that if his team were in the big game, he'd get a big chunk of that money. But he'd learned that the NFL front office had negotiated a collection of television contracts that totaled $17.6 billion over eight years, including the playoffs, and every team received an equal share. The $2.2 billion annual payment from the networks was split evenly between thirty-two teams, which meant that a team that went 1–15 during the regular season got the same sixty-nine million as the winner of the Super Bowl.

Revenue-sharing had been explained to Jonathan Kinneson when he was making the bid to purchase the Stallions, and it had been characterized as one of the NFL's greatest strengths. Kinneson was buying a fairly new franchise which would probably bleed money for a few years. Revenue-sharing guaranteed that he wouldn't lose too much. But now that the Stallions had become one of the best teams in the league, revenue-sharing felt like a communist plot to steal from the talented teams and give to weaker squads.

This revelation was just one of many shocking disappointments for Jonathan Kinneson. He had purchased the team in February against the advice of his accountants and lawyers. It wasn't a good investment, they had insisted. He would have to pay nearly half a billion dollars to buy the franchise, and the team wouldn't generate much cash flow. Jonathan Kinneson had shrugged off their concerns. Only thirty-two NFL teams existed, he reasoned, so he'd be part of an exclusive club. He had ignored his accountants, lawyers, brokers, and the chief financial officer at Kinneson Corp. The company's stock manager had pleaded with Kinneson to not sell off too much stock to purchase the Stallions.

"If you must do this," his various advisers had urged, "finance as much as possible."

But a few magazines had run articles challenging Jonathan Kinneson's real wealth. They had suggested that he was a smoke-and-mirrors billionaire with too much of his net worth attributed to overvalued Kinneson Corp. stock.

"Yes, Jonathan Kinneson may be a billionaire," opined one magazine, "and yes, you might think the house you bought for two hundred thousand is now worth five hundred thousand. But there's a wide gulf between perceived value and actual worth."

These articles, which had appeared with alarming frequency after Kinneson announced his intent to purchase an NFL franchise, caused some hesitation among NFL owners. They would approve the sale only if they had confidence in the financial solvency of the buyer. The league preferred independently wealthy people or ownership groups who could pay mostly cash for franchises rather than borrowing themselves into deficits that they might never escape. During one meeting, Jonathan Kinneson had ignored an accountant tugging insistently on his elbow, and boldly told the owners that he would pay three hundred fifty million in cash for the Stallions and finance the remaining one hundred twenty five million. The offer was nearly double the cash component the owners had demanded, and they quickly approved the purchase.

Jonathan Kinneson saw this victory as another exclamation point for the so-called experts to choke on.

That was February, just before Kinneson Corp. stock flagged in the ever-shrinking information technology market. To make the Stallions purchase, Kinneson had to sell millions of shares of company stock, which, as all of his advisers had predicted, drove the stock price down nearly forty percent in a terrifying spiral that lasted two months. Blessedly, it finally slowed, but the technology market continued to flail. Over the next few months, the stock lost even more value, and the magazines didn't waste any time attacking Kinneson as a foolish CEO whose ego had undermined his own stock.

Another unintended consequence of the stock sale was that control of the company shifted away from Jonathan Kinneson. Before the sale, Kinneson had held thirty percent of the stock, the board of directors had controlled not quite twenty-five percent, employees held eight percent, and the remainder was traded on the open market. When Kinneson started dumping shares, the board of directors had bought as much as it could in order to shore up the value. After months of buying, the board now held thirty-one percent while Kinneson had twenty-four percent, and his reign as president and CEO seemed to be coming to an end.

During the course of the past nine months, Jonathan Kinneson also had been stunned to learn just how little profit the Stallions returned each year. The gross numbers—the pork coming in the front door—were impressive, but high operating costs stripped the meat down to the bone. The $69 million the Stallions received from the television contract was consumed in one big bite by player salaries. The Stallions received $2.5 million from the local radio station that broadcasted the games, and just under a million from the local television station that called itself the official home of the San Antonio Stallions.

The city owned the Alamodome and controlled all of its revenue streams, which frustrated Kinneson to no end. The team's share of advertising, concessions, suites, and parking netted a paltry three million dollars a year, which seemed hardly worth the effort when other franchises were making twenty- to fifty-million in stadium revenue. The Stallions earned twenty-two million dollars in ticket sales, home and away, and paid four million a year to lease the Alamodome.

Jonathan Kinneson wanted a new stadium, paid for by the taxpayers, with revenue streams that would funnel straight to the team. He wanted a naming rights deal, luxury boxes, premium seating, personal seat licenses, inside advertising, and anything else he could squeeze out of the stadium.

The Stallions had other income from corporate sponsorships that yielded five million dollars annually, which put the team's annual revenue a couple of bumps under a hundred million dollars. But after the paying the players, chartering planes, booking hotel rooms, catering meals, maintaining the team at training camp for a month, running the Stallions Center, cutting checks for forty-eight additional staff members and paying the IRS, the team produced just five million dollars in profit each season. Finally, Kinneson understood the imprudence of paying three hundred and fifty million in cash for an asset that would produce so little cash flow. The true value of the Stallions, he had been told, was in the equity.

With a Super Bowl victory, a new stadium, and other amenities, Kinneson believed he could sell the team for a hefty profit and solve all of his problems in one swoop.

And so far everything seemed to be going according to plan. Thanks to Michael Gasca's manipulations and Trevor Deale's outstanding performances on the field, the Stallions finished the regular season 13–3, won the AFC South division, earned a wildcard bye, and secured home-field advantage throughout the playoffs.

In the divisional round, Trevor Deale threw for 288 yards and three touchdowns, while Caleb Alexander added 104 yards on the ground and another score. The defense produced two turnovers for a 31–10 victory over the Pittsburgh Steelers. The following week, the Stallions faced the New England Patriots, whom all the pundits believed was the best team in the AFC and possibly the best team in the league.

Despite the Stallions' exceptional record, many experts had believed the team was too dependent on Trevor Deale to be a true contender. As long as Trevor performed like an all-star, the Stallions would win. But if Trevor had a bad day, or even an average day, the Stallions would lose. The pundits had thought it would take a miracle for the Stallions to defeat the well-balanced New England Patriots team in the AFC Championship game.

Fortunately, Michael Gasca was a miracle worker.

He had devised his scheme days earlier when he and Roscoe were weaving through the jumbled road construction in downtown San Antonio. The city had known for five years that it would be hosting the Super Bowl, and the mayor had promised that this project would be completed long before the throngs of visitors arrived. But a series of set-backs had delayed the construction, and now a couple of weeks before the Super Bowl, downtown was a disaster zone.

"It's pretty confusing down here," Gasca had observed.

"Yeah, I bet the tourists have as much trouble finding the Alamo as Davy Crockett did," Roscoe said.

Michael Gasca hesitated and creased his brow. "I don't think Davy Crockett had trouble finding the Alamo. I think he was one of the men defending it."

"Oh yeah?" Roscoe asked. "Then why do they always say 'Remember the Alamo,' like someone forgot where they put it?"

Michael Gasca closed his eyes and rubbed his forehead wearily. He couldn't deal with Roscoe at the moment. He picked up his phone and dialed Dominic Sarcassi in Philadelphia.

The old man answered his private line himself. "Little Mikey!" he exclaimed with a gravely voice. "I've been missing you. How we lookin'?"

"Right on track, but I need a little help."

"Anything."

"If I wanted to get a particular driver on a particular bus, how would I do that?"

"We talking city buses or commercial charters?"

"It's a charter."

"You know the company running the bus you want?"

"Yes, sir."

Uncle Nick thought for a moment. "Union boss is probably the best bet. He's got a relationship with all the companies, and he can get a favor done when he needs it. You want me to find him and talk to him on your behalf?"

"I think we'll go talk to him ourselves. I just need a name and address."

"Where do you want to get him?"

"Out somewhere. Not his home or office."

"Give me half an hour."

■ ■ ■

"That's the guy, huh?" Roscoe was staring through the front window of Alita's Mexican Café. "Dude sure can eat."

Greg Uleman was working his way through a beef burrito smothered in green sauce. He represented all the bus drivers in San Antonio, wore leisure suits from Sears and ran the local 482 as if he were the dictator of a small country. In seventeen years as the union boss, he'd led three strikes and threatened a half dozen others. When negotiating with management, he liked to scream and slam his hands on the table for effect. When he had meetings with company executives, he'd show up late and walk out while they were in mid-sentence. Management hated him, but they had to work with him because he had complete control over the drivers.

Roscoe Evans and Michael Gasca walked through the sparsely populated restaurant, stopped in front of Uleman's table, and waited for him to look up from his food.

"Who the hell are you?" Uleman said. He didn't stop eating, but he gave Roscoe a careful top-to-bottom appraisal.

"Just wanted to talk to you." Gasca pulled out a chair and sat down across from Uleman. Roscoe moved into the chair next to the man.

Uleman looked at Roscoe again, but he didn't feel intimidated. He supposed that someone from one of the bus companies had sent this thug over to try to scare him before their next meeting. It wouldn't work.

"Mr. Uleman, there's a kid working for Continental Charters who's been dying for a break," Gasca said. "He's the nephew of a very important person, and this important person would like to see his nephew behind the wheel of one of the buses taking the Patriots to the stadium on Sunday."

"So call Continental." Uleman shoveled another forkful of food into his mouth, smacking aggressively as he glared at the two men.

Roscoe struck faster than Uleman thought possible. He snatched a fistful of hair on the back of the union boss's head and jabbed a meaty thumb into the hollow spot at the base of Uleman's neck.

The sharp pressure just below Uleman's Adam's apple forced his chin down; his mouth gaped open, and he made a choking sound as partially chewed food spilled out onto the table. Roscoe was compressing Uleman's esophagus in the most uncomfortable manner imaginable. Uleman's hands went up to grab at Roscoe's paw, but he couldn't shake the bigger man's grip.

"Put your hands on the table," Gasca advised. "You try to fight, and he's just gonna push harder. Put your hands on the table, and he'll ease up."

Uleman's instincts told him to keep fighting, but he knew he couldn't stop Roscoe. He put his hands on the table, and thankfully, Roscoe stopped pushing. Uleman's breath came back with a heavy congested cough. He spit out more food and felt as if he might vomit. Thankfully, the feeling passed after a moment.

Michael Gasca placed a thick stack of bills on the table. "This is five thousand dollars. It's yours, and all you have to do is call Continental Charters and make sure Chris Delgado is a driver on Sunday."

Greg Uleman looked at the cash. That was a lot of money for one kid to drive one bus for one day.

"Who's this kid related to?" he managed.

Roscoe jabbed his thumb back into Uleman's throat. The union boss tried to scream, but no sound came out. He clutched at Roscoe's hand with true panic. He couldn't move. He couldn't think. He couldn't breathe. Every blood vessel in his head was throbbing.

"Keep your palms on the table, Mr. Uleman," Michael Gasca said. "You keep your questions to yourself, and he'll keep the pressure off."

Uleman desperately lowered his hands back onto the table, and Roscoe eased off again. This time Uleman did vomit, spraying thick chunks of masticated Mexican food onto the table. Roscoe and Gasca backed up slightly, but Roscoe never completely released his grip. Uleman quivered in fear. He had always imagined how he would react if someone tried to strong-arm him, but now he realized that he didn't have the courage of his convictions. He didn't feel defiant or fearless. He just felt helpless and scared.

"This doesn't have to be complicated," Michael Gasca continued. "The money is a gift, as long as you make sure Chris Delgado gets the assignment. Are we cool with that?"

"Yes," Greg Uleman gasped.

"If things don't go according to plan, then my friend here will be coming to press an industrial thumb tack into your throat. He'll pin the front of your neck to the back of your neck and leave you to try to un-stick yourself." Gasca looked at Roscoe and said, "We don't want to have to do that, do we?"

Roscoe shook his head. "It's messy."

"So it's in all of our best interest to make this as painless as possible. You make some money, the kid gets a great opportunity, and we get what we want. It's a win-win-win."

■ ■ ■

"I just can't do it," said David Parker, CEO of Continental Charters. He had rosters spread out in front of him, and he had just read the file on Chris Delgado. "The kid's a rookie. Barely been here a month."

"Who cares how long he's been here," Greg Uleman said, still rubbing his bruised neck. "How hard can it be to drive from the hotel to the stadium?"

"This is an important contract," Parker said. "Nothing can go wrong." Continental had earned the NFL's business five years ago after Ferryway Lines was twenty minutes late picking up the Atlanta Falcons at the airport. While the team was sitting on the tarmac, an accident had forced the buses to take a detour. The president of Ferryway had called the team personally to apologize for the delay, but it didn't matter. The NFL was a results-oriented business. Either you got the job done or you were gone. Ferryway lost all of its NFL contracts the following week.

"Parker, I'm telling you the kid'll be fine," Uleman said.

"You know how much the teams talk to each other," Parker said. "If we make the slightest mistake, we'll be out of favor with the entire league. So I don't take chances. Only the most seasoned veteran drivers get these jobs." Parker knew that each NFL team had a director of operations who negotiated charter flights, buses, hotels, meals, meeting rooms, practice facilities, and anything else the team needed on the road. The directors were a flock of decision makers who negotiated separately but always moved together.

"You've got Johnson, Pruitt, Edwards, and Stephens working this one, don't you?" Uleman had already made calls, so he knew exactly who was on the crew.

Parker looked at his paperwork. "Yeah, those are the guys."

"I could tell all of them to take the weekend off."

"Come on! Why are you making threats?" Parker knew the drivers had so much loyalty to Greg Uleman that they *would* call in sick Sunday morning if Uleman told them to.

Uleman said, "I need this favor."

"I don't get it. Why this kid?"

"I promised a friend that I'd get his nephew on this crew. It's been the kid's dream to drive for the NFL, and this weekend is a good time to give him a shot."

"But on top of the pressure from the NFL, I've gotta deal with my drivers," Parker said. "They get paid extra to work these games. The assignment is a perk for veterans. How am I supposed to explain to my older guys that I'm replacing one of them with a rookie?"

"Tell you what," Uleman said. "Don't replace anyone, just put the kid down as an alternate."

Parker thought about this for a moment. "You're telling me that one of my drivers is gonna call in sick?"

"Yep."

"But not *all* of them?"

"One guy's gonna call in sick, and you'll put the kid in. It'll be no big deal."

"If anything goes wrong—"

"Trust me. Nothing is gonna go wrong."

■ ■ ■

Of course, something *did* go wrong. Chris Delgado got lost on his way to the stadium. It was not the first time a bus had taken a wrong turn while ferrying an NFL team, but it was the last time it would be done by a Continental Charters driver. The four buses left the team hotel, one at a time, at half-hour intervals starting three hours before kickoff. Some players and coaches liked to get to the stadium hours before kickoff, while others liked to get there later. Staggered bus departures accommodated everyone.

Chris Delgado, at the wheel of bus three, got completely turned around in the one-way streets, detours, and road-closures in downtown San Antonio. Eventually one of the Patriots coaches had ordered him to stop the bus, and everyone had scrambled down and raced twelve blocks in their designer suits and slick shoes, with their overnight bags slung over their shoulders. Thousands of pedestrians paused to watch this migrating herd of mostly large, black men sprinting down the sidewalk. A few people applauded, and soon drivers started honking their horns, women laughed and children screamed high-pitched encouragement. A camera crew doing a feature story on the River Walk caught the panicked players on tape, and soon the video of the New England Patriots sprinting to the AFC Championship game was being broadcast worldwide.

The unnerved Patriots lost 27–14.

Now the Stallions were a few days away from making the franchise's first Super Bowl appearance, and Jonathan Kinneson desperately needed his team to win.

■ ■ ■

Roscoe Evans had spent his entire life collecting from gamblers who couldn't or wouldn't pay. In the world of illegal gambling, a guy might get a couple of gentle reminders, but by the time Roscoe showed up, things had already passed all the reasonable stages. Most guys got behind because they honest-to-God didn't have the cash, and they'd do anything to square the debt. They'd sell property, steal, borrow from their families, work overtime, do anything.

Roscoe knew that Jonathan Kinneson was playing a completely different game. He *had* the money; he was just a deliberate slow pay. Usually Roscoe only had to visit a guy once to make a memorable impression. After one chat with Roscoe, they were set for the duration But with Kinneson, every payment required a fresh threat. Roscoe thought he could have saved everyone a lot of trouble if he had knocked the confidence out of Jonathan Kinneson the first time they met. Years of practice had taught Roscoe that the knee was a particularly persuasive joint in people who were confused about their loyalties. He didn't whack at it with a baseball bat or a pipe. That was too messy. Roscoe would just wrap one of his massive hands around a guy's knee and squeeze until he heard it pop. He never knew what it was that snapped inside, but judging from the looks on the victims' faces, it was terribly painful. The knee would swell up with furious speed and it made a lasting impression. In Roscoe's humble opinion, Jonathan Kinneson was ripe for a knee squeezing.

Kinneson glared at the two men in his office. Michael Gasca stared back with a look of amusement while Roscoe conducted a silent inventory of all the things he could do to the Stallions owner. The first time they'd come to Kinneson's office, they'd waited three hours. But when Michael Gasca called to set up the second meeting, he'd threatened to penalize the owner a hundred thousand dollars for every minute they waited. Since then, they always went straight back when they arrived.

"You're late," Gasca said, referring to Kinneson's scheduled payments.

"I've had some cash flow problems," Jonathan Kinneson smirked. "You know how it is."

Roscoe made a mental note: urine flow problems might help Kinneson get back in line.

"What we need right now is two million dollars," Gasca said. "That'll get you caught up, then three million after the Stallions win the Super Bowl."

Kinneson shrugged helplessly. "It's been a tough couple of months in the market. I can rustle up five hundred thousand right now, but I won't be able to get you the rest until after the Super Bowl."

"If I wasn't so trusting," Michael Gasca said. "I might think that you're planning to stiff me."

"My problem," Kinneson said, "is that I don't have the money right now."

"You've got plenty of money."

"But it's all tied up."

Dried up might be a better explanation, Gasca thought. He knew all about Kinneson's financial woes, and though the Stallions owner wasn't broke, he really did have cash flow problems. He couldn't sell any more stock without further eroding his position with the board of directors, and even if he could, the sale of more stock would only cause increased panic among other investors.

"You think I had eleven million dollars sitting in a drawer at home?" Kinneson asked. "When I want to get some money, I have to come up with a story for my accountant. I've got CFOs here at Kinneson Corp. and at the Stallions Center, and when I want to sell some options, my accountant has to deal with them. I can't come to them every week saying I need a million more. These things take time, but it'll be easier after the Super Bowl."

Michael Gasca nodded. "Tell you what. You give me one million now, and we'll let you hold off on the rest."

Kinneson released a weary breath. *Typical low-rent thug*, he thought. *Walks into my office and thinks he's going to just push me around, but in less than fifteen minutes, I've got him down from two million to one million, and he'll eventually leave with a lot less than that.*

"I just don't know how I'm going to do that," Kinneson said.

"I could make you lose the Super Bowl," Gasca said.

This oft-repeated threat failed to move Kinneson. *If you want to make us lose, then just go ahead and try*, he thought. The way his Stallions were playing, Kinneson didn't believe God could stop them.

"That doesn't change anything for me," he said. "It's not a question of motivation. It's just the practical reality of my situation. I don't have access to the money at the moment."

"Well," Gasca said, apparently out of ideas, "I guess if all you've got is half a million...I guess we'll have to settle on that for now."

Roscoe looked at his friend in disbelief. Was Michael Gasca really gonna let the guy skate?

"When can you get us the rest?" Michael Gasca asked.

Never, Kinneson thought. "Things will be a lot better for me in February."

Then Michael Gasca did something that neither Roscoe nor Kinneson expected. He stood and extended his hand across the desk.

"All right, Mr. Kinneson, you win."

Although the move caught Roscoe off guard, he knew exactly what was coming next.

Jonathan Kinneson, surprised by the gesture, stood with smug confidence and took Michael Gasca's hand.

Gasca pulled forward slightly, holding Kinneson upright and away from the gun mounted under the desk. Roscoe stood quickly, grabbed the front of the owner's shirt, and dragged him on to the top of the desk, pressing him down on his back, sending his calendar, organizer, and pens skittering on to the floor.

"No!" Kinneson said in a high-pitched squeal of pure panic.

Roscoe took the index and middle fingers of his left hand and jammed them into Jonathan Kinneson's nostrils Three Stooges style. He shoved them in as far as they'd go, then pushed some more as if he wanted to jab his fingers up into the man's brain. Kinneson squealed again; this time the sound was slightly muted. Roscoe's fingers were too large for Kinneson's nostrils; skin and cartilage ripped open and blood rushed down his face. A wave of pain washed over Kinneson.

"Mr. Kinneson," Gasca said, "aside from Roscoe picking you up by your feet at the country club in Philly, we've never touched you. Roscoe's been asking for permission to be more aggressive with you, but I've held him back. I told him that you were a businessman and you knew a good deal when you saw one. But at every turn you've resisted us, and now I think Roscoe might have been right all along. Maybe if he'd stepped on your hand at the beginning, we could have saved ourselves a lot of trouble. But no sense crying about it now. You've got until end of business today to transfer three million dollars into my account. I was willing to accept two million and let you pay the remainder after the Super Bowl, but I'm out of patience. If you don't transfer the money by the deadline, Roscoe will come to visit you again, only it won't be here at the office. He'll catch you at home, on your private jet, at the Stallions Center, at your girlfriend's house, or at a stoplight. He'll do something so horribly painful that you'll wish you were dead. Do you understand, or should Roscoe wiggle his fingers?"

"I understand," Jonathan Kinneson croaked.

Michael Gasca walked around the desk and removed the gun holstered along the left edge. He handed it to Roscoe, who tucked it into his waistband.

"If everything goes according to plan," Gasca said, "this will be our last meeting. You'll wire the money, we'll make sure you win the Super Bowl, and that will be that. But if you don't make the payment tomorrow, your quality of life will diminish significantly. Do you understand me?"

"Yes," Kinneson said. Even the slightest movement made his nose scream in agony.

"Let's go," Gasca said to Roscoe.

If Roscoe Evans had felt more charitable, he would have ripped his fingers from Kinneson's nose quickly. It would have given the Stallions' owner a sudden flash of pain, but it was far better than a slow removal.

But Roscoe wasn't feeling charitable; he eased his fingers out a millimeter at a time, which felt to Kinneson like a jagged knife being pulled out of a wound slowly, shredding fresh nerve endings as it went. The owner panted, trembled, squirmed, and moaned so loudly that someone outside the office might have thought he was having an orgasm. Fat tears dripped down the side of his face, but still Roscoe pulled slowly, taking a full thirty seconds to extract his bloody, snot-covered fingers. He wiped them on Kinneson's shirt and followed Michael Gasca out the door.

39

Jerry Powers called Steven Oquist from his pickup truck.

"What do you have?" Oquist asked.

"I got Keith Ramsey to climb through Kinneson's computers."

"Sneak-and-peek?"

"Quiet as a mouse. Kinneson'll never know we were there."

"Judging from your tone," Oquist said, "you must have got something good."

"Better than good."

"Give it to me."

"What would you think about an NFL owner transferring nine million into an account in the Cayman Islands?" Keith Ramsey had just called to tell Jerry Powers about a new three-million-dollar transfer.

Steven Oquist whistled. "Pre-tax?" His mind immediately raced to prosecution. He could sic the IRS on Kinneson.

"No," Powers said, "he ain't skimmin' it."

"Into a numbered account?"

"Ramsey says there's no way to know who owns it."

"Michael Gasca," Oquist said without hesitation. He could never prove it in court, but he knew the account belonged to Gasca. "What kind of chunks are we talking about?"

Jerry Powers consulted a printout Ramsey had provided. "It's one million here, two million there."

Oquist scribbled on a notepad. "When was the first one?"

"It was," Jerry Powers drawled slowly, "October fifth."

Steven Oquist didn't need to consult a calendar to know the

significance of that date. "That was week five," he said, "a couple days before the Green Bay game."

"The most recent one was three million about half an hour ago."

"That's crazy," Oquist said. "How could this possibly be worth nine million dollars to him?"

"Don't know."

"We should go chat with him."

"You know what might be interesting to ask him about?" Powers said.

"Something better than a meeting with Michael Gasca, a known member of the Sarcassi crime family?"

"It might be interesting to ask him about his ticket broker in D.C."

Oquist perked up. "You don't say?"

Each year, every NFL team received a block of Super Bowl tickets to distribute to players, coaches, media reps, sponsors, and season-ticket holders. Owners had enormous discretion in deciding how to release those tickets. Some focused mostly on season-ticket holders, meeting their minimum contractual obligations with players, sponsors, and media outlets, but saving the bulk of the tickets for their loyal fans. Other teams staged lotteries that gave a handful of tickets to fans, while reserving the majority to grease legislators, mayors, police chiefs, bankers, advertisers, and media personalities. The NFL front office had no formal protocol for the dispersal of Super Bowl tickets, but every team was reminded that it was against league rules to sell tickets for more than their face value.

Despite this prohibition, Steven Oquist knew that ticket scalping by players, coaches, and owners was standard practice during every Super Bowl season. The league turned a blind eye to it as long as no one got carried away. After the AFC and NFC championship games, every NFL player had the right to purchase two Super Bowl tickets at face value. Players on the two participating teams could buy more seats if they needed them. League audits over the years had revealed that nearly every player took advantage of this right to purchase two tickets, but the best estimates were that fewer than one hundred fifty men on the thirty non-Super Bowl teams actually attended the game. The rest sold their tickets to brokers, who paid as much as five times the face value. The NFL front office had long been mute on this trend because it was a relatively small problem. The ticket brokers sold the seats as part of corporate packages that were contracted long before anyone knew which two teams would make the Super Bowl. The corporate buyers weren't so much fans of particular teams; they just wanted to use a trip to the World Championship game to impress their clients. Late in the regular season, ticket brokers sent letters to players and coaches offering to discreetly purchase their Super Bowl seats. The broker FedExed checks along with return envelopes. The player simply extracted the check and put his tickets into the envelope. It was quick, it was easy, and once a player did it his rookie year, chances were, he'd be loyal to the same broker for the rest of his career. And since the brokers knew they'd be able to get tickets in late January, they could confidently sell corporate Super Bowl packages as early as July.

The league frowned upon scalping, but it knew that ticket brokers played an important role in the success of the game, so the front office purposely ignored the practice.

However, every now and then, a player, coach, or owner misinterpreted the league's silence as a license to get outrageous with scalping. During the early 1980s, Dominic Frontiere, the late, ex-husband of St. Louis Rams owner Georgia Frontiere, made a little over five hundred thousand dollars scalping Super Bowl tickets. The justice department tracked him down and sent him to prison for nine months for failing to pay taxes on his earnings. Since then, Frontiere had served as a cautionary tale for NFL owners about how to deal with their allotment of tickets.

"He's got ten percent of the seats as a participating team," Jerry Powers said.

"And another eight percent as the host city," Steven Oquist added.

They both knew that Jonathan Kinneson had contractual obligations to meet with his players and coaches, the Texas state legislature, the governor's office, the mayor's office, the council of state mayors, media outlets, corporate sponsors, and a host of other groups, but after doling out all those tickets, he could easily have thousands of seats left over to scalp.

"I wonder if he'd sell us a couple of tickets?" Steven Oquist asked.

40

Elizabeth Moya had seen it all in fifty-five years of life, marriage, motherhood, grandmotherhood, and career, and she'd spent thirty-three of her best years as an assistant for various upper-echelon executives. When Tracy called from the receptionist desk to warn her that two men from NFL Security were on their way back, Elizabeth had checked her calendar to confirm what she already knew—they didn't have an appointment. When they walked through her door, the first thing she noticed was that they didn't look very official. One had a huge belly overhanging his belt buckle, a bandana around his neck and spurs, of all things, on his boots. She did a confused doubletake on the spurs, and when she looked up again, the other one winked at her. Elizabeth watched them warily, and when they marched past her toward Mr. Kinneson's door, she barked, "You can't go in there!" and picked up the phone.

"Won't be but a minute," Steven Oquist called over his shoulder.

Jonathan Kinneson was sitting behind his marble altar talking on the phone. He had a thick, congested voice. A bandage covered the center of his face, a souvenir from the emergency room he'd visited after Roscoe Evans jammed his big fingers in his nose. The doctors hadn't believed Kinneson's story about running into a door, but Jonathan Kinneson thought they were even less likely to believe that a criminal had burst into his office and tickled the front of his brain with two meaty fingers, so he stuck with the door story.

Several blood vessels had ruptured, giving his nose a bulbous, alcoholic quality, and the attack had damaged the structure of his sinuses. He had dark purple bruises under both eyes, wooden splints along either side of his nose, and white tape splayed across his face. His mouth stood agape; the doctors said it would take a couple of weeks for his nose to clear enough for regular breathing.

Jonathan Kinneson had heard Elizabeth yell at the two men, so he barely glanced at them. This sort of interruption was not unprecedented. Many obstacles kept people out of Jonathan Kinneson's office and some salesmen—their sanity suffering in the sweltering boredom of the waiting area—convinced themselves that Jonathan Kinneson wanted go-getters who would flout convention and muscle their way into his inner sanctum. They believed that if they entered his office by force, Kinneson would smile, impressed by their tenacity, and give their hands a warm, congratulatory clutch.

But Jonathan Kinneson didn't want go-getters. He had adopted the practice of ignoring them when they made unauthorized entries. Elizabeth would call security, and after a minute or two peace would be restored.

When Steven Oquist and Jonathan Powers walked in, Jonathan Kinneson swung his chair around to face his overlarge windows and spectacular view of the city. He continued to talk in a low voice to a board member who was warning him that he might be ousted as president of the company.

"They can't do that!" Kinneson hissed.

The phone died in his ear. Kinneson stared at the receiver. He couldn't believe the board member had hung up on him. He turned around to redial and saw one of the intruders standing with his finger pressed on the off button.

Kinneson said, "That was an important call!"

"We won't take long," Steven Oquist promised. He fell into a chair and motioned Powers to do the same. "Looks like you got into a nasty accident."

Kinneson still had the phone in his hand and he pointed it at them. "I'll have you arrested!"

"We're from NFL Security, and we just wanted to know if we could buy Super Bowl tickets directly from you or do we need to call your broker in Washington?"

Jonathan Kinneson stopped for five full beats. He slowly placed the phone back on its cradle.

"What's the broker's name?" Oquist said, looking at Powers. "Jones? Chuck Jones? Something like that?"

Jerry Powers nodded. "Charles Edward Jones."

Three powerfully built men burst into the office wearing identical uniforms. They stopped for a moment, awaiting orders. With a nod from Jonathan Kinneson, they stepped forward and dragged the two NFL Security officers out of their chairs.

"We'll talk you to you soon," Oquist promised as they pulled him out of the room.

"Did you know that back in the eighties," Powers said, his spurs jingling, "there was an owner that went to prison for scalping Super Bowl tickets?"

When they left the office, Jonathan Kinneson snatched up the phone and dialed a number in Washington, D.C.

"Who did you tell?" Kinneson demanded.

"Who is this?" the voice wanted to know.

"It's Kinneson, you stupid schmuck! And I just had two guys from NFL Security in here asking about my ticket connection. Who in the hell did you tell?"

"I didn't tell anyone," the voice said. Then, cautiously, "You sound strange. You don't sound like Mr. Kinneson."

"I got in an accident and my nose got busted up. You must have told someone, because they knew."

"All I did was move the tickets. I never mentioned your name."

"Nobody asked you where they came from?"

"The people I sell to don't care where they came from."

Jonathan Kinneson drummed his fingers on the desk. "Well, how do they know, then?"

"You sure they were NFL Security?"

Kinneson shrugged. "They didn't show me badges or anything, but that's what they said. And I think I sort of recognized one of them. I think he's our local security officer."

"What did they say?"

"They wanted to know if they had to call you to get tickets."

"Maybe they don't know. Maybe they were just fishing."

"They knew your name."

"Seriously?"

"Yeah. And that you were in Washington."

The voice went silent. Finally, he said, "When were they there?"

"They just left. Came barging in here like they owned the place."

"And you called me first thing when they walked out the door?"

"They didn't walk out, they were dragged out by building security." Kinneson hoped they'd been roughed up.

"*How* they left isn't so interesting to me," the voice said impatiently. "What concerns me is that the minute they walked out the door, you called me."

They both paused then. "Yeah," Kinneson admitted, finally getting it.

The voice sighed. "I gotta go."

Jonathan Kinneson held the empty phone against his head until it beeped and told him that if he'd like to make a call, he should hang up and try again.

41

"Look, I know she was a bitch," Robo said, "but you gotta be joking." They were sitting in Trevor Deale's living room, talking about the Super Bowl. None of the boys could quite believe their amazing success.

"Where's that fine little woman of yours?" Rob had asked a few minutes earlier. And Trevor told his friends—Robo, Caleb, and Martin—that he'd broken up with her.

"Definitely not joking," Trevor said.

"For what?" Robo wanted to know.

"It just wasn't working out."

"What's her name?" Caleb said. They all chuckled.

"There's no other woman," Trevor said.

"Bullshit!" Martin coughed into his hand.

"You don't walk away from something as fine as Vanessa unless you got something else cooking," Robo said. "So what you got on the back burner?"

"Nobody," Trevor insisted. "I did meet a girl at the mall, but—"

"I knew it!" said Caleb.

Robo and Martin traded high fives.

"My man's a true playa for real," Robo said. "He met a girl at the mall and cleared the decks in a quick minute."

"What's her name?" Martin asked.

"It's not about the girl," Trevor said. "Seriously, I'd been looking at Vanessa differently for a while, and I knew I was going to break up with her. When I met this girl at the mall—"

"You notice he still hasn't told us her name," Martin said

"Must be serious, he doesn't want us to know who it is," Caleb said.

"Jennifer," Trevor said.

"Ooh…the lovely Jennifer," Caleb said.

"Is she fine?" Robo asked.

Trevor shrugged.

Martin said, "On a scale of one to ten—"

"Halle Berry's a ten," Caleb said, setting the standard.

"Shit, on that scale, Vanessa was an eleven," Robo said.

"True," Martin agreed.

"Jennifer," Trevor said, slowly, "isn't as pretty as Vanessa, but she's nice. There's something about her that makes her seem a lot higher on the scale."

His three friends stared at him.

"Trevor," Caleb said, "this girl is *nice*? Like when someone wants to hook you up and you say, 'What's she look like?' and they say, 'She's *nice.*' Is that what we're talking about here?"

"You dumped an hot, sexy, beautiful woman like Vanessa," Robo said, laying a fatherly hand on Trevor's shoulder, "for a *nice* girl?"

"I didn't dump Vanessa for Jennifer," Trevor said. "Jennifer was just a catalyst."

Robo grunted. "What the hell is a cat with a lisp?"

"He didn't say *cat,* you idiot," Caleb said, smacking the back of Robo's head. "He said, *cattle* with a lisp."

Martin shook his head. "I can't believe you two went to college."

"Hell," Caleb said, "when Robo graduated from high school his IQ was lower than the you-must-be-this-high-to-enter sign at Disney World."

"Ha ha ha," Robo said.

"A catalyst—" Trevor started.

"Don't explain," Martin said. "Make them go find a dictionary."

"Screw all y'all and the mothers you rode in on," Robo said with both middle fingers extended.

"So how many times have you seen Jennifer?" Caleb asked.

"Three times." Since their ice cream date, they'd gone to dinner twice. Trevor was surprised by how much he liked her. She was different from Vanessa in every conceivable way. She wasn't nearly as pretty, nor did she have Vanessa's incredible body. But she had a wonderful smile, and a gentleness about her that was real and intriguing. Trevor realized that's what had been lacking in his life—reality. For the past eight months, he'd been living in a dream world full of agents, pro scouts, the NFL draft, media interviews, packed stadiums, a palatial estate, millions of dollars, and a girlfriend who was too beautiful for words. But it had all felt so artificial.

But Jennifer Winesett was real. She was a kind, decent person. She'd grown up in rural Pennsylvania, had moved to Texas for college and never left.

"What did y'all do on your dates?" Caleb said.

Trevor shrugged. "We talked."

"And?" Robo asked suggestively.

"Talked some more," Trevor said.

"You didn't get any?" Caleb asked.

"No," Trevor said.

"Hey, good for you, man," Robo said. "I'm happy you found a nice girl." After a suitable pause, he said, "Can I get Vanessa's number?"

"You ain't right," Martin said. He grabbed a pillow off the couch and threw it at Robo.

"What?" Robo said. "He said they weren't right for each other. I happen to think me and Vanessa would be a perfect fit." None of them doubted that. Robo had the right mix of good looks and cocky confidence to match Vanessa beautiful bitchiness.

"If I knew where she was," Trevor said, "I'd be happy to give you her number."

"What do you mean, if you knew where she was?" Martin said.

"You didn't put her on the street, did you?" Caleb said.

"Damn, you's a cold-ass playa," Robo said. "You should have sent her over to my place if she needed a spot to crash."

"I took her to a hotel downtown, but when I sent her stuff over the next day, she wasn't there. They said she checked out in the middle of the night, and she called me the next day to say that she had left town."

"What stuff were you sending over?" Robo asked.

"Her clothes, jewelry and some cash."

"And she left without it?" Robo could hardly believe it. "There are a lot of women in the world who don't care about material stuff, but Vanessa ain't one of 'em. If you promised to bring her some jewelry and cash, you better believe she was gonna hang around to wait for it."

"She didn't really leave without it," Trevor said. "She asked me to mail it to an address in Chicago."

"What's she doing up there?" Martin asked.

"I don't know," Trevor said. He realized that he was glad to know that she was okay but he didn't care what she was doing or where she was headed.

"And she hasn't called you since then?" Martin asked.

As if on cue, the phone rang. Trevor smiled when he saw the name on the caller ID.

"Hi, Trevor," a female voice said.

"Hey there," Trevor said.

Robo stage whispered, "If that's Vanessa, tell her I'd like to—"

Trevor shook his head and covered the receiver with one hand. "It's Jennifer."

Robo frowned, disappointed.

"Are you busy?" Jennifer asked.

"Just chillin' with the boys."

"Oh, well I won't keep you—"

"Don't worry about that, they were just leaving." Trevor glared at his teammates theatrically; they grumbled and shuffled toward the door.

"I was calling to invite you to dinner," Jennifer said.

"Sure," Trevor said. "When?" He was still amazed at how comfortable he felt with her. When they were together, they talked for hours without ever running out of things to say.

"I'd like to cook for you next week."

"Sounds great," Trevor said. "But how about if I take you to dinner instead?"

"Okay," Jennifer said, "are you that afraid of my cooking?"

"Not at all," Trevor said, "But I'm going to be in Hawaii for the Pro Bowl. If you come with me, I'd like to take you to dinner."

Jennifer was stunned. "Wow," she said after a moment. "I think I could be persuaded."

Trevor and Jennifer talked for another hour. It wasn't until the following day that Trevor realized that he hadn't thought about Vanessa even once during the entire conversation.

42

The next morning the phone rang precisely at 8 AM. It was Mandy's boyfriend, William.

"I hate to bother you," he said nervously. "I know you're busy getting ready for the Super Bowl, but I wondered if I could stop by?"

Trevor could hear a slight tremor in his voice. He imagined this was how William must have sounded when he was in high school calling a girl to ask her to the prom.

"You're in San Antonio?" He wasn't expecting his family until the following day. They were coming down for Super Bowl weekend.

"I flew down this morning to consult with the sheriff over at the Bexar County jail, and I'll be leaving again tonight."

Suddenly Trevor knew what this was about. William Stoughton wanted to ask for Mandy's hand in marriage, and he wanted Trevor's approval. Trevor hadn't spent a lot of time with Mandy's beau, but William seemed like a nice guy. Trevor smiled. He knew Mandy would be thrilled.

"What time were you thinking about coming by?"

"I can be there within the hour," William said.

"That's cool. Do you know how to get here?" Trevor gave William directions and hung up the phone with a smile.

■ ■ ■

When Trevor answered the door, he didn't know what to think. William Stoughton was on the stoop with the biggest person Trevor had ever seen.

"Trevor," William said, "this is Roscoe."

Roscoe Evans smiled down like an affable giant.

"Wow," Trevor said.

"Yeah, I get that a lot," Roscoe said.

Trevor extended his hand, "Come on in." He suddenly knew that William's visit didn't have anything to do with wedding bells.

"Nice place you got here," Roscoe said. Their footsteps echoed off the marble floors. Trevor ushered them to a couch and sat across from them in an armchair. A heavy granite coffee table sat between them.

"I want to talk to you about the Super Bowl," William said.

"Yeah? You need some more tickets?"

William and Roscoe laughed. "No, we don't need any tickets," William said. "What we need is your help during the game."

The vibe in the room turned serious. Trevor had met William twice since Mandy started dating him, and both times, he had seemed nice but nervous, competent at his job but bumbling in life. But now William stared at Trevor without a hint of the shyness he'd exhibited in their previous meetings. He'd become a different person. Or perhaps, Trevor realized, he'd been acting the whole time.

"You're name isn't William Stoughton, is it?" Trevor asked.

"Very good," William said. He clapped his hands slowly. "My name is Michael Gasca."

Trevor put the pieces together very quickly. "You're the guy who gets planes for Caleb Alexander."

Gasca blinked, surprised that Trevor knew that.

"And you told him to fumble in the Green Bay game so that we'd lose, and Mr. Kinneson could fire coach Starnes."

Whoa! Michael Gasca and Roscoe Evans looked at each other. *How the hell did Trevor know all of that?*

"Listen, Trevor," Michael Gasca said. He was off balance. "We're here to talk about something very important."

"You were never interested in my sister?" Trevor realized. Mandy would be devastated.

Michael Gasca shrugged. "She's a nice girl, but not really my type."

They stared at each other for a couple of beats as terror built in Trevor's heart.

"Excuse me a minute," Trevor said.

He walked into the kitchen.

"Where you going?" Roscoe asked. He was worried that Trevor would come back with a weapon.

"Relax," Gasca whispered. "He doesn't own a gun. I asked him about that when he was up in Lamesa a couple months ago."

"He coulda bought one," Roscoe said.

"I doubt it."

"So what's he doing?"

"He's worried about his little sister."

In the kitchen, Trevor dialed his mother's number and closed his eyes. When she answered, he tried to be as casual as he could. He didn't want to alarm her.

"Hey Mom, how you doing?"

"Oh, I'm good honey, just getting ready to head down to the shop." Kathy Deale had found a job at the small bakery and sandwich shop in Lamesa. She worked part time during the lunch and dinner hours and proudly drove her new Honda Accord all over town.

"Is Mandy there?" Trevor pressed against the countertop so hard that the back of his hand went pale.

"No, she left with William yesterday. They were going off for a romantic evening, and they're gonna meet us at your house tomorrow. You could try her on her cell phone."

"That's okay," Trevor said. "I'll just talk to her tomorrow."

"All right honey. Well, I'd better run."

"Talk to you later, Mom."

Trevor shuffled back into the living room. Roscoe was watching him carefully to see if he was armed. Gasca smiled. So now Trevor knew the situation. It would make the rest easier.

Trevor studied Michael Gasca, trying to understand what sort of man could do what he had done. Gasca had met Mandy nearly a year ago, before Trevor left college, before he got drafted by the Stallions, and before he had any money. This man—this Michael Gasca—had targeted Trevor and decided that Mandy was the best route to get close to him. Gasca had started to date her, and she had fallen in love with him. All of this put Michael Gasca in position to set up this meeting so that he could...could what? Trevor wondered. What could be so important that it was worth investing a year of work to set up this one meeting?

Michael Gasca could almost see the gears turning in Trevor's head. Gasca smiled inwardly and reviewed everything he'd accomplished in the past couple of years. When Trevor was just a sophomore at Oklahoma, Michael Gasca knew that he'd found the player who could help him beat the NFL. The success of Gasca's plan depended on controlling a dominant, impact player, and Trevor was just that player. Michael Gasca did a great deal of research, trying to discover Trevor's strengths, weaknesses, and vices. What he loved, what he hated, what he would die for. It was then, nearly two years ago, that Michael Gasca had the conversation with Dominic Sarcassi in which he proposed that the family do something that was ordinarily forbidden—fix NFL games. A short time later, Gasca sent Vanessa to Oklahoma to start building a relationship with Trevor Deale.

In the middle of last season, the league formally stated that Jonathan Kinneson had been selected from a small group of candidates as the next owner of the San Antonio Stallions. That's when Michael Gasca had put his plan into action. He knew enough about Kinneson to know that the billionaire would be the perfect candidate for manipulation. Kinneson was greedy, egotistical, and accustomed to bullying his subordinates. One look at last fall's NFL standings told Gasca that it would be a pretty simple matter to get Jonathan Kinneson and Trevor Deale together.

As a fairly new franchise, the Stallions already had been one of the league's poorest-performing teams, so Michael Gasca had to fix only a couple of games to ensure that the Stallions ended the regular season with the worst record in the NFL. That gave San Antonio the first pick in the April Draft, which everyone in the country knew was going to be Trevor Deale.

Over the winter, Michael Gasca had flown down to Lamesa, Texas, a few times to meet and start dating Mandy. And it was Michael Gasca, through an intermediary, who had first planted the idea in Jonathan Kinneson's head about using outside help to get rid of Coach Max Starnes and get his Stallions into the Super Bowl.

Now, sitting in Trevor's living room, Michael Gasca was ready to execute the final stage of his plan.

"Where is she?" Trevor said with quiet venom.

"She's safe, and—"

"Where the fuck is she!"

"She's safe," Michael Gasca repeated slowly. "And she'll stay that way as long as you do what I ask you to do."

A funnel of raw rage swelled inside Trevor, breaking out of a deep and violent fissure in his brain, speaking to him in an urgent whisper. It leaked out of his eyes, poured out of his pores, and steamed out with every breath. His whole body vibrated as if he might explode.

He strode toward the two men; they stood to face him.

"Calm down, Trevor," Gasca said, trying to back away. "I know you're angry, but you need to just *calm down!*"

Trevor reached over the coffee table, nearly grabbing the front of Gasca's shirt, but Michael Gasca avoided his grasp and fell back into the couch. Roscoe grabbed Trevor's arm with a vise-like grip, and he was about to tell Trevor to take it easy when Trevor ripped his arm back with such fierceness that Roscoe lurched forward and nearly lost his balance. His shins were wedged against the heavy coffee table and he held on to Trevor's arm to keep from falling. Trevor swung his left hand and caught Roscoe just under the ear with a closed fist that struck like a hammer. Roscoe moaned, stunned. His grip tightened. Trevor swung again, twisting his torso to drive as much force as he could into his fist. He hit the same spot; the bones in Roscoe's jaw crunched audibly. Trevor angled his fist upward, hitting Roscoe with a powerful uppercut that clattered the big man's teeth together and snapped his head back. Roscoe's tongue got caught between his teeth and a triangular chunk was shorn off; it dropped to the marble floor like a fat, lifeless worm. Roscoe's grip on Trevor's arm finally slackened, and he tumbled to the ground gracelessly sending ceramic figurines tumbling off a bookshelf.

Michael Gasca jumped off the couch and ran, but Trevor chased him down in five quick strides. Trevor grabbed Gasca and launched him into the entertainment center. Gasca screamed as the back of his head struck the edge of the television. He crumpled to the ground and the entertainment center teetered forward and fell on top of him. Trevor grabbed Michael Gasca by the arm and dragged him—scraping the whole way—out from under the entertainment center.

"Wait a second," Michael Gasca managed.

Trevor punched Gasca in the face, which brought a mist of bright red blood from his nose and mouth. Trevor pulled Michael Gasca up and hit him again, this time catching him in the temple and nearly rendering him unconscious. Roscoe rolled over and tried to get up; Trevor walked over and kicked the man square in the face. Roscoe's entire body heaved backward. Two teeth flew out of his mouth and clattered on the floor, and a fresh surge of pain flooded his system; he writhed in agony. Trevor turned back to Michael Gasca, who had pulled himself up to his hands and knees. Trevor grabbed him, took a running start, and propelled Gasca through the big picture window at the front of the house. Heavy drapes hung along the sides of the frame and thin sheers stretched across the window. The glass and wood shattered as Gasca hit them. The sheers caught him in a gauzy net and wrapped around him as they came off the rod. Gasca tumbled into the yard on top of the sharp shards of glass and wood. Trevor jumped through the window, grabbed Gasca, and punched him through the sheers.

"Thstop!" a muffled voice said. "I havth tha gun! I'll thshoot!"

Trevor's chest was rising and falling quickly. He turned to see Roscoe Evans leaning out of the window. Roscoe's face was swollen and blood was spilling out of his mouth like water overflowing a dam. He pointed a blood-smeared chrome pistol at Trevor.

"Thdon't movf!" Roscoe managed. His tongue—missing a chunk— was swollen to the point of uselessness.

Trevor stared at Roscoe and waited.

"You'll newa thsee you thsista again ith you don't thstop!"

"Where is she?" Trevor demanded.

"Thshe's thsafe."

"Take me to her."

Michael Gasca rolled over onto his knees, coughing and spitting blood. "You might have just messed up, kid." Gasca spit out more blood. "I'll call you, and I'll tell you what you have to do to get her back."

Roscoe kept the gun trained on Trevor as he swung first one leg then the other over the window frame and eased onto the lawn. He moved past Trevor and hooked one arm around Michael Gasca, who looked as if he might collapse at any moment. He and Gasca limped back to the car, and when Roscoe looked back, Trevor had disappeared. The big man helped Gasca into the passenger seat, then gave him the gun and told him to keep his eyes open.

"He mighth be gonth thto getth a gun." Roscoe went around to the other side of the car, and began his slow slide into the driver's seat. He could barely move his mouth, and when he touched the side of his face a sharp bolt of pain streaked down his spine. He figured that his jaw was broken, but he put it out of his mind. There would be time to deal with that later. For now, he needed to get away from Trevor Deale.

■ ■ ■

Trevor dragged his fingers down a list of phone numbers on the front of the refrigerator. "Come on…come on…" *There!* Trevor stabbed the buttons on his phone, dialing the guest house that sat just two hundred yards down the hill from the main house. A golf cart, parked in a small garage, ferried guests to and from the mansion. Trevor waited impatiently while it rang.

"Hello." Caleb sounded surprised. These days, no one ever called him.

"Caleb, it's Trevor. I need your help."

"Anything," Caleb said, suddenly alert.

"A blue Lincoln Town Car is coming down to the gate in a couple of minutes. I need you to follow it."

"Really?" Caleb wondered if this was a joke.

"Michael Gasca is in that car. I need you to move right now! You've got to get out through the gate before them. Then follow them, but don't get too close. I need to know where they go."

"All right." Caleb's head was reeling. *Michael Gasca? Here on the estate?* He hadn't talked to the man since just after the Green Bay game.

"Go, Caleb. Go!"

■ ■ ■

Roscoe started the engine and watched Trevor walk out onto the front porch.

"Why don't you tell me what you came here to tell me?" Trevor said as he came down the front steps.

Michael Gasca breathed heavily through the open window. His face was covered in blood; his nose was swollen and crooked, he had a busted lip, puffy eyes, and knots along the left side of his head.

"Tomorrow," Gasca said weakly.

"Just tell me." Trevor didn't want them to leave without knowing where his sister was or what they wanted from him.

"Let's go, Roscoe," Michael Gasca said.

Trevor took a step forward, and Gasca raised the gun.

"You can't shoot me," Trevor said. "Whatever it is you want, you need me healthy to do it. So just tell me what it is."

"I'll call you tomorrow," Gasca said.

"You can call me this afternoon. I'll be here all day."

"About eight tomorrow night," Gasca insisted. "That's when I'll call you."

"Tell you what," Trevor said. "You call me *tonight* at eight, and when you call you'd better have my sister there to tell me she's okay. If I don't hear from you at eight, I'm gonna call the cops."

"You call the cops and your sister is dead," Gasca warned.

"If anything happens to my sister, *you're* dead," Trevor said. A cold rage lingered in his eyes and convinced Gasca that the quarterback would do everything in his power to follow through on that threat.

"Eight o'clock tonight!" Trevor said. He turned and walked back into the house, slamming the door.

"Thjesus Cwrist!" Roscoe mumbled.

Michael Gasca let out a breath and slumped back against the seat. His head was pounding. In all their years of dealing with murdering, lying, cheating, gambling gangsters, no one but Trevor Deale had ever gotten the jump on them.

"Let's go home, Roscoe."

■ ■ ■

Caleb Alexander jogged out to his BMW and looked up the hill to see if he could make out Michael Gasca's car, but a grove of trees standing between him and the house blocked his view. He drove down the driveway, hit his remote control to open and close the gate, made a couple of turns, and eased through the main gate. He pulled over among a group of cars parked along the side of the road and waited. After a minute or two, the Town Car emerged. Caleb waited a few seconds, and then followed the car.

◾ ◾ ◾

As Roscoe Evans drove slowly back to their house, Michael Gasca dialed Dominic Sarcassi's secure line.

"How are things going down there?" Uncle Nick asked.

"Not so good," Gasca confessed.

"Yeah?"

"We need a doctor."

"What kind and how bad?" Uncle Nick said without hesitation.

"Roscoe lost a couple of teeth, and he might have a broken jaw," Michael Gasca said. "I just need a general doctor."

"Who hurt Roscoe?" Uncle Nick asked incredulously. He could not recall a single instance in which Roscoe had ever sustained even a bruised knuckle. If Roscoe was hurt, someone must have gotten the jump on him with a bazooka or an eighteen-wheeler.

"Trevor Deale," Gasca mumbled, closing his eyes.

Uncle Nick waited, but nothing else was coming.

"Yes…Trevor Deale…" he led.

Michael Gasca coughed softly. "We went over to tell him that we had his sister."

"No, thhe thfigured it outh," Roscoe corrected.

"Yeah," Gasca said into the phone, "he figured out that we had his sister, and then he attacked us."

This was the most remarkable thing Uncle Nick had ever heard. "So Trevor Deale, by himself, took down Roscoe Evans?"

"Yeah."

"Did he have anything?"

"Like what?"

"Like a tank?"

"No," Gasca sighed.

"Just his bare hands?"

"Yes, Uncle Nick," Gasca said with eroding patience. "Just his bare hands."

"Anthd hiths thfoot," Roscoe injected, wondering what Nike put into the toe of their cross trainers to make them so damn hard.

Uncle Nick shook his head. "You want to head to the doctor now?"

"Can you get someone to come to us?"

"No problem." Uncle Nick hung up the phone and shook his head. Trevor Deale had beaten up Roscoe Evans. That was one for the books.

■ ■ ■

Trevor waited anxiously at the front door for Caleb's return.

"How'd it go? Trevor asked.

"I stayed back a long way, and they drove pretty much straight there without making many turns."

"Where?"

"I have the address here." Caleb handed Trevor a piece of paper. "It's sort of a creepy old house."

"Thank you, Caleb." Hot, angry tears rimmed Trevor's eyes.

"Are you okay?"

"They've got my sister." Trevor said, his body shaking.

Caleb didn't know what to say.

"They're using her to try to get me to do something in the Super Bowl," Trevor said.

"What do they want you to do?"

"I don't know. They're going to call me tonight."

"What are you gonna do?"

43

The adrenaline rush that had seized Trevor Deale was beginning to fade. He was in his Range Rover flying down I-10, and he thought about driving straight to the address Caleb had given him, busting down the door, kicking their asses again, and grabbing Mandy. But he didn't know if that would be smart. He needed to use his brain, not his brawn. He had the upper hand now that he knew where Michael Gasca and Roscoe Evans were living. He wasn't sure Mandy was in the house with them and he didn't want them to relocate to a new hiding spot.

He'd call the NFL Security guy who'd approached him in the locker room. Trevor pulled out his wallet, his eyes dancing back and forth between the road and his hands. His fingers flipped nimbly through his billfold until he found the card he was looking for: Steven Oquist. Trevor snatched up his cell phone and dialed.

The line in Jerry Powers's office rang three times, then automatically forwarded to his cell phone. Powers pulled the phone off his hip as if it were a six-shooter in a holster. Steven Oquist sipped a Coke as he watched his colleague pull a piece of hay out of his teeth and answer the phone.

"Howdy, this is Jerry…no…uh-huh…yep, he's right here."

Powers handed the cell phone across the table to Oquist, who gave him a quizzical look, but the big Texan just shrugged his shoulders.

"Hello?" Oquist said.

"Mr. Oquist, it's Trevor Deale."

The NFL Security officer perked up. "What can I do for you?"

"I've been contacted by Michael Gasca and Roscoe Evans."

"In person?"

"They came to my house."

"What did they look like?" Oquist wanted to be sure.

"Michael Gasca's a skinny little guy and Roscoe Evans is built like a cement truck."

"That's them." Steven Oquist's pulse was racing. "What did they want?"

"Why don't we meet in person to talk about this?" Trevor said.

"You bet."

"Where are you?"

"No, no, no. This isn't a good place," Oquist said. The last thing he wanted was for the Stallions' star quarterback to walk into a bar with an illegal bookmaking operation in back. He looked at Jerry Powers. "Is there a park around here anywhere?"

"There's McCallister Park up near the airport."

"Do you know where McCallister Park is?" Oquist asked Trevor.

"Yes," Trevor said. "There's a bunch of benches right in the middle near a statue. I'll meet you there in half an hour."

■ ■ ■

Trevor Deale watched the two men approach, and he wondered if he'd made a mistake. Steven Oquist, wearing khaki pants, a light blue button-up shirt, and a baseball cap, looked casually efficient, but perhaps a little old. Jerry Powers strode across the grass wearing a five-gallon hat. As they got closer, Trevor noticed the sprig of straw dancing from side to side in Powers's mouth, and he had spurs on his boots.

"Trevor," Oquist said when they reached him.

"Trey-va," Powers said with his twang.

The two men sat down.

"How do you drive with spurs on?" Trevor asked, honestly curious.

"I take 'em off when I get in the truck, just like my hat."

"And you put them back on every time you get out?"

"Yep," Jerry Powers said. Steven Oquist had watched with amusement as Powers fought against the pressure of his stomach to reach down and re-fasten the spurs every time he exited the truck.

"Seems like a lot of effort."

"Yep."

Steven Oquist detected a note of pride in Jerry Powers's voice, as if he were a jogger bragging about the distance he covered every day.

Trevor took a deep breath. "They've got my sister." He paused for a long moment. "They came by the house to say that she was a hostage and I had to help them in the Super Bowl."

"What do they want you to do?" Steven Oquist asked. He was concerned about Trevor's sister, but his first instinct was to protect the game.

"We didn't get that far," Trevor said. "I got pissed off and beat them up pretty bad. They left without ever telling me what they wanted from me."

Oquist stopped. "You beat them up?"

"Yeah."

"Both of them?"

"Yeah."

"Michael Gasca *and* Roscoe Evans?"

"Yes, Mr. Oquist," Trevor said impatiently.

"You're telling me you took down Roscoe Evans?" Steven Oquist had one arm stretched up to the sky with his palm right-angled about where the top of Roscoe's head would be.

"Look," Trevor said, "they're gonna call me tonight at eight to tell me what they want. Can you help me or not?"

"Of course," Oquist said. There was no way C.C. could deny Oquist's request now. A player had called NFL Security to report that he'd been contacted by known criminals. Steven Oquist would have the full authority to set up an operation.

"What would you do?" Trevor asked.

"Well," Oquist considered the options. "We'd put together a strike team of eight to ten security officers and a dozen FBI agents. We'd guard your house, find your sister, arrest Michael Gasca and Roscoe Evans, and keep them from doing anything to harm the Super Bowl."

"Wouldn't the SWAT team be faster?"

"Listen," Steven Oquist said carefully, "One of the things we have to consider is the media. We have to keep this out of the newspapers."

"Maybe it would help if the press knew," Trevor said.

"No!" Oquist said, a little more forcefully than he intended. In a measured tone, he said, "The fewer people who know about this the better." Oquist needed to keep this on a federal level, because the NFL had a very close relationship with federal legislators, justice department officials, and the FBI. On the federal level, Steven Oquist was sure he could keep this situation quiet. He feared what would happen if the local D.A. tried to make a name for himself at the expense of the NFL.

"The FBI," Oquist said, "can handle this far better than the SWAT team."

Trevor nodded as if he'd already thought it through. "Michael Gasca has been manipulating our games all season and you guys haven't been able to catch him, so he must be pretty sophisticated."

There was no reproach in Trevor's voice, but Oquist felt stung nonetheless. His intuition had been right all along, but C.C. had held him back so effectively that Michael Gasca had been free to move with impunity.

"What do you think we oughta do?" Jerry Powers asked, because it seemed to him that Trevor Deale had an idea.

"Two things," Trevor said. "First, we have to lull Michael Gasca to sleep by making him believe he's got more control over the situation than he actually does, and two, we need to rescue my sister as soon as possible."

"I don't see how we're gonna fool him," Jerry Powers said. "It seems like he's got control of everything at the moment."

"Maybe," Trevor said, "but we know a lot more than he thinks we know."

"Do we?" Powers asked.

"Mr. Oquist, you've known for months that they were down here fixing our games."

"True," Oquist said.

"And I've known that Mr. Kinneson was involved since the Green Bay game," Trevor said.

That was week five, Oquist realized. Somehow early in the season, Trevor Deale had detected this plot.

"How did you know?" Oquist asked.

"This part stays between the three of us, because it involves a friend of mine. I don't want him to get in trouble."

"We'll protect your friend," Steven Oquist promised.

"The week before the Green Bay game, I went to Mr. Kinneson's office to talk to him about a charity event, and I heard him tell someone on the phone that something would happen that weekend with Coach Starnes. Then after the game, Caleb Alexander told me that Michael Gasca put pressure on him to fumble in the red zone, which he did *accidentally*."

Steven Oquist had studied each of the Stallions's games but he didn't recall that play. "You lost that game, right?"

"Yeah, that's when Mr. Kinneson fired Coach Starnes on the plane when we were flying back to San Antonio."

"So you think—"

"Mr. Kinneson arranged the loss so that he could fire the coach."

Oquist hadn't considered that angle. He had thought it strange that Kinneson dismissed Coach Max Starnes in the middle of the season, but it wasn't unprecedented. It was odder that Jonathan Kinneson hired Trevor's college coach, but it hadn't occurred to Oquist that Jonathan Kinneson might have manipulated that game with the intent of getting rid of Coach Starnes.

"Was Caleb's fumble at a crucial point in the game?" Jerry Powers asked. He didn't recall anything particularly strange about that game either.

"That's the thing," Trevor said. "I can't figure out why they wanted him to fumble. He dropped it right at the goal line, so it robbed us of seven points, but we were leading at the time, and it was still early in the fourth quarter. So the fumble might have hurt us, but it didn't kill us. We had more scoring chances later in the game. After that game there were other suspicious plays, and we won three or four games that I didn't think we should have won. Now I realize they were trying to get us into the Super Bowl. But I still can't figure out what Michael Gasca could possibly want from me. He's been helping us win all season, so why would he have targeted my sister so many months ago?"

Steven Oquist was asking himself the same question. "Maybe this is the week they plan to make their big score. Now that the Stallions are playing so great, maybe they're going to ask you to throw a couple of interceptions to upset the balance. They can lay down some bets and get a big payday."

"After all the work they've done to get us here, you think they want us to lose?" Trevor said.

"They probably don't care if you win or lose," Jerry Powers said. "They just want to control the outcome."

"But they must want us to lose," Trevor said. "Kidnapping my sister will only distract me. It couldn't possibly make me play better."

"Maybe he wants you to accept his help winnin' the game," Powers said.

"What does that mean?" Trevor said.

"Well," Powers responded, "I was thinking you have the freedom to audible to any play you want, so maybe Michael Gasca's puttin' pressure on one of the Rams defensive backs. Late in the game the DB's gonna give you a signal. Then you'll audible to a certain play, and the DB's will fall down. You throw the ball to the open receiver and score a touchdown."

"Maybe," Steven Oquist said. "But if Gasca wants that to happen, he doesn't need Trevor. He could just tell the DB to fall."

"No, Jerry's right," Trevor said. "The best person to tap for that would be the free safety, and if Michael Gasca wanted it to work, he'd need to have me and the free safety on the same page. Just because the safety falls down doesn't guarantee that I'll see the open man. Or by the time the safety falls, I might already have thrown the ball somewhere else. Or maybe the receiver isn't running the right route to take advantage of the fall. The safety knows when he's got middle deep coverage with no help. He could give me a signal, and I'd call an audible to send a receiver down the middle of the field."

"But," Oquist said, "if the safety is signaling you, then everyone in the world is gonna see it. This is the Super Bowl. There are a million cameras out there. He can't be flapping his arms at you."

"It would be easy," Trevor said. "Every player who's ever worn a helmet adjusts it by grabbing the facemask and shifting it from side to side or up and down. If Michael Gasca wanted this to work, all I'd need to do is make eye contact with the free safety on every play."

"Every play?" Oquist said.

"I look at him anyway when I'm surveying the defense. When he's ready, he grabs his facemask and leaves his hand there for three or four seconds. That's all it would take. No one in the world would ever notice."

"And if the timing is right, you guys would score a touchdown," Jerry Powers said.

Trevor let out a long breath. "So what's our next step?"

"First we have to find them," Steven Oquist said.

Trevor reached into his pocket and pulled out a slip of paper with Michael Gasca's address written on it. "They're in this house."

Talk about stopping the crowd.

Jerry Powers shook his head in amazement. "Kid...you are something else."

Steven Oquist said, "I won't even ask how you know this."

"How soon can you get Mandy out of there?" Trevor asked.

Oquist thought for a moment. "You said Gasca's gonna call you tonight?"

"At eight."

"Demand to talk to your sister."

"Already done. Before they left my house, I insisted that they let me talk to her."

"Good. That'll help. I'll get over there and watch them. Either your sister is staying in this house," Oquist held up the piece of paper, "or they're gonna drive to the place she's being held when it's time to talk to you. One way or another, we'll find her."

Trevor shook his head. "They could have her somewhere else and get her on a conference call."

"True," Oquist agreed, "but unlikely. The reason we haven't been able to find Michael Gasca and Roscoe Evans here in San Antonio is that they're handling everything themselves. So my guess is that they've got your sister with them or she's by herself and they'll have to go to her."

44

Steven Oquist sipped lukewarm coffee in a darkened apartment and stared out the window toward Michael Gasca's hideaway half a block away. The manager of the complex had showed him three vacant units, before Oquist finally decided that this one provided the best view of the old house.

After meeting with Trevor Deale, Oquist had called Assistant Director Ken Parsley, knowing there was no way that C.C. could avoid a full-scale operation. A team of FBI agents had been dispatched from the San Antonio office, and now they had the house surrounded by plain clothed agents. Pedestrian and auto traffic continued to move past the house.

NFL Security Director Don Burke and Assistant Director Ken Parsley were sitting on the couch in the hotel room that had been turned into a command center. They'd already been in town for the Super Bowl, so it had taken them less than an hour to get to the command center after Oquist called.

Steven Oquist had told them everything he knew about Michael Gasca's movements during the season. He told them about the videotape in which Gasca mentioned Trevor Deale back in September. A short time later, Michael Gasca and Roscoe Evans had disappeared from the streets of Philadelphia. He explained the pressure that was applied to Caleb Alexander to get him to fumble in the Green Bay game, which allowed Jonathan Kinneson to fire Coach Max Starnes. He speculated that Michael Gasca had manipulated the outcomes of five, possibly six of the Stallions contests, and the reason no unnatural money showed up in the betting line was that Kinneson had paid more than $9 million directly to

Gasca. He told them about the security tape from Jonathan Kinneson's building, the sign-in log from the front desk, and the wire transfer records on Kinneson's computer. He told them about Michael Gasca's visit to Trevor Deale's home, where against all expectations, the quarterback had beaten up Michael Gasca and Roscoe Evans. And finally, Steven Oquist told his superiors that Trevor Deale's little sister had been kidnapped.

"How come I didn't know about this situation?" Director Burke asked.

"I'm not sure, sir," Steven Oquist said, throwing a small victorious smile at Ken Parsley. "I told C.C. about it pretty early in the season."

"I just. . ." Parsley started, not sure where to go from there. "I sent Oquist down to San Antonio to check it out."

"By then it was too late," Steven Oquist countered. "We should have been on this from the start."

"I agree," Don Burke said. "It should never have gotten this far."

"I just didn't want to upset the teams," Parsley said feebly.

Burke shook his head at his assistant director. "Steven, what's the next step?"

■ ■ ■

"You're late," Trevor snapped. It was five minutes after 8 P.M.

Michael Gasca didn't know what to make of the edge in Trevor's tone. He'd always believed the quarterback had a docile personality, but he was learning that he really didn't know the first thing about Trevor Deale. Gasca had started a relationship with Mandy mostly as a means of getting close to the quarterback and his family to discover what he might be able to use against him.

But somehow, Trevor knew about Caleb Alexander's fumble and Mr. Kinneson's involvement in the Stallions's success. Michael Gasca wasn't surprised that Caleb had confessed to Trevor, but how in the hell did the quarterback know about Mr. Kinneson?

"We've been tending to our wounds," Gasca said, explaining his tardiness.

"Put my sister on the phone."

Michael Gasca rubbed his temples and sighed. Roscoe was sprawled in bed, drifting on the combined effects of Novocain, nitrous oxide, and sedatives. An oral surgeon and a cosmetic dentist had been working on him for hours. They were making a mold for porcelain replacement teeth and wiring Roscoe's jaw shut.

"Hang on a minute," Michael Gasca said. He walked up the stairs and unlocked a bedroom door. Mandy stood up as he entered, looking at him expectantly. She seemed more confused than frightened. Michael Gasca handed her his cell phone.

"Hello?" Mandy said tentatively.

"Mandy!" Trevor's heart was racing. "Are you okay?"

"I don't know," she said. She didn't understand what was happening. She didn't know where she was or why she was being held. There were boards over the windows, a bathroom, and a small refrigerator stocked with sandwiches, fruit, and water. "William locked me in a room. He came back later all bloody, but he didn't explain anything."

"His name isn't William," Trevor said. "It's Michael Gasca."

Mandy blinked several times and shook her head. They had come to this house the day before, and an enormous black man had greeted them at the door. William had led her back to this bedroom and sat her on the bed. She'd laughed and asked him what he was doing. He didn't answer. He had walked out of the room and locked the door behind him. A few minutes later, she heard him leave the house, and she was left alone and scared for several hours. When William came back, his face was swollen. One eye was nearly closed, a dark purple bruise was blooming on the side of his head, and his nose and lips were fat with swelling.

"Oh my god," Mandy had said. "What happened?"

"Nothing," William had said.

"Honey, what's going on? Why are you doing this?"

"Just came to check on you." Michael Gasca had said, turning and walking back out of the room.

Now Mandy held the phone tight against her ear. "What do you mean he's not William?" she asked, as if she didn't believe her brother, though it was clear that she didn't know the man she'd been dating for the past year.

"He's holding you because he wants me to help him fix the Super Bowl," Trevor said.

Mandy's vision was swimming. It all seemed so surreal. Could she really have been completely fooled by William's intentions from the start? She replayed their relationship in her mind, wondering if she'd missed some signs. "So you're saying that William wants—"

"Michael Gasca."

"Trevor," she said, smiling desperately. "Is this some stunt that's going to lead to a proposal?"

Trevor clenched his teeth and wiped his eyes. "Mandy, I want to kill him. He is *not* William Stoughton, he is *not* in love with you, and he is not going to propose marriage. He's been using you from the beginning."

Mandy's face screwed up and tears streamed down her cheeks.

"I don't think she wants to talk anymore," Michael Gasca said, taking the phone.

Trevor's voice was trembling. "If anything happens to her—"

"Nothing will happen to her as long as you do what you're supposed to do," Michael Gasca said.

"And what's that?"

Michael Gasca suddenly realized that he'd missed something. He stood very still with glassy eyes focused in the middle distance.

"Hello?" Trevor said. "What am I supposed to do?"

"I'll tell you when the time is right," Michael Gasca said slowly, hanging up the phone. He continued to stand in the middle of the room with his arms slack against his sides.

Mandy watched him for a few minutes. "What is it?" she asked, tremulously.

Gasca seemed to snap out of a trance. He shook his head and steadied himself. He stared at Mandy as if he didn't know who she was.

"What?" Mandy said again, growing more nervous. She'd never seen William—Michael Gasca—this way. He was not looking at anything, just standing in one spot scowling with an angry, desperate expression on his face.

Gasca was clawing at a nervous idea that had blossomed in his mind while listening to Mandy talk to her brother. He thought back about everything that had happened in the past few hours. He'd made a mistake just now when he handed Mandy the phone. If Trevor were smart— and Gasca knew he was—the quarterback would have learned from this phone call that Mandy was in the same place as her captors. And she told her brother that Gasca had left her locked her in a room and returned hours later covered in blood. That comment revealed that Gasca and Roscoe had traveled straight from the quarterback's house to their hideout. *Had Trevor followed them?* Gasca wondered. *Could he have jumped in his car after they left and tracked them?* Michael Gasca tilted his bruised head to the side. When he and Roscoe had left Trevor's house, they'd been in pretty bad shape and focused solely on getting home and getting medical attention. They hadn't watched their mirrors closely or taken any deliberate detours.

"What is it?" Mandy asked again.

Michael Gasca shook his head and walked out of the room.

■ ■ ■

Trevor Deale immediately called Steven Oquist. "She's in the house with him!"

"I know," Oquist said. The NFL Security officer had listened in on the conversation.

"We've gotta get her out of there!" Trevor said.

"We're putting a plan together right now," Oquist said.

"What's to plan?" Trevor asked. "Let's just go get her."

"Trevor," Oquist said carefully, "this may sound crazy, but the safest place for Mandy at the moment is right where she is."

"Are you out of your mind?" Trevor closed his eyes and tried to stop the pounding in his head. He felt that he was losing control. It had started with Vanessa at the mall. He'd cursed at her, abandoned her, and then broken up with her. Then he'd attacked Michael Gasca and Roscoe Evans when they came to his house, and now he was ready to tear into Steven Oquist. A wild rage was building inside of him, and he wasn't sure he could contain it.

"Right now, Michael Gasca has what he wants," Steven Oquist said. "He didn't tell you what he wanted from you. So, for some reason, between this morning at your house and tonight he decided he should hold onto that information and give it to you later. Why do you think that is?"

Trevor realized the answer the moment he heard the question. "Because I'm unpredictable."

"That's right. They came to your house and you caught them off guard, so now they're worried about you."

"They don't want to give me too much time to think," Trevor said.

Oquist continued, "There's no reason for him to do anything except wait for the right moment to reveal his plan. If we go barging in there to rescue your sister, there might be gunplay, they might escape, anything could happen."

Trevor seemed to be thinking.

"Trevor, here's the situation from my perspective," Steven Oquist said. "We've finally caught Michael Gasca fixing NFL games. Thanks to you, we know what he's been doing all season, we know where he is right now, and we know that he's going to call you in a day or two with a specific request. We have at least another twelve to eighteen hours to come up with a good plan, and while we're waiting, Michael Gasca hopefully will become more relaxed."

Trevor let out a deep breath. "You'd better not let anything happen to her," he warned.

45

Roscoe Evans woke up groggy, disoriented, and incredibly hungry. He suddenly felt sympathy for bears, who must awake to similar feelings after their long hibernation. His jaw ached. The painkillers had worn off, and his head was throbbing. Roscoe sat up and looked around the room. He slowly climbed to his feet and shuffled to the bathroom, ducking under both the bedroom and bathroom doors. He barely recognized himself in the mirror. His head—normally an attractive egg shape—now had a distended jaw that looked as if it belonged on a prehistoric skeleton. The swelling had taken all the detail out of his expression. He tried to raise his eyebrows, then smile and frown, but his face remained a thick, unmoving mask.

Roscoe walked downstairs to the living room, where Michael Gasca had a bag of frozen peas pressed against his right eye.

"How you feeling?" Gasca asked.

Roscoe tried to say, "Like shit," but his jaw was wired shut, and his tongue was swollen to epic proportions. The sound came mostly through his nose. "Unnngh unnhhhh."

Michael Gasca nodded. "You won't be able to talk for about a week." He held up a notebook and a pen. "The doctors said you should carry this with you."

Roscoe accepted the tiny notebook and pen with what might have been wry humor, but Michael Gasca couldn't tell because the big man's face betrayed no emotion. Roscoe scribbled a message, ripped out the page, and handed it to Gasca, who read it and then studied his friend carefully.

"Roscoe," Michael Gasca said, "what does this have to do with anything?"

Roscoe jabbed his finger at the paper, and Gasca guessed that behind the swollen mask, Roscoe must be knitting his brow impatiently.

"Honestly," Gasca shrugged, "I have no idea why bears hibernate."

Roscoe scribbled again. He'd never been a good writer, but he felt suddenly energized. He handed a second note to Gasca.

"You're right," Gasca conceded, "other animals do stay awake all winter." He thought for a moment. "Maybe bears are just lazy."

Roscoe delivered a third note. This time Gasca smiled. He leaned forward to pat a small pouch on the table in front of him.

"Painkillers are right here. They'll have to be injected four times a day."

Roscoe wrote: "I'M READY."

After Gasca administered the medication, Roscoe sat down gingerly and scribbled, "NOW WHAT?"

"I think," Gasca said, "we're going to wait."

Roscoe nodded. Waiting sounded like a good plan. Wait for the swelling to go down. Wait for solid food. Wait for Trevor Deale to forget that there would be serious repercussions for this attack. Wait for the right moment to take Trevor Deale's jaw and massage it into roughly the shape of the state of Texas. Waiting sounded just fine to Roscoe Evans.

"He knows we have his sister, and he knows that we want him to help us in the Super Bowl," Gasca said. "We'll sit tight and let him sweat."

Michael Gasca said all of that for the benefit of surveillance devices—if there were any. He had no idea whether the FBI might have tapped his phone lines, snaked fiber optic wire through the vents or stationed men on nearby rooftops with parabolic listening devices. If the authorities were tuned in, he wanted them to think that he and Roscoe were settling in and weren't planning to make any moves.

Gasca nodded toward a piece of paper sitting on the coffee table, and Roscoe immediately noticed the change in Gasca's demeanor. He slowly dropped his eyes to the paper.

"FBI MAY BE OUTSIDE," the note read. "DID ANYONE FOLLOW US HOME YESTERDAY?"

Roscoe shrugged his big shoulders. He turned to Gasca and shook his head. Gasca arched his eyebrows silently saying *think about it*. Roscoe Evans closed his eyes and replayed the events of the previous day.

After the fiasco at Trevor's house, they'd climbed into the car. Trevor had disappeared into the house, presumably to get a weapon. But he came out empty handed and watched them drive away. Roscoe had studied the rearview mirror, but he hadn't seen Trevor's car leave the garage. They'd left the subdivision and got on I-10, driving slowly in the right lane. Roscoe thought hard. *Had anyone been following them?* He'd been Michael Gasca's driver for many years, and he'd been tailed by some of the best agents the FBI had to offer, so he knew what to look for. He tried to remember every mile of the trip. Every car. Every truck. Every lane change. Every exit.

After a few minutes, he opened his eyes and wrote a short note. Michael Gasca took it from him, then closed his eyes and crumpled it up. The note read: "BLACK BMW BEHIND US ON HIGHWAY AND BEHIND US AT A STOPLIGHT DOWNTOWN."

Roscoe scribbled in his notepad again, and presented the paper to Gasca.

"TREVOR WENT IN THE HOUSE AND CALLED SOMEONE," Roscoe wrote. Gasca nodded. That's what he'd figured, too.

46

It was the night before the Super Bowl, and Trevor Deale was holding Jennifer Winesett's hand over the breakfast table in his hotel suite. She had called earlier in the day to ask if she could come stay with him. He would have said no—first, because players were prohibited from bringing wives, girlfriends, or dates to their rooms the night before a game, and second, because Trevor was too upset about Mandy to concentrate.

But Jennifer seemed to be able to sense his angst and said she wanted to be with him to help him relax before the big game.

So they sat at the table holding hands, and Trevor's eyes kept getting wet, and Jennifer kept asking him what was wrong. She waited until he was ready to talk. Finally, he told her everything that had happened during the past few days. She had listened wide-eyed as if she had never heard of Roscoe Evans or Michael Gasca.

"So they have Mandy right now?" Jennifer asked, truly shocked. She'd had no idea that kidnapping was part of Gasca's plan.

Trevor nodded.

"And you know where they are?"

Again he nodded. "The FBI has their house surrounded."

It was a good thing for Jennifer that Trevor's head was bowed and his eyes were closed. If he had looked up, he would have seen the panic on her face. Michael Gasca had no idea that anyone knew where he was hiding; Jennifer needed to warn him.

Jennifer looked at her purse, which was sitting on the bed on the other side of the room. She could sneak into the bathroom and make a call.

"Thank you for being here," Trevor said, looking up at Jennifer. She tore her eyes away from her purse and turned to him with a quick smile.

"Of course, honey," she said, rubbing his hand gently. He held her gaze for a long time, and Jennifer felt herself soften inside. She'd never met anyone like Trevor Deale. He wasn't at all what she had expected. He was kind, loving, and generous, and it hurt her to see him so tortured. Jennifer knew he was worried about how his little sister was feeling and about whether she would escape from Michael Gasca unharmed. Jennifer wondered what it would be like to have a brother like Trevor, who really cared about her and would do anything for her.

When Trevor lowered his head again, Jennifer closed her eyes and tried to shake these distracting thoughts from her mind. She couldn't afford to engage in fantasy about what if. She had a job to do for Michael Gasca, and she felt tremendously loyal to him. She'd known Gasca most of her life, and he was the closest thing she had to a loving older brother. She had to let him know that he was in danger.

"Excuse me for a second," Jennifer said. Trevor barely looked up as she scooped her purse off the bed and walked into the bathroom. She closed the door and locked it before pulling out her cell phone. She stared at it for a long time. Her emotions were flip-flopping between loyalty to Michael Gasca and her feelings for Trevor Deale. What if something happened to Mandy? But what if Gasca were arrested and sent to prison? How would she feel knowing that she could have saved him with one phone call?

She stared up at the ceiling as if seeking divine guidance. A single tear rolled down her cheek as she made up her mind. She scrolled through the memory on her cell phone and hit the speed-dial for Michael Gasca.

He answered on the first ring, recognizing her on the caller ID. "Talk to me, girlie."

"Just checking in," Jennifer said as softly as she could.

"Where's Trevor?"

"In the other room."

"How does he seem?"

"He's pretty upset."

"Has he told you what's happening?" Michael Gasca asked.

"Yes," Jennifer said. "He didn't want to at first, but he broke down and told me everything."

"Good," Gasca said, "that means he trusts you."

The words stung Jennifer. She'd never purposely deceived anyone, and she couldn't believe she was doing this to Trevor. When Michael Gasca had called to ask a favor, Jennifer had agreed without hesitation. It had sounded fun. But now that she was in the situation, she found that she had no appetite for deception.

"You got some news for me?" Michael Gasca asked.

"No," Jennifer replied softly, making a decision. "I was just checking in."

"That's it?" Michael Gasca asked doubtfully. "How are you holding up?"

"I'm doing okay," Jennifer lied softly. "It's just stressful waiting for something to happen."

"Yeah," Gasca said. "It won't be long now."

She hung up the phone and sat with it in her hands for a long time, feeling even more miserable for betraying her lifelong friend and advocate.

There was a soft knock on the bathroom door.

"You okay?" Trevor asked.

"I'm fine!" she called, flushing the toilet. She ran some water over her hands, dried them and came out of the bathroom with a forced smile on her face.

"I thought I heard you talking to someone," Trevor said.

Jennifer said, "I called my mom. She said to tell you good luck tomorrow."

Trevor nodded. His tears were gone, but his face was still ashen.

"Trevor," Jennifer said. "I need to tell you…" She hesitated, realizing she was about to tell him the truth. What would Trevor think about her if he learned that she had lied to him from the very start?

"What is it?" Trevor asked gently.

"Will you pray with me?" Jennifer asked. That was one of the lessons she had learned as a child. Whenever she felt nervous or unsure of herself, she'd sit down, clasp her hands together, and say a quiet prayer.

"Of course," Trevor said.

"We'll pray for Mandy," Jennifer said.

Trevor's eyes grew moist again.

A few minutes later the phone rang, and Trevor looked at Jennifer nervously before picking it up.

"Hey there, superstar," Michael Gasca said.

"Put my sister on."

"In a minute. First, I want you to go to your door and pick up the package I left for you."

Trevor wondered how Michael Gasca had managed that. The Stallions completely occupied the twenty-second and twenty-third floors of the downtown Hyatt, and hotel security was standing guard twenty-four hours a day to keep fans away. FBI agents were stationed throughout the hotel, and another set of agents was watching Michael Gasca and Roscoe Evans. Trevor couldn't imagine how Gasca had managed to make this delivery. It would never have occurred to him that Jennifer Winesett had left the package outside when she had arrived earlier.

Trevor retrieved a small brown bag, which contained a razor blade and a tiny plastic bottle of a liquid that looked like water.

"Okay," Trevor said. "I've got it." He'd given a lot of thought to the question of what Michael Gasca would want from him, and he still didn't know. Watching the free safety for a signal seemed like a possibility, but Trevor wondered how realistic it was. Michael Gasca would have to convince Trevor *and* the Rams' free safety to participate, which doubled the number of people involved and increased the risk exponentially. Why tap two guys when Gasca could get the job done with one? The Stallions were three-point underdogs going into the game, and Michael Gasca probably wanted Trevor to make a couple of mistakes along the way to ensure that the Stallions didn't cover the spread. That would be easy enough. Late in the game, one bad play could take care of it.

"You're the best player in the NFL," Michael Gasca said. "MVP of your team, of the league, and you'll probably be the MVP of the Super Bowl."

Trevor wished Gasca would get on with it.

"You touch the ball on every single play. That's why we needed you."

"What do you want?" Trevor said.

Michael Gasca chuckled. "What I want is to make some money, and I need a little help. Just a little, not a lot. You do one thing for me, your sister will go on home unharmed, and you'll still be a hero to all your fans in San Antonio." Gasca lightly rubbed the outside edge of his swollen eye. It still hurt, but talking to Trevor made him feel a little better.

"In long history of the NFL, there haven't been many quarterbacks like you," Gasca continued. "Not many guys have meant as much to their teams as you mean to yours."

"I can understand greed," Trevor said, his body tense with rage, "and I can understand that you're a criminal, but how could you do what you did to my sister?"

"Believe me, Trevor, I didn't like tricking her, and I don't like having to threaten her now. But this is what I had to do. I had to provide you with the proper motivation."

"What do you want me to do?"

"Well, that's the sixty-four-thousand-dollar question, isn't it? There are a lot of possibilities. You could mishandle snaps, throw interceptions, call bad audibles, get sacked, turn the wrong way on a handoff. There are a million things you could do, and believe me, I've thought through all of them, but in the end, I decided that the best possible scenario for my particular plan is that you don't do any of those things. I don't want you to mishandle snaps, throw interceptions, call bad audibles, get sacked, turn the wrong way, none of that."

Trevor didn't get it. If Gasca didn't want him to make mistakes, why kidnap his sister? "So what *do* you want?"

"Don't play," Gasca said.

Don't play what? "What do you mean?"

"Don't suit up tomorrow," Michael Gasca said.

Trevor wrestled with the prospect of not playing in the Super Bowl. Could he really do that? Could he simply skip the biggest game of the year?

"Use the drops in the bag that I left at your door. What you do is put some drops in just *one* eye and wait about fifteen minutes. Then get in the shower and look around to see if there's anything particularly hard that your head might hit if you slipped and fell. Use the razor to make just a tiny cut on your head. Nothing major, just enough to produce a little blood."

Trevor held the phone tightly, hardly believing what he was hearing. Did Michael Gasca really expect him to do this?

"Make sure you lean over the hard spot to deposit a little blood there," Gasca continued, "then put the razor and the empty bottle into the toilet and flush them away. Then go knock on the head trainer's door. You tell him you slipped in the shower and hit your head. It's fluky, but it happens."

"You think I can tell them that I want to sit out of the Super Bowl because of a small cut?" Trevor asked incredulously.

"Quite the opposite," Michael Gasca said. "You should insist that you feel fine and that you want to play. But you're going to have *one* dilated eye, and that's going to drive them absolutely crazy. They have to assume the worst. They'll send you off for an MRI, and even though the tests will come back negative, they'll have to keep you off the field. It'll be a grand mystery. How did Trevor Deale slip in the shower and suffer a fluke concussion the night before the Super Bowl? It'll be the stuff of legend."

Trevor listened to all this numbly. *Could it really work?*

"I'm gonna let you talk to your sister now, and after you get off the phone with her, you need to get in the shower and take care of business. You have to visit the trainer before 11 P.M. So here's your sis, then it's off to the hospital you go."

"What did he say?" Jennifer asked as soon as Trevor hung up the phone, barely able to think straight. He'd been prepared to do something on the field to impact the outcome of the game, but he hadn't expected Gasca to ask him to do *nothing*. Trevor stared at Jennifer blankly for a long time before he told her what Michael Gasca had said.

"So what are you going to do?" Jennifer asked when he finished. But before he could answer, the phone rang again. It was Steven Oquist, who had listened to the whole conversation.

"Damn, he's good," Oquist said. He hadn't considered this possibility, but now that it had been presented it made perfect sense. "Jerry," Oquist said to Jerry Powers, "pick up the other line. Tell Trevor what you think."

Jerry Powers said, "I think Michael Gasca's looking to milk the line."

"What does that mean?" Trevor asked.

"Gasca hasn't put down any money on the games he fixed," Steven Oquist said. "But if you want to hide some unnatural money, the Super

Bowl is the best time to do it, because it's the biggest sporting event in the world and there's so much money riding on it, it's hard to spot unnatural money."

"We're talking seventy-five million wagered legally in Vegas," Powers said, "and another five to seven hundred million worldwide. So if Gasca wanted to float five, ten, even fifteen million dollars out there, he could probably spread it out enough so that no one would see it."

"So," Trevor said, trying to understand, "he bet on the Rams to win, and by keeping me off the field, he's trying to make sure his bet will pay off?"

"Sort of," Jerry Powers said, "But it's probably way bigger than that. He's insisting that you report your concussion to the trainers tonight, which means the team will have to report the injury to the league first thing in the morning—"

"—and the league will tell the media," Oquist said, "and when the casinos find out, they're gonna panic. Millions of people are going to try to make last-minute bets."

"I still don't get why this is such a big deal," Trevor said.

Jerry Powers said, "All week, the line on the game's been St. Louis by three and a half. My guess is that Michael Gasca initially bet on the Rams to win *and* cover the spread. When the casinos find out about your concussion, they're going to have no choice but to make a serious move on the line. Then Gasca will place a monster bet on the Stallions to cover the new spread without you."

"It's called middling," Steven Oquist said. "Let's say Michael Gasca bet five million dollars riding on the Rams to win by more than three and a half." Oquist was piecing it together as he went. "Now word gets out that you're not going to play, and Vegas has to scramble to change the line before a bunch of people run in and place new bets on the old line. You're the biggest impact player in the league, so you're probably worth four-, five- maybe even six-points in the line. To move the pointspread that much is unheard of for an NFL—"

"Especially the Super Bowl," Jerry Powers interjected.

"True," Oquist said. "I can count on one hand the number of times the line has moved more than two points. But the way Michael Gasca has played this thing out, I think he's going to create panic. Suddenly, the world will believe that the Stallions have absolutely no shot, and if the casinos leave the line where it is or even close to where it is, everyone will bet on the Rams and no one will bet on the Stallions."

Jerry Powers said, "If they bump the new line to St. Louis by say ten points, then Michael Gasca could lay down another five million on the Stallions to cover that spread without you."

"That's right," Oquist said, "If the new spread was Rams by ten, and the final score was Rams 27, Stallions 21, then Gasca would collect five million on the first bet because St. Louis won by more than three and a half, and he'd collect another five million on the second bet because the Stallions lost by less than ten. His worst case would that the game ended outside of that range. He'd win one bet and lose one, which would be no big deal."

"So what do we do?" Trevor asked.

"We go get your sister."

Trevor hung up his phone and sighed heavily.

"So?" Jennifer asked.

"They're going to rescue Mandy."

"When?" Jennifer said, alarmed. "Now?"

"Yes." Trevor looked terrified.

Jennifer did too, but for different reasons. Would the cops bust in and kill Michael Gasca and Roscoe Evans? She needed to warn them. She still had her cell phone in her hand. She was about to go back into the bathroom to call Gasca when Trevor spoke.

"Will you pray with me again?" he asked.

Jennifer closed her eyes and pinched the bridge of her nose. "Of course," she said after a moment.

They sat down together on the bed, clasped hands and prayed. It was the most fervent prayer of Jennifer's life.

47

A team of FBI agents entered Michael Gasca's hideout just after 4 AM on Super Bowl Sunday. They went in blind, without advance fiber optic surveillance, because Steven Oquist had feared that Michael Gasca might have electronic perimeter security set up.

"We start snaking cameras through the heating vents, and we might be in for a shootout. Our best bet is to just charge through the front door," Oquist had said. "By the time Gasca's equipment gives him a warning, we'll be inside and on top of him."

The FBI team, dressed in all black and brandishing Heckler & Koch MP5 submachine guns, smashed through the heavy front door with a battering ram and stormed into the living room

"FBI! Get on the floor!" they screamed, scanning the room for suspects, always keeping their muzzles and their eyes aimed in the same direction. Six agents went up the stairs, where they could be heard kicking in doors, screaming, "FBI! Get on the floor!"

It took several minutes to sweep the entire house.

■ ■ ■

"Where the fuck are they?" Steven Oquist yelled into his walkie-talkie. He was pacing back and forth in the command center. The FBI team had searched the house from top to bottom three times, and though a rooftop sniper had sighted Roscoe Evans through a window a day earlier, the house was now inexplicably empty.

But how? Oquist wondered. There was no way that Michael Gasca,

Roscoe Evans and a hostage could have slipped away.

Oquist closed his eyes and rubbed the back of his neck. Things always got this way when he was dealing with Michael Gasca. Somehow, Gasca always seemed to stay a step ahead.

"Search again!" Steven Oquist ordered into the walkie-talkie.

The officers went through the house half a dozen times, looking not just for the suspects but for some sort of secret exit that would allowed them to leave the property undetected. They found nothing.

After several hours, Steven Oquist left the command center and drove to Northeast Methodist Hospital, where Trevor Deale and his family were anxiously awaiting news of Mandy's rescue. As instructed, Trevor had left the hotel for the hospital just in case Michael Gasca had someone watching.

When Oquist walked through the door of the lobby, Stallions coach Joseph Repanshek approached. The coach had been sitting with his offensive coordinator, trying to devise a scheme for the Super Bowl now that it appeared that Trevor would be unable to play.

"Is she okay?" Coach Repanshek asked. He'd learned of the game-fixing and kidnapping just a few hours earlier.

Oquist shook his head wearily. "We don't know."

"What happened?" Repanshek asked. Since Repanshek was so new to the NFL, he'd had no idea whether this was a common occurrence in the league, but he'd been under the impression that NFL Security had the situation under control.

"They disappeared," Steven Oquist said. "We had them pinned in, but somehow they disappeared."

Coach Repanshek chewed on the inside of his cheek as he studied the NFL Security officer for a few moments. "Have you talked to Trevor?"

Oquist shook his head. "I didn't want to tell him over the phone."

"You should listen to him," Coach Repanshek said earnestly.

"Who?"

"Trevor."

"Listen to him?" Oquist asked, confused. "About what?"

Coach Repanshek looked around the room, then lowered his voice. "Trevor calls all of our plays," he confessed. "Even at Oklahoma, this kid knew exactly what to do in every situation. I learned to listen to him, and I think you should too."

Steven Oquist knew that Trevor Deale had a great football mind, but he thought the coach might be a little delusional if the though that would make Trevor good at tracking criminals.

"With all due respect, Coach," Oquist said. "I've been chasing Michael Gasca for years, and I know him better than anyone else. I know what he's thinking, what he's capable of, and what he's most likely to do."

"Yet, you lost him," Repanshek pointed out.

"We'll find him," Oquist said tersely.

"Mr. Oquist," the coach said. "I've been coaching Trevor Deale for four years, and he has more analytical ability than anyone I've ever seen. When you turn him loose on a problem, he solves it."

Oquist hesitated.

Coach Repanshek continued, "Now, I've just been brought up to speed on this situation, but as I understand it, Trevor is the reason you know the location of Michael Gasca's hideout, right?"

"Yes," Oquist said.

"Trevor is the person who told you that Jonathan Kinneson was involved in fixing games, and Trevor was the one who told you about Caleb Alexander's fumble in the Green Bay game."

Steven Oquist couldn't deny any of that.

"Trevor is the reason you're close to catching this guy," Repanshek continued.

Oquist nodded slowly. Maybe the coach was right. They climbed into the elevator and ascended to the fourth floor, where Trevor and his family were waiting.

▪ ▪ ▪

"You didn't get her," Trevor Deale said the moment Steven Oquist walked into the room. Trevor's family was spread around him, waiting anxiously for news about Mandy. Uncle Jim and Aunt Nancy were on the couch, holding hands with a glazed look on their faces. And Kathy Deale was standing at the window staring out at nothing. Jennifer was leaning against the wall, tapping one foot against the linoleum. They were all ragged from worry and lack of sleep. They'd been waiting more than two hours to hear the result of the rescue attempt, and as minutes had turned into hours, they had grown more certain that something had gone wrong.

Steven Oquist said, "They weren't in the house."

Everyone seemed to release a breath. This was better news than they had expected. When they hadn't heard anything, they had assumed the worst. They thought there must have been a shootout or a chase and something had happened to Mandy. But if no one was in the house that meant Mandy was probably still okay.

"I thought you had the house surrounded," Trevor said.

"We did," Steven Oquist replied. He ran a hand through his hair and fell into a chair. "Somehow they got out."

Kathy Deale sniffled quietly in the corner. Uncle Jim got up and hugged her tightly.

Trevor plopped down on the end of the bed with his head in his hands.

The hard bottom of Jennifer's shoe rattled against the floor more insistently. "Trevor," she said.

He didn't look up. Jennifer walked over and sat next to him. "I need to tell you something," she said.

"What?" Trevor asked wearily.

Jennifer took a deep breath and wiped her eyes. "It's not an easy thing to say," she said.

Trevor brought his face up and stared at her. "What is it?"

Jennifer cleared her throat and looked around the room. "I've been...I've been...working...for Michael Gasca."

Everyone in the room stared at her. Kathy Deale stopped crying.

"What do you mean, *working for?*" Uncle Jim asked.

Jennifer's bottom lip was trembling. Haltingly, she told Trevor and his family everything she knew. She told them about her lifelong friendship with Michael Gasca. She told them that Vanessa had been hired to seduce Trevor and get control over him. When it became clear that Vanessa wasn't making progress, Michael Gasca had asked Jennifer to come down to San Antonio. A few days later, she had followed Trevor and Vanessa into the mall and waited for an opportunity to meet him.

"At first, I thought the whole thing was just a fun gag," Jennifer said. She tried to take Trevor's hand, but he pulled away from her. "When Michael Gasca called, he made this project sound like a harmless joke. I honestly thought you might laugh about it when you finally learned the truth—like one of those TV shows where they pull pranks on celebrities. But then I met you, and I felt bad for tricking you. But I wasn't sure what to do. Then Gasca kidnapped Mandy, and I was horrified. I didn't know that was part of the plan, and I never would have agreed to participate if I had known." She hung her head, sobbing quietly with heaving shoulders.

Uncle Jim shook his head in disbelief. "*Vanessa* was on the payroll?"

Trevor studied Jennifer carefully.

"Is there anything else?" he asked. He wasn't sure he could handle any more surprises.

"No," Jennifer sniffed.

"Do you know where they went?" Steven Oquist asked.

Jennifer shook her head, and then paused.

"One time," she said, "I overheard them talking about a warehouse near downtown. Maybe that's where they are."

Oquist snatched up his walkie-talkie and told the FBI team leader to get his people into the downtown warehouse district and await further orders.

Trevor cradled his head in his hands, pressing his palms against his temples hard as if he was trying to squeeze out the pain and anger that clogged his brain. Then he moaned, quietly at first, the sound building in his lungs until it turned into a frustrated wail that filled the room.

"Trevor," Jennifer said, laying a hand on his arm. He ripped his arm away and stormed across the room, still screaming, still pressing his palms to his temples. He reached the corner and let his head fall against the wall. The room fell silent.

No one moved. Jennifer watched Trevor with tears streaming down her face; Steven Oquist kept his eyes on Jennifer, and everyone else seemed to be staring at the floor.

Trevor rocked his head back and forth against the cool wall and tried to think through this situation as if it were a defensive scheme. He'd always been able to see through the disguised coverages, bluffed blitzes and strange formations that defensive coordinators threw at him. What if Michael Gasca was just a defensive coordinator? Trevor pressed harder against the wall.

"I bit on the blitz," he said after a while, starting to piece it together. "Vanessa was a bluff. She wasn't real. Then they brought in Jennifer, and I fell for her, but she wasn't real."

Jennifer flinched as if she'd been slapped.

"Now," Trevor continued, "the FBI goes to the house where they're holding my sister, but no one's there." Trevor looked pointedly at Steven Oquist. "Michael Gasca knew you were coming."

Even though Steven Oquist knew this must be true, he didn't see how it could have happened. The surveillance on the house had been absolutely covert—no one inside the house or even in the neighborhood could have known the officers were there. But somehow Michael Gasca had known.

"So where do you think he went?" Oquist asked.

"A million places," Trevor said wearily. "And it would be smart for him to plant his helper among us to send us looking in the wrong direction."

They all stared at Jennifer.

"Is this what he told you to do?" Trevor asked, turning to Jennifer. "To wait until this moment, and then tell us that you've been working for him, and you overheard him say that he was going to a warehouse downtown?"

"No," Jennifer insisted, crying harder. "I swear, Trevor. He didn't tell me to do this. I don't think he even knows that I know about his warehouse. Please, Trevor. Please believe me! You know I would never gamble with Mandy's life."

Trevor watched her for a long moment. "I believe you," he said softly, surprised to realize that he actually did.

"I don't," Uncle Jim spat. "You need to tell us where he is right now!"

"Maybe we can figure it out," Trevor said.

"But they could be *anywhere!*" Steven Oquist protested.

"*Where* is probably the wrong question," Trevor said. "The question is *how?*"

"What do you mean?" Uncle Jim asked.

"The house was surrounded," Trevor said. "*How* did they get out?"

"You think they dug a tunnel or something?" Oquist asked.

Trevor shrugged. "Have you ever heard of a *zone blitz?*"

"Yeah," Oquist said.

"You know how it works?"

Oquist shook his head.

"The defense sends four rushers at the quarterback, but it's not the four he was expecting. So it looks like a blitz when it's really just a four-man rush. A zone blitz works because it looks like the opposite of what it actually is."

"So you're saying…"

"Maybe they didn't escape," Trevor said.

Steven Oquist said, "We've searched everywhere."

"But Gasca knew you were coming," Trevor said.

"So?" Steven Oquist said. "He still couldn't have slipped past us."

"He anticipated it months ago, maybe years ago," Trevor said. "Michael Gasca knew that eventually the FBI would come through his front door."

"So…"

Trevor said, "When Caleb followed them home from my house, he told me they were staying in a 'creepy old house.' I didn't think about it at the time, but now that they've mysteriously disappeared, I have to wonder why would they stay in a place like that? Why not get a hotel room, an apartment or a nicer house? There's no good reason for them to stay in a beat-up old house."

Steven Oquist was starting to get it. "But we've searched…"

Trevor continued, "*Unless* the beat-up old house was part of the game plan. If Michael Gasca wanted to run a zone blitz and make you think he had left when he actually hadn't, then he had to be in *that* house. He couldn't be in an apartment; he couldn't be in a newer home. It had to be *that* house."

"So we go running off looking for him all over the city…" Oquist said.

"Like in a warehouse downtown," Uncle Jim said, glaring at Jennifer.

"But he never left," Trevor said.

Oquist snatched up his radio. "Everyone back to the house!" he screamed, racing out of the room with Trevor close on his heels. "They're still in there!"

48

A torrent of nervous sweat ran down Roscoe Evans's face. He was seated against a wall with his legs stretched out, taking slow, deep breaths through his nose. His jaw ached; he was starving, and now he could feel a panic attack coming from being trapped in this small, possibly haunted room. He'd been unable to eat in a day and a half, and though he didn't have a scale, he guessed that he had lost about ten pounds. He'd written a note to Gasca the night before, complaining about the weight loss, but he'd received no sympathy.

"You weighed three hundred twenty pounds," Michael Gasca had said. "You needed to slim down."

Roscoe had scowled at him, but Gasca had missed the gesture; Roscoe's face was still grotesquely swollen.

"Maybe you can go on *Oprah*," Gasca had suggested, "and tell the women of America about the Broken Jaw Diet. I can hear you now, saying 'the only thing better than the Broken Jaw Diet is the Ebola Diet, but the Broken Jaw Diet is cheaper 'cause you don't have to fly to Africa to fill a prescription.'" Gasca had laughed and clapped Roscoe on the shoulder.

Roscoe had made a silent note to break Michael Gasca's jaw the first chance he got—see how funny he thought it was then. But before he could act on that idea, his stomach had rumbled again. Roscoe didn't know how much longer he could go without food. All he could have now was soup, but he wanted to rip the wires out of his mouth and chomp down on a porterhouse steak.

Roscoe's breathing in the darkened room was labored, but fortunately, the thick walls surrounding the secret space made it fairly soundproof.

They could hear the vibration of FBI's boots pounding on the hardwood floors, and they could just make out that people were screaming orders, but the words were unintelligible. Now the house was silent. Michael Gasca knew the agents were searching, but he wasn't worried. They would never think to look for a secret room, and even if they did, the entrance was well disguised.

Mandy was sitting next to Roscoe with her knees drawn up to her chest and her arms wrapped around her legs. She'd been quiet for more than twenty-four hours, watching Michael Gasca with hurt, angry eyes; she'd rebuffed all attempts at conversation.

When Michael Gasca had sent his advance team to San Antonio months ago, he'd told them specifically to find a Prohibition-era home with a secret room. A secret tunnel would have been nice too, but their investigation had revealed that few houses had had tunnels during the 1920s, and even fewer still existed. During the past few months, Gasca and Roscoe had stockpiled food, water, and even a small portable toilet in the secret room. They could stay hidden for several days if necessary. However, listening to Roscoe's labored breathing, Gasca realized that he hadn't counted on anyone having his jaw wired shut. They didn't have any food that could be sucked through a straw, so if they were forced to stay hidden, Roscoe would lose more weight.

Michael Gasca considered all the decisions he'd made during the course of the season, and though he was happy with most of the results, he had to admit that targeting Trevor Deale had been a mistake. The quarterback was the only piece of this puzzle that Gasca had failed to control, and ultimately, it was Trevor who had brought the authorities through the front door.

Trevor might be a rookie, but Michael Gasca thought he had played this situation like a wily veteran.

■ ■ ■

FBI agents moved through the house slowly, working in groups of three. One man tapped on the wall with the butt of his knife, listening for hollow spots, while the other two kept their guns trained on the plaster. They had already been through each of these rooms a dozen times, and they were convinced that this was wasted effort.

At about 10 AM Steven Oquist and Trevor Deale hustled down the sidewalk toward Michael Gasca's hideout. Trevor had demanded to go into the house with Oquist, and after an argument that had lasted the entire trip from the hospital, Oquist had finally agreed.

The moment they approached the front door, it swung open and two agents wearing flak jackets and brandishing machine guns looked them over suspiciously before backing away and letting them pass. The house was dingy, with hardwood floors, dark walls, pastel paintings, and antique furniture scattered about. The FBI had overturned just about everything in their search.

"Mr. Oquist," a FBI team leader said, walking up to greet the two men. His nametag read AGENT HARTMAN.

"This is Trevor Deale," Steven Oquist said.

Agent Hartman nodded. "We've searched every nook and cranny of this place, and it's my professional opinion that they're not here." He knew the *secret room* theory was Trevor's, and he didn't buy it. He thought his men had wasted enough time already, but he didn't want to insult the football player.

Trevor could sense the agent's cynicism.

"Look at all this," Trevor said, indicating the furniture, the pictures and the knickknacks. "Does this look like a dangerous criminal's hideout?"

Oquist and Hartman had to concede that the home looked more like someone's grandmother's house than the place Michael Gasca would choose as his base.

"There has to be a reason that they chose this house," Trevor said.

Hartman said, "But we've been through this place more than a dozen times, and we've found nothing."

Trevor thought about that for a moment. "Can you walk me through the house?"

Agent Hartman led them on a tour of the main floor. From the living room, they moved into a formal dining room, through the kitchen, into the den, a full bathroom, and a small bedroom and bathroom just off the kitchen in what appeared to be a servant's quarters. They climbed the stairs and inspected three bedrooms and two bathrooms on the second floor. They ascended farther to peer into the musty attic. They walked back to the main floor and marched into the basement. There wasn't much to look at—one large, mostly empty room, a small storage area full of boxes, a washer and dryer, a furnace, and a tiny washroom that housed a stained oversized sink that looked as if it had been used to dispose of paint. The house was at least ninety years old, but solidly built—it looked as if it might stand for ninety more.

Just two bare light bulbs hung from the ceiling, but the FBI had brought in bright klieg lights that illuminated the entire basement.

The boxes in the storage room were packed in tightly, and they looked as if they hadn't been moved in years. A sheet of dust covered most of the boxes and the floor, but it was disturbed in a few places.

"That's from my men," Agent Hartman explained. "When we first came into the basement, there was a perfect sheet of dust on that floor. We searched it anyway just to be sure, but it seemed clear that no one had entered that room in years."

"It has to be down here," Trevor said.

Hartman shook his head. "We've searched. There's nothing," he said tersely.

Trevor walked into the laundry room and inspected the washer and dryer. He looked at the walls from every angle, but he couldn't see anything that was different about them. He backed out of the room, and studied all the external walls. They all had cracked paint and discoloration from past water damage, but none of them looked as if they had moved recently or even *could* move. Trevor entered the small washroom, and tried the rusty handle on the sink. No water came out of the spout. He tried the other handle—nothing there either.

Trevor stomped his feet on the concrete floor of the basement, trying to feel for something that felt different from the rest, but it all seemed the same.

■   ■   ■

Michael Gasca's cell phone glowed green in the tiny, darkened room, but he had no signal. He held it out to his right, then off to his left, then above his head, but he got no reception. He needed to call Uncle Nick and give the order for the second half of his Super Bowl bet. Once he made the call, thousands of people all over the globe would bet money on his behalf, and Gasca would pull off the biggest middling scam in the history of pro sports. If he didn't make the call, he stood to lose everything he'd wagered already.

Despite all of Michael Gasca's preparations, he hadn't considered the possibility that he might be stuck in this room at the moment he needed to use his cell phone. He and Roscoe had awakened Mandy and entered the secret room last night. They'd fooled the FBI, but now Gasca was trapped with no ability to call out. What he needed, he realized, was a listening device that would tell him if the FBI had left the house. The downside of soundproofing was that it worked both ways—the FBI couldn't hear the suspects, but the suspects couldn't hear the FBI either.

But Gasca still had time. He figured the FBI eventually would station one man at the front door, while the rest left to scour the city. It was now past 11 A.M., and Michael Gasca knew soon he would have to take a chance and crack the door open.

Michael Gasca had purposely mentioned a downtown warehouse while Jennifer was in earshot, just in case she suffered a bout of conscience. If she switched loyalties, then she'd certainly mention the warehouse to Trevor, which would buy Gasca more time.

He would wait a little while longer, and then sneak out of the room, make the call, and hustle back in. It would take him thirty seconds at the most, and then they'd stay inside until midway through the Super Bowl, when most of the law enforcement agencies in San Antonio would be in or around the stadium.

■ ■ ■

Trevor Deale stood in the middle of the basement with his head down, concentrating.

Agent Hartman watched all of this impatiently. Somewhere in the city two criminals—he hadn't been told who they were—were running around with a hostage while he and his men were standing waiting for the star quarterback to confirm that the FBI had done its job. Hartman was insulted by this whole charade. Steven Oquist should never have let a civilian have this much input into the action plan.

One of the reasons Trevor could read defenses so well was that he understood what they *had* to do, and he knew how to turn those needs against them. If a receiver ran full-speed at the free safety, and the quarterback had not yet reached his drop point, the safety *had* to backpedal—he didn't have a choice. If a linebacker was covering a running back man-to-man, and the back went in motion before the snap, the linebacker *had* to run with him. So if Michael Gasca were hiding in a secret room what would he *have* to do?

"How do you breathe in a mostly soundproofed room?" Trevor wondered aloud.

"You open your mouth," Hartman said sarcastically.

"But if you're in a hidden room with thick walls," Trevor continued, "wouldn't you have to worry about getting enough oxygen?"

Hartman and Oquist stared at Trevor, thinking about this for a moment.

"There would have to be a vent," Steven Oquist said after a moment.

"Anderson! Thomas!" Hartman barked. "Go scout the outside of the house and see if you see anything that looks like a vent coming out of the basement."

The two officers raced up the stairs. They came back a few minutes later shaking their heads. The only thing they saw was the vent from the dryer.

Trevor walked back over to the storage room and studied it for a long time. *Could someone fake dust?* he wondered. He looked at the dirt and grime that covered everything in the room. He moved over to the laundry room and studied the walls again. He climbed up on the washer and looked at the connections behind. Everything seemed normal. He walked back out into the main room. All of the officers were watching him, waiting for him to say something. Trevor went back into the small washroom, and cast his eyes up and down the walls. He didn't see anything. He looked under the sink, inside a cabinet, and behind the door. He turned the knobs again, but still no water came out. He rested his hands on the sink and hung his head. *Where could they be?* he wondered.

Something tickled the top of his hand. He jerked his arm back, thinking that a spider had run across his fingers, but there was nothing there.

He put his hand back on the edge of the sink and felt it again. It took a moment to realize that he was feeling a breeze. Slight puffs of warm air were teasing the tiny hairs on his hand. He placed both hands fully under the faucets, and the sensation grew stronger.

Trevor beckoned the FBI agents; the rusted, non-functioning faucets were the vents.

■ ■ ■

Michael Gasca had his ear pressed against the thick wall of the hidden room, and one hand resting on the latch that would open the door, but he still couldn't hear anything. He wished he had thought to at least bring a stethoscope with him. That might have helped.

During Prohibition, this small room had been designed to hide liquor, not people, so the three of were sweating together in heat that grew more oppressive by the hour. They took turns sitting near the small ventilation holes.

Michael Gasca looked at his watch; it was 11:45 A.M., and by now everyone in the world knew that Trevor Deale was in the hospital and would not play in the Super Bowl. The casinos had undoubtedly announced a new point-spread, and millions of people were rushing into casinos or calling their bookies to make new bets.

If Gasca didn't make the call soon, he'd miss his opportunity.

He tried to slow his breathing and listen more intently. His ear was pressed flat against the wall, but he could hear absolutely nothing. Roscoe Evans tapped him on the arm, but Gasca waved him off and kept listening. Roscoe tapped again, this time harder; it was more of a jab than a tap.

"Can't you see I'm busy?" Michael Gasca snapped.

Roscoe handed him a piece of paper. "IT'S TIME FOR MY SHOT."

"Just wait," Gasca said. "I need to make a phone call."

Roscoe shook his head and jabbed Gasca again, even harder this time. His eyes were watering. It was clear that the previous dosage had worn off and the pain was back in full force.

"Jesus Christ!" Michael Gasca said, taking out his frustrations on Roscoe. "Where is your medication?"

Roscoe held the flashlight, while Gasca filled the syringe with fluid and tapped the needle to get the air bubbles out. Roscoe turned on his side and slid his jeans down.

Michael Gasca bent over Roscoe's ass with the flashlight in one hand the syringe in the other.

"Are you ready?" Gasca asked.

Roscoe nodded nervously. He was too squeamish to watch the needle go in, but he didn't like to be surprised either.

"All right," Gasca said. "Here goes."

Suddenly, the wall slid open. Gasca blinked in the light, stunned.

They were quite a sight—Roscoe Evans with his big ass exposed and Michael Gasca hunched over him about to do Lord knows what.

After Trevor discovered the vents, the agents had pushed him back into the main room of the basement and trained their guns on the wall. One officer entered the small washroom and started pushing and pulling on anything he could reach. He tried the walls themselves, looking for handles or buttons. He felt for anything on the floor that might be a release for the door. After several minutes, he put his hand on the faucet and pulled on it uselessly before trying to twist it. It made a quarter turn to the right, and the wall slid open.

"Drop what you have in your hands, and lay down on the floor!" the agents yelled.

Roscoe Evans wanted to grab his pen and pad, because he would need them to communicate, but with so many guns pointed at him, he didn't want to make any sudden movements. He wasn't even sure if he was permitted to pull his pants back up, so he just laid down flat with his ass hanging out, groaning because he still hadn't had his shot.

Michael Gasca wasn't too concerned about the FBI—as long as they let him make a phone call.

Trevor rushed into the room as soon as the suspects were handcuffed, stepping over them to get to Mandy, who was cowering in the back. He hugged her tightly. They both burst into tears.

49

It took four FBI agents to pull Roscoe Evans to his feet, and as he lumbered toward the door, he wondered how long he would have to wait before he received his medication. Without his pen and notepad, how would he tell them what he needed? As they led him toward the basement door, Roscoe stared back with profound sadness at the medicine sitting on the floor of the secret room.

Although getting arrested wasn't part of Michael Gasca's preferred plan, he was relieved to see the FBI emblem imprinted on the uniforms of the officers in the house. Throughout the season, he'd taken careful measure of the laws he'd broken, hoping that if NFL Security somehow managed to track him down, the prosecution would stay on the federal level not the state or city level. Michael Gasca knew that local district attorneys could be difficult to control, whereas the NFL's reaction to this fiasco was completely predictable.

The NFL was the most popular league in the country, and it wielded tremendous political clout. In most NFL cities, it took only the threat of relocating to convince local politicians that the taxpayers should finance a new stadium for the local franchise. The NFL was one of the few industries that enjoyed federal anti-trust exemption. The deal was renewed annually in a handshake deal with Congress. A representative from the league would visit the House and the Senate and ask for an extension on the right to violate laws outlawing collusion, price fixing and other anti-competitive measures, and Congress would respond with a question of its own: "Do you promise to keep broadcasting the games on network television where the citizens can watch them for free?" Every year the NFL responded yes, and every year Congress extended the exemption. Few football fans knew about this rule, but they'd often call their local television stations in confusion when the realized their team's game was being broadcast on ESPN and a network station at the same time.

"You have to buy cable to get ESPN," sports producers all over the country explain, "so that means it's pay-per-view. Anytime an NFL game is on cable, it has to be simultaneously broadcast on one of the networks."

The key to staying out of prison, Michael Gasca thought, was to keep his prosecution on the federal level, where the full weight of the NFL's clout could be brought into play. Michael Gasca knew that the NFL would never press criminal charges against him, and they would try to talk a federal prosecutor out of doing the same. The league simply could not afford to have the public watch a trial which would prove beyond a reasonable doubt that Michael Gasca and Roscoe Evans had manipulated the outcomes of a season's worth of NFL games. If the two criminals were convicted, it would be a pyrrhic victory for the league. Consumer confidence would fall, and soon every questionable call or mistake on the field would spark allegations of a fix. People would lose confidence in the legitimacy of the games; ratings would fall and revenues would follow.

Michael Gasca was counting on the league to be his advocate with the justice department.

But first, he needed to make a phone call within the hour. If he had to wait longer than that, it would probably be too late.

"I want to make a phone call," Michael Gasca said to the agents who were leading him out to a car. Steven Oquist was walking a couple of steps back.

"It's going to take a little while to get you processed," Oquist said, smiling. "You might not be able to call anyone until after kickoff this afternoon."

Michael Gasca gritted his teeth. He had millions riding on the game, and he might lose all of it if he didn't call Uncle Nick.

"You're violating my Constitutional right to have legal representation during questioning," he growled.

"That's why we're not going to question you," Steven Oquist said. "We'll just let you sit for a little while."

50

Jonathan Kinneson sat on the closed lid of the toilet in his suite at the Alamodome. He was breathing heavily with his mouth gaping open. He looked as though he'd been hit in the face with a baseball bat. His nose was swollen and covered in a thick white bandage. Only the narrow tip of his nose was visible, and it was the color of an over-ripe plum. The skin around both eyes was a mottled black and brown.

"Hey Mr. Kinneson," a Stallions' fan had yelled when he saw the owner going up the escalator toward his suite, "looks like the cheerleaders finally got tired of you pinching their asses and kicked the shit out of you!"

Hundreds of fans in the area had laughed at Jonathan Kinneson, and his face had darkened. He had wondered if there were any way to track down the loud-mouth and kick him out of the stadium.

Since then, Jonathan Kinneson had been holed up in his bathroom with the door locked, refusing to come out. He was watching the Super Bowl on a small TV built into the wall. The Stallions were up fourteen points in the second quarter, and every few minutes the roaring crowd rocked the Alamodome and the commode Kinneson was sitting on vibrated. Trevor Deale, whom everyone thought was out with a concussion, had made a miraculous recovery, and he'd been leading the Stallions up and down the field effortlessly.

Someone knocked on the door.

"Mr. Kinneson are you in there?" a voice called. "The commissioner is here. He'd like to talk to you."

Jonathan Kinneson watched with maniacal eyes as the doorknob jiggled impotently.

■ ■ ■

The St. Louis Rams never had a chance. Every time Trevor Deale walked to the line of scrimmage, he looked over the defense and read it as if its intentions were posted on a billboard. He called audible after audible and exploited every blitz, every coverage and every decision the defense made.

The commentators shook their heads. "This rookie quarterback," they said, "plays like a fifteen-year veteran." But that wasn't quite accurate—he played better than any quarterback they'd ever seen.

Trevor was at peace on the field. His family was tucked away in a luxury box with the FBI watching them, and though Mandy's heart was broken, she was physically okay and that was the important thing. He was going to take his whole family down to the Caribbean after the Pro Bowl. They could sit on the beach for a week or two and just relax.

During the game, Trevor continuously called audibles that put the ball into Caleb Alexander's hand. By the close of the fourth quarter, Caleb had 24 carries, 138 yards and two touchdowns. Thanks to Trevor, Caleb had the best performance of his professional career. The commentators named Caleb Alexander and Trevor Deale co-MVPs of the Super Bowl.

"Look at this fool," Robo said, in the raucous locker room after the game. He drenched Caleb with champagne. "You see him running that thang out there?"

"Yeah, I saw him," tight end Mike Griffin said. "Ran like he was Kunta Kinte trying to get away from a slave trader!"

"Like Kunta Kin-*tay* from way back in the *day*," Robo said.

"Uh oh," Martin McNeil said, "You feeling a little freestyle coming, Robo?"

"I might be feelin' it," Robo said, "wheelin' and dealin' it, spreadin' round rhymes like a doctor, I'm healin' it."

"Oh shit, Mike, give him a beat!" Martin said.

Mike Griffin started a percussion beat with his mouth, and everyone in the locker room got quiet, nodding their heads, waiting for Robo to pick it up.

"Caleb ran that thang like Kunta Kintay," Robo began, "a fool on the plains from way back in the day/I was standing on the side saying run nigga run!/the kid brought it home like he was number one/the star of the bowl/tried to make a fine show/showing everythang he knows/stepping all up on their toes/run nigga run/having fun up in the sun/the Stallions number one/ 'cause the one nigga run!" Robo paused then said to his teammates, "The Stallions number one 'cause the one nigga run!"

"The Stallions number one 'cause the one nigga run!" the other players chanted, slapping Caleb on his back and shoulders.

Caleb couldn't stop laughing. For the moment, his past mistakes were forgotten.

"You know what this means?" Robo yelled out.

"What's that?" someone asked.

"Caleb's finally gonna get that Nabisco contract."

"Nabisco wants to sign Caleb?" someone asked dutifully.

"They want to put his face on their *monster* cookie for Halloween. I mean, come on," Robo said, "if you as ugly as that you gotta use it right?"

As the celebration continued, Caleb Alexander stood on his chair and looked across the locker room at Trevor Deale, who was surrounded by television cameras. Trevor caught Caleb's eye and grinned. Caleb mouth the words "thank you," and gave his quarterback a thumbs up. Trevor returned the thumb without ever breaking stride in his interview.

■ ■ ■

When Jonathan Kinneson finally emerged from the bathroom more than an hour after the end of the Super Bowl, his lawyer and the commissioner greeted him with an offer he couldn't refuse: Sell the team and avoid prison. The commission said he was facing charges for illegal ticket scalping, racketeering, extortion, fraud, and conspiracy to commit fraud.

Initially, Jonathan Kinneson had had to contain his elation that the league wanted to punish him forcing the profitable sale he'd already been planning. But his bloated face, raccoon eyes and bulbous nose had turned sour when the commissioner had laid out the terms of the deal. First, Kinneson would have to donate to local charities every penny he made scalping Super Bowl tickets. He'd have to sell the team to a buyer approved by the NFL and pay a penalty of ten percent of the sales price; any additional profits would be donated to the United Way. In total, Jonathan Kinneson would surrender more than a hundred million dollars in penalties and would not make a dime in profit, which greatly offended his sense of fair play. His lawyer advised him to take the deal and count his blessings.

To the media, Jonathan Kinneson would claim that he was selling the team after just one season of ownership because he needed to spend more time at Kinneson Corp. However, this would soon prove to be a lie. At the next meeting of the board of directors, Jonathan Kinneson would be voted out as president, and find himself suddenly unemployed for the first time in nearly thirty years.

■　■　■

Michael Gasca had smiled all the way through his negotiations with the FBI. The feds had tried to use the charges of kidnapping, false imprisonment, racketeering, and extortion to compel him to surrender the nine million dollars he'd received from Jonathan Kinneson.

"You're looking at twenty years in prison!" an officer barked in the interrogation room.

Michael Gasca shrugged at the empty threat. He held out for several days, but finally relented after his attorney explained quietly that the FBI might be able to build a case on the kidnapping and false imprisonment charges without involving the NFL. Michael Gasca knew that keeping the league's name on the table was his ticket to freedom, so he finally agreed to donate half of his earnings to charity. He and Roscoe Evans walked out of FBI custody in San Antonio and flew first class back to Philadelphia. The were disappointed in the way things turned out, but they'd still made a few bucks, and learned a few lessons that might help them in the future.

When Michael Gasca reached his home in Philadelphia, he had a surprise waiting for him. The IRS had confiscated everything he owned and charged him with tax evasion. They were going to audit his returns for the past three years, "and depending on what we find, we might have to go back seven years," a surly revenue agent said.

The audit and subsequent trial would stretch on for nearly a year, at which time Michael Gasca and Roscoe Evans were convicted and sentenced to serve twelve and nine months, respectively, in a medium-security prison.

Roscoe Evans, whose jaw had healed by the time they went to prison, still had dreams about taking revenge on Trevor Deale.

"What are you gonna do?" Michael Gasca asked one day while they were standing in the yard at the Federal Corrections Institute in Ashland, Kentucky. "You gonna hold a grudge for the rest of your life?"

"Not the rest of my life," Roscoe growled. His voice, though deep as ever, didn't sound quite the same because he was still missing a chunk of his tongue. Now he had a slight lisp. "Just until I see Trevor Deale again."

"You think every guy you ever muscled is sitting around thinking about how to get back at you?" Gasca asked. "Trevor took us on fair and square. Let it go."

Roscoe grunted; it didn't sound as if he were letting it go.

While Michael Gasca was incarcerated, Dominic Sarcassi and the rest of the clan returned to the old methods. They ran bookies, took layoffs, collected from deadbeats, and stayed out of the gambling business as much as possible. When Gasca returned, Uncle Nick thought they might make another run at the NFL, but he'd have to wait and see what kind of scheme his young protégé came up with.

■ ■ ■

Ken Parsley, A.K.A. Fat Fuck, A.K.A. the Corpulent Copulator, A.K.A. C.C. got his fat ass fired, much to the delight of Steven Oquist. Director Ken Burke offered Oquist a promotion to assistant director, but Oquist had declined, choosing instead to return to the streets of Philadelphia, where he would resume his surveillance of Michael Gasca and Roscoe Evans as soon as they were released from prison.

FIVE MONTHS LATER

"You talk to Jennifer?" Caleb Alexander asked. They were speeding down Interstate 10, heading to Trevor's mother's house in Lamesa.

Trevor shook his head slowly. For months, he'd been so upset about the deception, that he couldn't bear talking to her. After the Super Bowl, when his life had started to return to some semblance of normalcy, it had become increasingly depressing to realize that everything from his relationship to Vanessa, Mandy's relationship with William, his success on the field and meeting Jennifer at the mall, had been manipulated.

As the weeks had passed, his anger had diminished incrementally, and slowly his feelings for Jennifer had started to resurface. There was something genuine about her that made Trevor realize that in many ways she too had been a victim of Michael Gasca's deceptions. He remembered the hours they'd spent talking and laughing, and he thought they had far more in common than he and Vanessa ever had.

Sometime in early April, Caleb Alexander had said, "Why don't you just call her and say hello. What's it gonna hurt?"

Trevor had seemed doubtful.

"She's a lot like me," Caleb continued. "I worked for Michael Gasca, but I didn't want to. The guy had me over a barrel. It sounds like Jennifer was in the same position. When it came down to it, she chose not to follow through because she didn't want to hurt you."

Trevor had moved out of the Mediterranean mansion, because it had never felt like a home to him. He'd purchased a twenty-acre ranch just east of San Antonio. The property was wooded with a beautiful one-hundred-year-old two-story house. The stairs creaked under Trevor's feet, the pipes shuddered when the water first came on each morning, and the walls moaned against the wind. It felt like a home, and Trevor loved every inch of it.

The biggest surprise of the spring had been the budding romance between Caleb Alexander and Mandy Deale. After the Pro Bowl in early February, Martin McNeil and his wife, Jessica, and Robo and his girl-friend, Marguerite (who was still saying "you-daddys" because she'd lost another bet), headed down to St. Croix. Trevor had invited his mother and sister, and Caleb, who'd been living almost like a monk since his run-in with Michael Gasca, came down solo. Everyone was amazed at how quickly Caleb and Mandy hit it off. They had stayed together the entire trip, sitting at the pool during the day and walking along the shoreline at night.

Their mutual connection to Michael Gasca seemed to be the force that had initially bonded them. Caleb told Mandy about the legitimate fum-ble he'd suffered during the Green Bay game, and Mandy shared with him the horror of being held hostage by the man she thought she loved.

They started a romance that would develop slowly over the next few months. When Trevor first met Caleb Alexander a year ago, he would never have expected the running back to be interested in his sister, and if Caleb had ever asked about Mandy, Trevor would have warned her away.

It had been clear from the start that Caleb was a superficial, material-istic womanizer who collected girls the way other players collected cars—he was always looking for the latest model. But during the past eight months, Caleb had proven that he truly was a changed man. He'd settled down, stopped living in the fast lane, and started attending church. He didn't go out at night, didn't invite anyone over, didn't do much of any-thing except lead a quiet, contemplative life.

When Trevor and Caleb pulled up in front of the house in Lamesa, Kathy Deale and Mandy were in their arms as soon as they climbed out of the truck. Uncle Jim and Aunt Nancy were there too, and everyone was smiling with tears in their eyes. It had been a rough few months, but they were getting through it.

Inside, Trevor and Caleb put their right hands on the dining room table so everyone could gawk at their enormous Super Bowl rings. The square faces of the rings were encrusted with diamonds and their names and jersey numbers were emblazoned on the sides. It had taken months for the jeweler to make the rings, which were presented to the players and coaches during a ceremony on May 15.

Uncle Jim spoke in a reverent whisper: "How much is one of those worth?"

Trevor turned his hand from side to side. "About fifteen thousand dollars."

"Damn!" Jim muttered, licking his lips. "That's more than my truck."

"That's more than you've spent on me in our whole marriage," Nancy said.

"Hush, woman!" Jim said.

"Everybody smile!" Trevor's mom said, squinting behind her camera. Caleb and Trevor raised their rings.

They all settled down in the living room to drink beer and sodas and get caught up on the local gossip. After a while, Uncle Jim asked, "When are we gonna get started on the house?"

"First thing tomorrow," Kathy Deale said. She was finally ready to tear down the old shack. They'd start early with hammers and crowbars, slowly pulling the boards away from the frame, piece by piece and memory by memory.

"It's time for all of us to put the past behind us," Kathy declared, sharing a meaningful look with both of her children.

Trevor excused himself and went into the back of the house, while everyone else continued to chat in the living room.

After a while, Kathy Deale got up to get more drinks. As she closed the refrigerator, she heard a low voice coming from one of the bedrooms. She cocked her head and listened for a moment, then eased down the hallway.

Through a half-open door, Kathy saw Trevor sitting on a guest bed talking on the phone.

"You should come visit me," Trevor said quietly. Then he paused and laughed in a tone that was so rich and warm that his mother closed her eyes and leaned against the wall, smiling. She hadn't heard him sound happy in a long time.

"Yeah," Trevor said, still chuckling, "We should definitely meet at the mall again, and then go out for ice cream."

Kathy Deale smiled and closed her eyes. Then she tiptoed back down to the kitchen.

ABOUT THE AUTHOR

Reggie Rivers played six seasons for the Broncos, and in 1993, his teammates selected him as Special Teams Player of the Year. In 2000, he self-published his first novel, *Power Shift*. He currently writes a weekly editorial column for *The Denver Post*, cohosts *Countdown to Kickoff* on KCNC Channel 4, and writes once a month for *Pro Football Weekly*. He also serves as emcee, auctioneer, presenter, and/or motivational speaker at more than two hundred events each year. He is the recipient of numerous awards, including the Broncos Community Action Award (1992) and the Colorado Association of Black Journalists Radio Journalist of the Year (2000), and supports many charitable organizations from The Multiple Sclerosis Society to Big Brothers/Big Sisters. Rivers lives in Denver, Colorado.